TJ Powar Has Something to Prove

Jesmeen Kaur Deo

VIKING

VIKING
An imprint of Penguin Random House LLC, New York

First published in the United States of America by Viking,
an imprint of Penguin Random House LLC, 2022

Visit us online at penguinrandomhouse.com.

Library of Congress Cataloging-in-Publication Data is available.

Manufactured in Canada

ISBN 9780593403396

1 3 5 7 9 10 8 6 4 2

FRI

Edited by Kelsey Murphy
Design by Lucia Baez | Text set in Petersburg

**Content warning: This book contains instances of negative body image
and body shaming, specifically in the context of body hair.**

***

To all the hairy girls

ONE
***

"You have six minutes."

The Speaker's voice rings out, clear and calm. An expectant hush falls over the room. It's time.

TJ Powar takes a measured breath and rises from her desk. Although she's done this countless times, she still gets a huge adrenaline rush right before starting her speech. It's a good thing. It focuses her, gives her a sharper edge. The downside is it also makes her palms so sweaty she has to keep a death grip on her cue cards. She really should've wiped her hands on her slacks before standing. But it's too late now.

She grips the cards a little harder and surveys her captive audience. In her peripheral vision, she can see her opponents—one of Whitewater's senior teams—across the floor, their legs stretched out under cramped desks. Facing the debaters in equally cramped desks are the three older judges and the time-keeper, a half-asleep ninth grader who probably got roped into the job. And, of course, the Speaker, a parent volunteer now staring out the window, having clearly zoned out the minute he finished his spiel.

This is it. One of the defining moments of her debating career, happening right now in a musty high school English classroom.

To her right, her debate partner, Simran, coughs. Her subtle way of telling TJ to get a move on and stop basking in the weight of the moment.

TJ clears her throat. "Honourable judges, *worthy* opponents"— she injects just a slight amount of derision into that last bit, not enough that the judges would notice, but enough that her unworthy opponents might—"and, assembled guests. We of Side Affirmative are debating in favour of the resolution before us today: *Be It Resolved That life today is better than it will be in a hundred years' time.*

"My partner"—she half turns and gestures to Simran, who's sitting there polishing her glasses—"has already presented two of our contentions: that climate change is making living conditions worse all around the world, and that current extreme polarizations in politics just forecast more societal turmoil in the future. I will now present two more contentions: that a growing population will only continue to strain resources, and that life is just getting busier and more disconnected. But first, I'll take a moment to point out the flaws in Side Negative's case."

TJ launches into her speech, starting with her rebuttal of the first Side Negative speaker, Nate Chen. It's easy to fall into the rhythm of it. The nice thing about this tournament is that it's held in Cross-Examination style—no one can butt in with questions while she's talking, so her flow won't get interrupted.

However, the mad scribbling coming from Side Negative is hard to ignore. This cross-examination will be a bitch. It always is with these two. When Simran finished her speech portion earlier, Nate used his entire two allotted minutes to grill her. As usual, Simran was cool under fire. TJ can only hope to do the same when her time comes.

The timekeeper is counting down the last fifteen seconds with his arm when TJ finally wraps up her speech. "Thank you.

I now stand for cross-examination," she says, grimly, and the second speaker for Side Negative stands, buttoning up his suit jacket as he rises.

"Thank you for your . . . most *interesting* speech," Charlie Rosencrantz says, his voice dripping with condescension, like always. "However, I do have a few questions."

Of course he does. TJ fashions her face into a blank slate.

"There was some talk about how life will become more disconnected in the future, but you didn't provide a specific reason for this."

He pauses. TJ arches a brow. "I didn't hear a question."

"Of course," Charlie says smoothly. "Because I wasn't done yet. Could you explain how we would become more disconnected in an age when I can FaceTime someone across the world at a moment's notice, when educators can teach anyone anywhere, and people can access medical care in even the most remote areas?"

"You misunderstood," TJ replies, which is her polite way of saying, *You're twisting my words.* "Advancing technology might let us have *more* interactions, but not better ones. Most teachers and doctors would prefer to do their jobs in person. And as for social media companies, they don't care about meaningful emotional connections or nuanced discussion. They care about *engagement.* And they'll do anything to get it, including encouraging harassment and outrage on their platforms. No wonder we're lonelier than ever, despite having the world at our fingertips."

"So you agree that the internet of *today* has already done the damage of lowering quality of life?"

She walked into that one. "Not to a large extent," she hedges. "But in the generations growing up with the internet in their cradle, it will."

"I see. That's already happened, but I will move on." Charlie has a slow way of talking, like he's explaining something to a toddler. And he definitely dials it up when questioning TJ because he *knows* it gets on her nerves. Her eyelid twitches with rage as he continues. "What are your thoughts on the state of social activism today?"

The question seems out of left field. If left field were full of landmines. TJ smiles brightly. "A vague question, but overall there are now more opportunities to speak up and be heard than there were in the past."

Nate, who is trans, makes a soft sound of disbelief. Charlie pounces on her reply. "So you feel you have all the same opportunities as your white, male counterparts?"

Oh, she hates him for this. "There are still problems, but—"

"Thank you. Do you not agree that those problems could be solved over time? Say, in the next hundred years?"

"Look at what's going on in the world right now," TJ shoots back. "We're repeating our history with women's rights, religious persecution, racial and LGBTQ+ discrimination in so many places. Same story, different day. Time isn't the cure to timeless prejudices."

"But the *cultural trend* over the last hundred years has been towards improvement," Charlie presses. "So if we extrapolate, isn't it reasonable to say that will continue?"

"Side Affirmative prefers not to base our arguments on guesswork, my *valued* opponent. Do you have any facts or evidence to support your claim, or is this just optimism?"

"I wasn't aware I was the one being cross-examined, my *esteemed* opponent," Charlie says. TJ idly wonders if the judges have started catching on. "In any case—"

The timekeeper thumps on his desk. "Time's up."

TJ starts a bit; she hadn't noticed the timecard warnings being put up. She sits. Charlie remains standing, since it's now his turn to give his speech.

"Honourable judges. Worthy opponents. Assembled guests. Side Affirmative has brought up a number of . . . curious points." TJ barely restrains herself from rolling her eyes—last time, she got docked on professionalism for that. "Their pessimistic view of the future relies on what they've seen in the past. They're relying on historical examples and facts to convince you. But the truth is, you can find a fact or statistic to support any claim you want. We on Side Negative understand that numbers mean nothing without context. So let's look at the context.

"Change doesn't come easy. It never has. But despite that, our society has overall become more progressive in the last hundred years. And all we need to continue that trend is pro-gressive people moving forward. Those people exist. They're in our schools, they're growing up, and they have more hope and drive to make a better, more inclusive future than anyone. It's because of them that the world will be better off in a hundred years."

Wow. He didn't have facts supporting his case so now he's making a case against evidence. The judges better not give him points for that. Hell, "Evidence and Analysis" is one of the columns in the scoresheet.

It's Simran's job to cross-examine him, so TJ flips over one of her cue cards and scrawls a note to point this out. She pushes it over to Simran, who reads it and nods. Meanwhile, their opponent has since moved on with his speech, painting Side Negative as a beacon of hope while Simran and TJ are just afraid of change. When it's his turn for cross-examination, TJ gives Simran a meaningful look, which she hopes communicates her desire for Simran to send him home crying.

Sadly, that's not Simran's style. As soon as she stands, the tone of the debate immediately becomes way less aggressive.

"Thanks for your great speech. I do have a few questions, though."

"Of course." Charlie's voice is warm. It's sickening, really, how nice they are to each other.

"You talked about how healthcare will be better in a hundred years due to medical innovation," Simran says. "But innovation has actually slowed as our world grows more risk-averse by the day. Do you not agree that the ever-increasing regulations imposed on STEM research will stunt future progress, as can be seen by the drastically decreased rate of drug discovery?"

Charlie has been studying the floor as she speaks, but now raises his brown eyes to Simran's and smiles. He leans against his desk and crosses one ankle over the other. Gestures that may seem casual to the judges, but TJ knows better. He's giving himself more time to think about a tough question.

"We of Side Negative," he says eventually, "would like to

point out that those regulations were added for a reason. To prevent unethical experimentation. So while innovation *might* be a little slower going forward, it will *certainly* be less harmful to its subjects. We would argue the overall societal benefit of that far outweighs any harm."

Simran hardly blinks. Instead, she continues pressing him on the point, this time going from the angle of bureaucracy smothering innovation. He stands his ground, then deflects when the questions get harder.

Soon enough, the cross-examination time is up. The Speaker announces the usual two-minute period for preparing a final rebuttal. Since Simran's first Affirmative, that's her job, so TJ leans back in her chair. The judges are scribbling on their marking sheets, faces impassive. Across the floor, Nate whispers in Charlie's ear like a soccer coach giving frantic advice to the goalie right before a shoot-out.

When the two minutes are up, Simran stands and walks in front of the desks to deliver her speech, pushing her wire-frame glasses up her nose and looking impossibly calm. While TJ is all fire and dramatics when giving a speech, trying to convince the judges that her way is the best way, Simran is logical and levelheaded, delivering her speeches with a matter-of-fact confidence that must make the judges wonder why there was even a debate to begin with. She and TJ make a good pair—in this arena, anyway.

Simran's two minutes are up in no time. Nate rises to present the final stand of Side Negative. He flicks a lock of jet-black hair out of his eyes and opens in typical Nate fashion. "There's been a lot of different narratives thrown around in this debate, such as our opponents' defeatist view of the future versus our faith in future generations based on activism that's happening now. But perhaps the most consistent narrative we've seen is Side Affirmative always being wrong."

TJ can't help it there—she rolls her eyes. But the judges smile, eating up his humour as always.

The rest of his speech is just as full of subtle and not-so-subtle digs at them. After Nate's done, he sits, looking smug. It's over.

All is silent for the next few minutes, except for the ticking of the wall clock and pencils scratching on the judges' scoresheets. As they wait, TJ doodles spirals on her notebook. They've been debating the same topic for three rounds now, against different teams, switching between arguing Affirmative and Negative each time. It's hard to tell how this one went.

After what feels like eons, the Speaker gathers all the scoresheets, looks down at them, and announces, "The judges have called this debate a draw. At this time, if any debaters have complaints regarding rule violations . . ."

TJ tunes out the formalities. A *draw*? What a cop-out. She props her chin in her hand and resists the urge to sigh. Well, it wouldn't be the first time she and Simran tied with White-water's star senior team.

Something on her jaw tickles her palm, distracting her from her thoughts. Frowning slightly, she rubs at the spot. What's that—?

Oh *god*. Instinctively she slaps her hand over her neck. It's a sudden motion, sudden enough that Simran, her opponents, and the timekeeper all glance her way. She ignores them, hoping they'll think she hit a mosquito or something. Never mind that it's December in Canada. Eventually they look away, but she keeps her hand where it is.

It's just, it's so embarrassing. There's a long, wiry hair coming out of a mole on the left side of her neck. Usually, she pulls it out before it can get this visible. But with the busy days leading up to this tournament, she'd totally forgotten.

With her hand still on her neck, TJ looks down at her purse. There are mini-tweezers in her to-go makeup kit, so she just needs a private spot to get rid of it. But god, what if people already *saw*? What if her opponents saw? What if everyone's been seeing that hair and not saying anything—?

"You okay?" Simran whispers. TJ blinks to find her partner staring at her. She nods. *It's not a big deal*, she tells herself firmly. No one would even see it unless they were up close.

Still, when it's time to cross the floor and shake hands with their opponents, TJ keeps her left side tilted away from view. Just in case.

"Do you think we did it?" TJ calls to Simran afterwards, while they're in the washroom in adjacent stalls. She's sitting on the toilet with her hand mirror and mini-tweezers as she plucks out the errant hair. *Finally*.

Satisfied, she shuts the mirror as she hears Simran's door open. "We'll find out in the cafeteria, won't we?" That's where the final, totaled scores of all the rounds today will be announced—both for teams and individual debaters. "If we earned it, we'll get it."

TJ grumbles as she flushes the toilet—not that she even

went, but to keep up the pretense that she did—and follows Simran to the sinks. "You know how tournaments work. Judges have bias."

Simran yawns pointedly. "They could just as easily be biased in our favour as theirs."

"No, *two* of those judges are Whitewater teachers. We've had them before. You want to know my theory?" TJ doesn't wait for a reply, since it would probably be no. "They got put in our debate on purpose."

Simran hardly blinks. "A theory by definition has a strong base of solid evidence. What you've got is a terrible hypothesis. And a lot of paranoia."

TJ waves her hand dismissively. "If Nate and Charlie win *again*, they're going to be insufferable." She rethinks that. "Even if they lose, they'll be annoying."

"Only because they know it makes you mad. Stop giving them a reaction and they won't bother."

TJ huffs but falls silent. She keeps forgetting Simran isn't the type to indulge her venting. She's more of the *here's the logical advice I know you won't take* type.

As they head into the cafeteria and join the lunch line, the volume is deafening. Sixty-something debaters from grades six to twelve are crammed inside, buzzing in excitement and milling from table to table to chat. Although their debating region—the Southern Interior—covers a decent chunk of the province, it's really only five schools in Kelowna, and a scattering of others from the surrounding towns. Nothing like the gigantic tournaments held in Vancouver. But tournaments here are small enough that everyone knows each other, and so, unlike at larger competitions, people cross school lines for post-debate lunches.

TJ scans further, her eye catching on a table held mainly by Northridgers. One of the younger debaters waves madly at them—Yara, a ninth grader with frizzy dark hair down to her shoulders, her pantsuit hopelessly wrinkled. Simran sets off towards the table, and TJ follows because, really, where else is she going to sit?

"Hey!" Yara exclaims once they reach the table. Her voice is so loud that several heads turn from the adjacent bench. Yara's a debating junior—meaning she competes in the grade nine and ten category—who TJ and Simran are well-acquainted with through their school club. "How'd it go? Do you think you'll make it to Provincials?"

"Obviously," TJ says. Yara blinks, and TJ realizes how rude that probably sounded. But there's no point pretending like it's in *question*. She and Simran go every year; their cumulative scores from this season are already enough to make it, even if they bombed this final qualifying tournament. The uncertainty today lies in whether they go to Provincials as the top team or as second best.

"Well, great," Yara says after a pause. She holds up a camera. "I'm taking pictures today for the school paper!"

"You're a photographer?" TJ asks, trying to make up for her jackassery.

"Oh. Yeah." Yara blinks. "I got promoted to photographer in journalism club this year. I took photos at your last soccer game, remember?"

Not at all. "Totally—"

"How did your debates go?" Simran jumps in, and Yara brightens up immediately. As she starts giving a highlight reel,

11

TJ pulls out her phone and checks her notifications under the table. Two new texts.

The most recent is from one of her best friends, Chandani, sent at 10:43 this morning: **dont forget movie night at Piper's place. you know i cant stand Alexa and Katie so you better not bail bitch.**

So lovely, that Chandani. TJ replies with a GIF of some guy getting slapped.

The other text is from TJ's boyfriend, Liam, coming in at 9:03. **Come over tonight?** along with an eyes emoji that implies a lot more. TJ grimaces. They haven't really had enough time alone for fooling around since summer. Now she's sort of avoiding it. Pretty much until the next time she can schedule a bikini wax.

Luckily she has an excuse tonight. **Can't, going to Piper's.**

Liam replies almost immediately with a sad face emoji. **Guess I'll just have to build these gingerbread houses myself.**

TJ's jaw drops. She'd mentioned offhandedly the other day how she missed gingerbread decorating. **Really??**

He sends a picture of his dining table, where two gingerbread decorating kits are sitting. **Lol relax. I won't start without you.**

A woman at the front of the room taps the mic. TJ looks up. It's Mrs. Scott, the Northridge debate coach and also the tournament organizer. She taps the mic again, her thick brows drawing together when it doesn't capture anyone's attention.

In fact, it seems like TJ's the only one not currently socializing. Even Simran is talking to some seniors from Pineview who've migrated over to gossip. The table one over, full of juniors and novices from Kamloops, is obnoxiously loud. TJ sighs. She just wants to get her results and go home.

"*Ahem,*" Mrs. Scott says from the mic. "If we're all finished eating, we can move on to results?"

The hubbub doesn't die down. Mrs. Scott adopts that fake-patience expression teachers probably learn as a requirement in their degree. "I'll wait."

The hubbub dies down immediately. She smiles and smooths away nonexistent flyaways from her bun.

"What a great morning of debates! You've all improved so much this season, and it's been a joy to watch over the past few months. Many of our judges have told me how impressed they were with you, so be proud no matter what your score is."

Right. TJ can't fathom such a concept.

Mrs. Scott goes on. "Now, this is our last Provincials-qualifying tournament. The cumulative scores have been tallied. Meaning we now know exactly who will be going down to Vancouver in February to face off against the best debaters from every region in BC." She pauses dramatically. "We'll start with novice results."

TJ's knee starts bouncing through the twenty minutes of novice and junior results. The wait is torture. She only jolts out of her stupor to offer awkward congratulations to Yara, who returns from the stage beaming with the news that she qualified for Provincials.

And then, finally . . .

"Senior results," Mrs. Scott announces, unfolding another paper. "I know the grade elevens and twelves have been waiting patiently. Just like with the novice and junior categories, the top six senior debaters in the region will head to Provincials.

Let's start with team rankings—but spoiler: everyone in these top three teams qualified for Provincials."

TJ's knee stops bouncing. This is it. Despite her supposed serenity, Simran sits up straighter, too.

"Third in the seniors category: Ameera and Saad Khan, from Northridge."

Two slim figures rise from a crammed multi-school table of debaters—Ameera in her white jumpsuit, paired with an art-fully wrapped rose-gold hijab, and her brother her opposite in all black. Both wear identical grins. TJ claps enthusiastically with everyone else. The third-place winner was the real wild card, and it's nice that it's been taken by another team from her school.

"Second . . ." Mrs. Scott pauses, and TJ could almost swear she winks at her. "Nathaniel Chen and Charles Rosencrantz from Whitewater."

TJ exhales as applause starts again. Thank god. Grinning extra wide, she joins the clapping enthusiastically. She's very supportive of them coming in second, after all.

Charlie and Nate rise from their chairs. Their Whitewater comrades bang on the table in support. TJ obsessively studies their faces for any sign of weakness, but they appear to take their loss with grace. Or at least, some semblance of it—as Nate walks backwards away from the table, someone tosses a grape to him, which he catches in his mouth to more cheers. Charlie simply straightens his silk tie like his picture today might make it onto the national news.

After photos and shaking hands with the tournament organizers, Charlie and Nate stand to the side of the stage with the third-place team, and Mrs. Scott goes back to the mic. "And first place, none other than Northridge's own Simran Kaur Aujla and Tejindar Powar!"

No surprise. Many of the Northridge students stamp their feet, hooting their excitement at one-upping Whitewater. TJ schools her features into indifference now that all eyes are on her. Simran flips her long braid over her shoulder.

"Congratulations," Mrs. Scott says with a warm smile once they reach her. She hands them their certificates just as Simran's mom approaches.

She's a big woman, with a navy-blue turban wrapped around her hair that makes her a notable figure in any crowd. But currently her most prominent feature is her wide smile. "So proud of you girls!" she says, snapping a photo on her phone. "Smile! Hug each other!"

TJ turns to Simran and they do a very awkward side-hug. The embrace is loose and brief, just long enough for Simran's mom to take the photo.

There are more announcements, closing remarks, and then all the podium winners stand for a group photo, arranged to stand in order for the most pleasing symmetry. They all elbow each other trying to get into place, the camera flash goes off, and then Yara insists on getting one of her own for journalism club.

Once the photos are done, the crowd begins dissipating. There's a flurry of activity as debaters rise from tables, volunteers stack chairs, and organizers pack away leftover food. TJ scans the room for her dad. He watched all her debates, but he prefers to blend into the background until it's over. While she's craning her neck over the crowd, Yara approaches with her camera.

"Can I get one of you and Simran? I'll get you two on the front page Monday morning."

Yikes. Being on the front page of the school newspaper is just inviting mockery. But Yara's grey eyes are bright with hope.

"You really don't have to," Simran says graciously.

"Like, *really* don't have to," TJ agrees. "Really, really don't have to—"

Yara just beams and raises her camera. She zooms in unnecessarily far, and TJ only has time to thank fate that she plucked that annoying hair out before the flash goes off in their faces.

"Thanks!" Yara scurries off.

TJ's still blinking from the flash when Simran elbows her. "See?" She points at her certificate. "First place. Nothing to worry about."

"Okay, but Nate got first place individually," TJ says sullenly. She looks down at the scoresheet. She's right behind him, Charlie behind her, and then Simran.

"But *we* won the tournament."

True. For pure gloating rights, having Northridge beat out the Whitewater team is the best outcome. "Don't pretend you're not relieved, too," TJ retorts. Simran doesn't reply, which is basically confirmation. "Nothing sucks more than coming second in your own territory—"

A whiff of freshly ironed shirts is her only warning before a familiar voice chimes at her shoulder, "*Your* territory, TJ? I wasn't aware you owned your whole school."

TJ whips around to glare at the eavesdropper. Charlie's eyes bore into hers without blinking, and it's kind of creepy. With his brown hair combed immaculately in its side part and his hands in fitted pant pockets, he's the kind of guy who looks like he was born in a suit. Before she can respond, Nate appears next to him, his shirt collar now popped up like a vampire. A smirk has taken over his angular features.

Great. Both halves of her longtime rival debate team, here to troll her. Simran gives TJ a meaningful look. Right. *Don't give them a reaction.*

"Get with the program, Charles," Nate says in his typical super-fast voice. "There's a commemorative plaque in the front foyer declaring her God's gift to Northridge. Didn't you see it on your way in?"

Charlie arches his eyebrows. Even now, in casual conversation, he constantly sounds like he's reciting a memorized speech. "Now that you mention it, I think I did. Wasn't there also a statue?"

"A big towering one, of her holding a gigantic soccer ball like she's Atlas. It was so accurate, right down to the nose stud. The proportions are weird, though, the head is massive—"

"Really? I thought that bit was particularly lifelike—"

"Do you guys need some Tylenol?" TJ interrupts. "It seems like you're *extremely* sore losers."

Simran sighs.

"Twenty bucks she practiced that one in front of the mirror last night," Charlie says to Nate.

TJ glares. "You know, you can be disqualified for talking shit about your opponents."

Nate wags a finger in her face. "The rules only say disqualification if you're talking shit *before* the debates, not after, my *worthy* opponent. And besides, did I not beat you out for top spot individually? Who's the sore loser here again?"

TJ opens her mouth, but Simran, perhaps sensing danger, beats her to it. "We can at *least* agree that was a good debate to end our last regional tournament. Right?"

Nate shuts his mouth, and Charlie delivers Simran a winning smile. They don't mess with Simran as much. Maybe they think she'll be tempted to shank them with her kirpan.

"I can't argue with that," Charlie says. "You coming to the meeting on Tuesday?"

Or maybe because they're friends from being on the school district student council together. TJ rolls her eyes and turns to leave. She'd rather pull out each of her teeth individually than listen to this.

Charlie pauses mid-conversation to say, "Provincials, TJ. It's going down."

TJ scoffs. "I'm sure that's what you'll tell yourself tonight. While crying into your silk tie."

He runs his fingers over the silk tie in question. "Thanks for noticing."

Inexplicably, she finds herself growing warm. "I just like the thought of choking you with it."

"Hmm. I like that thought, too." He grins at her expression and turns back to his conversation.

She recovers, but too late. There she goes, giving him a reaction again. What a weirdo. But he owns it. So does Nate. They just don't worry about what people will think.

And maybe that's a *tiny* part of the reason why she can't stand them.

TWO
✳✳✳

TJ's post-win buzz lasts all through the weekend, but as usual, school arrives on Monday to slap her with reality. The homework assigned in her pre-calc class alone could be classified as a form of torture.

By the time she enters her last morning class, TJ's dragging her feet. She sits and checks the clock. A whole seventy minutes until lunch. Winter Break may be at the end of the week, but it's starting to feel like eons away.

While she's checking the time again, a girl with brilliantly red, wavy hair drops her notebook on the desk next to her. Piper Anderson, host of Saturday's movie night and one of TJ's closest friends.

Piper sits gingerly. "My legs hurt."

TJ grimaces. Yesterday, she, Piper, and the rest of their soccer team were subjected to their off-season fitness boot camp. "My everything hurts."

Chandani Sharma slides into the desk behind them. "Tell me about it. Whoever invented the beep test should be in prison." She leans back and lets her waist-length black hair fall from her ponytail only to tie it up again, studying them from under her lids. Her eyeshadow today is a subtly smoky maroon that matches her tie-neck top. "Did you two get slammed in your last class, or was that just me?"

"Mr. Oyedele assigned like four chapters," Piper says

mournfully. "I swear last week we were still talking about mitochondria and tomorrow there's a quiz on frog anatomy. Maybe Ms. Schwab will have mercy on us?"

Chandani's sharp eyes shift behind them. "Might be our lucky day. Substitute teacher alert."

TJ twists back to the front and freezes in horror. Normally she'd welcome a sub, since it basically means they can screw around for an hour. Except the substitute teacher is Mrs. Banger, a Punjabi woman with a pixie cut in her forties. An *auntie*. And not just any auntie—when she comes over for chah with TJ's mom, TJ knows her as Rupi auntie.

TJ ducks her head, but too late. Mrs. Banger makes eye contact with her while setting her bag on the teacher's desk. Her pencil-thin eyebrows rise, and a smile promises a conversation later. Great.

Mrs. Banger turns her attention to the rest of the room. "Bonjour, class!"

Apparently Ms. Schwab is sick, so Mrs. Banger gives them a group assignment to make a French poster about their New Year's resolutions. They're told to form their own groups, causing immediate chaos. Chairs scrape back, people yell at each other from across the room, and Chandani pokes TJ and Piper in the back, saying, "Turn around," which is her way of asking.

They still need more people, but luckily, Piper is a well-liked social butterfly—it's easy with those big blue eyes, round angelic face, and guileless smile that have gotten her out of many late penalties on assignments. In no time, they've corralled two of her friends and a few guys from the boys' soccer team.

They get to work, and actually finish a decent amount of

the poster before everyone gets derailed from their task and starts goofing off. Everyone except TJ, that is. She's on her best behaviour, painfully aware that Big Brother is watching.

Chandani clearly notices. "So are you going out with Liam at lunch today?" she asks loudly as she cuts letters out of construction paper. TJ kicks her under the table.

"Ow!" Chandani is smirking, though. TJ casts a furtive look behind her. Luckily, Mrs. Banger is otherwise occupied across the room, talking to Simran, who's in a group with three other loners. It's looking pretty awkward over there. Maybe TJ should've invited Simran to be part of their group. Then again, Simran doesn't know TJ's friends, so that would be awkward, too.

TJ turns back to Chandani and finally responds in a low voice. "Yes, I am. And if you say another word about it, I'll start loudly remembering what you got up to at Jake's parents' cabin last summer."

Jake, who happens to be in their group, looks up from where he's inputting words into Google Translate. "Now *that's* a story."

Piper looks between them, blue eyes widening. "Wait, what happened with you two?" She sounds anxious. TJ has it on good authority she's been nursing a crush on Jake for months.

Chandani knows it, too. "Nothing. He was just hosting the party. You were on vacation that time, remember?"

"Oh. Well, what happened?"

Neither of them answers because Mrs. Banger has drifted over and is now within earshot. Jake, however, is oblivious. "Skinny-dipping."

TJ winces. Mrs. Banger shifts closer. "What is 'skinny-dipping'?" she asks.

"Hello, Auntie!" TJ says loudly. "How are you?"

Mrs. Banger glances her way with a bright smile, effectively distracted. "Tejindar! I'm good. How's your mom?"

TJ pastes a smile on her face. "Good."

"Congratulations on debate. Simran just told me."

"Oh. Thanks." She can feel her friends looking at her curiously. TJ hadn't really mentioned the tournament to them.

"Did you win?" Piper asks while Chandani returns to sorting through markers, bored already. TJ shrugs. She's not sure they understand how much she loves debate. Piper seems to think it's a weird quirk. Chandani assumes TJ's padding her résumé. Not that TJ's given them reason to think anything else. It just feels weird to talk about with them. There are two very separate parts of TJ's life, and she doesn't like them overlapping.

Mrs. Banger answers instead. "They did! It's wonderful that you and your cousin debate together. Your family must be very proud."

Jake looks between TJ and Mrs. Banger. TJ can practically hear cogs turning in his head. "Wait. Simran's your cousin?"

The room quiets a bit. Simran's spine stiffens from across the room.

"Um," TJ says. "Yeah."

"Whoa," Jake says, and squints across the room at Simran, who's bent even further forward now. "I, uh, don't see it."

Chandani makes eye contact with TJ and smirks. She and Piper already know TJ and Simran are cousins. But it's not common knowledge, and why would it be? TJ and Simran barely talk outside of debate. It's not that they have a problem with each other or anything—they just don't have much in common.

The bell rings, saving TJ from more questions. Jake throws their half-assed poster on the teacher's desk for marking and their group dissolves within seconds, everyone stampeding out the door.

TJ exhales as soon as she's a safe distance down the hallway. Piper and Chandani are already chatting away about something else, so TJ takes the opportunity to crane her neck over the lunchtime crowd and search for her cousin. She spots her instantly, exiting the classroom last and heading the opposite way. Her expression is perfectly neutral. All right, so maybe that was only weird for TJ, then.

Piper nudges her. "Hey. Look who must've gotten out of class early." TJ follows her gaze to spot Liam's car, parked in the drop-off zone just through the glass doors of the school. She brightens.

"I'll catch you later?"

Piper makes kissy noises and Chandani slaps TJ's butt. "Go get it, bitch."

TJ rolls her eyes. "We're getting *lunch*."

"Oooh, hope there's dessert after," Chandani says, which makes TJ roll her eyes again.

She heads to the washroom to touch up her makeup, then to her locker for her peacoat. Kelowna's not freezing cold in the winter, but it's still chilly enough to make her shiver when she steps through the double doors.

Liam's car is idling when she hops into the passenger side.

"Hey, beautiful" is the first thing she hears, before a hand snakes around her shoulders and a kiss drops against her hair. She scrunches her nose, pretending not to like it, although she definitely does.

Liam leans back. She spends a moment just looking at him, because, *damn*. He's tall, athletic, a member of the soccer team just like her; with mischievous green eyes and dark curly hair she loves running her hands through. He looks like bad news, and if TJ's parents knew about him he definitely would be.

Good thing she's a pro at this. She grins. "Hi."

He puts the car into drive. "Did French keep you late?"

It takes her a moment to realize he's been waiting. "No, I was just in the washroom."

"I'll never understand why girls take so long," Liam says good-naturedly. There have been many date nights when TJ was late with the outfit-picking. The hair-doing. The makeup-donning.

"I told you, I'm running on BST. Brown Standard Time." She snuggles into the heated seat. "Where are we going?"

"Your pick."

"No, your pick."

"Your pick—"

"Just *choose*—"

Twenty minutes later, they're back in the school parking lot, tearing into the bag of fries nestled in the center console between them. TJ has just finished ranting about the soccer practice from hell when he changes the subject. "So, how was Saturday? Your debate?"

She pauses mid-chew. She doesn't remember mentioning it, but he probably heard about it around school. He always somehow knows. Even though he's never actually come to watch. "Fine."

"Did you win?"

"First place as a team. Second individually." Her loss to Nate doesn't smart too much, though. He, TJ, Charlie, and Simran continually swap the top four spots between them each tournament. TJ once tallied their standings over the years and it all pretty much evened out. She'd never admit it out loud, but whoever does better on any given day truly depends on the topics and pure luck.

She pivots before Liam can ask more. "How was *your* Saturday?"

"Before or after you rejected me for Piper?" When she rolls her eyes, he grins. "I helped my dad set up an open house. Boring as hell, plus I screwed up my shoulder lifting boxes." He makes a face.

TJ splays her hand over his broad shoulder, trying not to laugh. Liam's realtor parents practically see him as free labour. "Aw, you big baby. Need me to kiss it better?"

His green eyes go dark. She has exactly one second to wonder if she tastes like fries before he leans in across the center console. But that thought quickly dissolves when their mouths meet. Who could blame her? The boy knows how to kiss.

She relaxes and draws closer as the kiss deepens. His hand drops to her waist, skims beneath her peacoat, and slides up to brush the underwire of her bra.

She pulls away, and Liam leans back, running a hand through his curls. "Sorry. You're just . . . so beautiful."

He says that all the time, but it never fails to make her heart flip. "It's okay. I just don't want to have sex in Northridge's parking lot."

His lips curve up. "What, that doesn't sound romantic to you?"

They share a grin and then—there's a sticky pause. She knows what he's thinking because she's thinking it, too. They've only had sex a few times; the first time was at the end of grade eleven, and it's been . . . a long time since summer, that's for sure.

"My parents have another showing tonight," Liam says, voice dropping in pitch. "You could come over, we could pick up where we left off in August."

Her stomach drops. Tonight? That's not enough time.

He must sense her hesitation. "Or we can just make those gingerbread houses. Nothing else if you don't want."

But the eagerness is still clear in his eyes. She's going to have to tell him.

"I haven't, um, *gotten things ready* down there." His eyebrows draw together in confusion. She's going to have to spell it out. Heat rises on her cheeks, and she ducks her head slightly. "Um. Full bush. I don't know if . . ."

Liam lets go of her so fast you'd think TJ had just announced she had pink eye. "Oh, okay. We can wait, then."

"You sure?"

"Yeah." He won't meet her eyes. His tone has changed from sultry to awkward in two seconds flat, and it leaves TJ wringing her hands together. That was way TMI, wasn't it? She should've just made an excuse.

The silence stretches between them until Liam says, all at

once, "I bet it's not that bad. It's not like you're even hairy." He waves a hand, gesturing vaguely at her. "You're gorgeous."

He says it sincerely, and she tries to smile. It falls flat.

Because she's a complete fake. She has been, since she was twelve.

That was when her and Chandani's moms finally caved to their begging. Chandani was tired of boys making fun of her unibrow. And TJ came home in tears for the third night in a row after a girl from debate—who's since moved away, thankfully—commented on her *gorilla arms*. Their moms took them to the salon that very night. Both TJ and Chandani cried during the excruciating full-face threading. But when it was done, they peered at their reddened complexions in the mirror and marveled at how *normal* they looked, how much *prettier* they looked. Finally.

But that wasn't the end of it, of course. They were about to hit puberty. So, off came the hair on their legs and arms, toes and fingers, and later, for the swimsuit season, their stomachs and bikini lines. Last summer, TJ added a Brazilian to her routine.

So yes, TJ's aware people at school think she's pretty. They just don't know how much *effort* it takes.

"Thanks," she says now, to Liam. She looks down at her fries. They don't look very appetizing suddenly. "I have to go to the washroom before class starts. See you later?"

Liam blinks. "Hold on a second and I'll walk you in."

"No, that's fine," she says, super fast, and opens the passenger door. But before she can escape, he snags her wrist.

"Did I do something wrong?"

He sounds worried. She suddenly feels guilty. This isn't his problem, it's hers. She forces another smile. "No, of course not. I just *really* have to go."

Liam waits an extra second before letting go with a sigh. "Don't forget your fries."

TJ nods and grabs them without really looking. She speed-walks into the school through the main entrance, knowing he's watching, and heads down the hall like she's going to the washroom. But when she's around the corner, she slows. With a furtive glance around, she pushes through one of the school's side exits.

The smell of cigarettes greets her immediately. This side of Northridge, facing the trees, is a notorious rendezvous for illicit activities. But no one's here right now, which suits her perfectly for this conversation. She leans against the graffitied wall and dials a familiar number.

After three rings, a heavily French-accented voice says, "Allô?"

TJ clears her throat. "Hi, Lulu."

The voice changes immediately from professional to warm. "*Darling.* How are you?"

TJ smiles inwardly. She and Lulu know each other well. Well, Lulu probably knows her much more intimately, considering she's been her beautician for years. At some point Lulu had just given TJ her personal number so she could dial directly instead of calling the salon's receptionist. "Good. Can I make an appointment this week?"

"Of course. For what?"

TJ checks to make sure she's truly alone before responding. "Brazilian."

A pause. Then, cheekily: "Ahh. It has been a while. Friday okay?"

"Yeah." They set up the details, and Lulu promises to bring a batch of her wife's homemade lemon tarts to the appointment. That's code for *this is gonna hurt*. Great.

Sighing, TJ tucks her phone back into her purse and heads into the school again. She's only got a few minutes to get to class.

She re-enters the same way she went out, and a group of eighth graders look at her and do a double take. Maybe they think she was out there smoking. Busybodies. She levels them with a glare, and they quickly look away. Once she passes them, she surreptitiously double-checks that there aren't giant ketchup stains down her front or something. But nope.

She heads to her locker to stash her coat. She checks her face in the mirror and touches up the lip gloss that Liam kissed off. In the reflection, she notices someone watching her from across the hall: Alexa Fisher, who plays defense in soccer with her. Alexa drops her gaze when TJ meets her eyes. She walks away, but not before TJ notices she's clutching the school newspaper.

No one reads the school paper. Well, except for the teachers, and the kids who work on it. Curiosity overtakes her. TJ closes her locker, glancing in the direction of the receptacle that normally holds the paper. It's empty.

This has officially entered freaky territory. The newspaper only came out today. And TJ knows for a fact that normally Yara takes four copies from each stand to make it look like people are interested.

A few feet away, a couple of tenth graders peer over the paper at her. That does it. She scans the crammed hallway for anyone she knows holding a copy.

There. Rajan Randhawa. The resident stoner and juvenile delinquent of the grade-twelve class, reading the school *paper*? Is she in a new dimension? As he swaggers past, a head taller than everyone else, she catches the sleeve of his ratty black hoodie.

Rajan lurches to a stop slowly, noticing her, and removes the toothpick out of his smiling mouth. "Hey, dude. Congrats on the debate thing." He waves the paper in her face, too fast for her to properly look.

Her anxiety skyrockets. So it *is* about her? "Can I see that?"

He shrugs. She snatches the paper out of his hand.

Sure enough, the headline Yara promised is splashed across the front page, along with a huge close-up photo of her and Simran's faces. TJ winces. It's one of those pictures in unflattering lighting where you can see every pore and flaw and imperfection and sweat shining on their foreheads. Simran definitely got the worst of it; she doesn't have the same beauty routines that TJ does.

Okay, so that sucks, but not a huge deal. She scans the article itself. Whoever wrote the story clearly had a minimum word count they were struggling with. Nothing special. So what's got everyone so excited?

She looks up to ask Rajan, but he's already wandered off into the crowd. She catches up with him. "Why were you reading this?"

He glances down at her again, and this time has the audacity to flick her forehead. "Just because I'm failing half my classes doesn't mean I'm illiterate, dude."

TJ POWAR HAS SOMETHING TO PROVE

She bats his hand away, irritated. She's had a low opinion of him ever since they were in seventh grade and he said she had a big Indian-girl nose. "Sure, but I've never seen you read the school paper."

"Usually it doesn't have anything interesting."

"But today it does?"

He tugs the brim of his cap a little lower over his eyes and shrugs. "Well, I just had to see it for myself."

"See *what*?" she demands, but he's already sauntering away again. Just then, her phone vibrates. Piper.

did you see it?? I can't believe anyone would say that.

Apparently, no one wants to be specific today.

see WHAT??? TJ texts back frantically. She waits an agonizing five seconds for Piper to finish typing.

check Northridge Confessions.

TJ's sense of dread skyrockets. The Northridge Confessions Instagram page is where everyone anonymously sends their dirt and their school-specific memes. TJ hasn't visited it in a while.

She braces herself and pulls up Instagram.

The most recent post on the Confessions page snags her attention immediately. It's that same unflattering photo of TJ and Simran, except it's been cut into two individual images, of the two of them separately.

#1022
Hot Persian girls: Expectation vs Reality

Under *Expectation* is TJ's photo. She looks fine—even pretty—in it, despite the sweaty sheen. Her makeup held up

31

well. And then, under *Reality,* there's Simran's photo.

It's blown even bigger than the one Yara had in the newspaper. And it's uncomfortably clear what difference between the two of them the caption is referring to: Simran's facial hair. Her eyebrows are bushy, closer to a singular rather than plural; there's visible hair on her upper lip and chin, and her sideburns are deep enough to meet her jawline.

Several things go through TJ's mind right then:

1. Simran's not Persian. She's Punjabi, like TJ. But then again, racists aren't exactly known for their accuracy.

2. Embarrassment for her cousin. There's no way around it. This sucks.

3. But at least they think TJ's hot?

4. Shame immediately following #3.

5. Rage.

All background noise fades as TJ clicks through the post's many likes and comments. She recognizes some usernames as students at Northridge, and some she doesn't—but it's a public page, after all. One of the most-liked comments is **Someone start a GoFundMe to buy this girl razors.** TJ sees red.

Sure, there are always insulting posts on the Confessions page, but she never imagined she'd *be* in one. It's probably a good thing Simran doesn't have a phone or Instagram, because she shouldn't see this.

Then again, it's only a matter of time until she hears about it. They need to talk.

✶

TJ doesn't see Simran for the rest of the day, despite being on the lookout. They don't share any classes apart from French.

So TJ fumes silently throughout the afternoon. Maybe she's imagining it, but she swears people keep looking at her. No one actually says anything, though. It drives her up the wall.

After the last bell rings, she's so busy scanning the hallway outside the AP Lit room for Simran that she jumps when someone puts their hand on her back.

"Sorry," Liam says from behind her, and moves to her side. "Something on your mind?"

She huffs. "Don't tell me you didn't see that Northridge Confessions post."

"Oh, yeah. It wasn't funny."

He's not having enough of a reaction for TJ's liking. "Some of the guys on *your* team were liking the post, you know."

"They're douchebags. I'll talk to them." He rubs her back. "Come on, it'll die down soon anyway."

TJ takes a deep breath, hoping that will calm her. It's working, at least until Rajan walks out from the classroom behind them and says, "Doubt it."

TJ glares at him as he passes. "What's that supposed to mean?"

Rajan whirls on the spot and whips out his beat-up phone. "Don't get all uptight about it if I show you, all right?"

She breaks away from Liam to grab Rajan's phone. It's a tweet. The same photo of Simran from the Confessions post, with a new caption.

When your man forgets to shave. It has several likes and retweets.

"See, I can see you getting homicidal right now, dude." Rajan pulls his phone from TJ's grasp. "Chill out."

"How am I supposed to chill out?" she hisses. "My cousin is becoming a *meme*! Everyone's laughing at her!"

"Since when do you care?" Rajan arches a brow. "It's making *you* look like the hottest girl at Northridge. Thought that'd be a win for you, to be honest."

TJ's jaw drops. "You little—"

Liam steps between them and shoves Rajan's shoulder. "All right, thanks *a lot*," he says pointedly. Rajan puts up his hands before backing away.

Once he's gone, Liam turns to TJ. "Don't let him get to you." He wraps an arm around her shoulders. "But he's right, you know. You *are* the hottest girl at Northridge."

TJ's irritation spikes. The problem is, Rajan's comments hit a little too close to the truth—for a split second when she first saw it, she *had* taken the meme as a compliment. Wow. She really is a horrible person.

She pulls away from Liam. "Great. I'm just going to go *celebrate* how much hotter I am than my cousin."

Liam sighs. "TJ, that's not what I meant—"

TJ ignores him and walks away. She's too mad. At Liam, or Rajan, or whoever submitted the Insta post, or everyone laughing at it, or herself? It's a *take your pick* situation.

She fumes all the way to the parking lot, where Piper is waiting. The two of them carpool a lot since they live only a few blocks from each other.

Piper unlocks her car, eyeing TJ. "You looked really ticked off."

"Liam said I was the hottest girl in school!" TJ shouts.

"Umm . . ."

Okay, maybe not her most eloquent explanation. TJ rakes her hands through her carefully curled hair. "Never mind. Hey, can you drop me off somewhere?"

There's no way Simran can evade her at her own house.

THREE
***

TJ's masi is the one who answers the door, all smiles and friendliness. TJ forces a smile back.

It's not that she doesn't like her. Her aunt's actually quite nice—but very traditional. So TJ instinctively keeps up a facade around her to avoid disapproval. The facade of a nice, respectable girl who doesn't party and definitely does not have a boyfriend. Luckily, she doesn't have to pretend often. Their families don't get together very much.

TJ clasps her hands together in greeting. "Sat Sri Akaal, Masi ji."

"Sat Sri Akaal, putt!" She pulls TJ into a saffron-infused embrace. Her turban is white today, and she's dressed casually in a sweater and joggers. "How are you, how's school? Come in."

TJ follows her aunt into the small but cozy living room, giving generic answers to her equally generic questions. They pass the khanda mounted on the wall, and the childhood photos of toddler Simran with her then-teenage sister Kiran, performing at the gurdwara. As always, a wave of—something—goes through TJ. Her own parents are culturally Sikh but not religious, so coming here feels like a surreal peek into the alternate life she might have led, if her and Simran's places had been switched.

"How's Kiran?" she asks her masi, running her hand along the photo frame of Simran and her sister. "I heard she moved to Ontario."

"Yes, that was a while back. She's fine. Will you have chah?" Her masi's voice is falsely bright. Clearly that's a sensitive topic.

"Uh, no thanks." Hastily, she moves on. Another photo on the wall catches her eye—herself and Simran. It takes her a moment to place it. Kelowna's Vaisakhi parade. They couldn't have been older than eight or nine. TJ's and Simran's faces are peeking over the edge of one of the floats, both giggling. TJ can't remember why. She can't fathom giggling with Simran over anything.

"You haven't come by in a long time," her masi says, a questioning note to her voice. TJ blinks back to reality. Right. She's on a mission.

She turns to the narrow staircase. "I'm just here to see Simran. Uh, about debate." A flimsy excuse, seeing as debate's over until the new year, but her aunt's confused expression clears.

"Well, let me get you something to eat—"

TJ's already taking the stairs, two at a time. "That's okay!"

She doesn't wait for a response. Once she's upstairs, she swings around the bannister and turns left into the hallway lined with doors. Here, the white walls are bare, the beige carpet paled with age and flattened beneath her toes. Nothing's changed from when they were little. She still remembers exactly where to go.

Simran's door, at the end of the hall, is closed. TJ knocks tentatively.

"Come in," Simran says from inside, voice quiet. TJ's imagination runs wild. Is she crying in there? Tissues strewn all over the bed? Having some sort of crisis of faith?

She bursts into Simran's room only to stub her toe immediately on the harmonium lurking behind the door. "Shit!" She hops on one foot, clutching the other.

"Watch it!" Simran says sternly, without looking up from whatever she's doing at her desk. TJ barely rights herself before she can fall face-first into a tabla lying on its side. Finally, she straightens and takes it all in.

Simran's musical instruments are only a few of the hazards that lie in her path. There are textbooks, pieces of loose-leaf, envelopes, pens and pencils, a tea-stained mug, hair bands, crumpled-up tissues, wrinkled clothes . . .

"Your room is a pigsty," TJ informs her cousin.

Simran swivels around in her office chair. "That's what you say every time."

"Because it's true. I don't understand you." TJ picks her way through the mess. The room is small enough that it's only a few paces to the unmade bed. She pushes a hanger off and perches on the edge. "Aren't smart people supposed to be organized?"

"I guess I'm not as smart as you think."

TJ scoffs. "Yeah, right. You're going to do a full sweep on academic awards night and we all know it." TJ watches her cousin sway slightly from side to side in her chair, her face completely devoid of emotion. "So, um, how are you feeling?"

"About what?"

TJ leans back onto her hands. "Come on. You must've heard about that meme."

Simran's expression doesn't change. "Yes. Someone showed it to me."

It's hard to get a read on her tone. "And? It's horrible. Whoever wrote it"—TJ's anger rears its head again, and her voice rises—"they're an asshole. And everyone who liked it, too. Seriously, who gave them the right—"

"TJ," Simran interrupts. "It's all right."

TJ blinks.

"I'm *okay*," Simran adds, looking her directly in the eye. "I'm not like you—I'm used to it."

TJ frowns. "What's that supposed to mean?"

"You know what it means. You're—you." She gestures to TJ, then lets her hand fall into her lap. "And then there's me."

TJ gawks at her for a moment, but even she can't deny the point Simran's trying to make.

They're polar opposites. There's TJ, sitting there in her designer jeans, lipstick, and layered dark hair with ombre highlights. Then there's Simran in her ill-fitting T-shirt, wire-frame glasses, and hair perpetually tied back in a braid so long she can sit on it.

There's TJ, a soccer player in the in-crowd, and there's Simran, who eats lunch in the French teacher's classroom when she doesn't have a committee meeting. There's Simran, who spends her Sundays in the gurdwara, while the thing TJ is most religious about is getting her upper lip threaded weekly. The only thing they have in common is debating.

Simran goes on. "People make jokes. You kind of stop caring after a while."

"Wait, what? People make fun of you?" Simran gives her a look like she should know this already. "So . . . the meme doesn't bother you at all?"

"Why should it?" Simran shrugs. "It says more about the people who made it than me. Such as that they are"—she starts counting on her fingers—"racist, misogynistic . . . not to mention *trans*misogynistic."

There Simran goes with her infuriatingly logical arguments again. But—TJ studies her cousin closely—there's no sign of hidden weakness. Simran's completely relaxed in her chair. She's just . . . totally fine with being the school laughingstock. This isn't right.

"Was there anything else?" Simran says lightly. "Because I have this music camp application to fill out—"

"If it bothers you," TJ bursts out, "I could help you, you know."

Simran's brow furrows. TJ struggles with the right way to word this.

"I could," she ventures, "teach you how to shave. Or I can take you to the salon. I know someone who's really good with threading for first-timers—"

Simran flinches slightly. "TJ. You know I won't do that."

The way she says it, you'd think TJ had suggested they drown some kittens together. For Simran, it's probably on the same level of offense; she doesn't remove hair or cut it. Never has. It's why her braid is long enough to brush the backs of her knees. She was in the local paper once for it when they were younger.

Too bad hair isn't so charming when it grows in other places. "Doesn't it bother you?" TJ asks. "All those people making fun of you for the hair—wouldn't it make life easier?"

"Maybe for people looking at me." Simran absentmindedly

strokes her glossy braid. "But letting other people dictate whether I cut my hair isn't a very Sikh thing to do. Besides, doesn't it hurt when they rip your hair out of your skin? Doesn't it take a lot of time to keep up?"

"Well, *yeah*," TJ says. "It also hurts when I pull a splinter. It takes forever to floss my teeth. I still gotta do it."

Simran's solemn expression breaks momentarily to let out an amused huff. "But you don't really *have* to get rid of it. You know that, right?"

"Of course I know that," TJ says, suddenly annoyed. "I *want* to."

"Okay. I respect that." Simran turns back to the paper on her desk, some form with a picture of a keyboard in the header. TJ squints at her.

"So you're really not upset?"

Simran looks up again, now with a hint of exasperation. "No. Are we done? I have things to do."

TJ stands, her irritation growing by the minute. Why'd she even come here? The meme's probably going to blow over by tomorrow anyway. "Fine. I was just trying to check in on you, but I guess I'm not welcome."

Simran exhales slowly. "I didn't say that. I'm just tired of you trying to work out your own issues on me."

"What?" TJ snaps. "I don't even know what you're talking about."

Simran shrugs. "All right. See you later."

TJ grinds her teeth and heads for the door. But when she flings it open, her masi's on the other side, holding a tray with three steaming teacups and a plateful of digestive biscuits.

"Oops," her masi says, clearly unashamed to be found snooping. "Stay for chah, at least?"

After gulping down hot chah, her masi drops her off at home. TJ spends the whole awkward drive cursing the fact that her father's on day shifts this week, using their shared car.

When they finally pull into the driveway, all the house lights are still out, and her masi sends her off with instructions to send her hellos to her parents. TJ nods, although she has no intention of telling anyone she was at Simran's house.

But at dinner that night, she finds she has no choice.

"Why were you at your masi's house today?" TJ's mom asks right when they sit down. Her shoulder-length hair is disheveled, clothes wrinkled, and yet her eyes are sharp. Too sharp for someone who just came back from thirty hours of hammering prosthetic hips into place.

TJ takes a bite of pizza. They ordered out because no one wanted to cook. Her father has sliced up some vegetables in an attempt to make the meal healthier, but no one's touched them. "How do you even know that?"

"Kamaljot uncle's their neighbour, and he saw you arriving. He told his wife, who told Reeta, who told me."

TJ privately thinks Kamaljot uncle should mind his own damn business. She turns to her dad, who's slouched beside her drizzling his pizza with ketchup. Disgusting. "How was work?"

"Oh, you know. Just cleaning up your mother's messes." He grins. It's his favourite joke, since he's a housekeeper at the hospital where her mom works as a surgeon. Chandani's mom, who's a nurse, once informed TJ that the two of them are often seen having coffee together mid-shift. It's sickeningly cute.

"Don't change the subject," her mother says.

TJ scowls. "I was there to talk to Simran."

Her father scratches his five-o'clock shadow. "I thought debate was over until the new year?"

TJ takes her time chewing. She doesn't want to explain the meme to *them*. It would be a nightmare. Even if she managed it, her mom would suggest going to the principal or something, and her dad would tell her to ignore it. "I just wanted to go over our scores. Um, to debrief. We didn't get a chance at the tournament."

Her mom's thick eyebrows are still drawn together in suspicion. Like going over to her masi's is a crime. Maybe it is, in her eyes. They don't get along very well. TJ holds her breath.

But instead of probing further, her mother just holds out the plate of sliced vegetables. "Have some cucumber. All you ever eat is junk."

When TJ checks the Northridge Confessions Instagram the next morning, the post has tripled in likes. She almost throws her phone across her bedroom.

School doesn't help her mood; the restocked newspaper receptacles are empty again by noon. Every time TJ sees one she wants to scream. But she keeps her mouth shut. Tries to ignore it. She avoids Liam during class—mostly to avoid saying something she'll regret while she's this mad—and tells herself to just get through the day. Then she'll have soccer and can finally work off all her pent-up frustration.

There's a bounce in her step when, later that afternoon, she finally arrives at the indoor field they use for off-season winter practices. Coach has already gotten started on his pep talk by the time she dumps her bag on the ground and joins the huddle. "Listen up," he shouts, impressive moustache bristling. "The UBCO scouts are here today, as you can see." TJ glances where he's pointing; on the other sideline there's a cluster of women in UBCO shirts she hadn't noticed before. They're the last thing she cares about today, honestly. But her teammates hang riveted on his every word. "They're going to watch some of our spring season games, too. So don't embarrass me. Ever since I started coaching this team, the rate of university team recruitment has gone up two hundred percent. That's a reputation I intend to keep."

"Really?" whispers Alexa Fisher.

"I'm pretty sure he made that number up," Piper whispers back. "He said six hundred percent last year."

"I can hear you slandering me back there, Anderson," Coach barks, making Piper go pink. "We're starting a scrimmage in five. Show them what you're made of." He glares at them all, longest at TJ, who ignores it and sits on the turf with Chandani to stretch her legs. Her limbs thrum with restless energy. She has to get on the field before she bursts.

Piper remains standing, biting her nails. "I'm going to suck today because these scouts showed up. They'll never want me on the team."

"Didn't UVic already beg for you?" Chandani asks. "Why do you care?"

"Yeah, but I want *choices*. I still want UBCO to like me."

Chandani rolls her eyes. "You always want people to like you. Chill out. They'll be begging us to join their team by halftime."

Entirely possible. TJ, Chandani, and Piper are a power squad of midfielders. They work well together, which is how they became friends. Still, TJ's in a mood, so she scoffs. "You have to keep good grades to be on a team. Remind me, what's your GPA again?"

Chandani kicks her in the leg. "Oh, are you finally done moping? Then remind me, who's the clown who didn't go to any recruiting camps last summer?"

Piper winces. TJ doesn't react. While the rest of the senior players on the team went to recruiting camps, sought out university coaches . . . TJ didn't. "How many times do I have to say I don't want to play university soccer?"

"Until it makes sense. What else are you going to do?"

TJ sighs, successfully distracted. Yet another problem she has to deal with. The official university application deadlines aren't upon them yet, but the deadline to make a connection with a soccer program is definitely closing in. Coach has been hounding her about it, despite her repeatedly saying she isn't interested. Whenever she entertains the thought of years more of competitive sport—and all the time, travel, politics, and injuries involved—she feels exhausted. She's not sure when this change happened, but somewhere in the past couple years, she began looking forward to debate tournaments more than soccer games.

Luckily, she's spared from *that* conversation because Coach starts splitting them into teams.

TJ's split up from Chandani and Piper. She jogs onto the field, and as she takes her position, her heart races in anticipation. Take away the competition of it, and soccer is still her favourite sport. Just like with debate, she loves the tension right before kickoff, when everything's silent, her muscles tense, breath held, that moment where *anything can happen.*

The game starts. And just like she wanted, she forgets everything else for the next thirty minutes.

By the end of the game, the restlessness TJ's been harbouring all day has officially burned out. Trying to out-dribble Chandani certainly did the trick. Still grinning about her goal, TJ returns to the bench only to find Coach handing her a business card.

It's like a record scratch as he says, "UBCO's assistant coach told me to give you this."

He must've been campaigning hard for her to get an invite after a scrimmage. TJ sighs. "I told you, I'm not—"

"I'll send you the details," Coach interrupts. "You should email them tonight."

TJ takes a swig from her water bottle instead of answering.

"Do you think you'll go to UBCO, TJ?" asks the girl at her side—an eleventh grader who plays defense. "Or are you going to join a team somewhere else?"

Chandani, who's on the bench scrolling through her phone, snorts. TJ ignores her and wipes her mouth. "We'll see."

Coach announces some passing drills to round off practice. TJ turns to stow away her water bottle, but pauses when she sees someone approaching from the entrance. Liam. What's he doing here? She hasn't talked to him since yesterday's comment.

She takes a few steps forward to meet him. He looks slightly wary, dressed in a soft-looking blue hoodie and sweats and . . . holding a bouquet of flowers.

While she's staring at it, he says, "I'm sorry."

She blinks. "For what?"

"For what I said yesterday." He swallows. "For, uh, objectifying you when you were upset about the meme."

"'Objectifying'? That's a five-syllable word, Liam. Where'd you learn it?"

"TJ," he groans playfully, while her teammates snicker behind her, "why do you always have to bust my balls like this?"

She presses her lips together to prevent herself from grinning. Truthfully, she's touched. "I might've overreacted a little yesterday."

"Never," he says at once. "Am I forgiven?"

Instead of answering, she leans forward to kiss him—briefly, because Coach barks "PDA!" after two seconds—and then sets the bouquet down carefully on the bench. Some of her teammates send her envious looks. Yeah, she's pretty lucky.

Her phone buzzes. It's Chandani. TJ gives her a sidelong glance; she's literally on the other end of the bench. Sending her Instagram links without any explanation. TJ sighs and clicks on the first.

The meme pops up on her screen. Her and Simran's faces again, except the caption is different. **Before and After Puberty.**

"What's that?" Liam peeks over her shoulder. She doesn't answer, just clicks the next link. Simran's picture, with the caption **when ya girl gets too comfortable in the relationship.**

Liam sighs. "Just ignore it. Chandani, stop stirring shit up." He presses the sleep button on the side of her phone, leaving TJ staring at her own furious reflection. "It'll die down."

She takes a deep breath. Yes, it will. She just has to get through it until then.

Waiting for the meme to die down turns out to be a challenge. The next day only brings a fresh wave of posts, which TJ knows because she obsessively checks several social media feeds. Even though she's always the one framed positively, every new iteration stings. She's addicted to that sting. It's like pinching herself to make another injury less painful in comparison.

Simran, however, seems unbothered every time TJ sees her, calmly walking through the halls as if the giggles and whispers aren't happening. How can she be so okay? And why is TJ so *not* okay?

The meme finally hits a peak on Thursday when someone manages to hack the school TV slideshow and insert it between the announcement for the Spring Break senior retreat and the latest school council fundraiser. TJ even hears that the meme has reached other schools in the city, including Whitewater. Charlie and Nate must be pissing themselves.

However, the slideshow hack makes the school administration take notice. There must've been an emergency lunchtime staff meeting, because for the rest of the day and Friday, the teachers give five-minute condescending lectures about bullying. The secondhand embarrassment is almost as bad as the meme itself.

It's a relief when Friday afternoon finally rolls around, and Winter Break is upon them at last. Immediately after the last bell, TJ hightails it to Lulu's beauty parlour for her appointment. She changes into the usual terry-cloth robe and waits in a spa room for Lulu, tea in hand, riffling through magazines. The lo-fi instrumental music playing in the background does nothing to soothe her.

The door opens. Lulu pokes her head in, her black-lipstick-stained mouth widening into a smile. "I'll be with you in a few minutes, darling. Would you like more tea?"

"No, thanks, Lulu."

"Well, lemon tarts are waiting for you when we're done! Just remember that." She winks and, in a blur of platinum-blonde curls, is gone again.

After the door swings shut, TJ's knee begins to bounce.

Liam's invited her over tomorrow because his parents aren't home this weekend, and TJ's are attending a work dinner, a rare coincidence on both their ends. Making it the perfect opportunity to get it on.

She runs through a mental checklist. She's been on birth control for years for heavy periods. Liam has a stash of condoms. They've both got clean bills of health. With all that taken care of, there's just one thing left to do: this Brazilian.

She still remembers her first. She was so nervous she called Piper while in the waiting room and told her to talk her down from leaving.

"What if I, like, pee all over the table?" she'd asked.

Piper had laughed. "Just go to the bathroom right before. Don't worry."

"What if I"—she lowered her voice despite being alone— "orgasm? Didn't that happen to Tiffany Presser last year?" It had been the talk of the school; Tiffany had told the story in confidence to some questionable people, and it had gotten out. That was a trauma TJ wasn't keen on.

"Hmm. Then I guess you like it rough."

"Ha, ha. What if they think my butthole is weird? Or too hairy?"

"Buttholes *are* weird. It does hurt, but it's not like there's really much hair around there anyway."

TJ had sort of deflated at that. She called Chandani next.

When she told her what Piper had said, Chandani had ugly laughed, which was exactly what TJ had needed to hear. "Piper's so white!" she'd declared, and she sounded both amused and envious.

TJ's phone buzzes with a text, pulling her from her memories.

It's Ameera, who she hasn't spoken much to since the last debate: You around? Mr. York got a professor to come to Whitewater today to talk about the science of the Provincials resolution with us. We're invited, meeting at four.

What? She glances at the time. It's quarter to four already. And she was told to block off half an hour for this appointment.

Even if she races out afterwards, she'll only catch the tail end of the meeting.

But . . . it sounds so useful. TJ always has trouble wrapping her head around science stuff. Having an expert explain it would be amazing.

The door opens. Lulu pokes her head in. "Ready?"

TJ rises, wrapping her robe tighter around her. As she sets down her empty teacup, she realizes she forgot to go to the bathroom like Piper had advised. Great. This is going to hurt like hell, *and* she's going to miss possibly the most important debate meeting of the season.

But does she really have to?

The thought makes her hesitate halfway to the door. She mulls it over. Is it really a big deal if she doesn't get the Brazilian this one time?

Duh, yes it is, a voice in her head says. *You're so hairy!*

She frowns. Yes, she's hairy, but Liam can see past that, can't he? They've had sex before. He's been her boyfriend for over a year, her friend for even longer. Her hair shouldn't really matter.

"TJ?"

TJ looks up to find Lulu staring at her with confusion. She should just go with her.

But then she imagines getting grilled with difficult scientific questions in a cross-examination. The words immediately fly from her mouth: "Cancel my appointment."

Lulu blinks. "The Brazilian isn't *that* bad, darling—"

"I have to go." TJ's already hurrying back to the changing

area. "If there's a cancellation fee, I'll pay. There's just some-where I have to be right now. Sorry!"

She leaves a bemused Lulu standing there. If she's fast, she might make it to Whitewater on time for the meeting. This could seriously up her game. Her boyfriend will understand.

FOUR
***

S he's still late.
Whitewater's almost twenty minutes away, a sprawling
building that looms over Kelowna from a hilltop. TJ parks in
the lot and treks up to the archway entrance. The place is more
window than concrete, with state-of-the-art sports facilities
that make Whitewater the envy of every other school in the
district. She scowls up at it. It was so much easier to make fun
of Whitewater when they were still housed in that decrepit old
building three years ago. Now Northridge looks like a barn in
comparison.

She resists the urge to kick lockers on her way to the gigantic band room, where their debate club practices after-hours.
Everyone else is already there when she enters. The music
stands have been pushed aside, and the students sit in a semicircle of chairs around the board where a middle-aged man in
jeans and a hoodie stands holding a piece of chalk. TJ hesitates
slightly at his casual appearance.

Nate, sitting in the semicircle, must notice her double take
because he speaks up. "You're in the right place, don't worry. He
dresses like garbage because he's got tenure."

"Nate, that's *enough*," the professor says with a tone of
exasperation. TJ blinks and the pieces slide together; Nate's
mentioned before that his father teaches at the university, and

they share similar features. Dr. Chen offers TJ a smile. "Please, have a seat."

TJ approaches the semicircle. It seems like everyone attending Provincials managed to make it. There are three teams each from the novice, junior, and senior categories. Simran's there, briefly nodding at her. Yara, too; she smiles at TJ, but it wavers. TJ attempts a smile back. Yara must know her photo has become a joke. With TJ and Simran as the butt of it.

The only vacant seat is next to Charlie Rosencrantz on the edge of the semicircle, so she sits, dumping her purse behind her, as Dr. Chen goes back to drawing a strand of DNA on the board. The prepared resolution for the provincial tournament is already written on the top: *This House Would endorse genome editing in Canada.* A familiar sense of panic rises in her before she squashes it. The prepared resolutions are always sort of panic-inducing, but that's the point of them being prepared. Each team will have until February to do their research and write speeches. And there will be help, like Nate's dad; for Provincials, the local clubs pool their resources and help each other because, well, they're *all* underdogs in this tournament.

While she's digging through her purse for a pen, Charlie mutters through the side of his mouth, "Too busy googling 'genome' to show up on time?"

She mutters through the side of her mouth, too. "While you were sitting here googling 'editing'? Or maybe 'Canada'?"

"Hey," snaps Mr. York from the corner of the room, making them jump. "Dr. Chen is donating his time to us, and considering he's done research in genome editing, he's a great resource. The least you could do is pay attention."

TJ nods silently. Curse Charlie for luring her into conversation. But Dr. Chen doesn't look annoyed. He just smiles again before returning to the board.

TJ finally finds a pen and starts scribbling down buzzwords on her notepad. However, somewhere in the explanation between DNA and CRISPR arrays, she gets lost. She's strongest in debates about culture or politics. She casts a look at Simran, who's listening attentively. TJ will have to lean on her hard for this one.

"So what you're saying," Yara says at the end of Dr. Chen's talk, her eyes wide, "is that you could change anything about a person by editing their DNA?"

"Theoretically, you could change things that are genetics-based," Dr. Chen says. "You could choose which genes are turned on or off. Add desirable traits or delete ones you don't like. What would you pick and choose from a list of traits? Dark hair, or blond? Brown eyes, or green? What if you could activate genes that enhance intelligence? Strength? Beauty? And what would you delete?"

The whole room is riveted. Nate's expression has become unusually pensive. Yara bites her nails, and Charlie stares into space. Even Simran pauses in writing her notes. TJ wonders if they, like her, are thinking of what they'd ask from the gene fairy. She already knows what she'd wish for. Wherever the hairiness is in her DNA, she'd *snip snip snip* it right out.

Dr. Chen adds, "This technology has the potential to improve a lot of lives. But the idea of playing with our own genome is still pretty controversial."

"Why?" Saad asks.

"Well, first of all, ethically, preventing things like genetic abnormalities may seem like an easy choice, but that logic gets shakier the more you examine it. What's really a disease, and what's just diversity? Who gets to decide?" His brows crease. "And it goes even further than that. We might not know all the consequences of deleting a gene from the pool until later down the line. You've heard of the Irish Potato Famine, right?" Nods. "That happened because farmers all bred the same kind of potato. When they got infected with fungus, they *all* got infected, because there were no resistant strains to fall back on. No diversity. What might happen to us if we start trying to achieve the same sort of genetic health ideal?"

The conversation continues for a while. Some of the others are clearly way more into the topic than TJ is. She just tries her best to keep up. Once Dr. Chen has fielded all the eager questions, he leaves, waving them farewell from the door.

TJ taps her pen against her lips. A headache is building as she stares down at her notes.

"Cheer up, TJ," Nate says, and she blinks to find him looking at her from across the semicircle. "The resolution's not that bad. At least it's not like that debate a few years back on euthanasia where you thought we were arguing the existence of Youth In Asia—"

"For about two seconds!" TJ snaps. "And I was *thirteen*—"

"Enough, Nate," Mr. York barks, and Nate's smirk fades. This is what TJ appreciates about the Whitewater debate coach. He may be a hard-ass, but he's an equal opportunity hard-ass. "Now, let's talk debate practice for the next few months. For

those of you new to Provincials, all our qualifying teams practice together as much as possible. You won't be facing each
other at the tournament. The competition is over. We're all on
the same side now."

TJ almost snorts. Yeah, right. The top two seniors from their
region will get spots at the national competition. They may not
be facing each other directly at Provincials, but they're still
competing.

Mr. York goes on. "After Winter Break, we'll be meeting once
a week to practice, rotating our sessions between all the schools
represented here. Since Dr. Chen has given us a lot to think
about, let's—"

"Go home for the holidays?" suggests one of the novice
debaters.

"—play a game of Word Salad."

Groans from the group.

Word Salad is a sadistic game Mrs. Scott crafted in which
everyone writes an object or concept on a slip of paper and puts
it in a basket. Then they take turns going up to the front and
freestyling a speech based on whatever subject they pull out of
the hat on the spot. But that's not all—thirty seconds in, you
draw another paper, and have to find a way to segue the speech
into *that* topic. And then once more, or however many rounds
Mrs. Scott feels like on that particular day.

They're doing three rounds, so everyone's tasked with filling out three slips each. TJ stares at hers and draws a blank.
Not a single subject is coming to mind. Finally she gives up
and scribbles down three words that Freud would have a field

day with: *Soccer. Hair.* And finally . . . *Beautiful.*

There. It's anonymous anyway. She drops her slips into the pot.

"Charlie, you'll start," Mr. York says. "You're closest to the front."

Charlie's never been particularly good at this game, from TJ's observations. But he gets up from his chair as if he is, straightening the black blazer he's wearing over a white tee. He'd probably call this dressing down, with those skinny pants rolled up at the ankle and pristine white Vans. TJ would wager he has a bigger closet than she does.

Plucking a slip from the pot, he reads clearly, "Underwear." Snickers arise from the crowd, especially one of the ninth graders, the clear mastermind behind the slip. That's another thing about this game. Everyone tries to make it as entertaining as possible.

Charlie, of course, hardly blinks. "Underwear. We all wear it, there's a whole section in the department store devoted to it, and whole companies designed to make us look our best under our clothes." His dramatic speaking style makes him sound like he's delivering a TED Talk. However, he's also pausing longer than usual, which TJ smugly notes to mean he's trying to run the clock until the next topic. "But for most of us, while underwear is crucial, we might not even think about it much. After all, it's rarely ever seen—"

"Speak for yourself," Nate heckles. Mr. York shushes him.

Charlie continues as if he hadn't spoken. "—and when it *is* seen, well, you don't see it for that long anyway."

"PG-13, please, Charlie," Mr. York says resignedly. His watch dings. Charlie reaches into the pot again. Withdraws another.

"But despite all that," he goes on, and looks up to make eye contact with TJ, "there's an entire industry built on it being *beautiful*."

TJ crosses and uncrosses her legs nervously. He recognized her handwriting? But of course. They've been debating since they were twelve. Maybe she should've stuck to getting the Brazilian. It'd probably be less uncomfortable than this.

Charlie, meanwhile, launches into his next point. "Why do people shop for beautiful underwear? There's the obvious reasons, of course, which I can't talk about without being thrown out of this classroom." Mr. York massages his temples. "But there's other reasons. There are people who say that wearing nice underwear makes them feel more confident, more right in their own skin, despite the fact that no one's seeing it. But why is that so empowering? Is it the knowledge that the underwear *would* be beautiful if someone saw it? Is it that wearing something beautiful makes you feel the same way? Why do beautiful things have such an impact on us?"

Mr. York's watch beeps again. He thrusts the pot in front of Charlie, looking like he sorely regrets this whole idea. *"Next."*

Charlie withdraws his last topic from the pot. He takes a quick glance at it and then again, longer this time.

"Charlie," Mr. York says after several seconds. "No hesitation allowed, remember? Just try to work it in."

Charlie's lips part, and he looks like he's about to speak—he inhales, and his shoulders sink, but no sound comes out. It's like the words are stuck in his throat. Then he shakes his head, crumples the slip in his hand, and tosses it into the wastebasket.

Everyone gawks as he says, "I'll take a different one."

"No, you won't," Mr. York says. "You use what you're given. That's the rule."

Charlie hesitates—*hesitates!*—for half a second. "I can't think of anything to say."

TJ's jaw drops. The classroom is dead silent for a second. Even Mr. York seems a little stunned, before he reacts.

"Just try. You should be able to do this with any subject at your level."

Charlie gives Mr. York a bored glance. "Give me a break."

"No." Mr. York's voice becomes sharp. "Clearly, you need more practice. Sit down. You'll do a full five later."

Charlie shrugs and ambles back to his seat with his hands in his pockets.

Saad elbows him. "Looks like you should've worn your lacy black thong. Maybe then you'd have a bit more confidence."

"I save that one for tournaments," Charlie replies with complete sincerity.

TJ doesn't join in on the ribbing, just watches with narrowed eyes. As Ameera goes up next, curiosity niggles at her. Charlie always seems so infuriatingly cool under fire. Everything bounces off him. What could have tripped him up so bad that he couldn't take it? She's got to know.

She endures the next half hour, including her own turn at Word Salad ("lemonade," "sex ed," and "frogs" were an interesting combination). When practice is done, Mr. York sends them off with warm salutations for the holidays and a reminder to work on their cases.

TJ waits for everyone else to leave, feigning busyness by scribbling on her notepad. However, Mr. York isn't having it.

"I have to lock up in here," he says. TJ smiles brightly.

"Right." She stands, walks by the little metal wastebasket on her way out, and drops her notebook in. "Whoops."

Mr. York doesn't comment on her less-than-stellar acting performance. He just watches her fish it out. "I'm not sure that's sanitary."

She dusts off the notebook. "It's fine. There's nothing but paper in here." Total lie, there's gum stuck to her hand. Gross. "Besides, I really need this."

She hurries out and flicks the gum with a shudder into the nearest garbage. Only then does she unfold the crinkled slip of paper she'd fished from the wastebasket along with her notebook. And finally, she sees what some comedian in the group scrawled on one of their slips: *Simran's moustache.*

FIVE
✷

TJ's mood is spectacularly bad by Saturday afternoon. She's staring up at the ceiling from the couch in the living room when her mother's face appears over her.

"What's the pout for?"

TJ tries to fix her expression. "You look nice, Mom."

She does. She's in a full face of makeup, her glossy hair extending past her shoulders. A stark difference from her usual look, which is under-eye bags and frizzy bun from working overnight at the hospital.

Her mother crosses her arms. "Don't change the subject. Shouldn't you be happy now that you're free from school until January?"

"Free?" TJ echoes. "I've got university applications, debate, *and* soccer to worry about."

Her mother's eyes clear in understanding. "Well, I bet Kiran could help you with your applications. She got into so many schools. Why don't you ask her?"

TJ nods half-heartedly. Her older cousin *would* be a good resource, but that's not why she's stewing.

Yesterday, she'd thrown the slip of paper away immediately and washed her hands of it, literally. But in a figurative sense, she has not washed her hands of anything in the past week. In fact, her hands are digging even further into the muck. She feels like she's one incident away from pitching forward and drowning in it.

There are several people who could have put that prompt in the pot. One of the debaters from another school probably thought it would be funny. After all, both of the meme celebrities were in the room with them. TJ almost wishes Charlie *had* used it, because then maybe she could confront someone.

"I'm not so sure that's the only thing bothering her," her father muses. TJ lifts her head to find him by the door. With his hair freshly buzzed and his special-occasions-only overcoat on, he looks almost as young as he does in the wedding photo behind him.

"Aren't you going to be late?" she says pointedly. Her mom looks at her dad.

"She wants us to leave so badly. I wonder why?"

"She's going to throw a party."

"Or maybe invite a boy." They both giggle.

TJ laughs weakly, then clears her throat. "I might go to Piper's. We'll see. Have fun at the dinner!" She directs this last part at her father. He scowls. They both know he hates work events; he'll be listening awkwardly and praying for an early exit as TJ's mom schmoozes.

After her parents leave, she texts Liam. **You can come pick me up in 10.**

Then she runs to the washroom. With military efficiency, she puts on some makeup. She examines her face in the mirror. No pesky hairs that need to be plucked. Skin gleaming with a little highlighter. Eyes popping with mascara and eyeliner. Her hair straightened. Tinted chapstick only because, well . . . kissing.

She runs a mental checklist. Deodorant, check. Perfume, check. Cute underwear—Charlie's voice pops into her head, and she irritatedly shoves it out—check. All freshly shaved and waxed, check. Well, except for . . .

Down *there*.

Oh well. She's still glad she skipped the appointment. She *did* pick up some things at the debate meeting, more than she would've on her own. Besides, Liam knows she's not a Barbie doll. There's nothing to worry about.

Her phone vibrates again. Liam: I'm here.

She exhales and exits the bathroom.

Once she's bundled up in her cute ski jacket, she leaves the house and walks the extra block it takes to get to Liam's waiting car. His eyes sparkle when she slides in.

"Hey, beautiful." He kisses her in greeting. "Ready to make some gingerbread houses?"

TJ sits up straighter. She'd almost forgotten about those. "*Finally*. Did you buy enough candy?"

Liam grins and reaches into the back seat to show her a plastic bag full of bulk candy. "You think I'd half-ass this?"

Instead of answering, TJ smacks a kiss on his cheek.

When they arrive at his house, Liam turns the fireplace on while TJ enters the gigantic living room and starts an assembly line for their gingerbread, icing, and candy on the coffee table. There's a lot more candy than she realized. "You really cleared out the bulk section, huh?"

He joins her on the floor. "I had a feeling you'd need it."

He's right. Over the next hour, TJ builds an intricate ginger-bread castle much larger than Liam's simple four-walled house, but it partially collapses while she's still decorating the roof. That doesn't stop her from heavily decorating the ruins, how-ever. The candy dwindles as the conversation shifts towards graduation. Liam's in talks with coaches at UBC Vancouver, where he wants to study biology. TJ, of course, doesn't know what she wants to do yet, so she quickly changes the subject. "Um—any fun holiday plans?"

Not her best segue, but he doesn't seem to notice. "Yeah, maybe. Jake was talking about doing a trip to Whistler. Get some skiing in. Wanna come?"

That *does* sound fun. But . . . things will get busy in the new year. Now's the best time to work on her debate speeches. "Um, I don't know."

"Why not? Debate stuff?"

She blinks. "How do you—"

"With you it's always debate." He shrugs, popping an M&M in his mouth. "Is this the last tournament?"

Embarrassed at her utter transparency, she refocuses on add-ing tiny gumdrops to the roof of her castle. "It might be the last official debate association one, yeah." Technically, there are plenty of other private tournaments, either in Vancouver or across other provinces. They're usually hosted by universities. TJ's attended a few, but in recent years, with the Southern Inte-rior debate numbers dwindling, Mrs. Scott has called it quits on those because of the time commitment.

"Might be?" Liam prods.

TJ shrugs. "Unless I qualify for Nationals." That's *the* tournament, going up against the best debaters from each province.

"When's that?"

"May. Kelowna is actually hosting it this year. At Northridge." She doesn't specify the timing further, although she knows the dates by heart. It's the same weekend as her team's final soccer tournament. And she knows exactly which of those she would choose to attend, but that's a later problem.

"Maybe I should come watch. I've been wondering how it works," Liam says. "For some reason I just picture arguing over a table."

TJ snickers. "It's not a *politician's* debate. There's rules. Like, in Cross-Examination Style, you can't interrupt people's speeches, but you have a whole two minutes at the end just to grill them. I love that one." It's so deliciously bloody. Too bad it's mostly used for novice and junior categories. "Then there's Canadian National Style, which lets you stand up in the middle of people's speeches and ask questions. They get to decide whether they *let* you ask, but it *is* more of an immediate clash. They say one thing, you stand up and question it right away, watch them put together an answer on the spot. It's fun."

Liam sets his bag of M&M's down, nodding along, but his eyes have darkened, and she suspects he's not really listening anymore.

"Then there's British Parliamentary Style," she blabs, because his proximity is suddenly making her nervous. "We don't do that one, though. It's more of a university-level debate thing. I did watch this taping of a debate at World's—"

He cuts her off by kissing her.

She relaxes almost at once. Why was she even nervous? She doesn't remember, not when his arms wrap around her waist almost reverently; she leans into his body, running a hand through his hair. He tastes like icing and candy. She wants *more*.

If only the hardwood floor wasn't torturing her knees. But he seems to sense her discomfort, because he pulls her flush against him. "Hold on," he murmurs, and then rises in one fluid motion. She squeaks in surprise, but he just deposits her on the couch and crawls over her. His hands drift under her sweater and then up. "This okay?"

TJ responds by pulling her sweater off. She gets drunk on the look in his eyes when he takes her in, mint satin bra and all. "See something you like?"

Liam's voice is a low growl. "Yeah. Everything."

He reaches down to trace the button of her jeans, popping it open. TJ's breath hitches as he drags the zipper down. The world slows and focuses all into one point—that is, his hand, dipping into—

His fingers still.

"What?" TJ says breathlessly.

"Nothing." He pauses. "I just . . . thought you, um, were getting this done."

Her heart drops. The world rushes back. And with it, the problem that she had somehow, momentarily, forgotten.

She props herself up on her elbows, her limbs suddenly feeling clumsy and awkward. "I didn't think it was a big deal," she says in a small voice.

His eyebrows rise. "Didn't you say you were making an appointment?"

Her heart drops further. "I cancelled it."

"What? Why?"

His tone is sharp suddenly. It snaps her out of her strange shyness. She narrows her eyes. "*Why?*" she repeats. "Why does it matter? Does a little hair scare you?"

He's quick to reply. "No. I just—uh, didn't expect this much." He clears his throat. "We could always do this later, if you want."

TJ's face burns as the full impact of his words hits her. Her own boyfriend can't bear to have sex with her if she has a full bush. He can hardly even look at her.

After the crappy week she's had, it's the last straw.

She shoves his hands away and sits up. "I'm going home."

He pales and reaches for her. She jerks away and yanks her sweater back over her head. It takes her a few tries, but eventually she gets it on and stands.

"TJ," Liam sighs, "don't be like this—"

She can hardly see through her blurred vision long enough to rebutton her jeans. "Go to hell, Liam." She practically runs to the closet to get her coat.

He follows. "I'm sorry, okay? I just meant if you weren't ready for tonight then you could've said so!" He sounds upset. "Don't leave. How are you even going to get home?"

She whirls around at the door. "Don't follow me!" She shouts it, pretty much, but her voice catches, so the effect is probably nil.

Still, it's somewhat satisfying to slam the door closed as she leaves.

It's less satisfying when she realizes he's right—she doesn't have a ride home. No way is she crawling back to beg for one. He's probably watching from the window right now.

She considers texting Chandani, but she's at her little brother's piano recital tonight.

TJ texts Piper instead. **Can you pick me up?**

Piper's reply is instant. **From Liam's??**

Yep.

Piper doesn't ask more; she just texts she's on her way. TJ pockets her phone and paces down the street, past houses bedecked with Christmas lights, until she reaches the stop sign at the end of the road. She watches her breaths puff in the cold air and, in the silence, replays her and Liam's parting words. He apologized to her. Maybe she's overreacting.

Then she remembers his expression when he touched her— just for a moment, really, but *revulsion* flickered in his eyes as he jerked his hand away. Her eyes burn with tears again. He knows now; he knows how *fake* she is. Why didn't she just suck it up and get the Brazilian?

Piper's car pulls up to the curb. TJ gets in. Piper's hair is wet, piled hastily at the top of her head, and she's wearing sweatpants. Her eyes are wide with concern. "What happened?"

TJ tries to speak, but with Piper looking at her like that, she can't. If she talks, she'll cry.

Piper seems to understand. "Oh no." She rubs TJ's back. "I'm sorry. Guys are the worst."

TJ still can't respond.

"What happened?" Piper whispers again, but TJ just shakes her head. It's too humiliating. Instead, she takes a deep, shuddering breath and looks up.

"Please, take me home?"

Piper scans her face, which probably betrays everything she's holding in. "You sure?"

TJ nods firmly. She wants to crawl into bed and have no one see her.

Piper doesn't probe further. She just pulls away from the curb.

The ride is silent, although Piper glances her way multiple times. When she finally pulls into TJ's driveway, TJ murmurs, "Thanks."

"Call me when you want to talk."

TJ nods mechanically. "Thanks," she says again.

"Or if you want to plan Liam's murder."

TJ tries to smile. "Okay."

She lets herself in. No one's home, of course. Those fancy work dinners usually run late. TJ doesn't bother turning any lights on. She falls into bed and stares at the ceiling for a long time, blinking back the tears in her eyes.

Eventually, though, she pulls out her phone to scroll through Instagram. Somehow she finds herself clicking back to the original meme. The side-by-side photos of Simran and her are such a contrast. She stares at the screen until she starts going cross-eyed and sees double of her own face instead.

The people who think she's pretty—they don't know how

much of her life is spent keeping up the image. Her best-kept secret is her real body. But why can't her real body be pretty, too?

The thought has her pulling up Lulu's number. Instead of calling, TJ hits block.

Then she gets up and goes to the bathroom. She roots through her drawers and makes a pile of her razors. Shaving cream. Her thread. Her jar of wax. Her epilator. The old tube of hair-removal gel. Everything she can find, every tool that has helped keep her secret. The floor is littered with items by the time she's done.

She puts it all into a bag. Then she lugs it out the back door in her flip-flops and throws it all in the outdoor garbage can.

She stands there, panting, waiting to feel satisfied, to feel freer, but all she feels is her toes going numb from the cold. This is useless. Throwing out all her stuff doesn't prove anything. She could wake up tomorrow less brave and buy it all again. And she doesn't *want* to go back to how it was. No. She's done hiding.

The problem, of course, is that it's so much easier to hide than face her greatest insecurity. What she needs is a way to force herself to commit.

And the idea comes to her, all at once.

She runs back inside and upstairs to her room. Her debate bag is on her desk where she left it, and she grabs it, dumping the contents on the bed. Her notebook, pens, and scoresheets from the last tournament clatter onto the comforter, along with an unused package of cue cards.

She rips the package open and pulls out a blank card. Bracing it on her notebook, she taps a pen against her lips, trying to think of the right wording. It has to be convincing. It has to be firm. Finally, she puts her pen to paper and writes. A smile stretches over her face as she does. This was definitely the way to go.

Because it's a debate resolution. And like with all debate resolutions, she reads it and *becomes* it, instantly. She will go to absurd lengths to prove it. She will shoot down every opposing argument with *evidence* to prove why her resolution must stand.

This House Believes That TJ Powar can be her hairy self and still be beautiful.

SIX
✳✳✳

TWO WEEKS LATER

lick, clack, click, clack.

C TJ's heeled boots echo as she walks through Northridge's halls on the first day back after Break. It's seven thirty in the morning, so the place is a ghost town. TJ wouldn't be here, either, if it weren't for the seniors-only debate practice happening. They're all so busy this first week of classes that the crack of dawn was the only time they could meet.

She throws her soccer bag into her locker and heads to Mrs. Scott's classroom, where muffled voices can be heard. She pauses at the door, grips her Starbucks mug harder, and walks in.

Everyone is lounging at desks in the front, while Mrs. Scott is on the phone. They all look up when TJ enters. She gives a vague nod to the room before finding a seat next to Ameera.

Ameera glances at her from where she's eating a wholesome breakfast of Cheetos. "Love the outfit."

Quite the compliment coming from Ameera, who looks like a hijabi model twenty-four seven. "Thanks." It'd better get compliments—the silk scarf her masi brought back from India, combined with her cream sweater and straightened hair, is her armour today. She's just trying to draw attention away from what is glaringly obvious to her:

1. Her unruly eyebrows.
2. The hairs growing on her upper lip.
3. Her sideburns, which have started growing in again.
4. The hair on her knuckles. Dear *god*.

She represses a shudder and reminds herself that it's only been two weeks; it's not *that* noticeable. Although fluorescent lights like the ones currently above her don't help.

And that's only what's visible right now in her winter outfit. She doesn't even want to think about when the weather warms. Truly, every time TJ looks in the mirror she wants to scream. She wants to unblock Lulu and beg her to fix her. But no. She *must* win this debate. Side Opposition cannot be allowed to take this from her.

Speaking of, she hasn't seen Liam yet—over Break, she'd left all his calls and texts unanswered, relenting only to tell him to give her space until January. She's not sure what she'll do when she sees him.

TJ digs out her notebook, making eye contact with Simran when she straightens back up. They nod at each other. TJ hasn't seen her since Christmas. Simran's family came over for chah just like every year, and the uncomfortable silences between their mothers were painful. TJ spent most of it talking to Simran's older sister, Kiran, who was home for the holidays and had looked over her university applications for her. She'd seemed puzzled as to why TJ was applying to so many Ontario schools, and TJ explained she was looking for an adventure in a different province. Which was partially true. And definitely easier than saying it was really because they had robust, decorated debate clubs.

Anyway, Kiran seemed to buy it. But Simran, who sat silently nearby, was harder to read. She'd already gotten early acceptance into several schools. Not that she offered any wisdom to TJ, but then again, TJ didn't ask.

TJ's brought back to the present when Ameera offers her a Cheeto. She shakes her head and again meets Simran's gaze. "Hi."

"Hi." Simran yawns.

TJ offers her mug. "Coffee?"

"I don't drink coffee."

She hadn't known that. "Oh, okay." She retracts her mug. There's a long stretch of silence. Everyone else has stopped talking, too.

"You know what I just realized?" Nate pulls at his blue hoodie strings. "You two make a somewhat-decent team, but when you're not debating you act like neighbours who keep awkwardly meeting in grocery store aisles."

"No wonder no one ever realizes they're related," Charlie says, his arms stretched back over his head.

TJ sneers at him. "Kind of like how no one realized your parents were related, Charlie."

Nate guffaws and Charlie laughs, too, which makes it far less satisfying. Simran presses her lips together. TJ can't tell if she's suppressing amusement or disapproval.

Mrs. Scott finally slams down the phone. "Good grief, admin is irritating me and it's not even an hour into the first workday. Are you all here? Good. Who has speeches for Provincials ready?"

Awkward. TJ's only made a half-assed start on those, despite the promises she'd made herself at the beginning of Break. No one else raises their hand, either. Mrs. Scott arches an eyebrow.

"That's what I thought. You all could stand to learn something from the novice debaters. I'm told *four* of the six of them already have rough speeches written out."

"Because they're scared shitless," Nate mutters, and everyone grins. Mrs. Scott hears him, though.

"Pride goeth before the fall, Nathaniel. Now, let's do some impromptu practice. Three of you per side." She strides to the board and writes *THBT traditional universities will be replaced with online learning.* "You have twenty minutes to prepare. And split up from your partners. Might give you some perspective." She marks an imaginary line down the middle of the room, effectively making TJ, Saad, and Charlie into one group and Simran, Ameera, and Nate the other.

"Which side are we arguing for?" Saad asks. Mrs. Scott waves a dismissive hand.

"Rock-paper-scissors for it."

Saad and Ameera eye each other like it's a Western movie showdown. Ameera puts down her Cheetos. Saad cracks his knuckles. TJ has no intention of getting in between this sibling rivalry, so she goes to find an empty classroom to take over for brainstorming. Charlie follows.

The neighbouring classroom is empty, so she dumps her bag on the floor and drops into a chair. Charlie does the same. Through the wall she hears Ameera complaining in muffled tones that Saad cheated.

TJ and Charlie stare at each other for a long moment.

Charlie's "debate practice at seven, executive meeting at eight" look is in full swing today, with a navy crew neck sweater, the pale-pink collar of a dress shirt peeking from beneath it. Nerd.

She can't help but think about the last time she saw him—when he threw away that slip of paper. TJ gets why; he and Simran are friends. But would he have done TJ the same courtesy?

Without breaking her stare, Charlie plucks a pen from his pocket and clicks it. It reminds TJ of someone flipping the safety off a gun. "Well? What do you think?"

Right. They're on the same side. In previous interschool debate practices, she's never been teammates with him. This will probably be a disaster. She tries for civility anyway. "We might as well brainstorm for both sides while we're waiting for Saad. Any ideas?"

He crosses one corduroy-pant-clad leg over his knee. TJ feels like he's just trying to show off his suede shoes. "What, does Simran usually write your speeches, too?"

Great. That civility lasted about two seconds. TJ smiles sweetly. "Jealous? We all know Nate doesn't bother. He just feeds you lines."

"You don't mess with what works."

Saad walks in at that moment, looking smug. "We got Side Opposition. Screw online learning, status quo for the win."

Charlie glances at the clock and seems to sober up. "All right. Stakeholders." He flips his legal notepad to a fresh page. TJ nods. Figuring out who's affected in any resolution is always a good starting place.

The three of them brainstorm stakeholders quickly—students, professors, researchers who get university funding, taxpayers . . . the list goes on. Over the next fifteen minutes, they split their contentions. TJ will handle the economic effects and quality of education for students. Charlie will do the philosophical pondering about the significance of the institution and the loss of research opportunities. Saad will wrap up with the rebuttal speech.

By the time Mrs. Scott pops her head into the classroom to bring them back, they've got a fairly solid case. As they stand, Charlie grabs TJ's hand. "You're bleeding."

She looks down. There's a paper cut on her first knuckle, welling with blood. It must have happened while flipping pages back and forth in her notebook.

"You should get a Band-Aid." His thumb swipes over her unscathed knuckles, almost thoughtlessly. The tickling sensation of it makes her breath catch.

There's *hair* on her knuckles.

Mortified, she yanks her hand out of his grasp. She waits with dread. The comment, or the smirk. Either one will make her die a fiery death.

But Charlie doesn't seem to notice. He picks up his notepad, now speckled with a few spots of red. "Your blood is all over my speech. Symbolism?"

"Definitely not." She brings her knuckle to her mouth and sucks on the cut, relieved he didn't notice. Just as she's thinking that, his eyes drop to her mouth. She lowers her hand quickly.

He gives her an indecipherable look and follows Saad out

of the room. She wants to smack herself. Twenty minutes into the first day of school since making her resolution, and she's already wavering. But did Charlie Rosencrantz *have* to be her first test? That's just unfair.

Yet, despite his talent for weaponizing her weaknesses, he hasn't noticed her hair. She's certain he would've said something, or implied it, if he had. He's never held back before.

Her shoulders sink from released tension. Maybe that's just it. Maybe no one will notice. Maybe it's all in her head.

A few minutes before the bell for first class, the practice ends. Charlie and Nate have late passes for their first period, but they promptly dip out to head back to Whitewater, leaving the Northridgers to move the desks back into place. When TJ finally leaves Mrs. Scott's classroom, she runs straight into Chandani and Piper in the foyer. They're lugging their soccer bags into the school.

"There you are," Chandani drawls. "How was debate practice?"

TJ shrugs. Her team won the practice round. Saad had poked fabulous holes in Nate's and Ameera's contentions in his rebuttal, and in a surreal turn of events, Charlie actively backed up TJ's arguments when Simran went after them. The whole thing didn't devolve into bad jokes and heckling until the final speeches, which is pretty impressive for a debate practice. "Fine, I guess." She squints. "Wait. How'd you know where I was?" She definitely hadn't told anyone.

Chandani's eyes glint. "Well, when I was coming into the

parking lot just now, I saw this guy driving out who looked *really* familiar."

TJ nearly groans aloud.

Last year, Chandani had volunteered as timekeeper at one of their more informal tournaments—only because Mrs. Scott had offered extra credit in her English class. Somehow Chandani found a way to be assigned to one of TJ's debates, which just happened to be against Nate and Charlie. She'd spent most of it on her phone. TJ was fairly sure she wasn't using it to keep track of time limits, either. Actually, she was *completely* sure, because Charlie had gone two minutes overtime in his first speech before she noticed.

TJ had been pissed. Especially since Chandani was clearly paying attention to *some* things, just not things that mattered.

Chandani smiles evilly. "It was that one guy with the brown hair . . ."

"Oh, great," TJ says. "That really narrows it down."

"Shut up, bitch. You know who I'm talking about. And let me say, Northridge just doesn't make them like that, honey."

Piper pulls out her phone. "Who are you talking about? Let's find him."

"His name is Charlie Rosencrantz and he's got Instagram," Chandani says shamelessly. Piper taps away at her screen. After a minute, her eyes go round.

"*Now* I understand why you're in debate club, TJ." She and Chandani cackle. TJ does not. "His profile says he's student president at Whitewater. Did you know that?"

"No." Of course she did. She's stalked his Instagram multiple times; last year when he got re-elected for the position, he posted a completely unrelated photo of himself hiking along with a long caption about how *grateful* he was to his team. Performative prick.

The warning bell rings, and Piper bids them goodbye to hurry off to art. Meanwhile, TJ and Chandani walk back to Mrs. Scott's classroom for English. TJ tries not to show her trepidation. This is a class she shares with Liam.

When they enter, her treacherous eyes seek him out immediately. He's at the back of the class. His friends are talking around him, but he's focused on folding a piece of paper methodically into smaller and smaller squares. A nervous habit of his.

As if sensing her stare, he looks up and sees her. He starts rising from his desk, but TJ looks away and sits in her usual place several rows away. She's still half-angry, half-embarrassed. They've never fought like this before.

Silent reading is the first thing on the schedule, so TJ digs her book on genome editing out of her bag. Hopefully debate research will take her mind off Liam. Besides, she needs all the extra help she can get for Provincials.

However, halfway through the reading period, Mrs. Scott gets distracted chatting with the teacher across the hall, and the volume in the room rises steadily. TJ's trying her best to focus when Chandani leans across the desk, voice pitched low. "Don't panic, but you need a threading appointment stat."

Colour floods TJ's face. She touches her jaw. "Oh."

It's not a very convincing show of surprise. Chandani's eyebrows rise.

TJ puts down her book and wipes her sweaty palms on her jeans. She hasn't told anyone about her resolution yet. But Chandani's clearly awaiting an explanation, and, well, it's not like she's going to *stop* noticing the more TJ's hair grows in.

She beckons Chandani closer, and Chandani ducks her head so TJ can whisper. "I'm letting it grow on purpose."

"What?"

Chandani's voice is loud enough to make people around them pause.

TJ speaks even quieter. "I'm not threading or waxing or shaving anything. I'm stopping all of it." The words are hard to get out. They feel strange to say.

Clearly, they're even stranger to hear. "Are you joking?" Chandani asks. "Why would you do that?"

"To prove a point." TJ swallows. If she can't even say this to Chandani, who she's been friends with since she was little, then who can she say it to? "That it's okay to be . . . you know. Not hairless."

Chandani stares at her like she just grew a new arm on her forehead. "This is about that meme, isn't it?" When TJ doesn't reply, she shakes her head. "Girl. The meme is *dead*. No one even talks about it anymore."

That's true. It pretty much died out over Break. But . . .

"It's not about the meme anymore," TJ says. "It's about me."

Chandani doesn't say anything. Her eyebrows arch up again, and her gaze slides away, like she's holding something back.

Dread coils in TJ's stomach. Chandani *never* holds back. "What? Say it."

Chandani taps her pastel nails against the table before speaking. "Um . . . okay. What you're doing makes no sense. There's nothing to prove. Unless you're trying to prove you're a freak."

TJ blinks and narrows her eyes. She'd expected support. Instead, Chandani sounds disdainful. "You think Simran's a freak, too?"

"Simran is . . . different!" Chandani snaps. "I don't even know her, really. But I know *you*. Why would you willingly go back? It's the twenty-first century. We don't have to look like that anymore."

That stings. It more than stings. "Look like *what*?"

"You know what I mean," Chandani says icily. "Your werewolf look in sixth grade wasn't exactly sexy."

A long pause, where TJ just stares at her, unable to stop the wave of rage coming over her. "You're such a *bitch*."

She says it louder than she means to. Conversations in the room falter for a moment. Chandani's eyes harden, but she doesn't say a word. She just turns pointedly back to her book. TJ turns back to hers, because she's *not* apologizing for that.

But in the following five minutes, she doesn't read a single word, and she's pretty sure Chandani doesn't, either, because she never turns a page.

Mrs. Scott finally comes back to end silent reading and begin the lesson. TJ barely pays attention through the period; she's too busy fuming.

Chandani's always been judgy, but this? It stings. They've been friends for a decade, ever since their parents first forced them together for a playdate. You'd think you'd give someone the benefit of the doubt after all that, or at least not call them a freak.

As the period wears on, however, TJ starts to feel the beginnings of a *tiny* amount of regret. Maybe she didn't explain things properly. Maybe if she does, Chandani will listen, and understand.

But when TJ turns to her at the end of class, Chandani's already picked up her bag and is leaving without a backwards glance. TJ's guilt instantly swings back into annoyance. So. That's how it's going to be, then.

"Can I talk to you?"

She looks behind her. Liam is at her shoulder, peering down at her with his gorgeous green eyes, partly obscured by his curls.

And . . . he's checking her out. She forces herself to straighten her shoulders as she stands. She still doesn't know what to say, but she'll hear him out at least. "Sure."

He falls into step with her as she walks out of the classroom. "I'm sorry for what happened before the break. I wanted to give you space, but I feel really bad about it."

She turns to face him in the hallway. "About what?"

"Making you feel bad about yourself. It was a complete dick move." He hesitates, then reaches for her. When she doesn't move away, he brushes his thumb over her temple. "You look really pretty."

That gives her a rush. Either he sees the hair and doesn't care, or he straight up hasn't noticed yet, which is also possible. Chandani is just sharp-eyed about that kind of thing.

But that's all speculation. The fact—the *evidence*—is he said she was pretty. *This House Believes That TJ Powar can be her hairy self and still be beautiful.* And Liam agrees.

Someone jostles against her on their way down the hall. Liam automatically reaches out to steady her. "Watch it," he snaps at the kid, turning curious eyes their way. TJ becomes aware of how many people are around, including Chandani just down the hallway. TJ makes eye contact with her, but her expression is unreadable.

TJ looks back at Liam. *Yeah, watch this, Chandani.*

"I forgive you," she says with her sultriest smile, pushing her chest out a bit. His eyes fall almost helplessly, and that's when she leans in for a kiss, determined. And she gets it, right there in that busy hallway. She hopes they all see her. The girl who's making out with the hottest boy at Northridge. Her first contention, delivered without a hitch.

And if she jerks away a little early because his thumb brushes the new fuzz on her chin, well, that's beside the point.

SEVEN
✳✳✳

Over the next few weeks, TJ can only watch with horror as her body hair grows relentlessly. Her legs haven't been this hairy in years. Same with her arms. And her underarms. And her stomach. And—she could go on. The weather is still cold enough that she's only wearing sweaters and jeans, so that part is still a secret. Her face and hands, not so much.

One morning, TJ's wolfing down a piece of toast when her mother breezes by her and says, "You need a face threading, putt." TJ nearly chokes, but her mother's already out the door. She forces herself to breathe. *Remember the resolution.*

And then there's soccer. Since it's still off-season, TJ wears her soccer pants and a long-sleeve workout shirt to practices, and has no plans to change that. At least, until one practice in mid-February.

Before they begin, Coach announces they're getting photos taken for the upcoming season. Everyone shuffles into formation for the team photo. Coach stops the photographer before he can raise his camera.

"TJ! Didn't I tell you to wear your uniform?"

Heat rises to her face. "I am." Her jersey *is* on. Just over a long-sleeve shirt. But she definitely sticks out; no one else is wearing extra layers.

"And what about your shorts?" Coach says. "And socks?

Didn't we get a bulk order of colour-coordinated team uniforms or did I hallucinate that?"

Chandani coughs in a way that sounds suspiciously like a laugh. A few of the others titter as well, following her lead. TJ's blood boils. Things have been frosty between them ever since TJ snapped at her. But she isn't exactly keen on apologizing, especially when Chandani does shit like *this*.

But Coach is staring at her, waiting. Everyone is. This is so unfair. Scowling, TJ stalks to the empty changeroom and peels off her pants to reveal her shorts. They're fitted, green, and stamped with Northridge's logo, her last name and jersey number. They're also . . . very short. The team had voted for this style because they were cute. Right now, though, TJ wishes they'd gone for the longer, shapeless ones.

She tugs down the hem and pulls her socks as high as they'll go. Her knees and part of her thighs are still showing, the black hair glaringly long and obvious against her sun-deprived skin. This is nauseating. Maybe she can pretend she couldn't find the shorts . . .

TJ shakes herself. No. She can't change how she dresses because of the hair thing. That would be a strike against her resolution.

Which means—she glances down at her long sleeves in dismay—the shirt under her jersey has to go, too. Her heart sinks. How did she not notice this before? She's been hiding her arms without realizing it, for *weeks*. Contradicting her own resolution.

That ends now. Before she can overthink it, she removes the

long-sleeved shirt, throws her jersey back on, and heads back to the turf.

"Finally," Coach says when she returns. The whole team glances her way. TJ realizes right then that not wearing her shorts for weeks has backfired, because everyone got used to her in pants, and now that she's stepped out in shorts again, well . . . they're all *looking*. It's so silent. TJ wishes the ground would swallow her up.

The photographer is oblivious. "Middle row, please."

TJ obliges. The girls move apart for her. She can feel the weight of their eyes. It's aggravating. Do they notice or not?

But no one says a thing. The photographer takes several photos, and then it's time for individual shots. TJ stands behind the others, waiting her turn. Alexa smiles at her when she passes for her photo. TJ takes a deep breath. Maybe she's just imagining things.

When practice finally begins, she's paired with Chandani on a dribbling drill. The two of them have been tasked with passing the ball back and forth between an intricate setup of cones and then getting it past the goalie. Normally this wouldn't be a problem. Except each time she tries to pass to Chandani, TJ keeps misreading where she's going, and then missing the ball Chandani sends back.

"Ladies!" Coach is losing it from the sidelines. "*Talk* to each other!"

Yeah, right. TJ doesn't look at Chandani, just races over to where the ball has rolled and kicks it back at her, fully intending for her to nudge it into the goal with her cleat.

Chandani doesn't get her foot on it in time, though, and the ball sails past her. TJ slows to a stop. She knows how fast Chandani can run, can react. But she *chose* to go slower, and make it look like TJ miscalculated.

Oh, that pisses her off. TJ ignores Coach's shouting and walks off the field. She tosses her water bottle on the ground after a few swallows, then kneels back in the artificial grass to re-lace her cleats.

A pair of pale, smooth legs enters TJ's vision, blocking her sight of the passing drills. Piper.

"Usually I'd stay out of it, but this has been going on way too long. What happened with you and Chandani?"

TJ tugs on her shoelaces with unnecessary force. "Nothing."

When TJ doesn't say anything more, Piper sighs. "Well, please figure it out. I can't stand being caught between you two." She continues standing there, and after a moment, TJ realizes it's because she's staring at TJ's exposed knee.

TJ sighs and pulls her soccer socks up higher. "I know my legs are hairy, all right?"

Piper grows pink. "I wasn't going to say anything."

TJ wishes someone would. Over these last few weeks, she's wished someone would say some truly insulting shit right to her face, because then at least she'd know what was being said about her. But the longer the silence lasts, the more she suspects that things *are* being said, just not where she can hear them.

"But since you brought it up," Piper adds, "um, is there a reason?"

TJ hesitates. Telling Chandani about her resolution hadn't exactly gone well. But something tells her Piper wouldn't react that way.

So she tells her the same thing she told Chandani.

"I think that's cool," Piper says. TJ's heart flutters with hope. "Really?"

"Yeah!" She picks up her phone from the bench. "Look, body hair is totally in vogue right now. It's, like, a feminist statement." She taps away for a few seconds and turns the screen towards TJ: a Google Images search result with cute photos of celebrities showing off the peach fuzz on their legs and underarms. "Honestly, I wish I had eyebrows like yours. I have to draw mine in. Rock that hair. Maybe people will stop being mean to Simran now."

TJ fake-smiles.

She might have taken Piper's advice with a little more oomph had it not been for the fact that the way her body hair looks is nothing like those practically hairless celebrities. Besides, Piper hasn't seen anything. TJ's legs are the least of it.

But Chandani knows. Because Chandani's a brown girl. They went through the crucible of getting waxed the first time together. She's the only person who remembers what TJ looks like without her routine. And she has condemned her as a freak for it.

TJ glances across to the second soccer field, where the boys' team is doing a scrimmage. Liam's tall outline is distinctive among the others, effortlessly scoring in the top corner of the net. Something's been off between them lately, and she has the terrible feeling she knows exactly why.

Not long after they made up in January, she'd gone to his house to do homework. Somehow, naturally, they ended up watching TV on the couch instead. Partway through, he pulled her legs towards him to give her a foot massage, and TJ let him. At least until his hands slipped under her yoga pants to her calves. She'd flinched away, feigning ticklishness, but it was too late. He'd felt her hair.

At the time, she hadn't thought much of it. He hadn't said anything. But he also hadn't . . . reached for her again. Not then, and not later, either. Like last week: they'd gone out for a dinner date, but he barely touched her, and she initiated all the kissing. There were more silences than usual. TJ supposes it could just be leftover weirdness from their fight.

But it doesn't feel that way.

"Come on," Piper says, jarring her from her thoughts. TJ looks over to see there's a team huddle on the field. She gets up and follows, trying to shake off her paranoia.

Coach glares at her as she joins them. "*Almost* everyone did great today. Later this week is our first game of spring season. We're aiming for gold this May, girls. It's ours. Unless you want Whitewater to get it again?" Boos all around. The Northridge-Whitewater rivalry is legendary—not only in athletics, but everything else. Even spelling bees are basically a death match when Northridge and Whitewater face off.

Coach dismisses them, and the team heads across the field to the changeroom, past the finished boys' practice. Jake, who plays midfield, gives Piper a once-over as she goes. She pretends not to see, but her hips sway more than usual. TJ smirks. Piper clearly has a plan in motion.

TJ heads straight for her center forward boyfriend as he's coming off the field. She wraps her arms around his middle. "Hey, you."

"Hey." He gives her a side-hug. There's an awkward pause. Those never used to happen. And she could swear his eyes flick to her arms before returning to her face.

He must see the hair there, too, by now. The space between her brows is beginning to narrow, and TJ feels the hair on her chin every time she leans her face on her hand in class. TJ waits again for him to ask about it. If he does, her explanation—about her resolution—is on the tip of her tongue. But he doesn't.

It's Coach who breaks the silence, yelling across the field at them. "No PDA!"

"Jesus Christ," Liam mutters, and then yells back. "We're not even doing anything!"

"Is that so? Then get your paws off my midfielder!"

Liam swears and lets go of TJ's waist, holding his hands up. Despite herself, TJ laughs.

"God, Liam, control yourself."

"He always acts like we're about to shoot a porno on the field," Liam complains, but his lips tug into a smile as he looks at her. TJ laughs again, more out of relief than anything. Thank god the weird moment is over.

"I have my first game on Thursday," she blurts, while the magic lasts. "Are you coming?"

Liam tucks a strand of her hair behind her ear. "Wouldn't miss it."

TJ beams, and all is well for exactly one second before Coach shouts "PDA!" at them again. Liam curses under his breath once more before they separate to their respective changerooms, TJ with a bounce in her step.

As usual for the past few weeks, she walks straight by the communal showers where all the girls are headed and just grabs her duffel bag. She's itching to wash all her sweat off, but it'll have to wait until she gets home. There's no way she's stripping down around her teammates.

Today, her mom is picking her up from the school's main parking lot, so she crosses the road back to Northridge. Since it's freezing, she takes a shortcut through the side door of the school. The halls are quiet at this time, apart from distant voices coming from one of the classrooms. TJ pays them no mind. At least until she passes by the slightly ajar door.

"—and every time I piss off Ms. Schwab, the next day Coach makes his gym classes run extra laps. They're definitely banging."

"That's circumstantial at best," says a second voice dismissively, one familiar enough to make TJ pause. "Ms. Schwab and the *principal*, on the other hand—"

"Seriously?" A chair creaks back. "You've got to be pulling my leg, dude."

This last bit is what jars TJ into finally placing the voice. Rajan.

"Let's just say I've seen some things," replies the other voice, quite seriously. *Simran.*

Without thinking, TJ turns back around and pushes through the classroom door.

Inside, Simran and Rajan are sitting next to each other at a desk at the front, Simran twiddling a pencil in her fingers, Rajan with his feet up. They both jump when TJ enters.

There's too much to unpack about this scene. "What the hell?" TJ manages.

"Hello to you, too," Rajan says. "Hey, do you think Coach and Ms. Schwab are banging?"

TJ ignores this and looks between them. "You two know each other?"

"Are you joking? We're *tight*." Rajan slaps Simran on the back like she's one of his bros. TJ has the urge to rub her eyes and look again.

"I'm a math tutor," Simran explains, setting her pencil down.

"And the school keeps forcing me to get help," Rajan pitches in, twisting his ball cap from front to back. "They think just because I failed a few times, it means I don't know what's going on. Kind of judgmental, right?"

Only then does TJ register the textbook, calculator, and papers strewn on the table. She looks at Simran. "I didn't know you tutored math."

Simran shrugs and closes the textbook, offering no explanation. "What are you doing here?"

TJ realizes how it looks. Her barging into the room, clearly eavesdropping. "Soccer practice. I was just on my way to the parking lot." She watches Simran put her pencil case away. "Uh, do you need a ride home?"

"With Liam?" Simran mutters. TJ shakes her head.

"My mom."

She relaxes visibly. "Okay. Sure."

Rajan snickers. "I wouldn't want a ride with Liam, either."

TJ gives him a bored glance. "Don't you have a bathroom stall to vandalize or something?"

"You wouldn't be giving me that look if you knew the shit Liam was talking the other day."

She rolls her eyes. If she had a dollar for every time the guys in Liam's circle were talking shit to each other, she'd be rich enough to bribe her way into an Ivy League college. "Yeah, right. Come on, Simran."

Rajan opens his mouth again, but hesitates.

Something about that catches her attention. It's instinct, maybe, the paranoia that's been seeping deeper into her thoughts, but she can't ignore it. "What?"

His eyes dart from TJ to Simran and then back. "I'm not sure you wanna know."

Well, now she definitely does. "Spit it out."

Rajan sighs, his default lazy grin fading for a second and becoming uncharacteristically serious. "He was asking some of the guys after gym class this morning how to hint to his girlfriend that she should shave."

Simran makes a sound behind her. TJ's face heats.

"Just thought you should know," Rajan says casually.

She forces her jaw open. "Liam would never say something like that."

"Not to your face," Rajan concedes. "You'd be surprised, the stuff some of the guys say about their girlfriends in the locker room."

TJ sneers. "Because you're such a saint."

"Oh, come on! I don't even *have* a girlfriend to talk shit about."

He's grinning again. This is all just a joke to him. "You're such a liar," she snaps. "Making a joke—about *that*—" She can hardly speak from fury, and instead chooses to turn on her heel, brushing past Simran.

"Don't shoot the messenger," Rajan calls.

TJ hardly notices Simran's following her until she's nearly at the parking lot, and sees her mom's car pulling in. She waves and waits for the car to draw near.

Simran's strangely silent, so TJ mutters, "Rajan's an asshole. I'm sure no one would force you to tutor him, if you didn't want to."

"He's actually quite nice."

"In the last week, he started two fights, broke a window, and set off a firecracker in the parking lot."

"He's not a star citizen," Simran amends. "But he's got a good heart."

TJ glares at her as her mom pulls up. "Are you defending him?"

"No. I'm just saying"—Simran swallows—"maybe he's telling the truth."

TJ's jaw drops as her mom rolls down the window. "Simran, putt! I haven't seen you in so long. Need a ride? Hop in!" She grins widely and barely acknowledges TJ. Classic.

Simran smiles. "Sat Sri Akaal, Masi ji. Thank you."

"Of course!" TJ's mom's smile has reached a creepy width.

She hadn't planned on having to drop off another person and is going to complain about it later, guaranteed.

Her giant work bag is on the shotgun seat, so TJ clambers in the back with Simran while her mom asks, "Simran, how's your mom?"

Naturally she would ask Simran this question instead of talking to her sister herself. While they make small talk, TJ stares out the window and tries not to think about what Rajan told her. The guy is a criminal. And a huge gossip, too, apparently. Why should she believe anything he says?

Aside from the fact that her gut is telling her to.

Which is ridiculous. TJ *knows* Liam. They've been friends ever since he moved to Kelowna in grade ten. He and TJ were always thrown together in alphabetical seating charts and group projects, since his last name is Portman. They spent a lot of time in classes muttering commentary to each other under their breath. Despite herself, she started crushing on him. It helped that he was so cute and turned the full effect of his smile on her constantly. Even more so after they got together.

She can't wrap her head around Rajan's claims. It just doesn't match with the boy she fell for.

Her mom's phone rings on the sound system, and she answers it in somewhat-resigned tones. Sounds like a call from the hospital. In the respite, TJ turns to Simran, casting her voice low.

"I just don't believe Liam would talk about me like that."

Simran eyes her warily. Instead of responding to that, she just says, "Why are you even doing all this?"

TJ instantly knows what she's talking about. Looks down

at her hands, the long hair covering the backs of her arms. "Because of the meme."

"It wasn't making fun of *you*," Simran says quietly.

"It wasn't about who it was making fun of," TJ argues. Her voice rises in volume, and her mom, still on the phone, turns slightly in her seat to glare at them. TJ waits a minute before it feels safe to whisper again. "It was about what it *meant*. And, well, I want to show everyone that I don't have to do it—shave or wax or whatever. I can still be pretty. I can still be me."

The words sound emptier now. If what Rajan said is true, and Liam really said that in the locker room, it's a major counterpoint from the other side of the debate. Her own boyfriend wants her to shave so she can be hot again.

Simran doesn't say anything. They sit in silence for the rest of the ride. When they finally pull up to Simran's house, she glances at TJ while unbuckling her seat belt.

"Rajan was probably exaggerating," she says quietly, and that's what gets to TJ—the *sympathy*. She can't stand it.

TJ's mom bids Simran a cheery goodbye, complete with "Say hello to your mom for me" and "You should come over for dinner sometime." The door closes behind her. TJ watches her go, stomach roiling, until her mother huffs grumpily.

"*Now* I'm going to be late."

EIGHT
✳✳✳

C urse Rajan's ability to worm his way into her brain, because on Thursday TJ's still thinking about what he said. The timing couldn't be worse—their group is headed to Provincials tomorrow, and with it, her shot at qualifying for Nationals. She'll have to be at the top of her game.

During the school day, she tries to scroll through the national news on her phone. Impromptu topics usually have a correlation to current events, so it's good to keep updated. But her mind keeps wandering back to the same thing.

In French class, she finds herself writing a resolution in the margin of her notebook. *Be It Resolved That TJ should confront her boyfriend.* The points supporting the resolution are simple:

> 1. Not knowing how Liam really feels is worse than finding out the truth.
>
> 2. Either way, having a weekend away to digest whatever Liam says is probably a good thing.
>
> 3. She's way too impatient to wait for later.

And then there is the point against:

> 1. Ignorance is bliss. Depending on what he says, having this all out could screw her up even *more*.

TJ meets Liam at Pineview after school for her soccer game. She can't muster a proper smile or the energy to banter with him, or feel *anything* but sliminess in her gut when he wishes her luck right before she jogs onto the field.

"Last first match ever," Piper comments as they walk to their positions.

TJ hadn't realized that until now. This is her last season with the teammates she's known for years. She glances down the midfield line. Chandani's the farthest away, staring straight ahead and stretching her quads.

TJ tears her gaze away and looks to the sidelines. Liam's sitting in the grass with his legs outstretched, typing on his phone. It occurs to her that he didn't give her his customary pre-match kiss.

So what? she scolds herself. *Get a grip. That doesn't mean anything.*

Except it feels like it does.

The whistle blows. TJ startles. She hadn't been paying attention.

Someone calls her name, and she has to take a second to orient herself before jerking into motion. The ball is sailing towards her, passed by one of Northridge's forwards. She goes for it, but one of Pineview's players gets her foot on it first and boots the ball down the field. TJ curses inwardly and tears down the turf to chase it down. *Great* way to kick off the season.

But it doesn't end there. She keeps missing passes, fumbling the ball, and at one point fails to block a shot on Northridge's goal that normally would have been a piece of cake. TJ wipes the sweat off her face as Pineview cheers. What's wrong with her?

Each mistake makes her more frustrated. The two teams trade the lead between them—the game's tight. At halftime,

Coach adds a fourth midfielder from the bench, a new tenth-grade recruit.

"Just for now, since the midfield line is pretty weak," he says pointedly to the team. "Maybe if *someone* showed up to more off-season practices . . ."

As if TJ wasn't aware of how much she's screwing up. But still, that's just unfair. "I missed *two*."

"Two too many, apparently."

TJ bites her tongue. She missed those practices for debate. Meanwhile, the team is dead silent. Even Piper's avoiding her eyes. Just perfect. On top of the whole team thinking she's a freak, they're annoyed with her now, too.

She finds herself getting into her head even more in the second half. They lose the game by one goal. Coach shakes his head from the bench, which pisses her off. And Liam's not at the sideline to greet her post-game like he usually is.

This isn't how it was supposed to go. Soccer is supposed to help her escape her problems, not add to them. She kicks her water bottle savagely. It tips over, loose lid falling off, and spills the rest of her water into the grass.

Great. Her throat is parched and she's overheating. She yanks her jersey off, leaving only her thin cami, not even caring about her visible underarm hair. She needs one thing to go right. Just one.

She finally spots Liam on the opposite sideline and jogs towards him.

"Good game," he says with a somewhat-fake smile. She scoffs. "Liar."

His smile becomes real. Encouraged, she jumps up for a hug.

He catches her easily, so she can wrap her legs around his waist. She leans her head on his shoulder. "Hey."

His hands are on her thighs, brushing up against her leg hair. "Hey." No *Hey, beautiful.*

She can't remember the last time he called her beautiful.

TJ slides down from the hug, struck with a bitter realization. In the end, it doesn't matter if Rajan was lying, if Liam said something in the locker room or not. What matters is something she's been wondering for weeks but has never had the bravery to ask straight-out.

"Liam," she says quietly now, as they walk off the field together. "Can I ask you something?"

"Yeah, what?"

She steels herself. "Do you have a problem with my hair?"

He's silent for a second. Then he looks at her long ponytail, the ombre highlights freshly done. "Your hair is beautiful."

"I'm not talking about *that* hair."

There's a silence. His expression is blank. She takes a breath.

"It's not going away, Liam. So I have to ask. Do you have a problem with it?"

He looks up at the sky for a long second. Then he stops in his tracks, making her stop, too, and says all in a rush: "Is this because of what I said before Winter Break? Because if it is, I said I'm sorry, okay? What else do I have to do to get you to start shaving again?"

She blinks. Wait, wait, wait. That's what he thinks this is— *punishment*? "I'm not doing this to get back at you."

"Then why?"

Because I need to prove you still want me like this. I need to prove my life wouldn't be different if I looked more like Simran. She doesn't say that, though. "Why does it matter?"

He exhales, dragging a hand down his face. "Because it's hygiene, TJ! You can't just stop doing it and expect your boyfriend not to care."

That hits her like a physical blow, but TJ takes a measured breath. The debater part of her wants to convince him. Then he'll apologize, the way he always does, and they can move on. "What does hair have to do with hygiene? Am I going to get sick from my body hair? And if that's true, shouldn't you be shaving *your* armpits, too?"

He doesn't answer right away. "That's not the same."

"Why *not*?" She reaches up to adjust her ponytail, and his eyes drop to—well, her underarms. She knows what they look like. They haven't seen a razor or wax in two months.

Liam looks revolted. He actually takes a step backwards.

TJ drops her arms, struggling not to cry. "You're looking at me like I'm disgusting."

Liam holds up his hands, heat entering his voice. "Don't try to make me feel bad about not being attracted to *that*. It's not going to happen. So if you're going to keep doing it, then maybe we should just end this now."

TJ's jaw drops. "What?"

"Just answer me, okay, TJ?" He drops his hands. "Are you going to shave, or not?"

She stares. An ultimatum? He's got to be bluffing. There's no way he'd . . . he'd . . .

She can't finish the thought. Instead, she braces herself to tell the truth.

"No."

Please, please say it's okay.

He doesn't. He just exhales. "Then I'll see you around, I guess."

A roaring sound fills TJ's ears, making it impossible to hear anything else. This can't be happening. This must be a nightmare. There's no way he'd be so willing to let her go for *this*. "Liam, wait," she whispers, struggling to keep her voice even. She grabs his arm. "Let me explain—"

He pulls out of her grasp, looking pained. "Just stop, TJ."

And he walks away from her.

She stares after him, shell-shocked. Her boyfriend broke up with her. Just like that. He doesn't even seem affected. And here she is on the verge of tears, heart splintering, begging him to stay. That's not how it should be. She should be going down *swinging*, damn it.

The roaring sound fades, and the real world comes rushing back in, along with TJ's anger.

"Fine!" she shouts after him. "Leave, then. I'm sure you can find something hairless to make out with, like a naked mole-rat or, better yet, your pillow. That'll be your only two options from now on!" He doesn't look back, although some people turn and stare. Not her best insult, but it still makes her feel better.

She spins and stalks to the parking lot, ignoring the whispers. The back of her neck is hot.

She drives home on autopilot, clutching the wheel in a death grip. What a complete asshole. She can't believe it. He's going to apologize later, like usual. He'll remember why he liked her in the first place.

At that thought, TJ's treacherous brain pulls her back to when they first started dating.

It had been a long time coming. But despite their flirtation in class, he didn't ask her out until grade eleven, at a home soccer game.

She'd come running off the field, jubilant after blocking the opposing team from scoring. Liam'd stepped away from his friends on the sidelines to congratulate her on a good game.

Her hair was a mess from her last slide tackle, and she pulled the elastic off to redo her ponytail. He watched her shake out her hair. "You're so pretty," he said. She paused while piling her hair back up. His words had more effect on her than she wanted to admit.

"Tell me something I don't know," she teased.

His reply was instant. "Okay. I want to go out with you."

She dropped her hands. "Didn't I say 'something I don't know'?"

His friends laughed. Liam shook his head.

"Damn, TJ. I was trying to be smooth."

"Try harder." She was grinning despite being nervous. "You were saying you wanted to go out with me? Why, because I'm *so pretty*?"

"No." He paused. "Because you're funny, and smart, and you make every class we're in a hundred times better. Pretty is just a bonus."

Past-TJ was sold. Present-TJ laughs out loud in the car. What a *liar.*

When she arrives home, the TV is on, a fact she barely pays attention to until she slams the front door behind her.

Her dad jolts into wakefulness, and she realizes he's been sleeping on the couch. "TJ?"

She hadn't been ready to see him. But now she remembers he was waiting for her to come home so he could take their shared car to work. He's in his housekeeping uniform with the hospital insignia, ready for another night shift.

TJ shucks her shoes off, trying to control the anger she knows is etched all over her face. "You can take the car now."

"Oh. Okay." He looks bewildered, scratching the top of his head. "You okay?"

"Yeah," she grits out. He opens his mouth like he's about to ask more, but she darts up the stairs before he can. She doesn't bother putting her bag away; she goes straight to the bathroom and locks herself in. She turns on the fan, lets her clothes drop on the floor, and gets in the shower, cranking the water to a blistering hot full blast. She leans her head against the tile. And finally, it's loud enough to drown out the sobs she would never be able to explain to her parents.

NINE
***

"You're having a crisis," Simran surmises.

TJ downs the rest of her coffee and wonders what gave it away. Was it how quiet she's been throughout this five-hour bus ride, or maybe how her eyes look red-rimmed and cried-out no matter how much makeup she caked on this morning, or maybe because the breakup was public and humiliating enough that everyone on earth knows about it and probably the Martians, too? Her phone's been blowing up all day, but she's too exhausted to check it. She barely slept.

But by sunrise, her emotions had dried up, leaving her numb enough to look at the situation in an entirely different way. That was, in the context of her personal debate resolution.

She'd pulled out her cue card to study the wording. *This House Believes That TJ Powar can be her hairy self and still be beautiful.* Never mind how she felt about Liam; suddenly, the breakup became a contention from the opposing side. Sure, his rejection was a devastating blow to her argument, but that doesn't mean she *lost*. She just has to rebut the point with something better.

What that something is, she doesn't know yet. And besides, she has bigger fish to fry at the moment. "I *am* having a crisis. It's about the fact that you're writing your speech an hour before our first debate."

"If you don't want to talk, that's fine." Simran lifts her pen from where she was scratching a bunch of stuff out, admiring the absolute carnage her edits have left behind on her notes. They're almost at the school where Provincials are being hosted, yet here she is still making drastic changes to her speeches. This habit of hers always gives TJ anxiety. Simran twirls her braid absently as she adds, "I just want to make sure you're okay. I know something happened yesterday."

"Oh? *Something*, is that it?" TJ snorts, then stops herself. She's keenly aware of all the other Southern Interior debaters on the charter bus with them. And sure, the engine is loud and Simran is quiet, but TJ's not taking chances. Especially when Yara's in the seat in front of them and probably only pretending to be absorbed in her book. "Never mind. It's not a big deal."

The bus turns off the highway and finally, the hosting school—a private school in North Vancouver—comes into sight. Everyone leaps up and plasters their faces to the windows to catch a glimpse of the war ground. Mrs. Scott yells fruitlessly for everyone to stay in their seats.

"Our school looks like a jail compared to this," one of the novices from Northridge comments as they pull in. TJ silently agrees. This building makes even Whitewater look like a shed.

"That's because Northridge's design was based on a prison," someone else says.

Someone else scoffs. "That's what *everyone* says about their school."

"But in our case it's *true*—"

From the back of the bus, Nate's super-fast voice floats over as he gives questionable commentary.

"Here come the elite kids," he whispers. A small group of debaters march by the bus, dressed to the nines. Charlie's sense of fashion would probably fit in well with them. "They're going to eat us all alive."

He pauses. Some poor sap takes the bait. "Why?"

"Their private schools hire debate instructors for twenty thousand a year." Nate lowers his voice further. "It's not just a club for them, it's a way of life. They're in another league."

There's a hush at the back of the bus before someone says, "Jeez. Any advice for if we have to debate them?"

"Yeah," Nate says. "Wear a jockstrap."

TJ rolls her eyes; scaring newbies is Nate's favourite pastime during Provincials season. She sorely wants to turn around and chip in, but decides against it. It's time to detach fully from the other senior debaters. Only two debaters from the Southern Interior region will move on to Senior Nationals. It all depends on how they rank against each other this weekend. It will be fiercely competitive; neither TJ nor Simran, Nate, or Charlie qualified for Junior Nationals back in ninth grade, so this is their only chance to make it all the way.

She side-eyes Simran beside her. Technically, Simran's the enemy just as much as Nate or Charlie, but she doesn't feel like one. They're a team. In TJ's dreams of going to Nationals, it's always Simran at her side. She can't imagine anyone else.

The bus jerks to a stop in the drop-off zone. The next few minutes are chaos, as the debate coaches and parent chaperones attempt to herd everyone off in an organized manner.

When it's her turn, TJ steps out onto the sidewalk, the chatter of hundreds of people reaching her ears. The bus behind them pulls away to drop their suitcases off at the hotel. She takes a deep breath. It's time to focus. No more thinking about what happened yesterday.

As they're walking up the school's steps, Simran nudges her. "Hey, look. Someone's handing these out already."

TJ looks down to see Simran's holding a sheaf of paper. The schedule for today's events. TJ scans it and groans. "Seriously? We're against the *Turners* tonight? Tell me I'm having a nightmare." But their opponents are printed on paper, clear as day: Jenna and Isaac Turner, from Brixton Academy.

"Should be interesting," Simran says, voice very neutral.

"Interesting?" TJ scoffs. She scans the schedule further. It shows only today's round matchups, with the other four rounds tomorrow. Nate and Charlie are facing some of the aforementioned elite private school kids. She almost envies them. "Yeah, that's one way to put it. Pricks."

Simran doesn't comment, which is the closest she'll come to agreeing. She just puts her earbuds in and pushes up the volume on her tablet, presumably to hide away in her cocoon of shabad kirtan. She claims it calms her before a debate. TJ wishes she had a similar strategy; maybe then she wouldn't feel like she's about to hurl.

They enter the school—just as fancy on the inside, with gleaming floors, a vaulted cathedral-like ceiling, and even a brick water fountain next to the registration desk she and Simran sign in at. Once they have their registration packages, Mrs. Scott beckons them over. "Group picture, over here!"

The rest of the Southern Interior group is already lined up against the wall. Mrs. Scott directs TJ to the end of the row as usual, since she's tall, where she's positioned next to Charlie.

"Say cheese!" Mrs. Scott says from behind her camera. One click of the shutter. "TJ, come in a little closer, please. Charlie won't bite."

Snickers from the debaters. Charlie snaps his teeth at her and grins. Making a face, TJ shuffles slightly closer. He puts his arm around her shoulders like they're buddies.

A few shutter clicks later, Mrs. Scott nods. Charlie pulls back his arm and takes his soothing ironed-fabric smell with him. The group relaxes, about to disband, when Saad nudges Yara. "Don't you want to take a photo?"

Yara shakes her head.

"What? Really?" TJ can't help but ask. She'd think North-ridge having so many students at Provincials this year would make it a good story for the school paper.

Yara looks up at her. "No, it's fine. I'll get pictures from Mrs. Scott if I need them." Her voice is unusually high-pitched. For the first time, TJ notices guilt flickering through her eyes as they dart between TJ and Simran. Oh.

There's a brief, sticky moment of awkwardness as everyone else seems to get it, too. Predictably, Simran recovers first. "Well, if you want to take some of your own later," she says kindly, "just let us know."

Considering what happened last time, Simran's kind of a saint.

"Yeah, feel free to ask for pics of me at any time. Not for the paper, but in general," Nate adds, striking a pose. As everyone laughs, breaking the tension, Simran shoots him a grateful look. He subtly nods. Okay, maybe Nate's not the worst.

The group finally disperses and TJ wanders to the snack table. She's too nauseous for the dinner buffet, but a pile of pastries catches her eye. She may as well at least have a snack to boost her energy. As she's biting into a glazed donut, someone speaks from behind her.

"Long time, no see!"

The bright voice creeps up TJ's spine. She stiffens, wipes her expression clean, and turns around.

A grinning Jenna Turner stands in front of her, looking impeccable in a tailored grey pantsuit. Stylish, but not quite to the level of the elite debate kids, much to TJ's satisfaction.

TJ pastes a smile on. "Hi, Jenna. How've you been." The last bit doesn't come out much like a question because, honestly, TJ doesn't care.

Jenna flips her pin-straight blonde hair. "Oh, good. I'm a little nervous. I didn't prep much for this tournament. I was just so busy. You wouldn't believe how many committees I'm on. I met with the Minister of Education the other day! It was productive, but I almost wish I was back in Kelowna sometimes. Life was way more relaxed there, you know?"

TJ resists the urge to roll her eyes. Yeah, Jenna's exactly the same.

Before Jenna and her twin brother moved from Kelowna to Vancouver at the end of tenth grade, they used to go to Whitewater. For a couple of years they dominated in their debate category. TJ, Simran, Charlie, and Nate were all fighting over second place back then, a fact she'd rather forget. "Right." She takes a step away.

"I seriously miss it," Jenna continues, forcing TJ to stay out of politeness. "I see people's Instagram stories and I'm like, I miss hanging out with you guys!"

TJ is starting to get a bad feeling about this. "Mhmm."

"Hey, speaking of Instagram, I saw you on my feed a while ago." She lowers her voice. "There was this meme going around, did you ever see it?"

TJ freezes. Jenna's eyes are wide and sympathetic, but TJ's not fooled. The Turners like toying with their opponents. And not always in the debate itself. It's a dirty play, and that's why TJ has always disliked them infinitely more than any fleeting irritation she's felt towards Charlie or Nate.

At TJ's silence, Jenna leans in conspiratorially. "I guess you didn't. It was this comparison image of you and Simran—"

"I saw it," TJ grits out.

"Oh! Why didn't you say?" She glances behind TJ. "It's just awful for Simran. I haven't seen her in a while. I should go see if she's okay."

Simran's laugh floats from behind them where she's still talking to Yara. She sounds happy, relaxed. TJ balls her fists. There's no way she's letting Jenna bring this bullshit back up to Simran. "Don't you *dare* talk to her."

Jenna's eyes get big. "Oh my god, TJ. Relax. I'm just curious what she thinks about it."

TJ steps forward and jabs her finger against Jenna's shoulder. She doesn't even care that she's playing right into her game. "If you say a single word about it, I'll—"

She cuts herself off, remembering the tournament rules of

interaction with opponents. Jenna seems amused.

"Okayyy." She takes a step back. "Oh, by the way, there's something on your—" She gestures to her upper lip.

TJ's hand automatically flies to her face—her brain catches up too late. Jenna's mouth spreads into a smirk as she backs away.

There's nothing on her upper lip. Just some obvious hair that's been growing there for several months.

Her whole face heats. But Jenna's already disappeared, leaving TJ alone with this overwhelming wave of shame.

It's like she's twelve again.

She vividly remembers standing with Chandani as they begged their mothers to take them to Lulu's salon. TJ was the one to initiate the idea. She couldn't wait another minute, not after what had happened that weekend.

It was a three-day-long debate training camp TJ had really been looking forward to. The auditorium of the university where it was being held was warm, and after they'd been given a practice resolution to work on, TJ took off her hoodie and started writing.

The blond girl next to her, Jenna, glanced over at her paper. TJ didn't say anything at first, but when Jenna kept looking at her notes, she covered her paper with her arms and told her to stop copying. Wrong move, apparently, because Jenna just glanced down again and asked why she had gorilla arms. Her voice was loud enough to carry, and that was it. The running joke continued all weekend even though TJ wore long sleeves for the rest of it.

So when she returned home, she put her new persuasive skills to good use on her and Chandani's mothers. It worked. And all that shame had gone away . . . until now.

TJ slams her half-eaten snack in the trash. Why'd she let Jenna get to her *again*? She should have just stood there and eaten her donut. Now Jenna got exactly what she wanted—to rattle her.

Shake it off, she tells herself firmly. *I can still be beautiful. I am still beautiful.*

She repeats that mantra to herself all the way to the classroom. The judges are just getting seated when she arrives. Jenna and Isaac are already there, whispering to each other. Simran's there, too, notes spread chaotically over her desk.

Mechanically, TJ pulls her cards from her bag, then writes her name and pronouns on the board under the second speaker title.

"I now call this debate to order," says the Speaker. "The resolution being debated today is *This House Would endorse genome editing in Canada*. Arguing for Side Proposition are Jenna Turner and Isaac Turner. For Side Opposition are . . ."

As he proceeds to trip over every syllable of Simran's and TJ's names, TJ sits down. Simran's giving her a funny look. TJ wonders if she looks how she feels—like she's not really there.

Isaac stands when called, buttoning his grey suit jacket. He's taller than Jenna with hair a darker blond, but otherwise he looks very similar to his twin. They've both got a straight nose, thin face, and smile TJ would like to smack off. He leaves his notes behind and walks in front of the desks empty-handed.

"Honourable judges, worthy opponents, assembled guests," he says in his usual self-important voice. "We of Side Proposition believe that pursuing genome editing could only be a beneficial venture for our country, and we will present several contentions to show you why."

As he drones on about their proposed plan for implementation, and how genome editing could help eliminate genetic diseases, TJ scribbles down their points so she can dissect them later. As soon as the timekeeper holds up the THIRTY SECONDS card, meaning protected time is over, both she and Simran stand, ready with questions.

Isaac looks them over with raised eyebrows before nodding at TJ. The general practice in Canadian National Style debating is to ask two questions and take two when it's your turn to speak. It seems he's taking the strategy of getting it over with at the get-go.

Jenna smirks when TJ takes the floor. TJ ignores it and directs her question at the Speaker as per the rules. "Honourable Speaker, how can Side Proposition be sure this process won't be abused?"

"Like I said, we'll have regulations," Isaac retorts. "Side Opposition is trying to create fear about hypothetical worst-case-scenario ways this technology could be used, before we've even gotten there. Imagine if people told the Wright brothers not to build the first airplane because it *could* be used for dropping bombs on people. We'd still be in the Dark Ages, honourable Speaker."

He continues on with his speech. TJ gets up again to ask her next question—their plan suggests there will be regulations and rules, but she wants to pin them on specifics. But Isaac's waving her down, clearly done answering to her. He takes a question from Simran closer to the end and that's it.

Then it's Simran's turn to deliver her speech, starting with a rebuttal of Isaac's (holey-as-Swiss-cheese) plan before she moves into her first contention. The debate continues uneventfully. TJ is viciously glad to find they're holding their own. Back in the day, the Turners always had a lead. But now Simran and TJ are on more equal footing. She can see it in the way Isaac tugs at his bow tie during Simran's rebuttal. How Jenna's smirk slips when TJ asks her a question.

They're afraid they might not win.

Finally, it's TJ's turn to make her speech. She gathers her cue cards but pauses when she sees a card that does not belong at the top of the stack. It's the one she wrote her personal resolution on. She must've shoved it in her debate bag during her last-minute packing. And now it's staring back, mocking her.

Against her will, her eyes slide to Jenna's. She's watching intently, chin propped up in her hand.

TJ's heart pounds, but not with her usual pre-speech adrenaline. Jenna's eyes drop. TJ realizes she's pulling at her sleeve with her free hand—an old habit to cover her arms, and one she hasn't indulged in years. *Enough.*

She lets go and faces the audience with renewed determination, glancing down at her cards to remind herself of her points. "Honourable judges," she begins, then launches into autopilot with the speech she has practiced a hundred different ways, her voice passionate and full of inflection. You could hear a pin drop in the silence.

It's only thirty seconds in, when the timekeeper indicates the end of protected time and no one stands, that she realizes this silence isn't a riveted one. It's a shocked one. Something's wrong. She glances at her cue cards. Focuses.

And the problem smacks her right in the face.

For the last thirty seconds, she's been giving her speech for Side Proposition. The *wrong side*.

TEN
✳✳✳

Her mouth goes dry. The clock ticks loudly behind her. There's a cough from the other side of the floor. She immediately puts her cue cards back on the desk and turns to flip through her notebook with shaking fingers. Where did the cards for her Side Opposition speech go? They're not here. Normally, she'd be able to recite her speech by heart, but her mind is blank right now.

A painful ten seconds tick by before she gives up and turns back around. The judges' faces are masks, but she already knows she's screwed up this debate beyond redemption.

She takes a deep breath. Behind her, Simran is sorting through her bag as if TJ's cards might've accidentally fallen in there. Determination fills her. She can at least try to give Simran something to work with for her own scores.

So she just starts talking again. "I'll begin with a rebuttal of the flaws in the Proposition's case," she says, like nothing happened, and launches into it.

Once she gets into the rhythm of talking, parts of her speech come back to her. She has to leave out plenty of statistics and evidence because she can't remember the source or exact numbers, which the Turners might pounce on. But the more she talks, the more confident she gets, and the more of her power returns, her ability to transfix a room, an ability that's gotten her through so many debates.

Jenna stands for a question midway through. TJ waves her down, as she's in the middle of a lengthy anecdote. From the corner of her eye, she watches Jenna scribble her question down for her brother instead. Isaac stands a minute later.

There's a gleam in his eye. TJ sighs inwardly. If she ignores them, she'll be docked points for not allowing questions. "Yes?"

"Honourable Speaker, we're just a little confused by Side Opposition's case," Isaac tells the Speaker in a puzzled voice. "Right now, she's talking about the potential for the bill to pave the way for 'designer babies.' But at the beginning of her speech, she herself said it's just fearmongering blocking progress. She herself said that other countries are already doing genome editing, so we should, too, or we risk falling behind and letting other countries form the ethical standards. So which is it?"

TJ gapes. That was from her Side Proposition speech—or at least, the bit of it that she said before realizing.

This is a low blow—everyone already *knows* TJ messed up at the start. Any classy debater would've ignored the mishap and let the judges dock the points for themselves. But Isaac went there anyway.

This just got personal.

And how can she possibly respond? She can't just say, *Sorry, folks, I accidentally started on the wrong speech, ha ha, funny, right*? That's like breaking the fourth wall of debating.

"Honourable Speaker," she begins, then pauses to think. "Clearly Side Proposition misunderstood. As my partner and I have emphasized throughout this debate, this isn't fearmongering, it's a real concern. As I was saying . . ."

It's a pitiful sidestep, but it's enough to let her jump right back into her speech. She finishes with fifteen seconds left on the clock and sits. It's totally silent as the Speaker announces the end of the debate. The judges scribble away on their score-cards. TJ stares at her hands, replaying the last seven minutes in her head.

All in all, it was a respectable comeback. But she could've delivered the best speech in the world after what just happened, and it wouldn't matter. She made too big of a mistake. Her shot at Nationals is gone.

The thought slams into her chest and sinks lower, dragging her down. She could kick herself. And Simran—did TJ hurt her chances, too? Technically, they're marked individually, but a poor performance from your partner can definitely affect your scores.

TJ glances at Simran for the first time since her mistake. Her gut twists. Simran's staring off into space with a stormy expression. She's *mad*? TJ's never seen her mad. But she can't blame her. Simran has the right to be furious. TJ just lost them this debate and made them both look like amateurs. And to the Turners, no less.

She scribbles in her open notebook: *I'm sorry.* Then pushes it over to Simran.

Simran glances at the note and her expression clears. She pulls the notebook towards herself.

Don't worry. It's OK.

Somehow that just makes TJ feel worse. And confused. At least until Simran keeps writing.

That was SUCH a cheap shot from Isaac. The judges have GOT to dock them for that.

Simran underlines the last bit several times, leaving no uncertainty about who she's really mad at. Then she draws a smiley face, as if to give her hope. TJ smiles weakly. Even if the judges agree with Simran, they're still not winning this one.

And sure enough, when the Speaker collects the scoresheets, he glances down and then in TJ's direction with something of a pitying look before announcing, "The judges wish to award this debate to Side Proposition. At this time, if any debaters have complaints regarding rule violations . . ."

It's close to seven in the evening by the time they get back to the busy front foyer of the school, where swarms of debaters have gathered to debrief. Relief and exhilaration mixed with nervousness for tomorrow is nearly palpable in the air. TJ is numb to it, even as they join a group of Southern Interior debaters. Yara's partner is grinning ear to ear because, as she tells Charlie, their team won their debate by a landslide. Ameera and Saad are laughing their asses off about their loss at the hands of one of the best teams in the country. TJ would bet neither of them started with the wrong speech, though.

"Okay, but how did it go for you two?" Ameera says once she's done wheezing, wiping a tear from her eye. "Won? Lost?"

A long beat. TJ pretends to be absorbed in her phone. Simran glances at her before replying. "Lost."

Ameera looks between them, but shrugs. "Oh well. Individual scores are all that matter for Nationals anyway."

"And even then," mutters one of the junior debaters as they walk towards the entrance together, "it's cool that we just get to be here."

Well, that kid clearly got roasted for an hour straight. TJ feels marginally better.

Outside, the charter bus pulls up in front of them in the pickup zone. The door opens, and Nate pokes his head out.

"Get in, losers. We're going to the mall."

One of the perks of any out-of-city club trip is, of course, making use of the downtime. Seeing as there'll be less of it tomorrow, today their group is getting driven to a large indoor mall to go wild for two hours. Or at least, as wild as one can get at the mall, while being sternly told to stay in groups and not to leave the building without a chaperone.

TJ endures the entire bus ride full of jokes and laughter, leaning her head back against her seat and only intermittently listening in. Saad and Ameera take turns roasting each other's debate skills for the entertainment of the whole bus. Some Whitewater kids are hyping Nate up about his new suit. Mrs. Scott and Mr. York are talking on their phones, trying to confirm the schedule for tomorrow. TJ keeps her eyes closed and lets Simran tell people she has a headache when they ask.

By the time they reach the mall, however, she's at her limit. She needs a moment alone.

The debaters split off into groups with their friends, and all the chaperones go off in their own group. TJ follows a random group until the chaperones have disappeared around the corner, then mumbles that she's going to the washroom. Nobody seems to hear. Good.

In the washroom, she locks herself in a stall and roots through her bag. After several minutes, she finds her correct cue cards in a side pocket. She doesn't even know how they got there. TJ's never made this kind of mistake before. But then again, that was exactly Jenna's aim—to shake her up.

TJ wishes she could text Chandani. Chandani would make her feel better by coming up with a bunch of cathartic nasty insults. Except TJ can't text her, because they haven't spoken in weeks. She's alone in this one. Officially hit rock bottom, sitting on a public toilet with her pants down and staring at stall graffiti. She racks her brain for a time when she was more pathetic than this but can't come up with anything.

Eventually, she leaves, deciding that taking a lap around the mall might help clear her head. But it's not to be. Because leaning on the wall across from the washrooms, ankles and arms crossed, is none other than Charlie Rosencrantz.

Charlie pushes off the wall when she appears. He's gotten rid of his suit jacket and rolled his sleeves up, but otherwise he looks fresh as a daisy. Not even a hair out of place from his styled side part. It kind of pisses TJ off. Why can't he be a mess sometimes? Why is she the only one ever falling apart?

Charlie pointedly checks his watch. "That bad, huh?"

"Ha, ha." She doesn't even have the energy to refute his assumption. "Why aren't you with the others?"

"We're all supposed to have a buddy, remember?"

Great. "And you just decided to be the sacrificial saint who stayed behind."

"Someone has to be." He falls into step with her as they walk down a well-lit, open hallway of the mall; there are hardly any other shoppers. They pass three clothing boutiques, a jeweler, and a specialty meats shop before he asks, "Where to first?"

"I'm just walking. If you want to shop designer suits, go find Saad. I think he went to some boutique."

In her peripheral vision, she sees him give her a long look. "Are you okay?"

She shrugs as they turn another corner. "Yeah."

A silence falls between them. Charlie doesn't leave her side, despite her suggestion. Their footsteps clack in unison against the tiled floors, and TJ stares listlessly into the shops they pass. On a different day, she might've been excited to check out the purses on sale in that last window, but today the prospect seems exhausting.

Charlie speaks up after a while. "Want to get something to eat?"

"I'm not hungry," she lies.

"Really? You didn't eat anything at the dinner buffet."

She narrows her eyes. "How would you know that?"

"I was watching you." He's totally unashamed of this, meeting her gaze squarely.

"Creep," she says, as though she doesn't stalk his social media regularly. "I think you might be obsessed with me."

"Aren't we all a little obsessed with our competition?" He points ahead to the cafeteria sign. "Look, we're here anyway. Let's get something. It's on me."

Her stomach pangs with hunger. Screw it. "Fine. But I'm going to get the most expensive thing on the menu."

"I wouldn't expect anything less."

They do a lap around the cafeteria, scoping out the vendors. Charlie seems content to let her choose, and she's tempted to follow through on finding the place with the highest prices, but in the end, she goes with a comfort-food sandwich from Subway. Charlie orders one, too, and true to his word, pays for them both.

Friday nights a half hour before closing aren't the busiest times, evidently, because almost no one else is in the cafeteria. They easily secure a cozy table by a faux fireplace. Charlie sets down their tray and says, "I saw on the schedule that you and Simran were up against the Turners."

TJ pauses halfway through unwrapping her sandwich. Is this why he's really here? To hunt down the story she wouldn't tell anyone else? Maybe he just wants some material to mock her with. "Yeah, so?"

"So how'd it go?"

Her suspicions solidify further. "Like any other debate. Why do you care?"

He's silent for a while as they eat. Then: "I guess I'm just wondering because I haven't seen them debate since they moved away."

Oh. Right. Charlie and Isaac were debate partners at Whitewater for years, before Nate came into the picture. She vividly remembers them goofing off at an adjacent table during that sixth-grade debate training, throwing paper balls at each other. Several of them had hit TJ instead and she wasn't convinced it was by accident.

She doesn't remember Charlie making fun of her hairy arms, though. Maybe she blocked it out. "Why don't you ask Isaac if you're so curious?" she mutters.

As Charlie shrugs, she realizes he totally *could* ask Isaac. And he'd probably love to tell Charlie all about TJ's royal screwup. It would provide months' worth of ammunition. Especially when he realizes it affected her to the point that she couldn't even say it herself.

They've fallen into a silence of just eating. TJ's ravenous suddenly, and she practically inhales her sub. Then she sips her Coke and weighs her options. Even if Charlie doesn't ask Isaac, Jenna will probably blab about this to anyone she can. Might as well get ahead of it.

"I started saying the wrong speech," she finally says in what she hopes is an offhand way. "We were Side Opposition and I used my Proposition speech for, like, a whole minute before realizing. Everything went downhill from there."

Charlie doesn't say anything at first, just keeps sipping from his straw and watching her thoughtfully. She waits. And waits. Once he gets to the bottom of his drink and his cheeks hollow out, the vacuum effect making obnoxious sounds, she loses patience.

"*Well?* I can feel you trying not to laugh at me."

His mouth finally pops off the straw. "I'm not. I'm just trying to figure out why this has you so upset. We all make embarrassing mistakes sometimes."

"Maybe *you* do," she scoffs, sinking lower into her seat. "But not me."

A trace of a smile crosses his lips before he's serious again. "If that's true, why did it happen?"

She looks away. He's sitting across from her, close in proximity, and Jenna's comment about her facial hair resounds vividly in her head. The obnoxious cafeteria lighting probably isn't doing her any favours, either. Insecurity creeps over her until she's hunching and practically tugging her jacket collar up over her mouth. "Jenna," she admits. "She said . . . some stuff to me before the debate. To throw me off-balance. And it worked."

"What'd she say?"

She tugs her collar even higher. Charlie must know about the meme and everything, but she doesn't want to draw attention to her newfound hairiness. He might look at her differently, and she's not sure she could handle that, for some reason. "It's not important."

"Fine. She got you wound up. You lost. So what?"

"So I screwed up. There's no way I'm going to Nationals." She tries to be flippant, but to her horror, her voice wavers. She glares at the floor, ordering herself to hold it together. "This is my last tournament."

"*Exactly*. So don't waste it." She looks at him sharply, surprised by the sudden fierceness in his voice. It's in his eyes, too, a fire that makes his amber irises burn brighter. "You've only lost one debate. There's four more tomorrow."

Something about the way he says it captures her. He sets his drink down and leans in, forearms on the table with his hands close enough to almost brush her fingertips. Leans in until his warm smell envelops her and he's filled her vision, and she can't think of anything else but what he's saying.

"I don't know what Jenna said to you," Charlie continues. "But it doesn't matter. Forget the Turners. Be your best tomorrow like nothing ever happened. Don't you dare let them ruin something you love."

He's always had an intense way of talking, particularly in a debate. But this is different. This intensity is strangely personal. She studies him. He's not blinking, but this time it's not creepy, although it does send a shiver down her spine.

Maybe he's right. There's very little chance of making it back to the top ranks, but if she plays her cards right tomorrow, she can still go out with a bang. She can still make this trip worth it.

The PA system turns on with a horrible scratching sound, jarring them into sitting back. Fifteen minutes until closing. Her phone buzzes with a text from Ameera: **We're meeting at the east entrance in five. Is Charlie with you?**

She texts back a quick yes, and they get up. Then something occurs to TJ that makes her frown.

"Why are you saying this stuff anyway?" she asks suspiciously. "We're competing for Nationals. You should be happy I screwed up."

Charlie looks off into the distance and takes his time answering. "I can't stand seeing you so pathetic. If I only beat you because you gave up, where's the satisfaction?"

TJ scoffs. Of course. "You're a dick."

"And you're . . ." He taps her nose condescendingly. "Welcome."

ELEVEN

***

The next day, TJ wakes up far too early. The sun has yet to rise. But she's too wired to go back to sleep, so in the dark of the hotel room she shares with Simran, she gets ready for the day. By the time her cousin's alarm goes off, TJ's fully dressed, propped against her pillows with her laptop.

Simran yawns and squints to turn off her alarm. "What are you doing?"

"Reading through a quotes website." She likes having some inspirational lines in her back pocket to end impromptu speeches on a snappy note.

Simran nods, then rolls over and promptly seems to fall asleep again. TJ has to fight the urge to laugh. When they were little, Simran took sleepover invitations quite literally, and no one could ever rouse her before noon. Clearly not much has changed.

"You know," she says, "for a religious person, you're not very disciplined."

Simran mutters something about how discipline has got nothing to do with anything.

"What's that?" TJ says with mock confusion. "Speak up. I can't hear you."

After a second, Simran twists in her cocoon of blankets, looking more awake. "You're bright this morning."

She looks a little unsettled by the fact. TJ grins. "Well, someone has to be. We've got four debates to get through."

Simran squints at her for another moment before smiling back. "I'm glad you're feeling better."

"I am," TJ says, and she finds that it's absolutely true. "Now, seriously, get up. Or we're going to miss breakfast."

Breakfast is hosted at the school. Today, TJ manages to eat a muffin and a few pieces of fruit. Schedules are passed around but she doesn't look at them. She double-checks that both her Proposition and Opposition speeches are in her notebook, colour-coded with green and red sticky notes. Those will be in the afternoon. The first two debates in the morning will be impromptu, meaning they're given a resolution thirty minutes before the first debate. Their resolution: *Be It Resolved That art can be evaluated objectively*.

TJ and Simran put their heads together, and a hush of whispers falls over the huge auditorium. No one's allowed to talk to anyone but their partner during this time. No electronics, either. They only have each other to rely on.

Once the thirty minutes are up, a timer goes off, and hundreds of chairs scrape back as debaters rise to go to their assigned classrooms. TJ swipes a water bottle for the road and tries to ignore the nervous flutters in her stomach.

The other team is already in the room when they arrive, two guys from the Lower Mainland West region in matching navy-blue suits. They stop whispering to each other and look up when TJ enters with Simran. They've never come up against this team before, but the smile the blond one gives her when she makes eye contact is a little too knowing. Friends of Jenna's, probably.

As the Speaker calls the debate to order, TJ mentally runs through facts about the debate. She and Simran are arguing Side Negative this round, which she triple-checked already. TJ is first speaker for their side. It's Cross-Examination Style, so she'll have to save her questions for the end. But she feels good about this topic. If she can keep her nerves in check, she'll be fine.

Side Affirmative's first speaker, the blond guy, stands when he's called. As usual for his role, he opens the debate with an introduction to the resolution and defines the terms. The definitions are pretty standard until he adds, "Scientific innovations are art as well, because they too require creativity and imagination."

This isn't unexpected. Including science in the definition strengthens their argument for objectivity in art. TJ taps her pen against her lips and bends to write.

A lot of his speech is stuff TJ and Simran already had planned for when they argue Side Affirmative later. Other things they haven't thought of, so TJ scribbles down notes on each new point to use later, even while she brainstorms rebuttals for them in this particular round.

Simran slides over extra notes, since TJ is the one who will be questioning him. And then it's time. The first speaker wraps up his speech. "I now stand for cross-examination."

TJ rises before she can give herself time to overthink it. She moves to stand in front of her desk. "Thank you for your speech, but I do have a few questions."

"By all means." He's smirking. She ignores it.

"You mentioned you believe scientific creations are somehow a kind of . . . art," she says slowly, just to make it sound extra ridiculous. "You also said these creations can be measured objectively by how they improve society. But how do you objectively measure improvement?"

His voice becomes patronizing. "Like I said earlier, all you need for an objective system of measurement is to set rules that can be reproduced by anyone anywhere, and get the same result. Look at the invention of the wheel and ask yourself: Does this move me forward? Does it move me forward faster, with less effort than what came before? The answer to those questions is yes no matter where on earth you're standing. Therefore, it's objective."

The judges scribble madly on their sheets, probably impressed with him. Not on TJ's watch.

Setting the sheet of questions down, she leans on her desk and crosses her arms. Enough of this STEM talk. It's time to bring this argument to *her* playing field. "Do you think the rules and regulations of soccer are objective?"

His brow furrows. TJ can practically see him analyzing all angles before he responds. "Yes. Because that's a standardized system of measurement—"

TJ cuts him off. "But we've all heard about refs making bad calls and missing fouls. By your definition, an objective system of measurement should reproduce the same result every time. But doesn't that depend on who uses it?"

"But that just means the system of measurement isn't good enough," her opponent answers eagerly. "If all the soccer games used technology like slow-motion replay and made it easier to see the foul, then it *would* be objective."

"You know something my soccer coach once told us?" TJ says. "Instant replay hardly makes a difference. English-speaking refs are more likely to call a foul when the direction of the play is going from right to left. You know why that is?"

His expression is still pleasant, but now there's a sharp edge to his voice. "I'm assuming you'll tell me."

"Because it's the opposite direction you read from. It feels uncomfortable. Even though they know the rules, depending on where the camera is, or where the ref is standing, or what language they speak, one team could be put at a disadvantage. So it doesn't matter if you've supposedly crafted a totally objective system of measurement, because the person using and interpreting the system is always going to be biased. Therefore, you can never truly measure it objectively. Wouldn't you agree?"

Out of the corner of her eye, she sees the judges look to her opponent for a response. His smirk is long gone. Suddenly, TJ's not bothered at all that people know about what happened last night.

Because now they're underestimating her.

The four debates go by like nothing—it feels like barely an hour has passed when it hits midafternoon and the last one is done.

The last event of the tournament is the celebratory banquet, held back at the hotel. TJ spends a little extra time in her room touching up her makeup and slipping on a dress, so she arrives in the foyer a few minutes late. Clearly she wasn't the only one with that idea, because the entrance to the ballroom is so congested that no one's really moving. TJ cranes her head to look over the crowd. Damn it. Final scores are going to be made public in a few minutes.

Someone squeezes next to her, and she looks up to find Charlie studying her. They haven't spoken all day.

TJ keeps her face expressionless. "Hey."

He leans in to whisper so no one else can hear. "How'd it go?"

She stares at him flatly for another second, and his eyes soften in sympathy. Then she breaks into a grin.

Because it went *well.*

She and Simran blew their first opponents out of the water. Their second round was against some friendly Island region kids that they'd debated before. That one was a tie, but TJ felt good about their performance.

That set the tone for the afternoon rounds. By the time TJ walked out of the last debate, she had a bounce in her step. Three wins and one tie, plus the loss yesterday. Not bad at all.

Upon seeing her smile, Charlie grins, too, a wide, even one. "Good."

"Good?" she echoes, raising her eyebrows. "You should be quaking in your loafers. I'm coming for your spot."

"You'll try."

He's still grinning. It's a little weird to see Charlie happy for her. Maybe he's confident he did well enough to beat her anyway. "How were yours?"

"Fine." He shrugs, looking unbothered. So he killed it. She

waits for the jealousy to overcome her, but strangely, it doesn't. She just feels warm and content. Charlie continues smiling at her. Like her, he's changed into fresh formal clothes for the evening—a violet three-piece, with a complementary striped tie. And with the suit jacket tossed over his shoulder, sleeves rolled up, dear god, he's *achingly* cute.

Wait. What? Where did that come from? TJ's smile falls. Charlie's eyebrows draw together in confusion as the crowd finally starts moving again. And then a familiar voice sounds out.

"Charlie! It's been so long!" Isaac appears in front of them, enveloping Charlie in a side-hug. Great. Before Isaac can spot her, TJ slips away.

She mentally dumps ice water on herself as she goes. Charlie? Cute? She's way too slaphappy right now. She needs sleep.

But first. The banquet.

Long, cloth-draped tables stand in rows in the ballroom, and Yara waves madly with a piece of paper from one taken over by Southern Interior debaters. Appetizers are set out, but that's not what TJ homes in on. She needs to know which two senior debaters will represent the Southern Interior at Nationals. She snatches one of the papers out of Saad's hands.

"Hey!" Saad protests. She ignores him, scanning the sheet. Novice scores. She flips it over. Junior scores. She glances at Saad, confused.

"Why do you have the novice and junior scores but not your own?"

He looks unrepentant. "I'm nosy."

"Here," squeaks Yara. TJ looks up to find the junior sliding another piece of paper towards her. Apparently everyone is nosy, because Yara's been reading the senior results.

TJ scans the sheet, heart in her throat. As per usual, the Vancouver regions and the Island fought over the top few spots. Then . . .

Simran. Coming in number six. TJ can't help the grin that stretches over her face—she didn't screw this up for her cousin after all. Simran's still going to Nationals.

She scans further. Four spots down, Charles Rosencrantz. He's sandwiched between Jenna and Isaac Turner, who are ninth and eleventh. Top ten is no joke.

Her smile lessens considerably. She hadn't thought she still expected to make it into one of the top two spots for their region—not with how badly she screwed up yesterday—but a part of her was apparently still holding out hope. Now she knows this is the end of the road. No Nationals for her. It'll be Simran and Charlie.

Saad coughs, reminding her she's not alone. She rallies herself immediately, scanning further down the column that declares which region the debater is from until she gets to the next *Southern Interior*.

And there. Number twenty—Tejindar Powar.

Top twenty! TJ's grin returns. Jenna couldn't take that away from her.

Twenty-one is Nate. Close call. Pride fills her. She was good enough to beat Nate, albeit by zero point two. TJ checks for the others. Thirty-five, Ameera; thirty-seven, Saad.

She looks up at Saad. "You two did great."

Saad shrugs. He doesn't look cut up about not going to Nationals. Then again, he hasn't been locked in a years-long death match with Whitewater over the top spots in their region. He didn't even qualify for Provincials last year. "Yeah, it's cool."

Yara peeks over TJ's shoulder. "The scores are so tight. There's only a ten-point difference between you and Simran."

It's true. A pang goes through her. If she hadn't messed up yesterday, she could've easily taken Charlie's place at Nationals.

But it doesn't matter. He won, fair and square. And at least TJ's in the top twenty. As for the Turners . . . they're above her. They're the two top debaters of their region—Lower Mainland North—so they'll be at Nationals. But no one can say their scores were far superior to TJ's. Maybe Simran was right and they got docked for unprofessionalism after all.

TJ exhales, exhaustion creeping over her now that the suspense is gone. She looks up to find Simran watching her, standing next to Yara in her pastel-blue salwar kameez. There's something in her eyes—trepidation.

TJ tosses the results sheet on the table. "You better beat the hell out of the Turners at Nationals."

Simran's face breaks into a relieved grin. "I'll do what I can."

Nate appears at the table with a loaded plate of food and Charlie in tow. "You know, the only thing standing between you and Nationals is Charlie."

"Thanks for the reminder." She glances at Charlie, but he's staring at the floor. He doesn't look pleased. If anything he seems tired suddenly. She frowns.

"Just saying." Nate elbows Charlie. "When your body washes up in the Fraser River, I'll know who to point the police to."

TJ plucks a spanakopita from Nate's plate. "Shut up. I'm happy for them. Really." Everyone at the table falls silent. "What?"

Nate clears his throat and looks around. "Who here expected TJ to be okay with not going to Nationals? Raise your hand." No one does.

TJ's jaw drops. "Traitors!"

Saad coughs into his arm. "You are, erm, a little competitive."

"Just a bit," Nate adds. TJ glares at him.

"I don't see *you* in the top twenty, you fetus." Nate's in grade eleven, so this is a top-notch insult.

"Greatness can't always be recognized, TJ. The sad truth is sometimes mediocrity wins." Nate shakes his head dramatically. He seems unbothered, but then again, he'll have another chance next year. "After-party in my and Charlie's room. Who's coming?" He glances at Simran. "No alcohol."

"Thanks," Simran says wryly. It's an unnecessary warning, since debate parties are glorified pajama parties. The thrill comes from defying school-trip rules about being back in their own rooms by eleven.

The chaperones make it back to the table. Mr. York suggests a toast to all the debaters from the Southern Interior. Everyone raises their glasses of sparkling juice amid cheers.

Simran nudges TJ's shoulder. They clink glasses.

"You did great," Simran whispers. "You should be proud."

TJ grins back. "You too." And maybe it's her exhaustion that makes everything seem so shiny and her heart so unnaturally giddy, so much more sentimental than it usually is; or maybe it's just that it's her last tournament, but she looks back at Charlie, who's on her other side. She never thanked him for his pep talk.

Just as she's thinking to say it, Charlie's phone buzzes on the table. The name *Andrew Yen* lights up the display, and he immediately picks it up, standing to excuse himself. Probably one of his student council henchmen.

Appetizers are served, then the main course, then dessert, and the atmosphere in their little group is joyful and energetic. Charlie doesn't return. Nate makes everyone laugh with his impression of the MC; one of the Pineview novices shares a story of how an opponent left for the washroom in the middle of the debate. Saad and Ameera nearly get into a shouting match over the last piece of chocolate cake, and by the time the speeches start, they're all in a lazy, contented sort of mood.

The organizers drone on and on about all the work that went into the tournament, and TJ finds herself nodding off. She whispers to Simran that she's going to the washroom and ducks out.

There's a public washroom in the corridor, but she gets in the elevator, telling herself she's just going to the one in her room. But then she gets off on the floor just under hers, and tells herself she's just going for a walk. And when she passes by Charlie and Nate's room, she tells herself she's just trying to delay going back downstairs and listening to boring speeches.

She knocks. No answer. She knocks again. Again, nothing. Giving up, she starts to head back down the darkened hall when she notices someone sitting on the couch at the end of the corridor, facing the floor-to-ceiling cityscape-view window.

Charlie doesn't react when she sits next to him on the couch, except to move his suit jacket to the other armrest to make room for her. His loafers are propped up on the low coffee table next to a plate that looks scraped clean. He must've taken food with him when he left.

She props her black heels up, too, and follows his gaze outside. The city view is really beautiful from here, the lights preventing the alcove from being too dark. She yawns and tips her head back, closing her eyes.

"Is the banquet over?" Charlie asks after a minute, and she jerks back into alertness. He must think she's a weirdo, wandering over here with no explanation and then practically falling asleep next to him.

The thing is, she doesn't have an explanation for why she's here that doesn't sound cheesy. She clears her throat. "Uh, no. They were getting to the 'patting ourselves on the back' stage of speeches. So I left. Why didn't you come back?"

He nods at his phone on the coffee table. "I got an important call."

"Oh? Did the clown convention finally get back to you?"

"Yeah, but the position I was gunning for was already filled by a more suitable applicant. Congratulations, by the way." TJ kicks his foot. He makes a show of rubbing the scuff mark off the genuine Italian leather. "It was this guy I've been trying to book for an event our school council is doing. A stand-up comedian. He's really busy and only just called me back."

She tilts her head. All these years, she's only really known

Charlie through debate, and whatever he posted online, which wasn't much. But suddenly, she's filled with curiosity about his life. "What event?"

"A fundraising dinner, for polio."

"*For* polio? Interesting side you've chosen to take."

He laughs under his breath. "You know what I meant."

"I never know with you." TJ realizes she's grinning. How disturbing. "Hey, I never said thanks. For yesterday, I mean."

He shrugs one shoulder. "I didn't do anything."

"No, you did." She needs him to understand what it meant to her to end this tournament on a positive note. "I just, well, I know you and Isaac are friends, so I appreciated the pep talk."

A small furrow appears between his brows. "We're not friends."

"What?" She stares. With the way Isaac acted earlier . . . "I thought you two were close. Didn't you grow up together?"

"It—it—it's old news."

That might be the first time she's ever heard him stammer. She waits for more, but he appears to have wired his jaw shut. "Meaning? You were *never* friends?"

"No, we were." His tone closes the matter despite the many questions she has. This is new; she's never heard him sound *bitter* before.

But if his experience is anything like hers, she understands being bitter. It's like with Chandani. In some ways, Chandani hurt her more than Liam. Because in the back of TJ's mind, she always thought she would have her friends no matter what happened. But apparently that's not true. And that . . . sucks.

The mood has soured slightly, so she tries to lighten it. "So. Nationals. Congratulations."

"And here I thought we were being honest with each other," he intones. She snickers.

"Okay, fine. Screw you for taking my rightful spot." He nods as if that's better. "At least I owned Nate."

"On paper, anyway."

She aims another kick at his foot. He pulls it off the table at the last second, and she twists to get him in the leg instead. He laughs softly. TJ smiles against her will; he seems less tired now.

They lapse into yet another easy silence. This time, though, they're half facing each other. She studies his face because she's never seen it so close. Charlie has gently rounded eyebrows, the edges fuzzy and indistinct the way natural brows are. His lashes are long, but not as thick as hers. There's the tiniest bit of stubble glinting off his jawline. She searches the strong lines of his throat for more, but there are too many shadows.

She raises her eyes back to his, and finds him staring back unblinkingly.

"I like the earrings," he says suddenly, reaching out to tap one.

She feels warm for no reason. He's complimenting the earrings, not her. She reaches up to steady the swaying earring, brushing his fingers in the process. "They were my grandmother's."

"Hmm. I knew you couldn't have such good taste." She scoffs. He drops his hand. "A ponytail would show them off even better."

Curse him and his fashion sense, he's totally right. This look would be much better with a slick, high-up ponytail. And she even tried it, back in the hotel room.

But. Then she took in the whole picture: Black dress with lace sleeves, matching tights and heels, killer eyeshadow, sleek ponytail, dangling Rajasthani earrings, and . . . *sideburns*. Long fuzzy caterpillar sideburns that completely killed her aesthetic. So she put her hair back down and curled it around her face. She's not proud of it. It's a point against her in her little internal debate. But given the last few days, she just let it go. Part of debating is deciding which hills are worth dying on, after all. And this hill . . . Well. TJ just didn't have the strength for it tonight.

She rearranges her hair to frame her face. "I don't need your subpar fashion advice."

"That would hurt if I didn't know how obsessed you are with my tie collection."

"I am not!"

"Then why are you blushing?"

"I don't *blush*." One of the many benefits to being brown.

"You don't turn red," he concedes. "But your skin . . . glows."

Her face gets hotter. Charlie even looks surprised at his own words. But then he smiles, and something in her chest flip-flops.

If she puts her pride aside, she can acknowledge Charlie *is* cute. Actually, he's . . . more than cute. TJ usually just chooses to focus on how annoying he is. But she'd bet he's got admirers at Whitewater.

She frowns, not liking that thought.

"What?" he asks.

TJ shrugs. "I just realized I don't know much about you."

"What do you want to know?"

Later, TJ will blame her lack of filter on her sleep-deprived state. But as it is she just blurts, "Are you single?"

He blinks. Then: "Yes."

TJ can hardly believe that. Not with those bright, intense eyes and the easy confidence in that grin. She craves that kind of confidence. She's craving a lot of things right now, actually.

"Was that it?" he asks, and she realizes—too late—she should've had more questions prepared to avoid sounding transparent. She scrambles for something, but her hesitation is too long.

"You know, I've had this theory for a while," Charlie says.

His voice sounds deeper than usual. She licks her lips. Her curiosity about him has suddenly expanded in all sorts of other directions. "A theory, you say?"

"Yes."

She draws her legs up under her. She's on the verge of doing something reckless, she can just tell. And yet, it's almost like she's outside of her own body, hearing herself talk. "Well, have you got evidence for it?"

"No. More . . . just a feeling."

"Then it's not really a theory, is it?" TJ challenges, remembering Simran telling her that. "A theory by definition has a strong base of solid evidence."

"Side Opposition makes a good point." Charlie shifts slightly on the couch to fully face her. Casually, he braces his hand on the backrest beside her head. "A hypothesis, then."

If she turned her head, her lips would brush against his knuckles. She inhales slowly, and his smell closes in, ironed linens that remind her of lazy Sunday mornings. She studies the waves of brown hair that cascade (carefully) over his forehead, that tie embellishing a throat she aches to touch. A button-down shirt that begs her to press her nose into it. A boy she's spent her entire debating career trying to make tongue-tied, and well, maybe she's been going about it the wrong way this whole time.

Her eyes travel back to his. She likes what she sees in his gaze. It's not the way Liam ever looked at her, like he couldn't help himself because she was hot. Charlie doesn't look at her like he thinks she's hot. He looks at her like he thinks she's weird, and he likes it. A lot.

And god, does it feel good to make his breathing turn uneven. To lean closer and not have him lean away. It feels good to be wanted.

And the thing is, this ridiculous impulse she's currently having could *work*. Zero complications or attachments, because after this weekend, they're going their separate ways. She's not going to Nationals; her last soccer tournament is that weekend, so she won't even be present. This is their last debate together.

She brushes away the wave of sadness that comes with that thought. Now is the perfect time for a little experimentation. Just a kiss with a guy who's attracted to her. Maybe it'll be nice. Maybe it'll be awful. Who cares? She can leave it behind, here in this posh Vancouver hotel, and never revisit it again.

Not only that, but this . . . this could be her rebuttal to the Liam argument. This could be the ace in the hole. All she has to do is close the distance.

"Do you want to hear the hypothesis?" Charlie asks quietly.

She doesn't even remember what they were talking about. She's just staring at his lips. Is she doing this? Wow, she's totally doing this. "Shut up, Charlie."

And then she bites the bullet and leans in all the way.

It's an awkward fumble at first. She goes in too fast and he's not quite ready and their lips don't line up properly. And TJ thinks, *Huh, it's a good thing I can leave this behind.*

But a few seconds in, he relaxes, tilts his head the extra degree they need to fit together, and everything falls into place. His hand drags off the couch next to her head and she doesn't know where his hands are at all for a moment. Then she feels them both at once, sliding, cupping her jaw, making her shudder.

And TJ thinks, *Oh no. I can't leave this one behind.*

Because they're kissing properly now: the toe-curling, sweet kind, mouths meeting gently and parting. His lips are soft, and his touch even gentler. One hand slides down her neck to her shoulder, down her arm. He draws her closer and she reaches for him, too, bunching up the material of his shirt. He makes a sound low in his throat when she runs her fingers through his hair—*so soft*—and something scorching hot flares to life in her body.

Holy crap. She's kissing Charlie Rosencrantz. Her heart speeds up giddily, leaving her brain and all her logical reasoning behind. The banquet they're missing doesn't matter. Liam doesn't matter. Her resolution doesn't matter. Nothing matters but this.

They break for air. Charlie starts to say something. TJ doesn't let him; she pulls him back in by the knot of his tie.

He doesn't exactly protest. His hands slide down her sides, and he kisses her with the same singular focus he brings to every debate. The warmth in her belly liquefies to something molten and heavy, sinking lower, pressing against her insides, burning her from within.

Mindlessly, she puts her hands on his shoulders and rises up on her knees to get closer. She only half gets in his lap before he presses his mouth against her throat. *Oh.* Okay. He ghosts his hand up the back of her neck and winds her long hair around his wrist, tugging her head back.

Her head tips to the side like a rag doll, lulled by his lazy movements. She's enjoying it, at least until one of her own long, dangling earrings taps against her jaw.

Her hair's pulled out of her face like a ponytail. Exposing her earrings, but also . . . everything she was trying to hide. Her limbs lock up.

Oh *no.*

Charlie's sensed her hesitation and has stopped. Now he's just looking up at her, and she hates it, because they're so up close and personal, he can see and feel how hairy she is. It's not something you miss. How did she totally forget about this earlier when they were staring at each other?

Is he grossed out? Or has he not really registered it yet? It's dark in here, after all. That must be it. She should pull away now before he realizes.

But. If she pulls away she'll lose her internal debate. The resolution *This House Believes That TJ Powar can be her hairy self and still be beautiful* would fall like a rock, because it would be proven beyond doubt that not even she believes her own argument.

She has to keep going. Resolution aside, TJ *wants* to keep going. Preferably in a private setting. She likes everything they're doing, and wants more.

But then her brain supplies her with a horrible image: taking off her dress, showing her happy trail, and watching the distaste flicker through his eyes—

TJ recoils—away from Charlie, and away from the thought. She can't—*can't*—go through that again.

She shakes her hair free of his hand and scoots to the end of the couch, breathless, heart still thundering, skin still burning. Finally, she looks up at him.

Charlie looks like a mess for possibly the first time in his life. His brown hair is disheveled and his tie loosened by her grip. His amber eyes are liquid dark. His hands, still half-outstretched from where she pulled away, flex as though he wants to touch her again. But he doesn't. He just speaks, voice raspy.

"*Now* it's a theory."

TWELVE
***

"So tell me," Simran says. "At what point during this makeout session did you start regretting it?"

"I didn't say I regret it." TJ frowns. She's not even done telling the story.

"No, but you only tell me stuff about your love life when you wish you hadn't done it."

TJ's jaw drops. "I do not!"

Simran stops playing her harmonium to give her a look. TJ sighs and fiddles with her scarf, which is hiding a little souvenir Charlie left on her throat. It's Sunday evening, and they're back in Kelowna, at Simran's house.

The whole thing is all kinds of embarrassing. After breaking off the kiss with Charlie, TJ had fled, muttering some excuse about needing to pack. She went straight back to her and Simran's hotel room, texted Ameera that she wasn't feeling well, and burrowed under the blankets. Nate messaged her later, wondering why she wasn't at his little after-party, but she ignored it. She couldn't risk seeing Charlie again. Then, the next morning, she kept her nose buried in magazines the whole bus ride home to avoid catching his eye.

At least they won't cross paths anymore. In any case, TJ had been bursting to tell someone what happened. Not Piper, who'd just get excited and wouldn't understand why TJ ran away. It had to be Simran. Someone who'd be able to give a calm and logical perspective on things and not judge her.

But apparently she's just going to get roasted. "You're just good at seeing angles I don't consider," TJ tries.

Simran gives her another look that makes it clear the attempt at flattery was obvious. "On what? It's pretty obvious what happened. You wouldn't even look at him at breakfast."

"Maybe he just wasn't looking at me."

"Oh, he was. He kept trying to catch your eye." Simran shakes her head. "Now I know why."

A bit of guilt curls in TJ's stomach, but she brushes it off. It's done, it's over. "Well, anyway," she says, pushing away from the door she'd been leaning against, "we were getting pretty into it, and then I stopped and basically ran away."

Simran plays a long sequence of keys on her harmonium. "Why? Was it a bad kiss?"

No. That's the problem. She can't stop thinking about it. She also can't stop thinking about how it was a perfectly PG-13 kiss until she tried to crawl *into his lap*. Cringing at the memory, TJ pushes aside Simran's not-yet-unpacked suitcase to sit cross-legged on the carpet next to her. There's not much free space elsewhere. "I just realized it couldn't go anywhere. And I couldn't stand being looked at like I was ugly and gross for being hairy."

Simran stops playing again. "Did he look at you like you were ugly and gross?"

"No!"

"Then why—?"

"I didn't want to wait around until he did, okay?" she snaps.

Simran's unmoved. "So, what happened to you proving something by being hairy?"

"That's just it." TJ glares at the wall. "I couldn't prove it. I can't."

She lost her debate against herself. Hairy TJ doesn't really believe she's beautiful enough to be desired. Because truthfully, she isn't, and Liam already proved that. She just couldn't bear to have it proven again with Charlie.

Simran's quiet for a long second. "For what it's worth, the right person wouldn't reject you for being hairy."

TJ snorts. "Do you believe that?" When Simran nods, TJ changes her question. "Do you really believe that, *for yourself*?" Simran lowers her eyes. "Exactly."

"In a perfect world—"

"There is no perfect world," TJ cuts her off, angry. "There's just the real, crappy world, where people laugh at jokes about my cousin's hair, and the guys I hook up with get turned off by mine."

Simran's quiet. "So what now?"

TJ shrugs. "Just gonna make an appointment with the salon. I'm three months overdue." She may as well, since she has nothing to prove anymore except what a loser she is.

Simran nods slowly. "I'm sorry things didn't work out."

"Yeah, well, that's life, I guess." TJ frowns. "When you and Charlie meet up to practice for Nationals, you better pretend you don't know what happened."

A pause. "Of course."

"When are you two meeting, anyway?" When Simran shrugs noncommittally, TJ gawks. "How do you not know? You have to figure out your arguments! Hasn't the resolution already been announced?"

"Yeah, but it's okay to take a break."

Debate club pretty much wraps after Provincials, since it's the last big tournament that lots of people go to. Plus, other clubs and sports become active in the spring. Only those going to Nationals keep at it. TJ had seen Simran and Charlie talking before they got on the bus and had assumed they were making times to meet. But apparently not. "Seriously?"

Simran's lips twitch. "We *just* got back from Provincials. Why are you getting so worked up?"

"I'm not," TJ retorts. "I'm just saying, if Charlie's being lazy—"

"It was my idea." Simran puffs more air into her harmonium, and then presses her fingers into a minor chord. "Okay? It's not Charlie's fault."

TJ wishes it was. She wishes it was *all* his fault. Then maybe she wouldn't feel like such a tool.

When TJ arrives home, she's greeted with the sound of laughter in the parlour. A quick peek confirms several aunties are over, including Rupi auntie, aka Mrs. Banger. Yikes. Employing ninja-like stealth, she manages to get up the stairs without being spotted.

Her room's nearly as messy as Simran's today—she'd torn it apart packing frantically for Provincials. Her soccer jersey is still draped over her chair from her last game. She tosses it in the hamper and checks the to-do list on her vanity. It's full of graduation stuff she's been procrastinating on. No thanks. She picks up the lifestyle magazine she bought at the hotel for the ride home. Aimlessly, she sits and flips it open.

She lands on a huge, two-page spread of a woman's face. The woman's a pilot, and there's a whole article about her that TJ already read, but right now all she can do is stare at the close-up picture and wonder if the woman's face is naturally that hairless, or if she's been plucked and waxed, or if it's been air-brushed out.

She throws the magazine on her bed. What's wrong with her, looking at an article about a woman's career and instead searching for visible body hair in the photo?

This isn't even the first time. For the past months, it's been the first thing she focuses on when she looks at women. Any time she sees arm hair or cheek fuzz sparkling in the sunlight, she feels victorious, like she found Waldo in the big confusing picture. It's something she used to do when she was younger. It used to help, knowing she wasn't the only one.

Yet, there's not a lot of girls walking around with the amount of hair *she* has. She lifts her shirt and looks down at her wiry happy trail. Isn't that just wrong? She's never exactly seen a woman at the beach sporting that.

TJ's hit with the urge to get rid of it. Immediately. She heads to the washroom and digs around in the cabinet under the sink. After her initial purge, she'd realized she'd forgotten to throw out a few items hiding in the cleaning supplies bucket. There was an unopened razor lurking here, but she can't find it now.

Whatever. She picks up her phone and unblocks Lulu in her contacts. Her thumb hovers over the dial button. But just then, there's a knock on the door.

"TJ." Her mother jiggles the doorknob. "Come downstairs and say hello to our guests." Her voice is fake-friendly with an undertone of *This isn't optional.*

TJ mouths several F-bombs at the mirror before replying. "Coming!"

"Now." Footsteps fade away. TJ takes her time putting away the stuff she'd haphazardly pulled from the cabinet in her search. When she has no other excuse to delay, she descends the stairs.

The tinkly laughter in the parlour stops abruptly upon her entrance. Four aunties all look at her in unison. They're dressed up in pretty salwar kameezes. TJ wishes she'd thought to change out of her ratty, off-the-shoulder sweater and capri leggings.

They all stand as TJ approaches them with her fake smile. "Sat Sri Akaal, Auntie. Sat Sri Akaal." She goes around the table greeting them.

Rupi auntie grabs her shoulders and kisses her on the cheek, smiling warmly. When she lets go, she says, "I was just telling your mom how I was teaching your class a few months back. It feels like it's been so long."

There's a bit of sunlight filtering through the window on Rupi auntie's face. No hair catches in the light. None at all.

Someone coughs, and TJ realizes she hasn't responded. She shrugs a practiced sheepish shrug.

"How are you, putt?" Rupi auntie tugs her down to sit next

to her. Her floral perfume is nearly overwhelming. "Your mom told us you went to a debate tournament this weekend."

"She was in the top twenty in the province," her mom brags. TJ filled in her parents this morning on how the trip went. Of course, her two big screwups of the weekend never came up. "It's very hard to achieve."

They *ooh* and *aah*, and TJ's mom smiles proudly. TJ spends the next couple of minutes fielding questions about debate, soccer, her grades, and then they finally move on to some scandal involving someone's wedding getting cancelled. TJ relaxes. Well, that wasn't so bad.

She starts to rise from her seat, planning to excuse herself, when one of the aunties laughs and says, "Hopefully TJ won't do such a thing at her own wedding!" They're still talking about the couple who cancelled their wedding last minute.

"Ha ha," TJ says weakly. If that's their idea of a juicy scandal, their brains would probably explode knowing what TJ gets up to.

"Find a nice Jatt boy to settle down with, putt," Rupi auntie advises, taking TJ's chin in a viselike grip. "Then separations like this won't happen. Too many differences destroy a marriage."

"Jatt? None of that caste nonsense here," TJ's mom says sharply. "She can marry whoever she likes." TJ smiles. Her mom coming to her defense for once is nice. Although, her brain would probably still explode if she knew what TJ got up to.

One of the aunties tuts. "Yes, yes, we know *you* had a love marriage, but it's so much harder to attract a good match that way." She scrutinizes TJ. "Your nose is so long. But to be expected, your papa has it, too. Tarleen's daughter has such a lovely nose."

Great. The newest comparison between her and Simran is the length of their *noses*. TJ bites the inside of her cheek hard.

Then Rupi auntie says, "Oh, but, putt, you have such big beautiful eyes! You just need to get threading done and you'll be gorgeous." She says it so casually TJ's sure she doesn't realize what a backhanded compliment that is. "I used to be like you. So hairy." Everyone in the room laughs. "But don't worry, it's just an awkward stage. I can't believe you haven't started removing it yet!"

"But she has," TJ's mom says, and leans forward to examine TJ's face. "TJ, I reminded you about this a few weeks ago, too. Did you forget to make an appointment?"

TJ can't speak. She's too busy sinking into the floor.

"You can get a full facial removal for a very good price where I go," another auntie suggests. "I'll give you their number."

"Yes, go, get rid of that pesky hair." Rupi auntie gestures to her chin, nodding at TJ. "It makes your skin look brighter and your face cleaner."

"And you won't have a bigger moustache than your husband on your wedding day," cracks another, eliciting laughter.

TJ just stands there numbly as they chortle. She knows they're not trying to humiliate her. In fact, they think they're being helpful. Just giving beauty tips to a friend's daughter.

She mumbles something about homework and excuses herself back upstairs, despite her mom's dagger eyes. If she stays in this room for a second longer, she might have a literal breakdown. That would sure give the aunties something to talk about.

The magazine she was reading earlier is still on her bed, left open to the same page. TJ closes it. On the back cover is an ad for women's razors with the caption *Free your legs*. Wow. There really is no escape.

She picks it up. A brunette woman sits in a pristine tub, shaving an already completely smooth leg. Would it kill them to show some hair? Wouldn't that show the razor worked?

She hurls the magazine into the wastebasket near the door. Then she pulls out her phone, bringing up Lulu's contact number again. Lulu usually manages to squeeze her in last minute. TJ could easily go to the salon tomorrow after school.

She lets herself fantasize about it for a minute. She'd start with the full facial for her first appointment. It'd set her pores on fire, and set her back thirty bucks. But on Tuesday she'd walk into school with that bright, clean face Rupi auntie was talking about. People would talk to her normally again. She would be admired, turn heads for all the right reasons. Liam would wish he'd never broken up with her.

Then TJ would go in the next day for her arms and legs. She'd buy some home wax for her underarms. She'd start saving to splurge on laser treatments. Slowly, methodically, she would fix everything. She would retake her place as one of the prettiest girls in school. She'd tell herself that all her time and money spent on hair removal was just personal preference. That would be so easy.

Except deep down she'd always know that it wasn't true.

That her real, hairy Indian body, the one she was born with, is considered unacceptable. So unacceptable that even in ads for hair removal, showing actual hair is a no-no.

And there's nothing *freeing* about that.

A familiar anger boils up in her. She paces over to her debate bag and finds her old cue card: *This House Believes That TJ Powar can be her hairy self and still be beautiful.*

She scoffs re-reading the naive words. She wanted *so badly* for her natural self to be seen as beautiful. But it's time to face the facts. The hair covering her body is never going to get anyone going. Least of all her.

But that doesn't mean she has to give up on the debate. She lost this round, sure. But who says she can't win the next?

She picks up a pen. Scratches out her old words and carefully writes something new beneath. A resolution that feels like something she can actually argue for.

This House Believes That TJ Powar can exist as a hairy girl and still be worthy of respect, beautiful or not.

THIRTEEN
***

The next morning, the weather forecast declares an unseasonably warm day, so TJ flings open her closet with a mission.

She checks herself out in the mirror after finishing her makeup. A floral-print sleeveless dress just barely brushes her knees. No tights underneath, either. Her arms and legs are on full display. And her hair is swept up into a bun, calling attention to the amount of fur she's accumulated on her face.

She grins savagely at her reflection.

TJ's mom is in the kitchen drinking coffee when TJ comes down the stairs. She spills some of it down her front. "TJ! What are you *wearing*?"

"What do you mean?" TJ asks innocently. "I've worn this dress a hundred times."

Her mother opens her mouth, glances at TJ's father, who's eating at the kitchen table (he's just returned from a night shift), and hesitates. Then: "It's March. Shouldn't you save the dresses for warmer days?"

"It *is* a warmer day. Have you seen the forecast?" TJ pulls it up on her phone.

Her mother again glances at her father, like she's holding back because of him. It pisses TJ off, but before she can call her out, her dad says, "Leave her alone, sweetheart." He gives TJ a thumbs-up. "I think you look great."

TJ beams. Finally, support from *somewhere*. Even if it's from the man wearing his shirt inside out.

When she gets to school, she turns heads, all right. Whispers follow her as she strides down the hall with her head held high. She spots Piper at her locker and waves at her, careless of the fact that her hairy underarms are now exposed. Piper waves back, and TJ approaches. She, too, is in apparel suited for the weather, a sleeveless blouse and jean shorts.

Piper takes a binder out of her locker. "How'd the tournament go?"

TJ waves this away dismissively. "Who cares? Tell me your thoughts on my outfit." She gestures down to herself, and Piper looks her over for the first time. Her eyes bug out.

"Oh my god." A pause. "I didn't realize you were *that* hairy."

What might have once pinched TJ now just makes her smile maniacally. "Appreciate my impressive armpit hair, too, please."

Piper does. "I didn't know you could grow that much hair."

Her tone has slipped into uncertainty, and she looks at TJ with new eyes. TJ's smile wavers before it comes back, hardened.

"Well, *now you know*."

"I'm sorry," Piper says quickly. "It's just—hard to get used to. I mean, you used to have the nicest legs of any of us. I was so jealous."

"I still have the same legs. They're just not hairless anymore." TJ leans against a locker, forcing eye contact with a boy blatantly staring from across the hall. He instantly looks away.

Piper nods rapidly. "I—I guess so." She seems a little shell-shocked still, but then her gaze shifts behind TJ.

TJ turns to see Chandani standing behind them at her own locker.

Clearly she was eavesdropping. TJ gives her the most scornful look she can manage. Chandani's lip curls, looking TJ up and down, before she spins on her heel—her skirt twirls around her, smooth brown thighs gleaming—and heads down the hall.

A lump grows in TJ's throat. That never stops hurting.

Piper sighs. "You two *need* to make up."

"That's like saying we *need* world peace," TJ replies tightly. "A nice thought, but just not gonna happen, as long as people are assholes."

"That sounds like something Chandani would say." TJ turns her glare on Piper, and she puts her hands up. "Just saying. You two are way too similar."

"We are *not*."

"Yes, you are. Most of the time *I'm* the odd one out." TJ opens her mouth to argue, but Piper holds up a hand. "Come on, TJ. You and Chandani have known each other forever."

TJ hesitates. It's true. Their moms are friends, and they grew up together. People always assumed they were sisters—probably half-based on the fact that they were two Indian girls with long hair, but still. They only befriended Piper when she became a starting midfielder on their soccer team in grade nine. Since then, they've been a trio on and off the field, but TJ has always been closest with Chandani. She hadn't realized Piper saw that so clearly, though.

"That doesn't mean anything," TJ mutters at last. "Let's go to class." She starts walking, but falters when she sees another problem approaching down the hall.

Liam.

"Oh no," Piper breathes. "Should we go the other way?"

Piper's not the only one who's noticed his arrival. TJ can feel eyes on her back. The news of their breakup has definitely spread.

TJ shakes her head at Piper and keeps walking. She's not going to give them anything more to talk about.

Liam avoids looking at her for as long as possible. And then, when he draws close enough for conversation, he meets her eyes. His are so startlingly green. Despite everything, her stomach does a funny dip.

But then he gives her a look-over. *The* look-over. The one usually followed by *Hey, beautiful.*

He continues on past her.

And TJ continues on past him, hoping no one can guess what she's thinking.

He just walked away, like it was nothing. Like he never used to get in trouble whispering to her in class. Like he didn't take her for ice cream every week last summer, like they didn't make matching Addams Family costumes last Halloween, like he didn't use to kiss her in the hallways just because. Like *she* was nothing.

Piper gives her a sympathetic look. TJ sets her jaw. No— Liam doesn't get to make her feel worthless. Not with her new resolution.

But damn it all, she can't help but look back once more. Just in time to see him stop near Alexa Fisher's locker down the hall to talk. Alexa smiles up at him, and there's nothing to really suggest they're flirting. For all TJ knows, they could be talking about a science project. But it still feels like someone put a cheese grater to her heart.

After a few days, the shocked stares and whispers following TJ around at school die down. An excellent start to her new argument.

But it's not *quite* back to business as usual. She still can't bring herself to use the communal showers after soccer practice. And although Piper keeps tight-lipped about it, TJ heavily suspects her teammates talk about her behind her back. She never paid much attention to her own social status before, but now she notices all the time. The silences that fall when she joins a group. The eye contact people make when they think she's not paying attention. She decides to ignore it. Eventually they'll get used to it—get used to *her*.

The following Monday, TJ checks her phone under her desk in class and sees several university decisions in her inbox, from the handful of Ontario schools she'd applied to for their thriving debate clubs. She scrolls through them. Rejection. Rejection. Rejection—Offer! At Western University. TJ restrains her grin, not wanting her phone to be confiscated. She'd been hoping for an Ontario offer.

When the lunch bell rings, she practically skips down the hall, bursting to tell someone. The first person she finds is Mrs. Scott—in her classroom, rooting through a drawer.

Mrs. Scott barely looks up when she appears. "Oh, hello, TJ. Can you help me with something? I need someone to get those boxes from the top of the cabinet. They're full of old magazines I'm donating to the book drive." She points.

TJ knows she's about to get roped into an entire lunchtime's worth of errands, but there's nothing to do about it now. The cabinet's too tall to reach, so she drags a chair over. "I got a bunch of Ontario decisions today," she says as she balances on the chair.

"Really?"

TJ tells her the details as she hefts the box off the shelf. God, that's heavy. She turns and hands it off to Mrs. Scott, who's smiling.

"Oh, congrats. Western hosts such excellent debate tournaments. While you're up there, can you also take down those other boxes? They've been there for years."

TJ sighs and turns back around. "Well, I just wanted to thank you for writing me a reference." She's suddenly feeling sappy, so she adds, "And for running the debate club all these years. It's weird to think it's over now."

"It's not over yet. Nationals are in May."

TJ frowns as she hefts an even heavier box off the cabinet. She wouldn't be surprised if these were actually just full of rocks. "Uh, I know? But I won't be able to help out. I have an away soccer game that weekend. I thought I told you."

Dead silence behind her. TJ turns around with the box in her arms to find Mrs. Scott staring. "What?" she says slowly.

"I have to say I'm confused," Mrs. Scott says as she accepts the box from TJ. "I thought you were going to Nationals."

TJ blinks, unsure if she heard right. "Uh, no, I'm not. I came third in the region at Provincials, remember?"

"But Simran is stepping out of the competition, *remember*?"

TJ loses her balance and nearly falls off the chair. "What?"

Mrs. Scott balks. "Oh my goodness, TJ. Simran said she would talk to you. I thought you agreed already!"

"Agreed to what? Simran dropped out? *Why?*" This doesn't make sense. Although . . . she *does* remember Simran acting off the day after Provincials, when TJ asked when she was meeting with Charlie.

Charlie. Her stomach drops. No. No no no no. Teaming up with *Charlie*? Who she thought she'd never have to see again?

Her train of thought shuts down before she can entertain that nightmare. She hops off the chair. This has to be a mistake.

"I'm going to talk to Simran," she hears herself say in an oddly high voice. "I'll be right back."

She doesn't even wait for a response from Mrs. Scott. She just hurtles out of the classroom.

Despite the fact that they rarely interact during the school day, TJ knows exactly where Simran goes during lunch hour— either some club meeting, or the French teacher's classroom, which is always open to people who want somewhere quiet to sit. TJ speed-walks there and bursts in. Rock music plays in the background. Ms. Schwab is on her computer, and a bunch of people have shoved desks together to play a card game. TJ scans further. Simran's in the corner with the student council cash-box next to her. She's riffling through bills, no doubt counting profits from the latest school fundraiser.

"Simran!" she basically yells, and Ms. Schwab looks up and says something rapidly in French.

All TJ understands is *s'il vous plaît.* "What?"

"She said keep your voice down, please," Simran says evenly.

Never mind that. TJ's *mad* at her. "What's this Mrs. Scott's telling me about you dropping out of Nationals?" she hisses, coming up to her.

Simran's eyes go wide and she sets the stack of money in the box. "Oh no."

"So it's *true*?" TJ's voice teeters to new heights. "Are you serious?"

Simran swallows. "I was going to tell you soon, I promise. I didn't think Mrs. Scott would bring it up so early. It's only been a week—"

"*Why?*"

"I have something going on that week."

"What could you possibly have going on?"

Simran gives her a flat look. "I got accepted into a weeklong music camp."

"Music camp? What music?" TJ's at a loss.

"Indian classical," Simran replies. "You should know, seeing how you trip over my instruments every time you come over."

Simran's harmonium *is* a damn menace. "But—what? Why now?"

"There's a musician from Singapore visiting Vancouver. He's offering a program while he's there. I applied."

Shit. TJ vaguely remembers her filling out an application months ago.

"I found out I got in on the way home from Provincials. It clashes with Nationals weekend. I was going to tell you when you came over that day, but . . ." She chews her lip. "I couldn't."

Of course. Because TJ spent the whole time ranting about

him. If certain events hadn't happened over Provincials weekend, TJ might even be okay with this. But certain events *did*
happen. And now TJ is losing it.

"You could always give up the spot to Nate," Simran suggests
quietly. "Tell them you want to go to your soccer tournament
instead."

TJ glares. "Everyone in debate would know that's bullshit.
Couldn't you have told me *before* Provincials? That there was
a chance this might happen?"

"What difference would it have made? I didn't think I was
going to get into this program. It was a long shot."

"The *difference* would be that I wouldn't have made out with
Charlie fucking Rosencrantz!" She keeps her voice to a hiss, not
wanting her words to carry to the table of cardplayers, all of
whom have been sending them curious looks since TJ entered.
"Now you're basically leaving me high and dry—"

"I'm not leaving you—"

"You *couldn't have told me*—"

"Not everything is about you!" Simran shouts, and TJ's
taken aback enough to stop talking. The cardplayers go quiet,
too. "I didn't want to say anything because I didn't want to give
myself hope that it would happen! But you never consider that.
No, obviously, it has to be about *you* and *your* problems. We lose
a debate, and it's about you. I get into a music camp I've worked
really hard for, and it's about you. I get humiliated on the internet, and even that *is about you*."

TJ's shocked into speaking again. "That's not what I—"

"Do you think I *like* leaving you with Charlie?" Simran
pushes her glasses up in a rather violent motion. "I don't. I was

trying to figure out some way to tell you. I even considered backing out of the music camp because I didn't want to put you in that situation. But eventually I decided—just this once—to make something about me. Sorry it's inconvenient."

She slams the cashbox shut and stands. TJ reaches for her. "Simran, I—"

Simran brushes past her. Leaving TJ alone with a bunch of nosy cardplayers and the equally nosy French teacher, staring at her. She huffs and exits, but her cousin's already somehow halfway down the hall. "Simran!" she yells, drawing stares from the horde of eighth graders loitering by the lockers, but she's disappeared around the corner.

TJ takes several steps forward to follow before she realizes she doesn't even know what to say.

Now that she thinks back, she can sort of see what Simran was talking about. TJ only ever came over to complain about stuff that was bothering *her*, after all. Has Simran always felt this way, and if so, why did TJ never notice?

She can't process this right now. One thing at a time.

Dazed, TJ heads back to Mrs. Scott's classroom instead.

Mrs. Scott looks up from where she's sorting through the book boxes. "Well? Who's going to Nationals?"

TJ hovers in the doorway and opens her mouth, then pauses. She *could* give the spot up to Nate. It'd raise some eyebrows, but she could probably convince most of the debate people that she's more passionate about soccer.

But why should she? It's not like *Charlie's* backing out of the tournament, although he must know TJ's next up after Simran.

She straightens her shoulders. If he's not backing out, neither is she. There's no way she's giving him that power over her. "I am."

Mrs. Scott nods, approval in her eyes. "You should text Charlie. We can set up some practices."

She's looking at TJ expectantly, like she's waiting for her to do it right now. God, this is going to be humiliating. Maybe it's the universe's way of punishing her for being an ass to Simran. Giving her something she wants so badly—Nationals—except adding a nightmarish twist.

TJ sighs and pulls out her phone.

FOURTEEN
✱✱✱

The following afternoon, TJ paces Mrs. Scott's classroom, sweat slicking her palms. She glances at her phone for the umpteenth time to reread her chat with Charlie.

It's only used on occasion, and always to fire off logistical questions during out-of-town tournaments when no one else is answering their phones. Stuff like **where is everyone?? Or what time are we meeting?** There's no correspondence at all since Provincials. At least, until TJ texted him yesterday:

Apparently I'm going to Nationals, not Simran.

Meet tomorrow?

His answer was immediate: **3:30 ok? Your school or mine?**

He didn't seem surprised. She'd bet her life he and Simran had already talked about it. But then why hadn't Charlie reached out to her? Floundering and confused, TJ had to scrounge some control out of the situation. **Mine.**

She'd thought Mrs. Scott would be here to play referee when he arrived, but Mrs. Scott said she had a quick staff meeting after school, and that they should do some brainstorming for their topic while they waited for her. So here TJ is, on the verge of a nervous breakdown.

That's not to say she hadn't prepared for this. She had. Yesterday afternoon, she'd started an email to Coach to tell him she'd be missing the last soccer tournament, but then imagined him blowing a gasket and decided it could wait. Instead she made a list of possible contentions for the resolution and rehearsed what she was going to say to Charlie. She has a game plan, but this is *Charlie*. He specializes in tripping her up.

The door opens. TJ freezes midstride like Bigfoot caught on camera.

Charlie steps through, bag slung over his shoulder, and closes it behind him. There's a second of silence.

She takes him in. His face is unreadable, his hair in its impeccable side part, and he wears his customary button-down and a pair of fitted chinos—no tie, but he still looks very put together.

She remembers pulling on his tie while they kissed. He wasn't so put together then. She zeroes in on the hollow of his throat, where the knot would theoretically sit. Right now, he's left that button undone, so she has just the barest peek at his collarbone.

Charlie clears his throat, and TJ drags her eyes hastily back to his face. Right. The plan.

She crosses her arms. "So, obviously, we need to clear the air. Let me be totally honest. Okay?"

Charlie nods slowly. TJ takes a deep breath.

"So, elephant in the room: We kissed. A lot. I ran off without telling you why and I'm sorry, so here's your explanation. Last weekend . . . I had just broken up with my boyfriend. I was a wreck and, um, not making the best decisions. Then with you I freaked out because it was all too much. That's all. It was fun, but it was a mistake."

Charlie barely blinks at any of this, but then again, he's a master of poker face. Once in tenth grade, TJ absolutely thrashed him in a cross-examination, but he looked bored the whole time she was cutting his contentions to pieces. "Okay."

"Okay?" For some reason she'd expected more.

"Yeah, okay." He raises his piercing eyes to hers. "But if we're clearing the air, you should know, it wasn't a mistake for me."

TJ tries to swallow, but her throat is too dry. "What's that supposed to mean?"

"It means I like you and I wanted to kiss you. You can do whatever you want with that information."

He says it so blandly he could be talking about the weather. But the way he looks at her is somehow more intense than usual, and his body is very still, like he's entirely focused on getting those words out rather than on less important things like breathing.

"You *like* me?" she squeaks, stunned.

Without breaking their staring contest, he lets his shoulder bag slide down his arm to the floor. "Yes, TJ. I *like* like you. Should I provide a definition?"

TJ resists the urge to fan herself. Her longtime debating rival is *into* her? It feels like a revelation, even though it probably shouldn't, given that the last time they were alone together he gave her a hickey.

And now they're partners for the biggest debate tournament of her life. Not two minutes in and he's already thrown her way off-balance. How can she possibly respond?

Finally, she bursts, "You're so weird, Charlie! Why would you say that? Are you trying to make this more awkward than it already is?"

"As much as I enjoy making things awkward," he replies, "I'm telling you in the interest of honesty, in case that was any part of the reason you avoided me afterwards. I won't bring it up again."

Her heart is beating so hard she can hear it in her ears. "It had nothing to do with you." That much is true—she never even gave him the chance to disappoint her.

Something flickers in his eyes but that's all. "All right. Should we brainstorm some contentions?"

That's it? They're diving right into debating? He's taking out his notepad, so he must be serious. He *did* say he wouldn't bring it up again, but now of course it's all TJ can think about.

She doesn't want Charlie to like her. Because if he does, there's only one reason why, and it's that he hasn't been paying attention to her appearance. Well, she can help him with that.

She collapses into one of the chairs and props her hairy legs on the desk. *Come on, look.*

Charlie barely gives her legs a glance before sitting next to her. "I've come up with some contentions—"

"I bet you have. I mean, you've had more than a week already. In which you never thought to tell me I was your debate partner."

Charlie flips through his notepad. "Simran said she'd do it. Besides, I wasn't sure whether it'd end up being you or Nate."

So he thought she might chicken out. Even though he was almost right—a fact she will be taking to the grave—she forces a laugh. "Let me get this straight, you were so conceited you thought I'd give up my chance at *Nationals* because of *you*?"

"I didn't say it was likely." He looks up at her. "But you're hard to predict."

TJ can't tell whether that's an insult, but the way he's staring into her eyes is extremely disconcerting. She crosses her legs again, but he still doesn't look away. So she yawns and stretches her arms above her head. Exposing *very* hairy underarms.

And this time he does look. She watches his face closely, but again, complete poker face. Maybe he's just not showing his distaste. That's fine. If she keeps this up, eventually he'll become so grossed out he'll *have* to slip up. Until then, she can be as much of a freak as she likes. It's actually kind of a freeing thought.

"Well, I came up with some contentions, too," she announces, and pulls out a piece of paper with a flourish. It's heavily scribbled on. He raises his eyebrows, voice settling into a familiar condescension.

"Did Simran write those for you?"

"Ha, ha. I notice you don't have any notes." She nods to his blank page. "Is Nate talking to you through an earpiece right now?"

Charlie taps behind his ear. "Nate, game's up. You might as well come out from behind the curtain."

The door of the classroom opens, and they both whip around, but it's just Rajan, holding an enormous stack of papers.

"What are you doing here?" TJ asks bluntly. She's not interested in talking to him, especially since he turned out to be right about Liam.

Rajan grins like he knows what she's thinking, but he doesn't comment. "Detention. I gotta file these away." He pats the paper stack. "Mrs. Scott said to tell you she's gonna be here soon."

"Okay," TJ says. "Go file, then."

Rajan just strolls closer. "So what basic human rights are we putting up for debate today?"

"We don't debate *human rights*," TJ scoffs, but Rajan's already bending to peer at her page.

"This House Believes That it is sometimes right for the government to restrict freedom of speech." He casts TJ an amused look. She sighs. Point taken.

Rajan straightens back to his full height. "Don't worry, dude, I agree with you. Some people just need to shut the hell up."

TJ's about to make a quip about Rajan being an expert on the right to remain silent when Charlie speaks. "Why do you say that?"

Rajan blinks as if surprised to be asked. But Charlie is looking at him expectantly. TJ sits up. Who knows, maybe he'll give them an interesting perspective to work with. "Give an example," she adds. "Something actually relevant."

He grins. "I was gonna start talking about Nazis, but now you asked for it." He hops onto the desk next to them. "That Northridge Confessions post about Simran Sahiba and you is pretty *relevant*, isn't it?"

TJ's smirk freezes. Charlie's sitting right beside her. She never thought it'd get brought up with him around. *Shut up*, she screams internally.

Rajan, of course, goes on. "So-called free speech on Northridge Confessions gave her a rough time. People say anything they want on there. People get hurt. You think that's a good thing?"

She realizes it's not rhetorical after a second, and clears her throat hastily.

"Well, good things can come out of that, too. Certain people exposed themselves through the comments of that post as assholes." Not to mention, also in the aftermath of it. Particularly Liam and Chandani. She takes a deep breath, finding more fire with every word. "And it brought up certain *issues* that otherwise would've never been addressed. Like, why are girls expected to be hairless beings? Does no one see how screwed up that is—"

The door opens again.

"Rajan!" Mrs. Scott barks. "Distracting my debaters, I see."

"Who says they weren't distracting *me*?" Rajan winks, but Mrs. Scott isn't charmed. As she starts laying down the law, Charlie taps his notepad with his pen.

"So *that's* why."

TJ looks at him. She'd been afraid to, until now. "Why what?"

He waves his pen in the direction of her legs, still propped up on the table. She blinks.

"So you noticed?"

"Well, yeah. It's hard not to."

TJ tries not to flinch at his matter-of-fact tone. Despite everything, some pathetic part of her fantasized that she would display her biggest insecurities and people would say, *Aw, but I didn't notice that at all!*

But no. Everyone sees it, including Charlie, who, until now, did an excellent job of acting like he didn't. It's there and it can't be swept under the rug or ignored by anyone. Why had she ever hoped for different?

She clears her throat. "Well, that's the point. I'm trying to prove something."

"And what's that?"

No way is she putting it in resolution form. "That I can exist as a hairy girl, and still be worthy of respect." She cringes anyway because it sounds so cheesy out loud, even without *This House Believes That* before it.

Charlie tilts his head. She waits with bated breath, until he says, "You need to work on your wording. That's not a very snappy resolution."

She scoffs, with relief more than anything. He's still looking at her the same. Not shying away or looking revolted.

Mrs. Scott walks up to them, now that Rajan's sorting the files. "Got your contentions ready?"

"Uh—" TJ begins, only to be cut off.

"Didn't think so. If there's one thing you two are champions of, it's wasting time." She crosses her arms. "But I want to make one thing clear right now."

They both sit up straighter at her tone.

"In just over two months, we're hosting Nationals at this school. You are representing our whole region at this event," Mrs. Scott says. "And I think you have an excellent chance of doing well—maybe even well enough for finals—but *only* if you're not at each other's throats the whole time."

TJ and Charlie look at each other, then quickly away.

"Um," TJ says. "Not a problem."

"Good. Then let's get started. I have a list of resources that might help you in your research . . ." She walks back to her desk, presumably to find it. Meanwhile, Charlie picks up their conversation again.

"So, how will you know when you've proved your resolution?"

It takes TJ a second to remember what they were talking

about. "I just have to gather enough evidence."

"Seems like a pretty big lifestyle change, until then." He sounds genuinely interested. Maybe he sees her as a fascinating oddity now.

And that's a good thing, she reminds herself firmly. "It is. But it's freeing, too. I used to plan my outfits around my body hair. Now I wear what I want, whenever I want, without having to plan ahead. It used to be so much effort. Especially in the summer."

"How long did it take you?"

She pats her hairy knee. "Guess."

He studies her legs thoughtfully. "Twenty minutes?"

She laughs. An ugly laugh.

"I'm just going off my mom," he admits. "She doesn't shave that often."

She ugly laughs again. "Shave? Do I look white to you, Charlie?"

"What's it like, then?"

It's a little odd seeing his innocent ignorance about an experience that was once routine for her. She remembers Liam complaining about how much time she spent in the bathroom getting ready. He had no clue, either.

An evil idea occurs to her. "Why would I tell you when I could show you?"

He blinks. "I thought you said you were keeping the hair."

"Oh, I am." She leans in, grin widening. "But no one said the demonstration has to be on *me*."

FIFTEEN
***

In true Charlie fashion, Charlie takes the suggestion to wax his legs with enthusiasm. After their debate meeting, he peppers their chat with questions about different wax brands. TJ tells him the brand she used, although that stuff *hurt*. But that's just something he'll have to find out on his own.

Which TJ will definitely not derive any satisfaction, whatsoever, from.

A few days later, TJ finds herself at his front door, juggling a bag of supplies from home and her laptop bag. They'd agreed to meet up next at his place so they could also follow through with this whole waxing thing. Because TJ sure as hell isn't doing that at her house. Just thinking about explaining it to her parents gives her a headache.

A dark-haired, bearded man wearing a coat opens the door and smiles. "Hello! You must be TJ."

TJ blinks. For some reason, she hadn't thought to ask Charlie if his parents would be home. She shifts awkwardly, eyes darting away, as though I MADE OUT WITH YOUR SON is stamped on her forehead. "Uh, hi," she says, mouth dry. "Nice to meet you, Mr. Rosencrantz."

He stares at her for a split second and then lets out a big belly laugh. He clutches on to the doorframe, shoulders shaking, and TJ feels immensely awkward until he collects himself.

"I'm the stepdad," he clarifies, pushing up his hipster glasses. "Call me Derek."

Oh. TJ's face heats. How could she be this dense? The man in front of her doesn't even remotely resemble Charlie. "I'm so sorry—"

Derek, still chuckling, leans back a little to shout into the house. "Mr. Rosencrantz! Your friend is here!"

"I heard her," Charlie's voice says from what sounds like the next room, and then he appears into view with his hands stuffed in the pockets of his chino *shorts*. She'd told him to wear shorts or they'd be doing this in his underwear. She'd also regretted saying it because he raised his eyebrows in response, but thankfully, it looks like he's taken her advice. Somehow he still looks refined. "Well, come in." He gestures for her to follow. Derek keeps the door open for her.

She follows Charlie through the cozy living room, squeezing past the well-loved couch to the adjoining kitchen, where a brunette woman with amber eyes is wiping her hands on a dish towel. "TJ. So nice to see you again."

TJ returns her smile. She vaguely knows Charlie's mom, because she used to volunteer at tournaments when they were younger and would bring mouthwatering latkes to debate luncheons. "Nice to see you, too."

"TJ, you should tell her your theory about how I'm the product of incest," Charlie says.

"Charlie!" TJ gasps, laughing nervously. Until right now, she'd totally forgotten ever making that comment, and now in the context of his parental situation it sounds about a hundred times worse. "I never said anything like—"

But then she realizes Charlie's mom is laughing, too. Joined by Derek's big, booming laughs.

"I see nothing's changed," Charlie's mom says when she's recovered.

White parents are a trip.

"All right, kids, we're off," Derek says. "Keep him out of trouble, will you, TJ?" He winks. TJ barely has time to stammer a goodbye before the front door shuts behind them.

Charlie hops onto a bar stool at the kitchen island. "Make yourself at home. No need to stand there looking uncomfortable."

There's a laughing note to his voice. TJ scowls. "One day, I'll introduce you to *my* family, and you'll have a whole new definition of uncomfortable."

"Looking forward to it." He beckons her to sit. "Should we start with the Proposition case? We still haven't figured out our plan."

TJ opens her laptop, and they spend the first hour hammering out their ideas for how they'd carry out the resolution if it became law. Then they switch to Side Opposition to figure out a counterplan. In this case, how to address the problems that come with complete freedom of speech without actually taking away freedom of speech. It's a tricky thing, and TJ's yawning after a while of trawling the internet for research.

After what feels both like forever and half a second, Charlie closes his laptop. "I'm going cross-eyed."

TJ pushes away her laptop, too, and stretches her limbs. The kitchen is encased in semidarkness. They hadn't bothered turning on any lights as it grew late. "Then I guess we should take a break. Did you buy the wax?"

She's giving him an out. But he doesn't take it. "It's in the bathroom."

"Then lead the way."

The bathroom down the hall is small and neatly organized. TJ is about to change that. She pulls items from her bag one by one and lays them on the counter. First, her wax warmer, then a roll of muslin fabric, scissors, baby powder, and a Ziploc bag of popsicle sticks. All stuff that's been collecting dust at home for the past few months after she tossed her wax.

Charlie picks up the sticks. "Are we waxing or doing a craft project?"

"One could argue that waxing *is* an art." She plucks the sticks out of his hand and puts them back on the counter. "Sit on the ledge of the tub."

He obeys. That's when she notices a problem.

"Your leg hair is too long," she informs him. "Do you have a trimmer?"

He points to a drawer. She finds it and hands it to him. "Work on that. It just needs to be a bit shorter." She shows him the length with her thumb and pointer finger.

He turns the trimmer on, the buzzing filling the room. "I didn't see this step in my research."

Charlie has no idea what he's gotten into. Trying to suppress her smirk, TJ plugs in the wax warmer and starts cutting strips of muslin fabric.

After a few minutes, he turns off the trimmer. "Are we ready now?"

"No." She hands him the baby powder.

"What's this for?"

"It absorbs extra oil on your skin. Just do it."

Shaking his head, he tips powder onto his calf and rubs it in. She can't help but notice the muscle definition in his legs, most likely a product of his regular hiking, if his Instagram photos are anything to go by. She turns to busy herself testing the consistency of the wax. It's ready.

She perches next to him on the ledge with her popsicle stick dipped in wax. "Stick out your leg."

He does. "I'm starting to have a bad feeling about this."

"Why?"

"Because you're grinning. Maniacally."

"I don't know what you're talking about." TJ finishes smearing her strip of wax and admires her handiwork. She reaches behind her and grabs one of her muslin strips, carefully smoothing it over the line of wax on his thigh. "Ready?" He nods. "Three, two—" She rips the wax off.

Charlie swears. Loudly. It's so uncharacteristic coming from him that she giggles.

"Beauty is pain," she informs him, pressing on the area to help the swelling. She holds up the muslin, now adorned with soft, feathery brown hair. Then she begins applying another layer of wax to the adjacent part of his leg. "Imagine doing that for both your legs every three weeks. At minimum."

"Does it get . . . better?"

"Sort of." She rips off the next layer and cackles when he

swears again. "But also not really. Sometimes, when I waxed my armpits, they'd even bleed."

"That's so . . ." Charlie trails off, sounding aghast. When she merely shrugs in response, he picks up the wax container and examines the logo. "These people must be laughing all the way to the bank. They're basically selling pain."

"Well, yeah." She climbs in the tub and kneels to apply wax to his knee. "They tell us we *have* to do it, because they need us to feel like shit about ourselves to make money. And we just listen to them." TJ can feel herself getting angry. "But you know what? I'm done buying into corporate bullshit."

Charlie sets down the wax container. "You really mean that?"

"Yeah." TJ rips another wax strip off his leg with unnecessary force. "What are you trying to say?"

Charlie doesn't swear this time. He just pauses before speaking again. "Well, there's more than one thing corporations have exploited to make money. Take makeup, for example. So are you going to get rid of that, too?"

She stops her work to glare at him from under her mascara-coated lashes. He barely blinks at the ferocity of her expression. God. He's supremely frustrating. If Liam was easy to talk to, Charlie is the opposite. He constantly challenges what she says.

But not to troll her. He's honestly curious about her answer, what he's missing from her rationale, so he can understand it better. And that, if she's honest, makes all the difference.

She carefully lays another muslin strip. "Can I ask you a question, Charlie? Why do you dress so formally all the time?"

He doesn't miss a beat, although the question probably seems out of nowhere. "I'm student body president at Whitewater," he says, and it's cute that he thought she didn't know that already. "I'm constantly in meetings with staff or students or administration. It's easier to just always be ready for one."

"Do you like looking professional? Or you feel like you have to?"

He smiles with a dawning understanding. "Both, I suppose."

"But it's kind of hard to separate after a while, don't you think? Whether something is your personal style or if society has just conditioned you to think it would look good?"

"Point taken. What came first? My personal style or the societal expectation? Chicken or the egg?"

She leans her elbow on the top of his knee. "I'm not going to pretend me wearing makeup is some feminist empowerment statement. It's not. It's still fitting into an expectation of what girls are supposed to look like. But I *like* makeup. And yeah, part of that is advertising, but that's true for literally every product on the planet."

"So you agree, then," Charlie says, "that some people might like hair removal as a preference, too, even if they can't disentangle it from societal expectations."

She glances at him curiously. He sounds like he has someone specific in mind. "Like who?"

He shrugs. "A friend of my mom's is trans, and she told me the first time a cashier called her 'miss' after getting laser, she was really happy. For her, anyway, that felt right. Being seen as your gender is pretty neat. I think maybe you and I take it for granted."

TJ hadn't thought about that before. "True," she says, *very* slowly, because she's loath to agree with him. "I guess we just get to choose which brand of corporate propaganda we sub-scribe to."

He nods. This may be the weirdest conversation she's ever had. She rips off another wax strip. It's been longer than usual since the last one, and he lets out a string of curses so foul she reaches up to pat his cheek. "You kiss your mommy with that mouth?"

He laughs breathlessly. "Not my mommy, no."

He looks down at her and she only now realizes how she's basically crouching between his spread knees and—wow, her mind is *not* in PG-13 places.

She busies herself again with the wax. By the time the whole leg is done, he's wiping away tears and has long since stopped swearing, or talking at all, really. His leg is pink and raw, but ever so smooth when she runs her finger down his calf. He jerks away from her touch. TJ snickers.

"One leg done," she says in a singsong voice. He rubs his eyes. She surreptitiously checks her phone. As much as she'd love to continue, it's getting late. "Tell you what. I'll let you off here."

Charlie lowers his hand to look at her. "But I signed up for the full TJ waxing experience."

"This is it," TJ admits. "I almost never do both my legs on the same day. It takes forever. And mine are way hairier than yours, so it takes even longer."

He glances at her legs, then her arms. "Yeah, you're pretty hairy." She flings the waxing stick at him. He bats it away. "To tell you the truth, I've been wondering about the texture of yours." He reaches for her leg.

"Don't!" she shrieks, laughing, scooting away. Unfortunately, she scoots right back into the tap of the tub. Pain shoots through the back of her head and she sees stars.

Then there's hands on her shoulders. "You okay?"

His touch is sudden and distracting. She needs to get away. Now. Panicking, she tries to get up by reaching for something to grasp on to. Of course, when she tries to put her weight on it, she realizes it's the tap. And she just turned it on, full blast.

Within seconds, Charlie is drenched with ice-cold water. Because she's right at the wall, she only gets a bit of the spray, but it still makes her gasp and fumble with the tap. Charlie bats her hand away when it becomes clear she doesn't know what she's doing. He screws it off again, and then there's just the *drip-drip* of the faucet in the background. His normally perfectly fluffy brown hair is spiky and dark, hanging over his eyes, his black button-down clinging to shivering shoulders.

He meets her gaze.

I like you and I wanted to kiss you.

She nearly flinches at the sudden memory. No. He doesn't. He can't. She won't let him, and she certainly won't let herself.

"Huh," Charlie says thoughtfully, and she realizes his hand is on her shin. "Your hair feels the same as mine."

She jerks away. Clearly their thoughts were in entirely different places. "What did you think it would feel like?" she snaps. "Barbed wire?"

He laughs, the skin around his eyes crinkling. "I—I—I—" He stops midsentence, and his jaw works. She watches him curiously. It's not like he's shivering that badly. It's more like he can't get the words out. His mouth shuts. This has *happened* before. She's noticed it so many times.

When he says nothing else, she asks, "What's that about?"

He takes a deep breath before speaking. It still takes him a second, it seems, to get the sentence started. "I—I—*I* have a stutter."

She stares at him. In the silence, she hears the front door down the hall open and close. "No way."

The side of his mouth ticks up. "Way."

How could he have a stutter she never noticed? She frowns, suddenly in doubt of herself. If she's really as self-absorbed as Simran said . . . "Is this one of those things everyone except me already knew?"

His smile vanishes. "No. Not many people notice anymore."

"Anymore?"

"It was more noticeable when I was a kid," he says. Carefully. "As in, 'people laughed whenever I read aloud in class' notice-able."

TJ blinks. She can't even picture that. Charlie goes on.

"I went to speech therapy for a while. They told me to try public speaking, to train me to think about what I said before I said it. That's where debate came in."

His slow, deliberate way of speaking suddenly makes sense. And she's just now realizing in the conversation leading up to her blasting them with water, he'd been talking much more casually, more quickly, too. As if . . . less self-conscious.

"It doesn't come out often. Except when I'm tired, or emo-tional, or caught off guard. Or—or—or—or just talking to people I know really well." His eyes bore into hers, tempting her to ask which it is right now.

There's a knock on the door and before either of them can

respond, it cracks open. Charlie smoothly pulls away from her and is sitting on the edge of the tub again by the time Derek's head pokes around the door. He takes in the two of them sopping wet, TJ sitting against the tub faucet. The mess all over the counters. Charlie's mismatched legs.

He looks at TJ. "Didn't I tell you to keep him out of trouble?"

SIXTEEN
***

The following afternoon in biology, TJ's phone buzzes. She glances up to ensure the teacher isn't in her vicinity, but Mr. Oyedele is in the opposite corner of the room, berating someone for vaping in class. She props up her textbook to hide her phone and checks the notification. It's a photo from Charlie.

Someone else must've taken it for him. He's striking a pretentious pose, leaning against a Whitewater classroom doorway, one ankle crossed over the other. Navy pinstripe shorts show off his shiny, smooth waxed leg along with his natural, hairy one. He's gazing off into the distance as if he's a model.

A text follows. **Last night I finally understood what they mean about how good bedsheets feel on smooth legs.**

TJ types back, **so what I'm hearing is,,,, you want a repeat???** He leaves her on read.

"TJ."

TJ jumps a little in her seat to find Mr. Oyedele in front of her desk, one eyebrow raised.

"I didn't realize your textbook was so funny," he says, and TJ realizes she's grinning ear to ear. "Although I suppose everything is more comedic when you're reading upside down. You're excused from class."

TJ's jaw drops, at least until he continues, "No, not for that. Amy's pulling you out."

He points to the door, where Amy West, Northridge's very own student body president, is waving a pale hand at her. TJ gets up hastily. She's only ever spoken to Amy in passing, but she's never been so happy to see her.

Amy grins as TJ joins her. "Looks like I showed up just in time. Mr. Oyedele loves confiscating phones."

"Much appreciated." TJ smiles back tentatively, relief turning to confusion as she follows her down the hall. She and Amy, while on amicable terms, have never actively sought each other out. "Um . . . What's this about?"

Amy gestures for her to follow into the admin area, and into a smaller office that's clearly been vacated for this meeting. TJ stops at the door.

Simran is there, in one of the hard-backed chairs. She looks up, catches sight of TJ, and immediately looks away again.

Amy, oblivious, settles into another chair and tosses her wavy brown hair over her shoulder. "TJ, have a seat."

TJ sinks into the remaining chair, willing Simran to make eye contact. But apparently something on the floor is extremely interesting to her. TJ's heart shrivels a little. Is she really still that mad?

Amy says, "So, TJ. Simran already knows this, since she's on council with me. But I just want to tell you about something we've been discussing a lot lately at the school and district level. About bullying."

Simran starts winding her braid around her wrist.

"You and Simran were victims to a pretty vicious social media storm that brought to light how bad it is out there," Amy adds. "We developed a really exciting initiative and the administration is on board. A body-positivity campaign in school newspapers around the district. To show that all different kinds of bodies can be beautiful. And we'd like you to be one of the models."

TJ's eyebrows shoot up. She glances at Simran, who's still avoiding her gaze. "Are *you* doing this?" Somehow she can't imagine Simran puckering her lips for a photo shoot.

Amy answers for her. "No. I was actually hoping *you* would, TJ. Simran's helping behind the scenes, but she doesn't want to be a model." A wry smile touches Simran's lips, and Amy goes on. "If you agree, we'll schedule you for the photos pretty soon. We're hoping to roll out the campaign before Spring Break, before the senior retreat and all. Thought it would be good timing for a body-positivity campaign."

TJ blinks. The senior retreat? It's completely slipped her mind until now, but she had put down her deposit months ago. This year it's on Vancouver Island. TJ had been looking forward to lounging in the sun and surfing with her friends and boyfriend. Now she's barely got any friends at all.

Amy jars her from her thoughts. "Not just body-hair positivity, but other things, too. Different body shapes, skin colours, abilities. We're thinking of using the slogan 'Every Body Is Beautiful.' What do you think?"

A few weeks ago, TJ might've said it sounded great. But now . . . "I'm not sure I like the message. Why does being beautiful matter?"

"What do you mean?"

TJ crosses her arms. "I just think who you are is more important than what you look like, that's all. Maybe that would be better to focus on."

Amy snaps her fingers. "I've got it! You can be our rep for *inner* beauty." TJ stares at her until she explains. "We'll do an article on you as part of the campaign, you know, since you're one of our school's star soccer players. To shift the focus off your looks and let people get to know you for who you are and all the hard work you've put into it. How does that sound?"

Sounds like the exact sort of fluffy bullshit the school loves to do instead of real work, but TJ doesn't say that. At her silence, Amy looks to Simran as if waiting for support. That's probably why Simran was dragged here, TJ realizes. To help convince TJ. Which is clearly not going well.

But if this is a school council project . . . it's Simran's project, too. Maybe helping with it can get TJ back into Simran's good books.

"Okay," TJ says. "I'll do it."

One week later, TJ shows up at the multipurpose room after school as scheduled. She expects it to be set up as a quiet space for the interview, but instead, the expansive room is bustling with activity. Black curtains have been hung up, there are racks of props and clothes everywhere, and the theatre club's lighting equipment has been put to use, making the area bright and welcoming. Students mill around in assorted outfits.

This must be the photo shoot. TJ doesn't really know any of the models, though. At least two of them are from different schools. She casts a look around for Simran, but she's nowhere to be found.

"Hi, TJ! Ready for your photo?"

TJ whips around to find Yara approaching, holding her camera. TJ frowns. "I'm here for an interview, though."

"Yeah, I know. Amy just wants a photo to go with the article. It's weird to have a profile on somebody without a picture going along with it, you know?"

No, TJ doesn't know. Would've been nice if Amy gave her a heads-up so TJ could refuse it right then and there.

Yara's smile wavers at TJ's silence. "Someone else can take your picture, if you want. It doesn't have to be me."

Her voice is uncertain, and TJ instantly changes her mind. "Nah, let's do this."

"Are you sure? Simran asked me to help with camerawork after Amy turned me down as a model, but I just didn't know if people would want me to photograph them. Especially . . . you."

"Of course I'm sure." TJ smiles, hoping what she isn't saying comes across. Even if Yara took the most horrendous photo in the universe, it's not her fault it snowballed into what it did. Then she catches up to what Yara said. "Wait. You wanted to be a model?"

Yara shifts on her feet. "They were looking for plus-size models for one of the posters, and, well, I volunteered."

"Amy said no?"

"She said she already found someone. I probably wasn't a good fit to be a model, anyway."

TJ looks back at the plus-size model who's currently on her

phone in the corner of the room. She's not willow-thin, but Yara is definitely heavier. "Why wouldn't you be a good fit?"

Yara looks down, touching the acne scars on her cheek self-consciously. "My face isn't very model-worthy."

"That's exactly the opposite of the point we're trying to make." TJ frowns, but she's distracted from her thoughts when Amy enters the room.

Amy looks up from her clipboard and spots TJ. "You're here! Let's get started."

Her voice carries through the room. TJ's alarmed to see her descending with a small army wielding makeup brushes and hair curlers.

"I don't need all this," TJ says, when really she wants to say, *I don't need a photo*, but Yara's right there, and it's too hard to explain.

Amy waves a dismissive hand. "They're not doing much, don't worry. Just sit down, okay? While they're working on you, we'll do the interview."

TJ looks at Yara. Yara beams. TJ sits down.

While her hair gets curled and her skin touched up, she answers Amy's questions about soccer: how she got started (her parents enrolled her in rec soccer as a kid and it turned out she was naturally gifted), how much work it takes (several practices a week during the season), how many trophies the team has (a lot), and whether she's joined a university team (um . . . no). She never did email those scouts. The deadlines passed a while ago. If she tells Coach she's not going to the final tournament, either . . . Well. She's putting that conversation off.

There's a pinch over TJ's right eyebrow. She flinches and finds the makeup girl holding a pair of tweezers. She just plucked a hair.

"Hey!" TJ snaps. "Don't touch me with those things."

"I won't anymore," Makeup Girl promises. "It's just, that hair was *really* long and in my way, that's all."

TJ glares, ready to give her a piece of her mind, but Amy interrupts before she can. "Now I want to talk about debate."

TJ goes still. Amy definitely hadn't brought *that* up when pitching this interview. "Oh, it's nothing."

"Really? But you've put a lot of time into it, too, haven't you?"

Clearly Amy's done her research. TJ hesitates. A few months ago, she would've rather had a tooth pulled than talk about this. But now . . . What's the point of hiding who she is anymore? Everything else is out. What's one more thing?

Sighing, she reclines in her chair. "Fine. Let's talk about it."

She doesn't wait for Amy to ask questions. She stares straight ahead and just starts from the beginning—that day in sixth grade when she first saw the poster advertising debate. She tells Amy about how when she started out, she was all fire and passion with no substance. That it took years to build her skills. She talks about the tournaments she's attended, the training she's done, and some of the better stories she's collected over the years.

Amy's expression has changed by the time she's finished. Even the hair and makeup volunteers have quieted to listen to TJ. "You love it a lot."

She sounds surprised. How many people really thought TJ was just in it for her résumé? "Yeah, I do."

"Why?"

TJ sits back, stumped by the simple question. She's never really thought about it.

She thinks back to the poster that convinced her to join debate. It was a joke, of course—COME ARGUE WITH US. But to sixth-grade TJ it was a lifeline. It was a strange time, because she was becoming very aware of not just the hair on her body, but the colour of her skin, the way she was a *girl*, and she was realizing life would be very different for her just because of those things. And that was so unfair. She wanted to fight against it but couldn't.

But she *could* fight against something else. Something new every week, with a bunch of other kids after school in a musty English classroom.

"For a long time," TJ says slowly, "debate felt like the one place I could make a difference. If I worked hard enough, I could convince people of something, and it was proof my voice mattered. And that it could do something good."

The group is silent. Even Amy doesn't have anything to say. She just scribbles it down, and looks back at TJ like she's not quite sure what to make of her anymore. Then she seems to shake it off, setting her pen down. "Time for your photo!"

At Amy's instruction, TJ perches on a white block. She expects Yara to take charge from here, but instead, Amy continues to oversee everything, peering at Yara's pictures before okaying them or asking for another shot. Yara stays quiet while

Amy tells TJ to *Tuck your hair back, look in this direction, sit up straighter*. When she finally gives a satisfied nod, TJ hops off the block, then pauses to glance at Yara. "Are *you* happy with it?"

"Um," Yara says. "I don't know. I haven't really looked at the photos properly."

Amy pats her shoulder. "Don't worry, they're spectacular. We're going to do such cool things in editing."

Yara smiles tentatively. TJ glances between them. There's something off about this whole operation. "What if Yara had some photos taken, too? For the plus-size section?" she suggests. "She'd be great—"

"Oh, we already have a plus-size model," Amy says.

"And what, you can't have two?"

A pause. Amy's smile dims for a second before returning even brighter. "Everyone has a role here, TJ. We need Yara as a photographer. Speaking of which, the next model just arrived. See you later, okay?"

And she turns on her heel to head back to the entrance, where a new arrival is being swarmed by the hair and makeup crew. Frowning, TJ turns to Yara, but the younger girl is already hurrying after her. TJ lets them go, even though there's a bitter taste in her mouth. She did her job. And now, clearly, she's been dismissed.

SEVENTEEN
***

The body positivity campaign goes from photo shoot to an almost completely designed pamphlet within the week. TJ only knows this because Yara provides regular updates. Clearly she's working hard in the editing room.

"What's Simran's part in this project?" TJ finally asks, two weeks before Spring Break, when Yara shows her the layout they're going to run. Yara shrugs.

"I'm not sure. She was a big part of getting the campaign approved, though."

"But nothing after?"

Yara frowns. "I haven't seen her around the editing room, no."

Well, that says a lot. By the time TJ heads to Whitewater for her after-school soccer game, she sorely regrets participating in the whole thing. It feels like Amy played her.

She dumps her bag at the side of the bench and glances towards the school building. Speaking of annoying student council people, she's supposed to meet Charlie today. They agreed to rendezvous in Whitewater's library after her game and his council meeting. It's been hard, squeezing debate sessions in between all their schoolwork and extracurriculars, but they make it work. And if she's not lying to herself . . . well, she sort of looks forward to it.

A shadow falls over her while she's stretching. When she leans back, Coach is standing there, blocking out the sun and mountains behind him. "So," he says. "Were you ever going to tell me you're not playing the final tournament?"

TJ nearly chokes on her own spit. "I—what? How do you know that?"

Coach crosses his beefy arms, the result of afternoons spent in the weight room, bench-pressing to intimidate his eighth-grade gym class. "Mrs. Scott." At her confused look, he says, "Teachers talk to each other, you know."

Something's not right. He's too calm about this. "Listen—"

"First you started missing practices," he interrupts. "Then you ignored your opportunities to go varsity. You blew off the scouts. Now I hear you're not even coming to our final game because of this"—he waves a hand dismissively—"speech contest."

"Debate," she automatically corrects, but he goes on.

"I can't keep ignoring this, kiddo. You've stopped taking this sport seriously. This speech thing—it trumps everything, doesn't it?"

TJ swallows. Well, he's on the money. "Yes."

He nods slowly. "I was afraid you'd say that." TJ's brows furrow, at least until he adds, "I'm taking you out of play."

TJ's standing before she realizes it. *"What?"* Her voice is loud enough to carry to the others, but she doesn't care.

Coach hardly blinks at her outburst. "There are players on this team who want to get noticed by scouts. They can't do that from the bench."

TJ's jaw drops. "You're saying I can't play? That's so unfair! I've been on this team for years—"

"So what?" Coach says. "My newer recruits work twice as

hard as you do, and it shows. Jesus, kid, don't look at me like that. I'm not saying you can't play at all. You'll just be a substitute from now on."

"But, Coach—"

"Don't you think someone who actually wants to play should be on the field?"

TJ opens her mouth to argue—*of course* she wants to play—but then she notices how quiet it's become around them. She glances towards the bench. Piper gives her a helpless shrug, but several of her other teammates look away, going back to their stretches. They're who Coach is talking about. Some of them won't even be on the field today, but they're here anyway, warming up. Looking for any chance to prove their worth. To convince people that they deserve to be here.

And that's a feeling TJ knows a little bit about.

She glances back at Coach. He's standing there, expression guarded, clearly waiting for her to keep arguing. Everyone is.

TJ goes back to stretching without another word.

After the game, TJ sits on the floor of one of the long aisles of Whitewater's library, books piled around her. She stares into space as Charlie reads across from her. They're in a corner farthest away from the checkout desks and the study tables, so can talk freely without being shushed. Or, in her case, wallow in self-pity without being disturbed.

Usually at soccer, she plays the whole match. But this time, thanks to her new benchwarmer status, she was only on the field a few minutes. She didn't even break a sweat. So after the game, instead of using Whitewater's fancy private shower, she headed straight to the library. Now she's wishing she'd changed out of her jersey at least, but she couldn't bear to hang around for another minute.

It had never occurred to her before that Coach might bench her. It should have. It made sense, with her performance this season. She's almost surprised Coach didn't try it earlier; maybe he expected her to argue more. Hell, *she* expected herself to argue more. She's done so many out-of-character things lately, but this one takes the cake. Who even *is* TJ Powar if she walks away from a fight?

"I'm getting the sense you're not listening," Charlie says. TJ blinks. She was definitely not listening.

"Of course I'm listening."

"Then answer my question."

Shit. "Can you . . . rephrase your question?"

Charlie raises an eyebrow. "There was no question." Damn him. He holds up the Canadian history book he'd been reading. "I was just saying the War Measures Act is a good example of loss of freedom of speech we could use. Since you love *evidence* so much."

She knows he's referring to their debate back in December, but she can't seem to muster up a comeback for once.

He sets down the book. "You're off today."

The way he says it, so sure of himself, pisses her off. "Maybe you're just not funny."

Charlie doesn't even smile, so intent is he on studying her. She fights the urge to hunch, to hide. She hates it—the uncomfortable sense that he sees right through her. Right to her soul.

I like you and I wanted to kiss you.

She rubs her temples. Those words pop into her head at the strangest times. Sometimes she could swear he said them just to mess with her.

The other option is that he meant it. She can only hope she's done enough to make him change his mind. Whenever they meet, she makes a point of dressing in more skin-revealing clothes, and *not* in a flirty way. In a look-at-my-shockingly-hairy-body way. She's still waiting for a reaction; the final evidence she needs to get over him. But his poker face is too damn good.

"Does this have to do with your game?" Charlie asks finally. "I saw the first few minutes before my meeting, but you weren't playing. Aren't you supposed to be a starting midfielder?"

His creepy observation skills are starting to get real annoying. "I didn't play the first bit," she says shortly. "Coach wanted to give other people a chance."

She thought she was fine until she said it out loud. But the realization crashes into her again. Never again is she going to get that adrenaline rush right before kickoff. She hadn't appreciated it enough at the previous game. She hadn't realized it would be the last.

To her horror, her eyes start burning. No way is she letting Charlie see her be a baby about this. "It's hot in here, hasn't Whitewater heard of air-conditioning?" she mutters, and pulls up her jersey to wipe her face. Really, to wipe the tear that was threatening to spill.

Charlie has gone suspiciously quiet. That's when she remembers something that slipped her mind while desperately trying to hide her distress: her stomach is *hairy*.

She peeks over her jersey hem. And there it is. His poker face has slipped.

It's almost nothing, but because she's searching for it, she sees it. He looks . . . uneasy.

It brings her back to her breakup with Liam, and his face when he saw her hairiness. The way it *hurt*, the way it burned into her memory so she could remember it over and over and hurt every time. His disgust was more obvious than this, but Liam's also just easier to read. For Charlie to slip at all means exactly the same thing.

He recovers quickly, but too late. It already hurts.

She presses deeper into it. "What, does my hair bother you?" She says it so boldly he probably wouldn't guess she's holding her breath for his answer.

"No."

But he won't look at her. He's lying. She's never known him to lie before.

Charlie thought he could handle her hairiness. But he didn't really understand, did he? She needs to paint him a nice vivid picture so they can both move on. "That's the least of it. I'm hairy *everywhere*," she informs him with a bitter laugh. "Do you get it now?"

He actually looks pained. "Yes, TJ. I get it. Can we get back to debate now."

She drops her jersey. He exhales. There's a silence.

Well. She's officially cured him after weeks of hard work being a freak. Mission accomplished. So why do her insides suddenly feel like lead? She should be *happy*. Finally, they can just be debate partners.

After a pause, Charlie says, "By the way, I ran into Amy West today at district council."

TJ blinks. His tone is casual again. And he's looking at her now, the same as before. As if the awkward moment never happened. That's good, isn't it? Even if he finds her repulsive, he's still able to talk to her like a normal person. She's one step closer to proving her new resolution. *Still worthy of respect, beautiful or not.*

She feels a little better at that. Then she catches up to what he said. "Amy?" She makes a face. Thinking about the photo shoot will do that. "What'd she say?"

"That you participated in her campaign." At her surprise, he explains, "She's going through district student council to get it into the other schools. I just wanted to ask how it went."

TJ scoffs. "She's pretty set on her creative vision, if you know what I mean." At his silence, she wonders if she's being harsh. Just because Simran's not involved doesn't mean the project is automatically trash. "Um . . . but, I guess it's still a good campaign. To get the message out there."

Her words sound half-hearted even to her. Charlie arches a brow.

"I think that's the most diplomatic thing you've ever said." She scowls, but he goes on. "I've known Amy a long time, and in my experience, her main motivation is usually to pad her own résumé."

TJ nods slowly. Amy *does* seem obsessed with the campaign's success.

"Just . . . be careful with her. That's all I'm saying." His phone buzzes on the floor next to him. He flips it over and stares at the caller ID.

"What is it?" TJ asks.

"It—it—it's nothing." He flips it back over. She reaches across the aisle and takes it before he can stop her. Andrew Yen. It takes her a second to place the name. From Provincials. The banquet.

"Isn't this your comedian for polio night? Shouldn't you pick up?"

"No."

That one word is crisp, deliberate. She waits for him to explain. But he doesn't, just eyes the buzzing phone in her hand like it's a grenade.

"Why not?" she asks.

He swallows, but again, nothing.

"Charlie?" she prods, and he looks back at her. His lips part as if to speak, but nothing comes out. His expression clouds over. And she realizes then that it's not that he *won't* talk to her, but that he can't. He's blocking.

TJ immediately pushes his phone back. It's stopped buzzing. "Never mind. Um . . . what were you saying about the War Measures Act, again?" Awkwardly, she reaches for the book he'd been reading, but then Charlie speaks.

"That night at the Provincials banquet, I—I—I never actually got around to asking him to be a speaker."

TJ immediately drops the book. "What? Why not?"

He hesitates. "Remember how—how Jenna Turner messed with you before your debate?" TJ nods grimly. "Well, Isaac does the same thing. I avoided him the whole tournament, but he—he—he showed up just before the banquet."

"What'd he say?"

He shakes his head. "Doesn't matter."

There's a pang in TJ's chest. She hadn't shared Jenna's words with him, either. Because they hurt too much.

He goes on. "Point is, he's good at bringing out my stutter. And I've never been great on the phone—I try to avoid it, if I can. So w-w-w-when I got that call right after, I got anxious, and I couldn't *talk* suddenly. I was just stuttering. Worse than I have in a long time. He said—he said he thought our reception was breaking up." Charlie laughs hollowly. "Hung up on me."

Her heart sinks. No wonder he didn't come back to the banquet. "Charlie, that sucks."

He shrugs. "The problem is, we still don't have a speaker for the event. He keeps calling me, but I just can't. I keep thinking about how I'll ruin it again."

TJ stays silent. She doesn't know what the answer is—she can't guarantee he won't stutter again, or that the guy he's talking to won't hang up. But she can tell this is important.

"Then let me talk to him," she says finally.

He blinks. "What?"

"Come on, how hard could it be? I'll pretend to be the council secretary or something."

Now he looks on the verge of a smile. "You? A secretary?"

TJ narrows her eyes. "Why not?" He gives her a look, and yeah, he's right. She'd probably throw her laptop at someone halfway through taking meeting minutes.

"I guess you'll have to choose," she says, holding his gaze.

"Who'll bomb this call more, me pretending to be on council or you having a stutter?"

After a second, Charlie starts dialing.

"Dickhead," she stage-whispers. But really, she's glad. Once he puts it to his ear, she's practically vibrating with anticipation.

A tinny voice on the other end. She stills. He listens. "Hi. This is Charlie Rosencrantz speaking. I'm—I'm—I'm sorry I haven't been able to pick up your calls." He pauses. "Yes, ab-ab-about the polio event."

TJ mouths, *Ask!*

"The reason I—I was getting in touch with you is—" He pauses, swallows. "Is—"

A long silence. He's blocking again. The tinny voice in the phone is saying *Hello? Hello?* over and over. Charlie's expression shutters. He pulls the phone away from his ear, and TJ knows he's about to end the call.

She leans over and once again snatches his phone. "Hi, sorry," she says into the receiver, dodging Charlie's swipe. "I'm the, uh, secretary for Whitewater's student council. Charlie just dropped something, but basically we were hoping we could book you for our event?"

"Well, of course." The voice on the other end sounds pleased. "I was hoping that was it. It sounds like a great cause."

"Great!" TJ smiles. "We'll be in touch to sort out the details. Um, can I get your email?" She has zero idea what she's doing. This is Charlie's realm.

As if on cue, Charlie takes back his phone.

"Actually, can we meet to talk more?" Pause. "Today? In an

hour?" He glances at TJ, who nods rapidly. "Yes, that works. See you then."

He ends the call. There's a pause.

"I think you might have a career in school politics ahead of you," Charlie says.

"Ha." Her jokes die on her lips, though, when she sees how warmly he's looking at her. Maybe she should be a nice person more often. "So you're meeting him soon?"

"Yeah. I'm sorry to cut this short." Then he pulls an *actual tie* out of his bag and drapes it over his shoulders. She would make fun of him for having an emergency tie, but she's too riveted by his deft fingers. He stares into space as he smoothly weaves a Windsor knot. She looks away and wishes the librarian would turn down the thermostat.

But as he's reaching for his bag, she stops him. "Wait."

He turns to her. His tie is slightly crooked, just as she thought. He must really be preoccupied. She scoots across the aisle on her knees to his side, reaching for the tie knot. His breath hitches when she wraps her fingers around it. She's not sure why her heart is beating so fast as she straightens it out, carefully, her hands brushing his chest. He holds absolutely still in the seconds she's touching him, as still as the bookshelf he's leaning against. He may even be holding his breath.

She withdraws her hands and places them in her lap. "There." Her voice sounds strange.

Charlie, who still hasn't moved, exhales. His eyes are dark pools. "TJ."

"What?"

"Thank you."

She flushes. She's not even sure why. Maybe because she just made a clown of herself on the phone, to some rando, for *him*. "You should go."

He nods. "Let's pick this up again later?"

Yes. *Absolutely*, her brain screams, although it seems to have a different idea of what they'd pick up. This is a new level of pathetic. She knows he's not attracted to her anymore—she can't forget his face, the revulsion at her hairiness—yet here she is sweating over his tie.

Some dormant self-preservation instinct kicks in, and she scoots away again, her back hitting the bookshelf opposite him. "We've figured out our cases. All that's left is to write speeches. Do we even need to meet up on our own like this anymore?"

His smile has faded as she talked, and now it's settled back into a poker face. "I guess not." Pause. "Good night, then."

He gets up and shoulders his bag. TJ pretends to be absorbed in her notebook until he finally walks away. Once she hears the library doors swing closed behind him, she exhales. This—distance—will be good. She's already played herself enough when it comes to Charlie. The less she sees him, the better.

Because what she feels for him isn't warm and light anymore. No; her heart is beating too fast, skin flushing too hot, hands trembling too much to be that. And all those symptoms are terribly familiar. TJ can't keep ignoring it. Just like debate, and soccer, and all the rest of the things she loves, Charlie Rosencrantz gives her an adrenaline high.

EIGHTEEN
***

TJ's favourite method of dealing with things she'd rather avoid is simple: just stop thinking about it. It's working for both the soccer jersey gathering dust in her duffel bag and Liam, so why not Charlie, too? The longer she ignores them, the easier it'll be.

For the next two weeks, she throws herself into school, and all the graduation to-do's she can't avoid anymore. She writes extensive pros-and-cons lists for each university she's been accepted to (Western is still winning). She shows up to every soccer practice, and spends hours on her Nationals speeches, often with her father, who helps her write arguments. She works herself until she's too exhausted to think at the end of the day.

And then Spring Break arrives. Before TJ knows it, she's on Vancouver Island with the rest of her class on the Northridge senior retreat. Thankfully, there's plenty to keep her busy here, too.

"We should go on a whale-watching tour tomorrow," Piper says one afternoon early in the week. It's chilly but sunny on the beach of their Tofino resort; she and TJ are lugging their surfboards through the sand after a bout of surfing lessons. "Chandani gave me extra tickets."

TJ frowns at the reminder that Piper and Chandani still talk. Meanwhile, Chandani barely acknowledges TJ's existence, and even then, only when forced. But it doesn't seem smart to accuse her last remaining friend of being disloyal. "I don't think she'd want *me* using her ticket."

"I asked her for two and she didn't react. I don't think she cares."

TJ tugs at the neck of her wetsuit, privately doubting that very much.

They return their surfboards to the rental room, where most of their classmates are collected doing the same. Piper's just telling her how she's going to accept UVic's offer to play for their team when they pass a group of boys, Jake included.

Jake doesn't acknowledge TJ, but he gives Piper a grin. "Hey, Pied Piper."

Piper gives him a sly look and saunters out. TJ follows, and as soon as they're out of earshot, she says, "You two are hooking up, aren't you?"

Piper whips around, eyes wide. "Why do you think that? Did I seem desperate?"

TJ restrains the urge to laugh. "So you haven't?"

"No." She sighs and runs a hand through her red tresses. "But last night we made out in the hot tub."

That explains why TJ didn't know about it. She hasn't made any appearances in the resort's pool area. Well, good for Piper. TJ's glad for her. Even if Jake has ignored TJ ever since she broke up with Liam. But what does it matter what Jake thinks of her if he's into Piper?

"It was really hot," Piper adds. She has an expression on her face like she's remembering certain details she will never quite share in their entirety. TJ used to know the feeling.

She wrings her hair out, trying not to sound bitter. "The water, or the kissing?"

Piper snorts. "Both. Seriously, the pool is amazing. You should come." TJ hesitates, and Piper notices. "Oh! Sorry, I forgot."

Her eyes flicker to TJ's body, currently hidden in a wetsuit. TJ frowns. Until now, she hasn't really examined why she was never interested in an evening swim like the rest of them. But now she entertains the thought and is slammed with a wave of anxiety, the same one she gets every time she considers using the communal showers after soccer.

Damn it. She's *scared*.

She wishes she could take the realization back. Because now there's no choice. If she lets her fear stop her, she's once again disproving her own resolution. And she is *not* doing that again. "You know what? I think I *will* come to the pool tonight."

"Oh. Okay." Piper blinks. "I guess you could wear the wetsuit."

TJ scoffs. "I'm not wearing the *wetsuit*. I'll get something else." The same kind of swimsuit she would've worn before. Why shouldn't she enjoy the hot tub? She squares her shoulders. "I'll see you there."

That night, after dinner, she stands in front of the bathroom mirror and tries to envision herself walking out wearing the black two-piece suit she bought from the shop next door. And she just—can't.

It looks horrible. And it shouldn't, because it would've looked fine months ago. But now . . . the hair is just so unmissable.

Oh, there are the usual places, like on her arms and legs and underarms, but this suit also showcases other things. Her chest. Her tummy. Her bikini line—and god, this is the worst part, it really is. These aren't even the most revealing kinds of bikini bottoms, they're closer in cut to booty shorts, and yet the hair on her thighs is so obvious and *gross*.

Her body is totally gross.

Her vision blurs with frustrated, hot tears. There's nothing cute about this. Not a single thing.

Why can't she ever seem to make up her mind? Some days, she's able to stride down the hallways without giving a shit—in fact, reveling in the freedom—and then there are days like this.

She tugs a little on the hem of the bottoms and considers backing out. She could text Piper and tell her she feels sick. Piper wouldn't question it.

Her phone buzzes. Piper? TJ snatches it from the counter, but it's just her mom. TJ hesitates. She's not in the mood, but then again, if she's in here talking to her mom, at least she's not out *there*, wearing this ridiculous swimsuit.

So she answers. "Hey, Mom."

She thinks she sounds fairly casual, but not according to her mother. "What's wrong? You sound different. Are you okay?"

TJ opens her mouth to say yes, but instead, she just grips the phone harder. Hearing her mom's voice makes her heart ache suddenly. It's only been a few days away from home and yet TJ suddenly wants to run into her arms and never leave. God. She's going to be a wreck when she leaves for university.

"What are you doing right now?" her mom asks worriedly.

"Oh." TJ looks around, and then settles on a half-truth. "Getting ready for a swim."

"A swim?" Her mom is dead silent for a second. "Did you have a waxing appointment before you left?"

TJ holds it together for about one second and then, to her absolute mortification, bursts into tears.

It's just—once again, her fears are confirmed. Being rejected by her own *mother* . . . the jokes write themselves.

Instantly, her mom is practically shouting on the phone: "Oh no, putt, don't cry!" TJ sinks to the floor, her shoulders shaking so hard from crying she almost drops the phone. Her mom makes soothing sounds, the same she used to make when TJ was a little kid and inconsolable over a minor inconvenience. "It's just—it doesn't look good. I don't understand why you suddenly stopped waxing. You used to beg me to let you do it."

That pulls TJ out of it. With a hiccup, she sits up straight and tries to keep her voice firm. "Because I want to show people it exists. That *I* exist and it's okay, and normal." Her mom is silent again, and TJ's certainty wavers. "It *is* normal, isn't it?"

She hates how pathetic she sounds, but she has to ask. Her mom's a doctor; she'll know.

"It *is* normal. There are hormonal disorders that can cause more hair, too, of course. I don't think you have one, but even if you did . . . it would be okay. It's very common. More people than you think have hormonal differences they can't do much about. We just don't talk about it because we find it embarrassing."

Well, colour TJ shocked.

"Body hair is normal. Especially for us." TJ can practically hear her wry smile. "We've been removing it since ancient times. In medical literature, they call our hairiness idiopathic hirsutism."

"Gesundheit."

As usual, her mom misses the joke. "It means it's inherited. With no known cause or other symptoms. That's all."

"If it's not a problem, why does it have a medical name?"

"Some white doctor probably made it up so they could call us something." TJ can practically hear her shrug over the phone. "They are clueless. When I was in medical school, we were taught hirsutism in cisgender girls is if they have to tweeze facial hair more than twice a month."

TJ scoffs. She knows for a fact Chandani does her eyebrows weekly. So did TJ, when she was doing them. That was their normal. Their hair grows back quicker, thicker, longer. She thinks back to Dr. Chen's words: *What's really a disease, and what's just diversity? Who gets to decide?*

White people, apparently. "If that's true, and it's normal, why do you want me to get rid of it?"

"Oh, TJ." She sighs. "I just don't want people to say nasty things about you."

TJ angrily wipes tears from her cheeks. "I shouldn't have to change my body for that to happen."

"I know. But the world is harsh."

The world *is* harsh. TJ doesn't have to subject herself to it. But if she's going to prove her resolution, then she does. She can't stop living her life because of this.

She glances at the door and takes a deep breath. "Mom, I have to go."

It's time to do this.

NINETEEN
***

No one notices her at first.

When she arrives poolside in her terry-cloth robe, most of her classmates are wading in the pool, or splashing and shrieking from the waterslide. Some are in the hot tub. Including Liam, with Alexa Fisher tucked in at his side. TJ's stomach curdles.

She could still leave.

Except then Piper's voice rings out. "TJ! Over here!"

Piper's waving from one of the hard-plastic tables, wearing a polka-dot bikini and eating nachos. Next to her is the Northridge goalie, Angela Stevens, in a red one-piece and currently tying her shoulder-length hair into a bun. She glances at TJ and pauses, as if surprised to see her here.

This is it. The moment of no return.

For her last resolution, she was a coward. Not this time. With gritted teeth, TJ pulls off her robe, draping it over the back of an unoccupied chair at the table. Dead silence. She wants to wrap herself in her robe again, but instead she forces herself to sit.

Finally, she raises her eyes. Angela has a nacho half-raised to her mouth. Piper's the first to say, "Um, what's up?"

"Not much." Piper tries not to stare, TJ can tell. But her eyes keep flicking down. TJ sighs. "Just say what you want to say. I'm Bigfoot, ha, ha. Are we done?"

Angela titters nervously and excuses herself.

"No! I mean, yes. But, no," Piper says quickly, while Angela disappears. "It's just hard to get used to."

She's said that before, too, but TJ finds she can't really blame her. When would Piper have ever seen people like TJ? Razor ads don't exactly show women shaving their moustaches. It's always either legs or underarms. Anything else isn't supposed to exist.

TJ reaches for a nacho. "Would it be hard to get used to if I were a guy?"

Piper blinks. "I guess not."

"And if I were a guy who waxed my legs?" TJ asks curiously. "Would that be weird?"

Piper mulls this over. "I've never thought about it before, but I guess so."

TJ munches on her nacho thoughtfully. So the double standards aren't just for girls, then. Wax, body hair . . . on the right person, they're considered normal. Expected, even. But stop or do something differently and suddenly it's a big deal.

Piper's gaze shifts behind TJ. A second later Jake strolls by on his way to the hot tub. He gives Piper a rakish grin.

"Hey, Pied Piper."

Piper casually bites into another nacho. As soon as he's passed them, she turns her head and watches him go. TJ could throw up from the cliché-ness of it all.

She immediately chastises herself. Just because she's bitter about her love life being dead in the water doesn't mean she can't be a good wingwoman. "Maybe we should move to the hot tub," she suggests.

Piper squints in thought. "You know what? I think I will."

TJ starts to stand as well, but Piper turns to her quickly.

"Oh, no, you don't need to . . . You can stay here. The hot tub is kind of crammed anyway."

TJ blinks. "Um, okay." She sinks back into her seat and tells herself it's not personal. Piper just wants Jake to herself. That's fine.

Alone at the table now, TJ relaxes more with each minute that passes. It's warm and humid, and she's suddenly glad for the two-piece rather than the wetsuit. She'd been so worried about people's reactions, but that wasn't so bad, was it?

A classmate shoots out of the nearby waterslide and into the pool with a thunderous splash. Droplets spray at TJ's feet and remind her that she came here to have *fun*. So she pushes the nachos away and heads up the stairs to the top of the slide.

Someone starts climbing the stairs right after her, and it's funny how self-conscious she becomes knowing someone's staring at her back (and everything else) as she ascends. She focuses on moving forward. As she nears the top, voices from the slide's platform float down to her. She recognizes them as guys from the soccer team, right before she registers what they're saying.

". . . if you're going to be like that, at least cover it up."

"Right? No one wants to see that shit. It's really making me appreciate the girls who take care of themselves."

"I'm not even sure that *is* a girl. She's hairier than my dad."

"Dude, she's hairier than my dog."

Snickers. TJ stays frozen to the stair rail, cheeks burning. She can't. She can't go up any farther and face them. Maybe she could turn around and go back. But this stairwell is too narrow, and she has no idea how many people are behind her.

As if to prove her point, a voice at her back snarls, *"Move."*

Chandani. Too shocked to snap back, TJ takes the last few steps to the platform. The two guys loitering by the waterslide look up, see her, and she *knows* they know she heard. They don't say a thing, no apology, no chagrin, nothing. They look through her like she's not even there.

Chandani pushes past TJ so brusquely she's knocked forward a step. She's got her hands on her hips, looking scorching hot in her tiny yellow bikini, ponytail swaying as she sashays up to the guys.

One of them—tall, gorgeous—smiles at her. "Hey, Chandani."

"Hi, Trent," she purrs. Twirls her ponytail with one finger. TJ decides it's time to go, before she barfs. She brushes past them and clambers into the slide. But before she can push herself down, Chandani says to Trent, "Do you think I'm pretty?"

Wait. What? TJ turns to listen.

Trent doesn't seem as confused by the uncharacteristic question as TJ is. His eyes do a slow perusal of every inch of skin Chandani's bikini reveals. Wow, he really wants in her pants. "You're the most beautiful girl I've ever seen."

"I know." Chandani pauses. "I'm also hairier than your dad."

His smile starts to fade. TJ's jaw drops as she continues.

"If I don't wax every other week, I'm even *hairier* than TJ here. Which is why I take offense at the shit you just said." She gets in his face. "Grow up, Trent. Girls don't look like the actresses on the porn sites you've got bookmarked. They look like fucking human beings."

The platform is dead silent. No one moves, the soccer players or their classmates on the stairwell witnessing the whole thing.

Chandani, unbothered, turns towards TJ, who's still sitting at the top of the slide.

TJ opens her mouth, to speak, she doesn't know what—but before she can, Chandani gives her a strong shove.

TJ loses her grip and tips into the slide. The water instantly sweeps her away, and then she's whipping through the tunnel in an ungainly heap, her limbs colliding with the walls at every turn. It should be thrilling, but she can't process a single thing that's happening. All she can think is: *What the hell just happened?* Since when did Chandani—

She crashes into the pool. She turns her head back where she came from, just in time to see Chandani hurtling through the tunnel after her. TJ dives away to avoid getting smacked in the face with Chandani's leg.

When they resurface a little ways away, TJ splutters, "What the hell? You're supposed to wait ten seconds before you go down the slide after someone!"

"I got impatient." Chandani readjusts her ponytail and gives TJ a baleful look. The effect is somewhat diminished because her mascara has smudged all over her face.

"You look like a raccoon," TJ informs her.

Chandani's hands fly to her face. She dabs under her eyes, then looks at the black smear on her finger. The edge of her mouth turns down in displeasure.

They look at each other, both unsmiling. Then TJ breaks into a grin. Chandani follows suit. And just like that, three months of radio silence fall away.

"I knew that waterproof mascara on clearance was too good to be true. That saleswoman is gonna meet my chappal when

I get back." Chandani wipes under her eyes. Pauses. "Listen. What I said to you after Winter Break . . . that was uncalled for."

It's as close as Chandani will ever get to an apology. TJ takes it as such. "I'm sorry I called you a bitch."

Chandani arches a perfectly threaded brow. TJ crosses her arms.

"Okay, fine, I'm not actually sorry for that. But you call me a bitch all the time, so I don't see why you were so offended."

At her teasing tone, Chandani's mouth quivers. "Come here."

TJ reaches in to hug her, and as she does, she notices the tiny black dots on Chandani's jaw that signal hair growing back in. She embraces her; her heart melts. Under the chlorine spray she still smells faintly like expensive perfume and mehndi. God, TJ's missed her.

Chandani's arms tighten around her once, tight enough to make her lose her breath, and then let go. People are staring. TJ ignores them; and wow, it's so much easier to do that with a friend at her side.

They sit at a nearby table, one where the nachos are still untouched. Chandani plucks one out, digging it into the dip, and it's all very surreal, seeing as this morning TJ still thought they were enemies. Their friendship generally seems volatile to outsiders, but they haven't had a *serious* spat since seventh grade when Chandani spilled red nail polish on TJ's favourite white jacket. That time, it took their moms staging an intervention to get them to talk to each other. So, this time, it begs the question . . .

"Just ask," Chandani says, raising the loaded nacho to her lips. "I know you're dying to."

TJ snatches the nacho from her fingers and pops it in her own mouth. "Why today?"

It's a testament to the weight of that question that Chandani doesn't even react to the nacho steal. Her eyes become distant. "I've been thinking about it for a while. It bothered me that you were choosing to be hairy, but it also bothered me when people made fun of you for it. And I couldn't figure out why, at least until I overheard you talking to Piper. After the weekend you came back from your Provincials."

TJ pauses in her chewing. She hadn't known Chandani was even aware of her debate schedule. As for Piper . . . TJ glances towards the hot tub, but she and Jake are gone.

Chandani flutters her hands irritably. "Piper was all surprised by your leg hair. And it made me remember something that happened in grade seven. Before we were properly friends with her."

TJ nods. "What happened?"

"Remember Gaya Kumar?"

"Yeah, of course." TJ's intrigued now. Chandani had been closer to Gaya, seeing as they knew each other from events at the Hindu cultural society. "She moved away before high school."

"Right. But she was one of those girls that only *ever* wore pants. Never shorts or skirts or even capris. Anyway—you weren't with us that day, you were at debate practice or something—me, Piper, and Gaya were hanging out at recess and somehow we started talking about shaving. And Gaya said she never shaves her legs or her pits because she never shows them anyway, so what's the point? And Piper actually *shrieked* and said that was so gross."

TJ's mood sours slightly. She reaches for another nacho. Chandani steals it out of her hand and goes on. "Gaya didn't say anything. I didn't, either, because I hadn't shaved in a few days myself. It was cold out, why would I? But Piper—look, I know she was joking around. I doubt she even remembers this. But I went home and shaved my legs anyway. And from then on, every single hair I let grow on my skin felt dirty. Even when I forgot that conversation. That feeling of *gross*—it's always there."

Chandani's words strike home in a way TJ would never be able to explain. Yes, it's bitter to hear this story, but it's also a relief—a reminder that she's never been alone in this. Her best friend has always dealt with it, too, even when she acted like she didn't. "That's the thing, isn't it?" TJ says softly. "Those little comments are the hardest to shake off. It just cycles through your head forever."

"And you start believing it." Chandani studies her manicure. "Next thing you know, *you're* the one making the comments. Making people feel like shit."

TJ smiles, a little sad at how much time they've lost. Not just in their friendship, but in their lives; how much time they've spent eating up every horrible thing the world told them about themselves.

Chandani looks up again, and there's almost a pleading look in her eye, which TJ doubts she realizes she's doing. But if TJ says she forgives her, Chandani will deny having made an apology in the first place. So instead TJ grants her forgiveness another way. "Speaking of Provincials, you would not believe what went down that weekend."

Chandani's expression clears immediately, and she straightens up. Gossip: their eternal love language.

The nachos between them disappear as TJ catches her up on the drama that ensued with her breakup, at debate with the Turners, and after with Simran. Minus a crucial Saturday-night detail about Charlie that TJ can't bring herself to talk about. Within the first few minutes, Chandani's already called Jenna Turner the human personification of period cramps, Isaac a bhenchod, and Liam "an incel in another life."

At the end of it, Chandani pushes the empty bowl of nachos to the side to focus her entire attention on TJ. "So, you're missing our last soccer tournament for Nationals."

TJ bites her lip. "Yeah." She waits for Chandani to laugh.

Chandani doesn't. "I read that article about you in the school newspaper, you know. Where you talk about debate."

TJ swallows. The special-edition pamphlet with Amy's campaign had come out right before Spring Break. TJ hadn't taken a close look at it beyond what Yara had shown her. "And?"

"I didn't learn anything new. We always knew you were a nerd."

And that's it—that's all she says. Relief unfurls in TJ's stomach. "Really?"

"Yeah. So stop pretending you're not. Anyway, you're debating with Charlie Rosencrantz?" TJ nods, and she sits back. "Oh my god. Jump him."

TJ covers her face. Chandani misunderstands.

"What? You can't tell me you've become a prude now. Dating white boys is a line you've already crossed."

TJ uncovers her face. "And look how that went."

"So you *are* interested, just scared."

TJ glares. "That's not what I said."

"Touchyyy," Chandani drawls, but drops it. "Wanna go for a swim? No one will see your hairy bod underwater, so you can stop acting like a self-conscious little freak for a bit."

TJ actually chuckles despite herself.

"Let's go. And forget those assholes," Chandani adds, nodding towards the top of the waterslide. "They're nothing. They can't touch you."

A lump is growing in TJ's throat. "I missed you, Chandani."

Chandani looks up at the ceiling and dabs delicately under her eyes. "Stop ruining my makeup, bitch."

TWENTY
***

Now that TJ and Chandani are back on speaking terms, the rest of their time in Tofino flies by. Piper is elated to find the two of them together the next day. It's almost like old times.

Except, as Piper tells them about her night with Jake through giggles, TJ catches Chandani listening with a strangely cold expression. Oh, great. She may have made up with TJ, but the freshly dug-up seventh-grade incident with Piper has opened a different can of worms.

Piper seems oblivious, however, and Chandani says nothing. So they spend the next few days together, ziplining, exploring hot springs, and laughing at each other's surfing wipeouts. They spend their evenings at the pool—TJ becomes comfortable lounging in her two-piece—and dodging supervisors to stay in each other's rooms past curfew.

Their final day on Vancouver Island comes sooner than seems possible. The last hurrah is a sailing trip around the shoreline and peninsula; TJ dresses for sightseeing, but it turns out they actually have to help haul the sails. Chandani spends the majority of the morning laughing at TJ tripping over the rigging in her wedge sandals, for which TJ retaliates by refusing to lend her a hair tie when the strong winds blow her hair into her face. It feels like old times. TJ's almost disappointed when the trip is cut short to catch their shuttle back to the ferry terminal.

Except, as they find out once they've docked, the shuttle is late. The chaperones go to sort it out with the tour company, leaving the group to their own devices in the small indoor seating area. TJ hobbles to sit next to Chandani, who's wrangling her windswept hair into a hair tie Piper gave her, and scrolls through her social media. She's been so busy she's barely looked to see what other people have been up to on Break. Ameera, who didn't come on the trip, is ranting about a show she binge-watched that had a crappy ending. Nate accompanied his father to a work conference in Australia and has posted unflattering photos of Dr. Chen at each destination with the caption #professorbae. And Simran's sister got a new tattoo, which just reminds TJ that Simran's still avoiding her. She's not on social media, so TJ can only imagine what she got up to.

Chandani elbows her. "My mom says hi." She shows TJ the text. "Apparently her and your mom knew we weren't talking for a while."

"Wow. They didn't say anything?"

Chandani snickers. "They never do, anymore."

TJ smiles, too. Their moms have seen them get into countless fights. They just didn't realize how serious this one was.

Just then, the volume level rises considerably. "What's going on?"

TJ looks behind them. Most of her classmates are crowded around Jake. He's sporting several gift shop bags, handing out cylindrical bottles. Piper's next to him doing the same. TJ squints to read the label on them. Silly String. She and Chandani exchange confused looks.

The group around Piper and Jake begins to thin; they're all heading to the exit of the terminal. At that moment, Piper spots TJ and Chandani and waves them over.

"Weren't you paying attention? Whitewater's here, too," Piper explains. "They just docked. We're playing a prank." She shoves cans of Silly String into their hands.

"Whitewater?" TJ manages, but Piper's already turned away.

Chandani shakes her can experimentally. "Of course it's Whitewater. Who else would we stoop to cringey pranks for?" She sets off to follow the group at a brisk pace. TJ scowls at her back. Her aching ankles can't keep up and Chandani knows it.

For a minute, TJ considers just staying behind. Because Charlie might be there.

Then her stupid, traitorous body moves anyway, because: Charlie might be there.

She exits the shuttle area, following the Silly String trail. Lined up at the dock are several of the sailing company's near-identical boats, each with tall masts, canvas sails, and complicated systems of ropes and pulleys that could've come from a different century. TJ's eyes are drawn to the last two tall boats in the line. They're still full of people—swarming, really—and also very . . . colourful.

By the time she hops onto the first Whitewater boat from the dock, it's clear there's nothing much left to vandalize. Silly String hangs from everywhere; the mast, the rigging, the cabin, the railing. And of course, from the Whitewater students milling about. But no one's spraying anyone anymore. The Northridgers and Whitewaterians are just hanging out on deck. TJ sprays some Silly String onto a tarp without enthusiasm.

Then she turns and finds herself face-to-face with Liam.

He's holding three cans of Silly String and pauses upon seeing her. They haven't spoken since the breakup. She doesn't know what to say. He doesn't seem to, either.

"Hi," she says finally.

"Hi." He runs a hand through the dark curls TJ used to love messing up. Funny how things change. Now, she can't look at his face without remembering his disgust. She can't hear his voice without thinking of the things he said.

Liam shifts on his feet awkwardly. "Look, TJ, I'm not into you anymore."

She snaps out of her staring and realizes he thinks she's checking him out. She opens her mouth to correct him, but he goes on in an infuriatingly apologetic tone. "It's for the best we broke up. We're not compatible."

TJ has a feeling he's mentally patting himself on the back for his oh-so-mature speech when in reality what he wants to say is that she's a freak. She snorts. "You think I care whether you're into me?" She steps around him, but he stops her in her tracks.

"I'll give you a tip, TJ, since I know I was your first boyfriend. *No one's* going to be into you when you look like that."

Her jaw drops. "Says who?"

He throws up his hands. "It's not an insult, okay? I'm just trying to help. See you later." He brushes past her.

Anger beats through her skin. No way is she letting him have the last word. Before he can get too far, TJ raises her Silly String can at him, aiming for his precious curls, and lets the multicoloured goop fly. It hits her target perfectly. Liam yelps, cradling his head.

"What the hell, TJ!"

Cackling, she turns and walks away, farther down the deck. Well, that was satisfying.

But her amusement fades the more his words replay in her mind. He didn't say them angrily; no, he almost sounded *sympathetic*. Which is worse. It wasn't enough to break her heart, he had to make her feel like anyone else would've done the same?

Suddenly drained, TJ stops at the other end of the boat and leans against a mast. People pass by her but she barely notices. How is it possible Liam can still hurt her this much? Even though she *agrees*. No one could find her attractive like this. It's not fair to ask them to.

Another group of Whitewater students passes. TJ's snapped out of her thoughts when she hears Charlie's name.

". . . thinks he's such hot shit because he came up with the sailing trip idea, but it sucked."

TJ turns slowly. The boy who spoke is sandy-haired, wearing a grey windbreaker and shorts.

"Nah," says another. "This was way better than the past few senior retreats, at least."

Sandy-haired guy crosses his arms. "Don't let Charlie hear you say that. He's a smug enough little prick as it is."

TJ shifts. The wood under her creaks loudly. The whole group whips their heads around to look at her. Caught.

She gives them a jaunty little wave and pushes off the mast to head back the way she came. It's actually kind of bizarre to hear someone bad-mouth Charlie. But then again, she doesn't go to his school. She doesn't know what he gets up to.

"Hey."

She nearly jumps out of her skin. Speak of the devil; Charlie has materialized in front of her. And—whoa. He's wearing a T-shirt and athletic shorts and sneakers. His hair is the furthest thing from neat, blown out of place by the wind.

While she's staring, Charlie draws closer. "I'm half-surprised you're not spraying me with Silly String by now."

She automatically raises her can, but it's empty. Then she blurts, "I heard someone call you a smug little prick."

He grins. "Were you thinking out loud?"

"No!" She glances behind her, but the Whitewater group has moved on, out of earshot. "It was some guy from your school."

She doesn't know why she's telling him this. Maybe she just wants him to know. Maybe she wants an explanation. In any case, his smile fades slightly as he follows her gaze.

"I think I know who you're talking about. Blond? Grey windbreaker?" She nods. His voice becomes wry. "That'd be my nemesis in every school election, Brandon Fletcher."

"Nemesis?"

Charlie shrugs casually. "Not really, but he seems to think so." He turns towards the ocean, setting his phone down on a crate. "How's debate prep coming along?"

TJ decides not to point out the obvious swerve. She sets down her Silly String. "Fine. You?"

He nods absently. "I've been bribing Nate into helping me brainstorm impromptu topics."

She wishes she'd thought of that. It must show on her face, because he adds, "You could join us, if you want."

His tone is neutral. And despite the fact that she was the one to decide they shouldn't meet anymore, she finds herself wanting to say yes.

She dismisses the thought immediately. *No.* Why is she so weak? Ameera or Mrs. Scott can help her brainstorm. Better than seeing Charlie more than she needs to. "What are you bribing Nate with?" she asks instead.

"He's in the table tennis club. They've been lobbying for a new table for a while now—I can expedite their application so they get it before the year's up."

"Wow. Very ethical, Mr. Student President." She shakes her head, drifting closer to lean her arms on the railing. "If I went to Whitewater, I would actively vote against you."

That makes him grin. "But what if I did something for you?" Her mind goes to all sorts of imaginative places, but he's clearly not as deep in the gutter. "I could get more travel funding for the soccer team."

"That makes it even worse. You're just another corrupt politician."

His politician's smile widens further. TJ looks away and forcibly reminds herself of his disgusted expression at her stomach back in Whitewater's library. It's so frustrating—how easily she *forgets* her reasons to stay away from him, the moment he simply stands next to her.

Irritated, she pushes her hand through her hair. But her fingers snag on a piece of Silly String. She's not sure how it got there. Probably from one of her overenthusiastic classmates.

Then Charlie's hand wraps around hers, nudging it away, and she lets him gently pry the goop out of her hair. Her legs turn to jelly, at least until he says, "Just a tip, point the nozzle away from yourself when you're spraying."

"It wasn't *me*, you dick."

He laughs and drops the string into the ocean below them. That's when she notices—a bit of a hush around them. Like the background conversations have petered out. She peeks behind them, and there's Liam. He's standing not too far away, with some of his friends. And he's staring at them.

Realization dawns. Charlie's standing rather close. He just put his hand in her hair. To anyone watching, it might've looked like something was . . . happening.

Liam's humiliating advice from earlier pulses through her head. *I know I was your first boyfriend.* No one's *going to be into you when you look like that.*

The *gall* of it—to assume that just because he found her gross, everyone else would. Doesn't matter that he's right. It's the cockiness of it. Like he owns her. He thinks he's the only one who's known her so intimately.

Charlie's fingers tap a pattern on the railing, right next to her hand. An idea forms.

He was so supportive of her resolution to prove herself respect-worthy. Doesn't matter if she's too hairy for him; he could fake it. She could explain afterwards. But how to get that across to Charlie?

Just like this: "Hey, remember when we kissed?"

His fingers still. Then resume their pattern. "Am I supposed to pretend I don't?"

"Well, I need you to kiss me again. Right now."

His hand slides off the railing entirely. *What?*

"Do I have to ask twice?" she mutters, flustered now but unable to back out. Is he really that repulsed by the idea? Meanwhile, Liam's drawing closer. Soon he'll be able to hear the conversation. "Just a quick one, promise. I'll explain after."

Charlie seems to hear the plea in her voice. His lashes sweep down, considering her mouth. "And you call *me* weird."

She glares. "You know, I'm starting to think Brandon Fletcher was onto something—"

But he leans in and presses his lips to hers, right there on deck, in clear view of everybody, Northridgers and White-waterians alike.

It starts out chaste. His hands circle her waist politely. Good. She doesn't want to overdo this, or make it look like they're trying too hard.

Except her heart still rapidly swells and rises in her chest like a balloon, giddy with his touch, his proximity. Her hand slides up his chest until it reaches his sternum, where she grasps at empty air and only then does she realize she was searching for a tie.

Their lips part and linger, and she feels his shoulders shake. He's laughing. At her. To shut him up, she grips the back of his neck, nails digging in, and hauls him back to her. His mouth is still open mid-laugh, so, yeah, maybe she puts a little tongue into it. But *he's* the one who escalates it, instantly, as if he's been waiting for this exact moment. His kisses become deep and scorching and all-consuming, to the point where she's just holding on for dear life, and her whole universe seems narrowed down to where their mouths are meeting, again, and again.

A wolf whistle is what breaks them apart, and people laughing. TJ pivots half-around, passing her free hand shakily over her mouth. People are staring. Liam included, his jaw slack. Mission accomplished.

She should feel victorious, but it's hard when her legs are on the verge of collapse.

"TJ," Charlie says, a question in his voice. She whips back around to look at him, to realize she's still gripping his shirt-front. She lets go and lowers her voice to a whisper.

"Where can we talk?"

"Follow me."

She trails behind him. When he takes her down a set of stairs, belowdecks, she thinks they must be headed for the living quarters, but then they hear laughter from farther down that hall.

Charlie hesitates. TJ yanks him back, shakes her head, and opens the first door she sees. A storage closet? Good enough.

He follows her inside. The door swings shut. She immediately regrets walking in—it's crammed in here. He's right up against her back, and when she tries to turn around, she nearly runs into him, and her butt smacks against some kind of big storage box. Their chests nearly touch in the tiny space. Neither speaks for a moment.

"I—I—I guess this is the part of the movie where we make out," Charlie says, and laughs at his own joke.

"Oh, shut up!" Her voice sounds squeaky. She can hardly think. She tries to squirm away from him but there's no space to go—her thighs press against his. Too. Much. Touch.

"Sit up here," he says, a bit gruff, and then his hands are on her waist. She yelps and grabs his arm in surprise. But he just hoists her up onto the storage container, putting her above his eye level and a tiny amount more space between them. His hands don't drop from her waist. He doesn't look amused anymore.

TJ tries to find the words to explain but her brain keeps short-circuiting when Charlie looks at her like that. It just does not compute. Despite her disheveled state, Silly String remnants gumming up her hair, he's looking at her like *that*.

"Y-y-you're," he stutters in a ragged voice, hits a block, and stops. He touches the corner of her eyebrow the same way Liam did, right before he said, *You look really pretty*.

"You're," Charlie begins again, but she freezes him with a look.

"*Don't* say I'm pretty." She grips his bicep tighter. She doesn't want to hear lies from him. Never from him.

His golden eyes darken. "'Pretty' is the *last* word I'd use to describe you."

And then, like he can't help it, like he's falling, he kisses her again.

All thoughts of explaining dissolve right there. The intent in this kiss is dizzying, but she won't be outdone. She wrenches him in by his shirt and gives back as good as she gets. The darkness seems to make both of them bolder, and the more they kiss, the more frantic it gets. She becomes greedy. It's total instinct when her legs wrap around his middle to draw him closer than he's ever been to her. His body responds in a way that is both thrilling and terrifying.

Here Charlie pauses, his mouth pulling slightly away. TJ leans closer—she's enveloped in the small world between them and doesn't want to ruin it by opening her eyes—but her lips only graze his jaw. His breath stutters.

When he turns his face back to hers, the kisses are slower. Deeper. He moves, one knee balancing on the storage container ledge as if he might join her up there, but no farther. Their harsh breathing fills the silence in between, harsher still when TJ wraps her arms around him and buries her face in his shoulder. He doesn't smell like ironed linens today; he smells like the sea, but it's just as overwhelming. Her blood heats and heats and heats with every second until it seems impossible it hasn't evaporated. She's so ensnared in the sensation, and his hands guiding her movement, that she doesn't think at all, at least until there's a crash from right outside the door.

They jolt apart. Whoever's right outside laughs, and someone else swears, laughing, too. Footsteps pound down the hall and then, just as quickly as they were interrupted, they're alone again.

But the spell is already broken. Oh *no*.

TJ unhooks her ankles from behind Charlie's back. "Stop, stop, stop."

Immediately, he backs up until he hits the door. Which is really only a half-step back. "I—I—I—I'm sorry. I'm not trying to—I wasn't—"

She shakes her head. "It's not that." She shakes her head

again, more vigorously now. What is she doing? She came into this closet to explain herself, not to pounce on him and—and—

She can't even finish that thought, she's so embarrassed.

And how is she supposed to explain now that this was all for show? He'll never buy it. Liam wasn't in this supply closet with them, after all.

"TJ," Charlie breathes, but she's already surging towards the door, shouldering him aside to reach for the handle. She has to get out—

But he grabs her arm. "Oh, no, you don't. Not this time." She tugs but his grip tightens. "I don't want to hear the rehearsed speech you come up with a week later. I want to know what's going on in your head *right now*."

Shit.

She debates making a run for it anyway. But he's rightfully pissed. She owes him answers. Taking a deep, terrified breath, she turns around and presses her back against the door. Charlie hops onto the storage container and leans back on his hands. His hair is falling over his eyes. She fights the urge to brush it back in place.

"I'm sorry. I didn't mean for this to go so far." Words are failing her, despite her ability to spin speeches out of nothing in impromptu rounds. This is different. She can handle Charlie's piercing gaze across the floor in a debate, but not when he's a foot away, his lips still reddened from her mouth. "I asked you to kiss me out there for a reason."

"Which was?"

She swallows to work a little moisture into her mouth. She

can do this. She'll explain, and they'll laugh about it and move on. "Because Liam—my ex—was there. Watching."

She dies inside a little as soon as she says it—it sounds even more laughable out loud.

"You kissed me to make your ex jealous?" Charlie asks slowly.

"No!" She cringes. "He said no one could ever be into me like this. He acted like he owned me. I wanted to prove him wrong."

"You wanted to prove it," Charlie repeats. "You felt the need to prove yourself to your piece-of-shit ex-boyfriend. Am I getting that right?"

His condescending tone has returned. She glares at him. "*Proving it* is the whole point. That's my resolution, remember?"

"If I remember right, the resolution was that you should be respected. I don't see the correlation here. You *know* I like you and y-you—you—you—you just used me to make some stupid point."

She stares, stunned. Her brain latches on to only one part of his reply. "You . . . you still like me?"

His cold expression shifts. "Why would that have changed?"

"Because . . ." Her face bursts into flames. She has to push her next words from her mouth. She has to close her eyes to avoid seeing his reaction. "I'm . . . so *hairy*."

The words are whispered into the darkness. Dead silence follows them. She keeps her body rigid, hunched. She's never felt more exposed.

Charlie finally speaks. "I don't understand how you can be this dense."

His voice is icy. Her eyes fly open just in time to see him jab a finger at her. "You think you're delivering some kind of ground-breaking news right now? Do you think I walk around with my eyes closed? I know you're *hairy*, TJ. How could I not? You're one of the hairiest people I've ever seen. It just isn't relevant to how—how—how I feel about you."

Her anger flares. So that's how he wants to play it? Pretending he's better than that? "But back in the library, when you saw my stomach, you looked grossed out!"

Charlie hardly blinks. "Yes, TJ. You got me. I must've been grossed out. What other reaction could I possibly have to you *pulling up your shirt* in front of me?"

TJ flushes, hating his slow, enunciated sarcasm, and hating even more that she's no longer certain she was right back then. She scrambles to stay on top of the argument. "You say all that. But you think it's a quirk," she accuses. "You think this is a phase. I'm trying to prove a point but eventually I'll go back to being hot."

"What?" His voice becomes slightly more heated. "Y-y-you want to make any more baseless claims?"

"It's not baseless!" she shouts. If he wants evidence, she'll give it to him. "Answer me honestly, Charlie. You claim to be into me, *that* way?"

"What 'way'?"

"You tell me!"

"Romantically? Yeah. Other ways?" He glances pointedly down to his lap. "I thought that was obvious."

Her cheeks burn, but she won't let him throw her off from her line of questioning. "Well, doesn't that imply some sort of surface-level attraction to my body?"

A long pause. Charlie's eyes sharpen, and TJ knows what he's thinking. He recognizes a blatant leading question from a mile away. It doesn't matter whether he answers yes or no because TJ has a logical trap planned for both instances. After a long silence, Charlie simply says, "You don't understand just how attracted to you I am."

She lifts her arm and points to her underarm. "Do you think that's attractive?"

"I don't think it matters how I answer that question," he says, his voice hardening. "You're hell-bent on—"

"Just answer it! Is my armpit hair, objectively, pretty?"

"I don't know," he says, exasperated. "Is mine? It's just hair!"

"So you're saying you're into me . . . *despite* my body hair."

He drags his hands down his face. "Can you not twist my words?"

"I'm not. That's what you said." She points a triumphant finger at him. "You don't think it's attractive. Which means you think it's ugly."

"That is not even—" He stops and shakes his head. "You just want me to think that so you can be *right*. Fine. Say I do think it's ugly and disgusting and a huge turn-off," he says savagely, his words cruel and biting enough to make her flinch. "Say I think that. Then what? You still shouldn't care."

"Well, it's *wrong*, so of course I should!"

"No, you shouldn't!" he shouts, loud enough to make her balk. He rakes his hand through his messy hair and laughs, darkly. "You know, the fact that you think you have to *prove* you're worthy of respect in a *debate resolution* is pretty pathetic. Get it through your head. You can't control if people like Liam respect you. If someone wants to hate you, they're going to find a reason. The only thing you control is whether *you* respect yourself. And—and—and—and you clearly don't!"

She gapes, shocked as if he'd slapped her. Did he really just say that? "I'm done," she snaps. "*Done* with you."

He smiles without humour. "The feeling's mutual."

Now she really does feel like he slapped her. She whirls and grabs the doorknob. "Good!"

"Fine."

"Fine!" She slams the door shut behind her.

She stalks up the stairs, her heart thundering with rage and eyes burning with tears she doesn't understand. When she reemerges on deck, the bright sunlight almost has her recoiling. She'd forgotten it was still the middle of the day. She shields her eyes and, as her vision adjusts, notices people staring.

She drops her hand and ignores them all on her way off the boat.

TWENTY-ONE
***

The worst thing about dramatically running away is that she has to come back eventually.

When she gets a single text from Piper that Northridge's shuttle has arrived, she skulks back to the waiting area and joins the line, keeping her eyes trained on the ground, trying not to feel paranoid that people are staring.

She glances up and finds Angela Stevens hastily looking away. Okay, so she's not being paranoid. Of *course* everyone is talking about this. It's going to be hot gossip for ages.

She could kick herself. Was it really worth it to get back at Liam if she had to lose Charlie? If she'd known he still had feelings for her . . . but she had been so *sure*. She'd seen his discomfort as disgust that day in the library because that was the only reaction to her happy trail she could imagine. But apparently she was wrong.

It doesn't matter now. He said it himself—he's done. Not because she's hairy, but because she's a total bitch.

Chandani steps beside her, hip-checking a few people aside in the process. TJ braces herself for an interrogation, but she doesn't acknowledge her while they're in line. Once they get on the bus, though, Chandani drops into a seat at the front and pats the spot next to her. TJ gives her a confused look. Chandani raises her brow meaningfully at the bus driver, who's blaring his personal radio loudly.

It proves to be the right choice. Everyone else goes to the back of the bus, or as far back as they can get. But Piper clambers into the seat behind them, propping her chin on the top of the seat, apparently having disentangled herself from Jake for the sake of gossip. They're silent until the bus pulls onto the highway. Once the music and engine are loud enough to rattle their eardrums, Chandani speaks.

"He kissed you like he's done it before."

TJ swallows. Hard. "So you saw?"

"Of course I saw. I was looking for you. And there you were, taking my advice to jump Charlie Rosencrantz, except in broad daylight—"

"Shut up!" TJ casts an anxious glance around. Piper giggles.

"Everyone knows, TJ. It's not a secret anymore. Give us the details."

"It's not a— There was never any *secret*," TJ sputters. "We were never a thing. We'll never *be* a thing. He was being an asshole, just now."

"Right." Chandani sounds wholly unconvinced. "How so?"

"He told me to get some self-respect!" TJ hisses, then hesitates. It's time to come clean. Quietly, she relays the whole story, leaving nothing out, including the first kiss. Piper's eyes are round as saucers. Chandani looks, if possible, even more unimpressed.

"He's not wrong about you being pathetic. You messed up what sounds like the best makeout session of your life, and for what?"

TJ groans and sinks lower in her seat. A part of her is wondering the same thing. But even though it was perhaps a *slight* overreaction, there was a reason why TJ had to slam the door on him. Why she's always slamming the door on him.

She hesitates. And then it comes out in a rush: "I don't want to set unrealistic expectations for my love life. I just know there must be a part of him that doesn't like how I look. There's no way there isn't. And I can't handle the suspense of waiting until the day he proves it."

The look on Chandani's face is comical. Piper frowns. TJ shakes her head. Her greatest fear sounds so ridiculous out loud. "Never mind. It's over anyway."

Chandani snorts. "Don't you still have a debate with him?"

TJ shoots her a dirty look even though she's right. She picked a fight with Charlie at the worst time, with Nationals just weeks away. Hopefully things will cool down, but the anger etched in his face when she left doesn't seem likely to just disappear.

Guilt overcomes her again. She pulls out her phone and starts drafting a text to him. She agonizes over her wording for several minutes, not wanting to sound desperate or, on the opposite end, like she doesn't care at all. She shows the finished product to Chandani and Piper. **I'm sorry about what I did. Can we call a truce? For the debate?** When they nod, she hits send.

He never responds.

School starts again. Rumours fly in Northridge's halls about what happened with TJ and Charlie (some of which she kind of wishes were true). Although there are plenty of whispers and smirks, no one dares ask her about it directly. That makes TJ sort of glad for her bitchy reputation.

Then some other couple becomes the subject of school gossip, and her own little scandal becomes old news.

The next few weeks pass in a blur. The one benefit to being benched most of the time in soccer is she suddenly has much less responsibility, and more time for other things. With graduation looming, her class is in a frenzy to get every last school thing done; there's yearbook quotes to be submitted and gown fittings to be attended and outfits to be put together and RSVPs to be submitted and of course, somewhere in there, studying to do. Not to mention debate; Mrs. Scott recruits Ameera and Saad to help TJ practice as Nationals loom closer.

"I asked Simran, too, but she said she was busy," Mrs. Scott says at their first session. TJ almost snorts. Since their time debating together is over, they barely see each other, and when they do, Simran heads in the opposite direction. Maybe after years of their relationship being one-sided Simran is content to leave it in the past. It's a horrible thought.

As if determined to highlight all her failures, Mrs. Scott adds, "Is Charlie coming? I thought we agreed we should do more practices with both of you together."

Like that's going to happen. The last time she checked, her text to Charlie had gone from unread to read. The unspoken message is loud and clear—leave him alone. Maybe that will help cool things down so she can properly apologize at Nationals. "He's busy, but we're meeting outside of school to practice," TJ lies. Ameera and Saad say nothing, although they probably know she's full of it. Time for a subject change. "Um, can we brainstorm impromptu topics?"

"Of course," Mrs. Scott sniffs. "Current events are key, so let's take a look at the news."

Just what she needs. More homework.

Speaking of extra work, Mrs. Scott ropes the members of the debate club into helping prep for the tournament. There's a lot to do in hosting a huge event like Nationals. She and the others are constantly on the phone securing caterers, wrangling schedules, and booking hotels and buses. Because TJ's actually debating at Nationals, she's only given the relatively light task of finding volunteers for timekeeping. But even that is difficult.

Chandani offers up her little brother, who's in eighth grade, for the position.

TJ's skeptical. "Did you even ask him?"

"No, but I'll give him a swirlie if he doesn't."

Desperate for volunteers who aren't being threatened by their older sisters, TJ even attempts to recruit Rajan one lunchtime just over a week before Nationals.

He's already shaking his head. "It's a no from me."

"What else could you possibly have to do? Weekend detention isn't a thing."

He gives her a lazy grin from where he's lying across one of the benches in the foyer, hands tucked behind his head. He's so tall that his legs hang over the edge. "I have . . . social plans."

A date with his drug dealer, probably. "What if I let you cheat off one of my tests later?"

Rajan yawns theatrically, but before he can respond, someone calls TJ's name. She looks behind her, and there's Amy at the newspaper stand, restocking the special body-positivity edition and waving.

"These pamphlets run out so quickly. Isn't it great?" Amy says when TJ leaves Rajan's side to come over. Without waiting for an answer, she adds, "They're going to be distributed throughout the school district. I had to do some convincing to get Whitewater on board, though. Charlie can be so stubborn sometimes." Pause. "I guess that might have to do with you being on them."

So that's why TJ's been summoned. For gossip. "Why would you think that?" TJ asks evenly.

"Oh, well, everyone knows you two have history after the Spring Break trip," Amy says in an apologetic whisper. "But it didn't end well, did it? At least, that's the impression I got from Charlie at the district council meeting yesterday."

TJ knows she's being baited. But suddenly she has to know. "What'd he say?"

"Nothing. He flipped through the pamphlet and looked at your page for a really long time. Then tossed the whole thing back at me and said no." Amy watches her closely.

TJ keeps a poker face. Well. Charlie's angrier than she thought.

When she gives no response, Amy goes on. "I had to go around him and ask Whitewater's principal directly for approval. Charlie didn't like that, but that's fine. Personal feelings shouldn't get in the way of a good campaign." There's an annoyed undercurrent to her tone. Probably not the first time she and Charlie have clashed.

But for him to make a fuss over *this* . . . TJ doesn't want to think too much about it. Keenly aware Amy's still studying her, she busies herself picking up a pamphlet from the stand. EVERY BODY IS BEAUTIFUL, the title reads in a cute font. She's seen it many times now, but has never been able to stomach moving past the cover. Now, bracing herself, she flips it open.

She lands right on her own photo, positioned next to the text of her interview. The image has been put through a black-and-white filter that makes the hair on her face less obvious. Her head is tilted thoughtfully, neck long and graceful as a ballerina. Her skin gleams in a way TJ wishes it would in real life.

She flips a page, and there's the *no makeup* representative, a close-up of a tenth grader with curly hair blown into her face—by a fan, TJ recalls from the photo shoot. Her hair strategically hides the zit on her forehead. Her freckles are on full display, blue eyes wide and makeup free. She looks wild and delicate, a spirit from the wood.

It almost makes TJ smile to think about how the girl had been at the actual shoot, irritably pushing her hair out of her face between photos, sprawling in her chair and picking a poppy seed out of her teeth during her break. And the plus-size model: TJ had seen her breathe a sigh of relief after her shoot was done and she could take off tight shapewear.

The photos are gorgeous. But they're not very real.

TJ looks up at Amy, who's beaming, as if waiting for praise.

TJ hesitates. It doesn't feel right, sending this out to other schools. "Before we distribute these through the district, what if we revamped it? Made it even better?"

Amy's smile falters. "Oh? In what way?"

"Well"—TJ nods at the photos—"wouldn't these be more impactful if they showed the less pretty parts of ourselves? Because honestly they don't even really look like the people I saw at the photo shoot."

Amy looks down at it. "I'm a little lost, TJ. We were *trying* to make everyone look pretty. That's the point of the campaign. 'Every body is beautiful.'"

TJ closes the pamphlet. "I told you I wanted inner beauty to be emphasized if I was going to take part."

Amy shifts on her feet. "TJ, the project is over. I really do appreciate you being part of it, but I have to go to class. See you around, okay?" TJ opens her mouth to argue, but Amy's already walking away.

TJ throws the pamphlet back into the stack. Well, that went about as expected.

Rajan's still on the bench when she heads back, eyes closed and looking so relaxed she almost thinks he's asleep. At least until he says, "Maybe you should ask *Amy* to volunteer at your debate. Bet she'll do it if she can put it on her résumé."

TJ stops. He couldn't have heard that conversation; they were on the other side of the busy front foyer. "How do you know about that?"

"Simran auntie."

Of course. "*Simran auntie* does a lot of gossiping in your tutoring sessions, huh? What else did she say?" She's dying to know what Simran thinks of the campaign.

Rajan's eyes open. "Why don't you ask her yourself?" At TJ's hesitation, he nods. "Because you don't talk to her. Right."

She doesn't like his tone. The assumption there, which maybe hits a little too close to home. "I *would* ask her," she snaps. "But . . . she's mad at me right now."

"She said that?"

"Well, kind of." TJ crosses her arms. "She basically said I was a self-serving ass two months ago—"

"Damn, she just went right out and said it."

"—and we haven't really talked since," TJ finishes, choosing to ignore his comment. "Because every time I try, she runs off."

"Then give her a reason not to."

"What's that supposed to mean?"

The warning bell rings. Rajan winks at her and then closes his eyes. Clearly he's got no intention of going to class. Or of answering her question. Grinding her teeth, TJ spins on her heel and heads down the hall. What's he trying to say, anyway? That Simran's scared of her or something? That's ridiculous.

Except . . . TJ *did* blow up at her the last time they spoke, so maybe not.

She sighs. Rajan sure knows how to mess with her head.

Her dad picks her up that afternoon. "How was school?" He's just finished his shift, still in his wrinkled uniform and sporting a greying five-o'clock shadow.

"Okay." TJ climbs into the passenger seat. "Can we go to the mall?"

"Why, what do you want to buy?"

"A gift for Simran." She'd been thinking all afternoon of how she could send a message to her. A peace offering Simran can choose to take or not, the same thing TJ did with Charlie. And maybe like Charlie she'll ignore it, but at least then TJ will know for sure. "She's going to a music camp next week. She doesn't drink coffee, so I looked up some herbal teas that are good for singers. You know, for sore throats." She cuts off her rambling because her father's looking at her oddly.

"That's . . . thoughtful," he remarks as they pull out of the parking lot. "I didn't know you and Simran were that close." TJ winces, but he doesn't seem to notice. "I still remember the two of you butchering dolls when we did playdates. Barbie heads all over the floor. Gave me nightmares."

TJ smiles slightly at that. "Why'd you stop the playdates?"

A pause. "You got old enough to make your own friends."

TJ senses that's not the whole story. "Did it have anything to do with the fact that Mom and Masi ji can't stand each other?"

He slams the brakes a little harder than necessary at the stop sign. "Where'd you get that idea?" When TJ gives him a look, he sighs. "Okay, fine. But they're sisters. They just get on each other's nerves."

In the past, TJ had accepted this half-assed explanation, but now she crosses her arms. "About what?"

His eyes dart from the road to TJ and back. "Maybe you should ask your mother about this."

"I have. She always changes the subject." TJ sits up. "If you tell me, I promise I'll act like we never had this conversation."

He seems to consider. "Pinkie-swear?"

TJ solemnly extends her pinkie. Without looking away from the road, he links pinkies with her. Then he rests his hand back on the wheel. "Really, you already know why. Your aunt is so much older than your mother. She grew up in the village, but your mom grew up here. That's like being raised on two different planets." He chuckles to himself. "Which is why they never agree on anything. The friendliest I ever saw them was when you and Simran were born. Finally, some common ground."

"So what happened to that?"

His amusement fades as they turn into the mall. "You got older. And your mothers had very different ideas on how to raise a daughter."

TJ stares at him. "Are you saying it's about . . . me and Simran?"

"I'm saying that's probably part of it."

She has so many other questions. But she only asks, quietly, "Why didn't they ever work it out?"

He shrugs. "Maybe they think it would just fall apart again. Having a relationship with someone so different from you is a lot of work."

TJ nods glumly. She's starting to understand that feeling.

The next day, Friday, TJ finds Simran in her usual lunchtime haunt: the French classroom.

The room is loud and busy, a card-playing group clearly in a tense part of their game. Ms. Schwab appears too busy giggling with the principal to tell them off. TJ walks past them straight to Simran in her usual corner. She's got her head bent over a notebook, pen moving furiously. Probably doing last-minute homework for her afternoon classes.

She doesn't seem to notice TJ until she plunks the gift bag she'd bought on the desk. Then she looks up. Her eyes widen slightly.

TJ says, "Good luck for your music camp," very fast. She hovers on the edge of saying more, but hesitates. She and her father had taste-tested several teas before buying anything, but what if Simran hates them? TJ's only ever seen her drink chah.

And as for the travel mug she'd added, that was probably too much. It'll seem desperate. Like she's trying to buy Simran's friendship.

Simran looks at the bag. A second ticks by, then two. That's all TJ can take. She spins and leaves before her cousin can say anything. Whatever. Olive branch officially extended.

When Saturday comes, TJ busies herself with her weekend plans: last-minute Nationals prep. She wonders if Charlie feels as anxious as she does, but each time she thinks about texting him, she reminds herself to leave him be. Everything will be fine.

And everything *is* fine. Until Wednesday morning, when she walks into school and gets a text from Piper.

check Northridge Confessions.

Dread prickles up her neck. She stops in the middle of the hallway, people jostling her as they go by. Is she imagining it, or is that group of eleventh graders staring at her from their lockers?

She gives them a frosty look and makes a beeline for the washroom, the one people rarely use because it smells like mildew. It's empty, which is perfect. Once she's locked herself in a stall, she opens the Northridge Confessions Instagram on her phone.

Her stomach drops as soon as the page loads. There's another picture of her.

Well, two pictures. One is from the old meme, where she was the Hot One. TJ looks at her and doesn't feel connected to her at all.

Then there's the other photo. Someone must've taken it during Spring Break, when she was stretched out in a lawn chair in her swimsuit. It's . . . not flattering.

The caption: What it looks like when you buy it online vs when it arrives

She scrolls through the top comments. Need a refund STAT, this one's defective, says one. Is that even a girl???? says another, to which someone's replied, Bro that's a sasquatch.

It's still absolutely vile to read these comments. They're as bad as they were the first time about Simran. Most of them are even the same commenters.

She sighs and exits the app as the warning bell rings. This isn't anything new. It's just another step in a long journey, although the endpoint isn't entirely clear to her anymore.

Her phone buzzes again. Chandani, asking where she is. TJ answers, then leaves the stall. Just as she's drying her hands, Chandani bursts in, Piper in tow.

"Did you see?" she asks without preamble.

TJ doesn't bother pretending. "Yeah. So what? We're going to be late for class."

Chandani looks at Piper. "She didn't see."

"She didn't look?" Piper squeaks. She's clutching her phone with both hands. "Oh my god, she didn't look."

"Look at *what*?" TJ whips around, irritated. "I told you, I saw the post already."

"Show her, Piper," Chandani commands. When Piper doesn't move, Chandani snatches the phone out of her hand. "She deserves to know."

She shoves it in TJ's face.

TJ focuses on the screen. It's a list of all the likes on the post. Forty-nine of them so far. So what? They're all assholes, they—

Something catches her eye.

charlie_rosencrantzzz is listed.

Her eyes refuse to send the signal to her brain at first, and then her brain refuses to interpret the signal, so it takes several seconds of staring uncomprehendingly before it sinks in.

This has to be a mistake. She takes the phone from Chandani. Her friends are silent as she counts the number of *z*'s in the handle. Three, like always. She taps his username to make sure it's his account. It is. She refreshes the page to see if his like will go away. It doesn't.

No. No way. TJ's already shaking her head as she looks up. "He probably accidentally liked it."

Piper nods vigorously. "Yeah, maybe."

Her brain is going a million miles a minute. "He got hacked. Or he misread it."

"Are you even hearing yourself?" Chandani crosses her arms. "He *misread* it? It's a photo, bitch. And besides, I thought you were a debater. Shouldn't you be looking at the facts? Why are you making excuses instead of considering the simplest—"

"Because *he wouldn't do that*!" TJ's voice rises loud enough to make Piper flinch. She takes a breath, willing herself to calm. "He's not that kind of person, he's good, he's—"

"Isn't that what you thought about Liam?"

Chandani's words, said so coolly, slide between TJ's ribs like a knife. And she's not even done.

"Listen, TJ. In those last few weeks you were still dating

Liam, I had to listen to people talk about how stupid you must be for not seeing that he wasn't into you anymore. How desperate you acted. And when he broke up with you, how you were screaming your head off at him, completely losing it—"

"Shut up," TJ whispers.

"No, you need to hear this—"

"*Chandani,*" Piper says sharply.

There's a pause. TJ can't look up from the floor. She feels like she's choking.

When Chandani speaks again, her voice is unusually gentle. "I just don't want to see you get hurt like that again. Think about it, okay?"

Pity? From Chandani? That's it. "I'm going to class." TJ's voice sounds robotic.

She hands the phone back to Piper and brushes past them.

"TJ," Piper says, "Are you—"

"Leave me alone!"

They go silent as TJ storms out.

The hallways are empty. At some point the last bell had rung, but TJ hadn't noticed. She goes to her locker first. But as she opens it, she finds herself lingering on Chandani's words.

I thought you were a debater. Shouldn't you be looking at the facts?

Nausea roils her stomach. Well, here are the facts:

1. The last time she saw Charlie, he was furious with her.

2. He called her pathetic.

3. Said he was done with her.

4. Tossed away Amy's pamphlet after seeing her photo on it.

5. Ignored her feeble apology text.

And yet here she is, counting the *z*'s in his username like a loser.

But of course. At Spring Break, she had finally ripped away the rose-coloured glasses he was seeing her through. And he could finally fully appreciate her ugliness—both outside and in. All this time, she's been waiting for him to fail her impossible test, and he finally did. So why does it hurt so much?

You know why, a small voice whispers in her head.

Because in some twisted way, she'd started seeing Charlie as the judge in her personal debate. He certainly acted like one—listening without preconceived notions from the very beginning, open-minded when she ranted to him, logical when he evaluated her contentions. When he bought her arguments, she felt victorious. Validated. She was in the right, what she said was true, and her resolution *would* stand.

Except now he's clearly changed his vote. The judge she respected the most decided she was unworthy of respect.

It's so humiliating that everyone can see that he liked that post. After they *kissed*. She has to hand it to him, it's a masterful revenge.

Her vision blurs with tears. She tried everything. For months. God, how she wanted to prove her resolution. But she failed every time.

Maybe that's because there's no winning. Maybe she was just . . . wrong.

Mrs. Scott had once told the debate club that when tournament organizers brainstormed possible resolutions, they first made sure both sides had strong potential arguments. If it seemed too unethical or one-sided, they tossed it out. *Not everything can be argued*, she'd said. *Not everything* should *be*.

TJ looks into the mirror on her locker door. She stares at her almost-unibrow, her moustache, deep sideburns, and hairy chin, and suddenly hates them more than she's ever hated anything in her life. She wants to scrub it all off. She wants it gone and she wants a fresh, clean slate.

She wants to forget this all ever happened.

TWENTY-TWO
***

Her dad is the only one home when she arrives, not half an hour after she left. She tells him she has a bad stomachache. He doesn't question it, just spends the next several hours bringing mugs of saunf water to her bedroom.

TJ chokes them down, and by late afternoon announces she feels much better. Also, that she's taking the car to Piper's to get her homework.

And that's how TJ finds herself back at the waxing salon.

She's sure her eyes are red as she walks in, but the lady at the front desk smiles at her like always. TJ sits in the waiting area. Her phone buzzes relentlessly. She turns it off.

"TJ?" Lulu's voice drifts in from the hallway. Numbly, TJ rises to follow the sound to the appointment room.

Inside, Lulu's back is to her as she rinses her hands in the sink. "It's been such a long time since I last saw you. How've you been?"

TJ tries to say "fine" but can't seem to muster up the lie. Instead, she says, "I was hoping we could start with the full-face threading."

Lulu turns around. TJ tries to smile. She thinks she's doing a good job until Lulu speaks.

"What's wrong, darling?"

Her voice is soft. TJ's smile wavers. "Nothing."

Lulu sits next to her and puts her hand on TJ's shoulder. That's all it takes. TJ's vision swims with tears. "It's," she begins, shakily, "not nothing."

Maybe it's because she's at her breaking point, or maybe it's because she needs an adult who's not her parents, or maybe it's because Lulu's already seen the worst parts of her, literally. Whatever it is, as soon as Lulu sits next to her, the whole story pours out. From the meme that started it all, to what's brought her in today, TJ leaves nothing out. Somewhere in the middle, she starts crying and can't stop. Lulu silently passes her tissues.

When her words and tears have petered out, Lulu sighs, her black-painted lips pulled into a frown. "My girl. My lovely, foolish girl."

That wasn't quite the response TJ had been expecting. Lulu wraps her arm around TJ's shoulders.

"Let me tell you something. I have been in this business for nearly fifteen years, yes? Waxing, threading, laser, all that. My clients—my darlings"—she winks—"come from all walks of life. Women, men, nonbinary folks—of all racial backgrounds, all facing different kinds of expectations for body hair—and all having different things they actually want. Here, they can design themselves how they like, whether that means fitting into society's standards or their own. It's a joy helping them do that. Don't you think so?"

TJ nods slowly. It makes sense that Lulu would help people navigate that. All the same, though, she's somewhat lost the thread of this conversation. "Yeah, but, um . . . what does that have to do with me?"

"I'm getting there." Lulu tuts. "So impatient. Like I was saying, the world has these ludicrous expectations of how much
hair a man or woman is supposed to have. Hardly anyone fits
them naturally, but we feel the pressure to, don't we? Some
more than others." Her voice has become knowing. "Why do
you think you hate your hair so much? I have just listened to
you talk about it for ten minutes. You, like all the people who
have said unkind things about you, cannot reconcile your body
hair with your womanhood."

TJ blinks, opens her mouth, ready to deny it. That can't be
true. It can't be that simple.

But—she hesitates—can't it? Yes, she's observed gendered
hair expectations before—but she's never connected them to
herself. Maybe she should have. It *has* always felt like the hair
somehow made her look like less of a girl; and wasn't that what
the most hurtful comments said, too?

Lulu must see it dawning on her face, because she says, very
gently, "Hair has no gender, darling. It's just hair. Do what you
want with it, but it does not make you less of a woman. It does
not make you less interesting, less worthy, or less deserving of
desire. Understood?"

Frowning, TJ holds up her hands and examines the hair
growing on the knuckles. She tries to see them as feminine,
which of course they *are*—because they're hers.

But after so long seeing them as something else, it's hard.
She drops her hands. "I know, Lulu. Logically, I get what you
mean," she says desperately. "But it *just doesn't feel that way*.
I still can't help that I look at myself and feel like . . . I'm not
pretty. I'm not normal."

She whispers that last bit, that fear she has tried so hard to ignore. But Lulu only nods wisely. "Many of my clients feel that way. And it breaks my heart, darling, because after seeing so many different kinds of bodies, I know the truth."

"Which is?"

"Normal doesn't exist," Lulu says bluntly. "I've seen hair everywhere, on all kinds of people. Not only that, but I've seen every manner of skin condition, and lumps and bumps in places you couldn't even imagine. Sometimes I think I've seen it all. The truth of it is that humans are ugly little creatures by our own standards, and no one's immune to being human, although some of us try to hide it."

TJ thinks back to Amy's pamphlets and fights a laugh. "So . . . everybody is ugly?"

"So, so ugly. Trust me." Lulu beams. "Once you accept that, you can finally be free of those ridiculous expectations. And start seeing beauty in the things that really matter."

TJ smiles bitterly. "That would be so much easier to accept if other people did, too."

"Are you still thinking about *that boy*?" Lulu sniffs, although TJ isn't sure if she's talking about Liam or Charlie. "Forget him. Do you think you're the first person to come into my business afraid their partner won't like the way they look? I always tell them the same thing: I can sell you smooth legs, or coochie, or face. Whatever you like. But I don't sell lies. So listen to me, darling." She taps TJ's chin, making her look up. "You can't spend your life being afraid no one will love you if you are yourself. If you cannot be yourself with someone, that is not love. That is settling."

The words sink deep into TJ's chest. "You're right."

"Of course I am." Lulu reaches towards her desk and pops a lemon tart into her mouth. "Now, do you still want the threading? I've got everything ready."

TJ looks up at her. Lulu shrugs.

"What? I still have bills to pay."

When TJ gets back in her car, she adjusts her rearview mirror to look at herself out of habit. This would normally be when she admires Lulu's handiwork, but today she just sees her own facial hair, the same as she saw in her locker mirror earlier today. She looks for a long time, and then turns her gaze to her hand, to the hair on her knuckles and arm.

And for the first time . . . she doesn't hate it. She doesn't feel anything towards it, actually. Nothing positive, nothing negative, either. Her body is just that. A body.

It lasts only a moment, but it's magic.

She arrives home to the sound of clanking dishes from the kitchen. The living room is empty, but the lamp is on and the TV muted. She settles on the couch, rearranging the cushions, and tucks her feet under her. Then she turns her phone back on.

There are about a million texts and missed calls from Chandani and Piper. She sends them each a single message. I'm okay. It's only partly true. But it's what matters—she *will* be okay.

She scrolls through Northridge Confessions again. Charlie's username is still in the likes. So is Jake's, now that she's scrolling through. She wonders if Piper knows that. Or if it even matters.

But the comments section is different since the last time she checked. There are now more people reacting angrily to the post than there were a few months ago. Piper's one of them. Meanwhile, Chandani has personally replied to every nasty comment to rip them a new one. TJ grins. Maybe some things have changed after all.

"Feeling better?"

TJ jumps a little. She hadn't heard her father come into the living room, but there he is, slouching in the doorway, wearing a T-shirt and shorts and holding a steaming mug in his hand. He's looking at her expectantly.

It takes her a few seconds to remember her alleged stomach-ache. "Uh, yes. I'm great."

He smiles and raises his mug. "I told you saunf water works. Good thing, too. Isn't your tournament starting tomorrow?"

Tomorrow. That's when debaters from different provinces will arrive for Nationals, with plenty of sightseeing activities organized for them to tour the area. TJ shrugs. "I'm not partici-pating tomorrow. Friday and Saturday are the actual debates."

He sits next to her on the couch, propping his feet up on the coffee table. "Are you nervous?"

Of course she's nervous. It's *Nationals*. There are five rounds in this tournament; it will wrap up by Saturday afternoon. Then the scores will be tallied, and the top four teams will tackle one more round each—the finals—to determine the podium. The competition structure is about all TJ knows; the rest is out of her depth. Her only goal is not getting destroyed.

It must be written on her face, because her father nods. "I bet it's odd to do this tournament with a brand-new partner. You've been with Simran so long."

TJ blinks; she hadn't even thought about *that* angle. Early in her debate career, she did tournaments with different partners all the time. But Simran was the one that stuck. They just worked so well together, even though they were so different. No—they worked *because* they were different.

Her father asks, "What'd she say about your gift?"

"Nothing, yet." A pang goes through TJ. She misses Simran more than ever now.

He pats her leg. "Patience."

That strategy doesn't seem to be working for their moms, but TJ doesn't point that out. She just sighs and tips her head back. She's so used to debating with Simran that she hadn't, until now, considered what her dynamic with Charlie might be. It's one thing to work with someone in a practice; something else entirely in a tournament. After everything that's happened between them . . . how will it work?

"Do you want to practice your speeches?" her father asks.

TJ rolls her eyes. "Dad. We've gone over those a million times."

He pretends to be affronted. "So what? Come on, I'll pretend to be the opposition and ask you questions. This might be the last tournament I watch you in. We should make sure you're prepared."

That hits her like a train. The *last* tournament. The last one he'll watch, the last one he'll stay up late helping her with; the last debate experience her father will be part of with her. Her next ones will be half a country away at Western in Ontario. She'd accepted her offer there a few weeks back, partly *because* it was far away. She wanted to go somewhere new. But she's been avoiding thinking about how her life will change, because the truth is, the idea of her leaving home is terrifying.

And—she shoots her father a curious look, but he's taking a long sip from his mug—maybe she isn't the only one who feels that way.

So even though TJ doesn't need to practice, she nods. "I'll go get my cue cards."

TWENTY-THREE
***

Friday quietly rolls around. TJ has the day off from school for Nationals, but only if she partakes in the morning's social event . . . a hike.

So here she is, sitting on a rock along with everyone else who's made it to the summit already. She admires the view down on the valley, how tiny the city seems from here, and the waters of Okanagan Lake sparkling in the sun. The view almost makes the fact that her glutes are on fire worth it.

She spent the long hike chatting with debaters from the other provinces. Now she's winded from both exercise and conversation. She tucks her water bottle back in her bag and looks around. Some debaters are already headed on their way down.

Nate is among them—it takes her a second to recognize him with his hat and sunglasses. When he sees her, he sends her a sunny middle finger. She responds with two. He clutches at his chest and keels over like he's sustained a mortal injury. Other hikers step around him on their way down. Grinning, she gets up and walks over, giving him a light kick to the leg.

"Volunteering for the weekend?"

He lifts his sunglasses up into his hair. "Volun-*told*, more like. I've been directing people up trails all morning. But what really sealed the deal was the idea that I could watch you and Charlie embarrass yourselves in the debates."

Hearing his name takes the light edge off her mood. "I'm sure *Charlie* will."

"Oh, that's a given." But there's a question in his eyes. He wants to ask about them, she can tell. Luckily, at that moment an out-of-province debater walks up to them, looking at the VOLUNTEER sticker stuck on Nate's jacket, and asks him to take a photo.

Relieved, TJ leaves them to it and wanders off. Alone again. Idly, she checks her phone. Piper's sent her a selfie from the bus to Abbotsford with the rest of the soccer team, with the caption **Coach misses you :(.** TJ grins. Coach looks disgruntled to be captured in the photo, but that's about it.

She's so engrossed in typing a response that she nearly runs into someone. She halts, mouth opening to apologize—

It's Charlie.

He jerks back to avoid crashing into her, clearly also distracted. They stare at each other for a moment.

She hasn't seen him in weeks, and her treacherous eyes catalogue every detail. His hands are stuffed in the pockets of the same lightweight blue jacket he wears in his Instagram profile picture, and it's jarring to see him in mud-caked hiking boots, his brown hair spiked with sweat.

Then he says, "Hi."

She doesn't answer right away. How *is* she supposed to react to him now? Her common sense tells her to be disgusted. Her body strongly disagrees.

She ignores that and crosses her arms, offering a bland, "Hey."

Expressionless, Charlie looks past her, to the trail he was

headed down. "See you tonight." A sticky pause. "At the impromptu topic release, I mean."

She wonders if he knows she saw the Instagram post. Well, if he's not going to bring it up, she won't, either. No way is she giving him the satisfaction of getting to her.

Just then, someone throws an arm around Charlie's shoulders. Isaac Turner, seemingly appearing out of thin air.

"Well, well, well. If it isn't Kelowna's dynamic duo," Isaac drawls. "Hopefully we face each other this weekend."

"Hopefully," Charlie echoes with a smile. Most people probably wouldn't notice how strained it is, but TJ can tell. As if by instinct, her heart warms for him instantly. Maybe he didn't like the post, maybe it was a misunderstanding after all—

She shakes herself and reminds herself firmly of what Chandani told her. *Don't get hurt again.*

Isaac goes on. "I'm feeling nostalgic, Charlie. Remember when we used to hit up that bakery near Whitewater for the killer croissants? We should go there after this. For old times' sake." Charlie's silent. Isaac looks at TJ, then back at Charlie, and she knows from his smirk, right away, that he *knows*. "Your girlfriend can come, too."

TJ inhales sharply.

"*No*," Charlie says.

Isaac tilts his head. "No to what part? TJ doesn't have to come."

"To—to—to—"

"No to . . . ?" Isaac prompts. His eyes are laughing.

Despite the fact that Charlie has turned out to be a tool, TJ

TJ POWAR HAS SOMETHING TO PROVE

finds herself unamused. She speaks over Charlie's stuttering. "No to all of it, obviously, weirdo. Get lost."

She doesn't wait around for Isaac's response. She brushes past both of them and heads back to her ledge with the brilliant view of the lake.

Once sitting comfortably,facing the horizon, she takes a deep breath. She can't afford to feel anything about Charlie right now. Because if she does, it'll become anger. And if she gets angry, she'll get reckless. No way is she letting impulsivity get the best of her this time. Not with Nationals on the line.

Charlie is still her debate partner. And this weekend, whether she likes it or not, they have to be a team.

Later that day, TJ dons her freshly pressed white blouse and black slacks, wraps her hair into a bun at the nape of her neck, and picks out a pair of heels. She studies herself in the mirror. The look is just about perfect. Powerful in its simplicity. Her facial hair is clear as day.

In a burst of inspiration, she paints her mouth a deep, dark red. When she puts down the lipstick, the effect is dramatic. It draws attention to her mouth, and makes the hair above it stand out even more in contrast.

She smiles, and it feels revolutionary.

Her parents drop her off at the Northridge entrance before going to find parking. Today's the only day this weekend they got off work, and they wanted to spend it watching her debate. Even her mom, who normally doesn't take interest. TJ suspects she, like her father, is starting to get sentimental.

TJ walks through the double doors. To her surprise, the first person she runs into is *Rajan*, holding programmes. Someone has forced him to take off his hoodie, and it's strange seeing that he actually has a shape to his body rather than a vague baggy cloud around his middle.

"What the hell?" she demands. "You said you were busy this weekend!"

"I was busy until Simran Sahiba asked," Rajan says, popping his toothpick out of his mouth. Before TJ can give him a piece of her mind, Mrs. Scott's voice blares over.

"Rajan! You have to actually *give* people these programmes, you know, not just stand around and look pretty."

Rajan salutes and moves on. Mrs. Scott shakes her head as she walks up to TJ.

"I don't know what to do with that boy." She looks TJ over. "Ready? I'll be watching as many of your debates as I can. I can't wait."

Oh, great. TJ's stomach flips.

"You'd better get in line for registration," Mrs. Scott adds, her eyes shifting over TJ's head. "The Alberta group is here, I'd better go greet them . . ." She vanishes from TJ's side.

It's at this time that TJ spots Isaac and Jenna Turner signing in. She looks the other way, praying they won't see, or they won't interact.

No such luck. Jenna's sugar-sweet voice floats over.

"Fancy meeting you here."

TJ tears her eyes away from the wall to look into Jenna's. She doesn't bother forcing a smile. "Yes, well, this is my school."

"I meant more that you're here at Nationals. Someone must

have cancelled and given you their spot. Am I right?"

Jenna has got to know Simran was originally top debater in the region—everyone had the scoresheets, after all. She's just asking to make a point of it. TJ sets her jaw. "Yep."

"Aw, that's great! So nice that you got the opportunity!" Jenna smiles, big. "It's a cool experience. You'll see."

TJ's dentist would cry if they knew how much she's grinding her teeth right now. "Mhmm."

When she doesn't say more, Jenna shrugs. "Well, see you around!"

Once she's gone, TJ releases a relieved sigh. No comments today, although she'd been prepared for it. Maybe Jenna's done toying with her.

When she makes it to the front of the registration line, she finds Yara on the other side of the desk, smiling widely. "TJ!"

TJ smiles back—genuinely. "Hi, Yara. I didn't know you were doing registration today."

"Well, someone was sick, so I got pulled from the kitchen to help, and honestly, I'm still figuring it out. Uh, sign here. I'll get your itinerary and everything . . ."

She digs around in a large cardboard box while TJ writes her name and pronouns on a name tag. When Yara finally collects all the registration stuff, TJ tries to take it from her hands, but Yara keeps a firm grip. "I saw you talking with Jenna Turner."

"Yeah?" TJ mutters. "So?"

"So don't let her get to you." TJ blinks. Yara's voice is fierce. "You know she sees you as a threat, right?"

TJ snorts. "That's ridiculous. I've never gotten her scores at Provincials."

"Then why does she spend so much time trying to mess with you?"

TJ frowns. Someone coughs behind her. "Hey. The impromptu resolution is being announced in ten minutes."

Right. She's holding up the line. Yara lets her take her registration package with one last meaningful look. TJ shakes her head as she goes and descends the stairs in the direction of the gym, where folding chairs and tables have been set up to accommodate the hundred-something debaters, and a large stage is set up for announcements. She scans the room automatically, picking out people she knows from the crowd, and far more that she doesn't. All these unknowns from across the country packed into one room. This weekend should be interesting.

Of course, possibly the biggest unknown is the one she knows best. Charlie sits at a table alone. He's already watching her in his unabashed, clinical sort of way. Then he seems to dismiss her, glancing back down at the itinerary in front of him. She tamps down on the anger that again threatens to rise, steels herself, and marches over to slide into the seat next to his. Neither of them acknowledges the other, but he tugs at his bow tie as if it's strangling him. She hopes it is.

She opens her programme. Two impromptu-topic debates tonight, then three tomorrow for their prepared topic. Tonight they'll be facing teams from Ontario and Manitoba. Nobody they know. This is uncharted territory.

The speakers blare with the sound of a microphone being tapped.

Mr. York stands on the stage, waving. "Welcome to the Canadian Senior National Debate tournament. We're so happy

you're here and we can't wait for a weekend of great debates . . ."
He drones on for a bit with welcome words, and TJ zones out.
She only comes back when he says, "Be It Resolved That there
should be a mandatory retirement age."

As he speaks, the entire auditorium rises in volume as everyone madly scribbles it down. Furious whispering starts as Mr.
York adds, "You have thirty minutes to prepare before your first
round. You know the rules: No electronics, no conversations
with anyone but your debate partner. Good luck."

As he turns off the mic, there's a flurry of activity as debaters rise to find quieter spots to work. TJ and Charlie stay in
their seats, in unspoken agreement. TJ doesn't want to be in a
quieter spot alone with him anyway. Here, there's no chance for
personal talk.

Charlie draws a line down the center of his page. "I'll brainstorm contentions for one side and you can do the other. Then
we'll split them. Does that work for you?"

Usually in impromptu debates, she'd work with her partner
on contentions for each side, but this strategy guarantees mini-
mal interaction with him. "I'll take Side Negative."

He nods, and they bend their heads down to their respective notepads. The whispers of other teams around them only
make it more starkly clear how silent they are. How things have
changed.

Although, as she's working away, it strikes her how much
implicit trust there is in letting the other mold the entire argument for one of the sides. She tries not to think too much about
that.

Five minutes later, she sets down her pen. They share their

contentions, split them, and lapse into silence again to plan their speeches in the remaining minutes. With this time crunch, TJ writes bullet points only. The finer details will be made up on the spot. While she's thinking, she side-eyes Charlie, who's been staring at his page as well. Then all at once he starts furiously scribbling. He's probably just thought of a good point. She wonders if he'd tell it to her if she asked. But no. She'll find out at the debate, just like everyone else.

She ignores the pang in her stomach and bends over her notes again. When the clock shows five minutes till showtime, they gather up their things wordlessly and head to their assigned classroom, to their first debate and the rest of the evening.

They emerge from their second round only to be cornered by Mrs. Scott. "We need to talk," she says, and beckons them to an empty classroom.

Uh-oh.

As TJ and Charlie follow her in, she closes the door and says, "What's going on? This isn't working."

TJ frowns. "You realize we won, right?" There was an electric energy in the room back there. Every time Charlie drove home a point, she felt the need to one-up him. She imagined the judges thinking, *He's good*, and resolved to make them think, *She's better*. The result was a terrifying, aggressive debating style that did them strangely well.

"You were good," Mrs. Scott agrees. "But you weren't *great*. You had every opportunity to blow them out of the water and you didn't."

TJ waits for more, but there isn't. Charlie sips from a juice box, an odd contrast with his tailored waistcoat and bow tie. "So . . . how do you suggest we do that?"

"Get over yourselves," Mrs. Scott says bluntly. "I know you both want to do well. And to do that, you need to actually communicate. I thought I told you two to work out your issues *before* Nationals. Act like a team."

"We *are*," TJ says hotly. "It's not like we ever contradicted each other."

"Are you two familiar with British Parliamentary Style debating?" Mrs. Scott arches a brow. "It's what university teams do. Four teams total are in the debate, with two teams per side. Sure, they never contradict each other, but the two teams don't interact much, and they don't come to each other's aid. Because they're still competing. And that's how you two are acting. Like two separate teams, arguing for the same side."

TJ scowls, but suddenly she's re-evaluating. In that first round, they'd been Side Affirmative. She was first speaker, and so her contentions had been rebutted thoroughly by the other side throughout the debate. Charlie hadn't bothered re-defending many of her points when his turn came, even though he could have.

In the next round, TJ had thought of a good counterpoint to their opposition's plan, but she hadn't given it to Charlie for his final rebuttal—and so it went unchallenged.

They didn't even write notes to each other during the debate. She couldn't figure out what he was thinking, or where his speeches were going until he got there. She may as well have been another member of the audience instead of his partner.

Mrs. Scott must see the epiphany dawning on her face. "See? The style you're using might win you these debates, but it won't get your scores high enough for finals."

Finals. TJ blinks. "Who said anything about finals?"

"I did."

Even Charlie lowers his juice box at that.

TJ waits for Mrs. Scott to say sike. She doesn't. "You think we could make it that far? We're not even the best debaters in BC, let alone all of Canada."

"That's not necessarily true," Mrs. Scott says. "Provincials scores are . . . Well. We all know judges aren't totally impartial in how they mark. Whether they realize it or not. They're used to the debating style they see most often, so they tend to reward that. Which has consequences."

"Are you saying there's maybe a tiny bit of judging bias?" Charlie asks wryly.

Mrs. Scott points at him. "You said it, not me." Wow. If Simran ever talks to TJ again, she'll have to rub this in her face. "My point is, Nationals tends to shake things up. The judges are different, the style is different, the competitors are different. You have the chance to prove yourself on a fresh playing field. If you can stop trying to one-up each other, that is." She heads to the door, opening it. "Come on. Your parents are waiting to congratulate you."

She ushers them out. TJ doesn't have time to fully digest her words, or even look at Charlie to see what he's thinking, before she's swarmed by her parents.

"That was great," her dad says. He's wearing a rumpled tie

for this occasion, a rare sight. "I never thought you and"—he glances in Charlie's direction, where he's several feet away with his mother, and lowers his voice—"what was his name, again?"

TJ smiles, pleased. Her mother elbows him with a frown.

"Why can't you remember anything? That's *Charlie*."

Charlie and his mother look over at the sound of his name. TJ's mom waves them closer. "We were just telling TJ, you two make a good team." She elbows TJ's father again. "Right?"

TJ's father, who gets shy around people he doesn't know, nods jerkily and extends a hand to Charlie. "Yes. Good job."

"Thank you," Charlie says with an easy smile, and shakes her father's offered hand. TJ starts to sweat. Every instinct in her brown-girl body screams for her to escape this situation.

Charlie's mom, meanwhile, pats TJ's back. "You always give my son a run for his money," she says warmly. "I like seeing you together."

This is hell. "Thanks. I'm really tired," TJ says quickly, looking to her parents. "Early morning tomorrow. Can we go?"

Thankfully, their parents agree. While they're bidding quick goodbyes, TJ makes eye contact with Charlie. His face is unreadable. She can't tell what he's thinking. Does he agree with Mrs. Scott?

He doesn't break her stare. TJ wonders suddenly if he's searching her expression for the same thing she is. But then the goodbyes are over, so TJ turns away from him and falls in step with her parents. As they head to the exit, her dad side-hugs her. "Too bad we can't watch tomorrow." He winks. "Don't worry, I'm sure even without me there, you'll win."

TJ rolls her eyes even though there's a lump in her throat. He's always been invested in her debate career, helping her with speeches, brainstorming, and research. Of course he wants her to get to finals; of course he believes she can do it.

And now so does she. TJ may have her issues with Charlie, but if Mrs. Scott thinks this is the way, well, she's never been wrong before.

Which means . . . it's time to make nice.

The next morning, TJ arrives early to their first-round classroom. The three rounds today are for the prepared resolution, the one everyone has had months to research: *THBT it is sometimes right for the government to restrict freedom of speech.* Charlie sits down next to her without comment, flipping open his notepad.

Being the bigger person is not TJ's forte, but she'll try. She pushes her plate at Charlie as the timekeeper finally enters the room. "Muffin?"

He looks at the plate of breakfast food she's brought from the refreshments table.

She points to one of the muffins. "It's blueberry." That's always the one he chooses in any given breakfast spread.

"Are you trying to give me food poisoning?"

"These are fresh, dickhead."

A beat. Then he takes it. Accepting the truce.

"I was thinking," he says, peeling the muffin liner away, "about our plan for this side. There's a hole in it."

TJ blinks at that, and listens while tapping her pen against

her lips, growing more and more glad she offered him the muffin. She's first speaker and was going to present the plan. He
could've held on to this mistake. Could've let the other team—
two girls from Alberta—poke holes in it, then swoop in as second
speaker to clarify everything, making himself look good. And he
was going to do it. Right until she extended the olive branch.

A dick move, really. But one she would probably make herself. "So," she says casually, scratching things out of her speech,
"we agree that Mrs. Scott was right yesterday?"

"Yeah." Charlie shrugs, voice even. "There's only one way to
win. Together."

The idea chafes against her instincts. Normally, for her to
win, Charlie has to lose. That's been the nature of their relationship for years. But not anymore. She nods, just as the Speaker
calls the debate to order.

TJ stands to present. She delivers her speech without a hitch,
revising where Charlie suggested, and easily fields a few questions. Then the first speaker from Side Opposition starts, and
another point occurs to TJ that she wishes she'd brought up.
She scribbles it on a cue card and pushes it to Charlie.

He reads it. Raises his eyes to hers. She meets his gaze
squarely, knowing he's trying to figure out her motive. It's a
good contention—she can't use it, since her speech is over. He
can, though. It'll give him more points, but it'll strengthen their
team standing.

Finally, he nods. And something between them clicks into
place.

It's the first of many notes they slip each other. Questions, last-minute ideas, and changes to their arguments as their opponents shift the ground under their feet. Half the time, when they stand in unison to ask a question and Charlie gets chosen to speak, he asks the same thing she was thinking. The other half, he asks something that never crossed her mind.

And so, they add another win to their record. And then, in the next round, another.

In their last round of the day, Charlie's pen runs out of ink; TJ puts hers on the table, and they share that one pen between them, writing notes on the same piece of paper, thoughts running together, for the rest of the debate. They still win it. In fact—TJ suspects it was their strongest showing yet.

Mrs. Scott finds her after lunch, in the quiet lull of the aftermath. Everyone's still waiting for results, and TJ's sitting on the stairs with Ameera, who's telling her some of the drama she overheard from other debaters while volunteering in the break room. Mrs. Scott stops in front of them. "TJ, a word?"

A second word in twenty-four hours? TJ exchanges a look with Ameera and gets up to follow her teacher. "What's up?"

"Good job," Mrs. Scott says. Whoa.

"Uh . . . thanks."

"Don't tell anyone this, but I have it on good authority you and Charlie made it into finals."

TJ stares. "You're joking."

"Not at all." Mrs. Scott seems to enjoy her shock. "We're not talking bronze here—we're talking first place."

TJ leans against the wall, dazed. Mrs. Scott adds, "The third-place round will be in an hour. It might be fun to watch. Or rest, if you need to. Yours will be at the banquet."

"The *banquet*?"

"It's entertainment for everyone while certificates are printed." Mrs. Scott's phone buzzes. She looks down at it and frowns. "Saad's got a spreadsheet crisis going on in the results room. You'll have to excuse me."

As Mrs. Scott starts to walk away, another thought occurs to TJ. She calls after her. "Wait. Who are we up against?"

"Oh, right." Mrs. Scott half turns around, an afterthought. "A pair from Vancouver, who used to live here. You probably remember them: Jenna and Isaac Turner?"

TWENTY-FOUR
***

"A re you worried?" Yara asks at the banquet. TJ pauses in reapplying her lipstick to shrug.

"No, actually. I'm good."

"Really?" Yara sits back, doubt lacing her voice. The third-place debate finished two hours ago; the last event of the weekend is taking place here, at a local hotel. TJ, Yara, and a few other Northridgers have taken a table together, waiting for the final resolution to be announced. "Well, good luck anyway."

"Thanks," TJ says. Once Yara's attention is turned by someone else at the table, she drops the fake smile.

She glances at Charlie, halfway across the ballroom. Like her, he's spending the remaining time with people from his school. Mrs. Scott told him the news, too, but he seems perfectly calm. Chatting away. Then again, he's not the one who got *obliterated* the last time he faced the Turners.

TJ snaps her mirror shut, feeling ill. If only she could talk to Simran. She was there the last time; she'd understand. But Simran's not here, and besides, TJ doesn't have the right to unload her problems on her anymore. Simran still hasn't responded to the olive branch.

At the front of the room, Mr. York taps the mic. This is it.

"Welcome to the final round of the Senior Canadian Nationals," he says grandly. "The two teams facing off tonight will have thirty minutes to prepare and will debate in Canadian National Style. Are you ready for the resolution?"

TJ pulls her notebook towards her and clicks her pen. Mr. York unfolds a sheet of paper.

"This House Believes That inner beauty is more important than outer beauty."

TJ's fingers pause midway through writing, and it takes her brain a little longer to catch up.

Murmurs begin to rise in the room, and her face grows hot. What the hell?

Yara shifts in the seat beside her. TJ knows she's thinking the same thing: This is too much of a damn coincidence. She looks up, seeking out Mrs. Scott.

Her debate coach is standing at the back of the stage, staring straight at her. Like she's trying to tell her something.

The resolutions are prepared ahead of time by a team of debate organizers, but Mrs. Scott would be the only one who could've suggested this. She knew about all the taunts and Amy's campaign and everything that went down this year.

TJ should've seen it coming. Mrs. Scott even warned her that the impromptu topics would be related to something current. TJ just assumed it would be something related to the news or something—not a current event in their *school*. And she has to know TJ was involved. What is she thinking? Why would she do this?

TJ suddenly notices the other Northridgers turning her way, gauging her reaction to the topic. She forces her expression into stillness.

Mr. York goes on, putting his hand into a jar with two slips in it. "Side Proposition will be . . ."

TJ sits up straighter. *Us. Let it be us.* She's spent the whole year, really, preparing to debate that.

Mr. York draws a slip. "Isaac Turner and Jenna Turner. Leaving Side Opposition to Charlie Rosencrantz and TJ Powar."

No. No, no, no.

Mr. York goes on to announce the rules, and a volunteer motions for TJ to follow her. TJ rises numbly. Her head's full of a screeching noise that doesn't allow any other thoughts in. She barely feels the eyes on her, barely notices Charlie joining her.

The volunteer takes them down the hotel hallway, then opens a door to a boardroom. "You can prepare in here."

Inside is a long table with office chairs clustered around it, a flat-screen TV, and not much else. TJ sinks into a chair. Charlie follows a moment later.

"Good luck," the volunteer says with a bright smile on her way out. TJ doesn't return it.

"Thank you," Charlie says after a lengthy pause, even though it was clear she was talking to TJ. The door shuts.

TJ watches Charlie scribble *Outer beauty is as or more important than inner beauty*, their assigned stance, on his notepad. Her head starts to pound. This is like one of those dreams where you're talking in front of an audience and your pants drop, except worse. She's about to be *humiliated* in front of her whole school and debate community. "We're screwed," she says to herself more than to him.

Charlie replies anyway. "We can do this."

"Did you even hear that resolution? And the *Turners* got

Side Proposition!" She still can't believe it. Jenna's going to be insufferable.

Charlie gives her a look. "So what? We've all had to argue sides we didn't like before." He reaches into his bag to retrieve his Oxford dictionary. He flips through it. "'Beauty: A combination of qualities such as shape, colour, or form, that pleases the aesthetic senses, especially the sight.' That's actually not bad."

"As if *they're* going to use that definition," TJ retorts. "They're just going to say beauty means 'pleasing qualities' or something vague that can apply to personality traits, too." They could counter it, but at some point the parties have to agree on definitions, and the judges usually prefer the vaguest one to allow more clash. Besides, it just makes Side Opposition look bad if they keep resisting reasonable definitions.

"That's fine," Charlie says. "Let them pick the battlefield. We'll adapt."

TJ scoffs. "I think we'd have better luck winning if you chucked your dictionary at their heads and knocked them out."

Charlie snaps the book shut. "If you'd stop feeling sorry for yourself for one minute, you'd realize we have some great angles to work this resolution from."

TJ knows she's being annoying but can't stop. Besides, she is definitely not in the mood to be condescended to by *him*. "Of course *you* think it has great angles."

He gives her an irritated look. "What are you even talking about?"

"Never mind!" TJ snaps, highly aware of the ticking clock. "Let's just get this over with."

And they both bend over their own notes, resentment

fogging the air between them. It's as if their truce earlier never happened. Their words to each other over the next twenty minutes are clipped. They decide who will be first speaker (Charlie) and who will give the closing argument (TJ), quickly splitting contentions. It's bad. TJ knows it's bad. But not even the prospect of losing is stopping her pride now. They're going to lose anyway. The only question is how badly.

There's a knock on the door. TJ glances at the clock. They still have ten minutes. What—

The door opens, and a middle-aged woman with curly brown hair and steely eyes steps through. TJ recognizes her from the opening remarks; she'd been introduced as one of the tournament organizers from the national debate association.

"Hello," she says. "I'm Mrs. Grayson. We need to speak with Charlie Rosencrantz."

"What's going on?" TJ asks, as several other organizers filter inside. "We have a debate in ten minutes."

"It's being delayed until we sort this out. A rule violation has to be addressed."

TJ glances at Charlie. He looks just as confused. Something's not right. "Where's Mrs. Scott?"

Mrs. Grayson sits in one of the office chairs. "For unbiased assessment of this issue, both your debate coaches have been left out of the process. They're aware. Ms. Powar, you can leave. This is about Charlie."

Charlie? Violating tournament rules? TJ frowns. That doesn't seem likely. "He's my partner. Whatever's happening with him affects me. I'm staying."

And she leans back, crossing her arms. Mrs. Grayson doesn't seem impressed.

"This is to protect his privacy while we investigate. You'll get another debate partner if need be. And a new topic. There's no need to worry."

Another *partner*? TJ opens her mouth, but before she can speak, Charlie says, "TJ can stay. I don't have anything to hide."

Mrs. Grayson gives him a skeptical look and shrugs, directing her next questions at him. "Were you aware of the tournament rules and regulations? They're standard. One of the clauses is: No public slander of your opponents before debates."

"And I haven't done that."

"We've been tipped off that you did. On social media." Silence. She adds, "Instagram."

Charlie's answer is immediate. "I haven't used my Instagram in months."

TJ looks at him sharply. What?

Mrs. Grayson appears to have similar thoughts. "Then why is there activity from this morning?"

"There can't be. How would you know?"

"I can't disclose my source. But here." She slides over a phone. Charlie leans over it. Distracted, TJ leans with him. She has to see for herself if he's lying right now.

It's a post on Isaac Turner's account, a photo at the summit of their earlier hike with the caption At Canadian National Debate. Can't wait to argue with some of the best this weekend!

Mrs. Grayson scrolls down to a comment by none other than charlie_rosencrantzzz. Some of the best? Idk about that lol

TJ's struck with the urge to laugh. This is fake. She's sure of it. Even *if* he was going to say something that cringey, Charlie Rosencrantz would never be caught dead using acronyms online.

And if *this* is fake . . .

Wait.

Charlie says slowly, "I lost my phone recently. I couldn't find it, but . . . maybe someone took it."

"*When?*" TJ bursts.

Everyone in the room looks at her. Charlie replies, "The end of our Spring Break trip."

"So you didn't like that post?"

He gives her an odd look. "What?"

TJ exhales shakily. So that means . . . that means . . .

No, no, no. She's not allowed to change her mind about him again. It's safer to stay firmly in the world where she has a reason to hate Charlie.

Except she can't. She can practically feel her heart singing, *He didn't like that post!* And she can't shut it up. All she can do is stare at him, until she starts noticing little details she didn't see before. The shadows under his eyes. His ever-so-slightly crooked tie. His fingers, smudged with ink. And . . . trembling, very slightly where they rest on the table.

"Forgive me if I don't find this convincing," Mrs. Grayson says dryly. "We take these kinds of comments very seriously."

TJ wheels on her, her determination to prove Charlie's innocence even stronger now. "Who was the accuser, anyway?"

"Like I said, that's private."

"It's okay," Charlie says quietly. "I al-al-al-already know who."

He shuts his mouth after stuttering. Mrs. Grayson gives him a curious look. TJ, however, feels like she's been whacked over the head with a realization.

Isaac Turner, that tool—all this time she thought the Turners were going to mess with *her*. But they've decided to mess with Charlie instead.

But Isaac wasn't at the Whitewater Spring Break trip. So how could that have happened?

"Let me call my cell phone provider," Charlie says suddenly. "They'll be able to confirm that I got a new phone. Could that work as evidence?"

Mrs. Grayson blinks a few times. "I suppose—it could."

Charlie takes the phone and starts dialing. His expression is calm, but his hands are still trembling. He hates talking on the phone. This is going to shake him. *All* of this is. As Isaac knew it would.

TJ excuses herself from the room because she's starting to see red.

Outside, she stops short. Nate is leaning against the wall. He pushes off when he sees her. "What's going on? Everyone's waiting for the debate to start."

"Charlie's being interrogated," she says angrily. "And I'm pretty sure Isaac had something to do with it." And because she's pissed, she tells him the whole story. Nate's eyebrows climb higher with each word.

"Wow," he says when she's done. "Well, doesn't surprise me. Isaac has it out for Charlie."

TJ crosses her arms. "I wish I understood why. But Charlie doesn't talk about it."

"Wait, you don't know?"

TJ gawks at him. "Are you saying *you* do? You're not even in their year."

"So what? Even eighth graders at Whitewater know this one." Nate spreads his hands dramatically. "The Day Charlie Rosencrantz Snapped."

TJ leans in. "Snapped? How?"

Nate puts a finger on her forehead to push her back. "Patience. You need the backstory to fully appreciate it." TJ resists the urge to throttle him. "Charlie and Isaac used to be friends. But in high school Isaac got obsessed with his university applications and started looking out for number one."

Sounds like someone else TJ knows.

"Charlie rolled with it. So he didn't say anything when Isaac started using his ideas to move up school council. Charlie was still in some shitty notetaker position when Isaac became student president. And in debate, during their Junior Nationals qualifying season, I hear Isaac took the best contentions without asking and Charlie had to slap together arguments at the last minute. Stuff like that. And then Isaac announced he was moving away, so the president position opened up. Isaac decided to help Brandon Fletcher with his campaign instead of Charlie."

"Why? How did that help his résumé?"

"Word on the street has it, Fletcher's dad was on a scholarship committee. Isaac was trying to suck up. Even if it meant giving a big public middle finger to his best friend. It's not like Charlie ever cared anyway. Famous last words, if you ask me."

"Get to the *point*."

"This is where the story gets murky," Nate warns. He pauses

dramatically. "There was a student council lunch the day before the election where Charlie confronted Isaac. No one knows exactly what tipped him over. But depending on who you ask, he either told Isaac to go to hell, broke one of his trophies in the foyer display, or, in my favourite version, shoved him into a chocolate fondue fountain. Whatever it was, Charlie got his one and only detention, and Isaac's still butthurt about it."

Wow. TJ rubs her temples. "And then Charlie won the election anyway."

"Yeah, and Brandon Fletcher's a sore loser. I bet he stole Charlie's phone for Isaac." Nate sighs contentedly. "Don't you just love high school drama?"

The boardroom door opens. Mrs. Grayson pokes her head out, looking disgruntled. TJ and Nate straighten, waiting with bated breath until she speaks.

"The debate will go on as planned."

They're given ten more minutes to prepare.

TJ closes the door behind her after everyone files out. Charlie's still sitting in the same place, elbows on his knees, staring at the floor. He doesn't look up when she comes in.

She sits next to him, unsure what to say. "Should we go over our—"

"He did this to get to me," Charlie says. "And it worked."

Her heart plummets at the bleakness in his voice. "Charlie. Don't say that." If *he's* not ready for this debate that will surely be a disaster, how can she be?

"I should've known," Charlie mutters. "This is what he does."

TJ's had enough. "Then *why* did you put up with it, Charlie?"

she bursts. "Why were you friends with him for so long?"

"Because he was my *best* friend," he retorts, finally looking up to glare at her. "He's in every childhood memory I have. But he—he—he—he changed, and I didn't know how to let him go. I kept hoping things would go back to how they were. I could excuse everything he did. Ev-ev-ev—" He makes a frustrated sound and abandons whatever phrasing he was going to use. "There was this school election. You remember Fletcher—?"

"Yes," TJ says hurriedly. "Isaac backed him instead of you? And that pissed you off?"

"No. I—I—I already knew he was going to back Fletcher. I just told myself he needed more help than I did. It wouldn't affect the outcome. But . . ."

"Something happened," TJ prods.

"Yeah. There was a luncheon." His jaw works for a second. "I didn't know about it until the last minute, although apparently everyone else on council did. I'm pretty sure Isaac wouldn't have said it if he knew I was there."

"What'd he say?" She wants to cover her ears, almost. Hearing what hurt Charlie will almost certainly hurt her.

There's a long pause. She thinks maybe, like before, he won't tell her.

But then he smiles grimly. "I only heard the tail end of it. 'At least Brandon can speak in full sentences.' Funny, right?"

TJ's speechless for a second. Now she gets why Charlie got detention for however he reacted. TJ's pretty sure *she* would have landed a suspension. "Please tell me you actually dunked him in the chocolate fountain."

Charlie gives her an odd look. "What?"

"Um, never mind. You were saying?"

He returns to staring at his hands. "Well, I lost my temper. Said some things I regret, and—"

"Why would you regret it?" TJ demands. "He's just pissed you didn't stay his doormat."

"I regret it because every time I think he's going to let it go, he does something else to remind me he hasn't. And the thing is, he knows everything about me. He knows how to trip me up. W-w-w-when that happens, I'm done." He waves a hand irritably and takes a deep breath before speaking again. "I'm already stuttering. I can't do that onstage."

"Why not?"

A pause. His voice changes, less conversational, now crisp and controlled. "It makes me sound incompetent."

Wow, okay. TJ stares at him. "I thought you didn't care what people think."

"I care what some people think."

There's something weighted to his words that, while TJ doesn't totally understand, she grasps enough to know intuitively that her next words are very important. "So you have a stutter. So what? It's got nothing to do with your level of competence. And if anyone thinks differently, screw them. Screw *anyone* who tries to tell us we're less than they are." She jabs her finger at him fiercely. "No more apologizing for who we are or for things we can't help. The only thing that matters is whether we can debate—and we are *damn* good debaters."

She falls silent, strangely out of breath, her cheeks hot. Charlie doesn't say anything for a few moments. Then he meets her eyes.

"I'm going to miss debating with you."

TJ, caught off guard, drops her hand. She hadn't expected him to say that, but now he's left an ache in her chest. She's going to miss him, too. It's funny how much her feelings towards him have changed in the course of an hour.

But she has to make sure. "So you really haven't used your Instagram all this time?" He shakes his head. "Did you seriously never change your account password?"

"Why would I? I thought I dropped my phone in the ocean. I didn't think it got *stolen*."

"Why would you have dropped it into the ocean?"

"I was . . . distracted."

His voice is wry. Oh. Heat blooms on her cheeks as she very vividly revisits the moment she joined Charlie at the railing of the boat, when he'd set down his phone.

When she'd basically ordered him to kiss her. She blushes at the memory, and then she remembers him saying she glows when she blushes, and she blushes harder. *Get a grip, TJ.* But it's so difficult when he's looking at her like that.

Her heart makes a dizzying lurch when his eyes drop to her mouth.

But then he says, "What post were you talking about earlier?"

He may as well have dunked her in ice water. She grabs her notebook. "I don't know what you mean. Come on, let's go over our contentions—"

"When Mrs. Grayson was here, you said I liked some Instagram post."

"We only have a few minutes left, Charlie—"

"What was it? I can tell it's bothering you."

TJ grinds her teeth. She's forgotten how annoying his questioning can be. But it's too embarrassing to admit now. "It's *not* bothering me."

"Sure," Charlie replies condescendingly. "But don't I deserve to know what else Isaac did on my Instagram?"

He's not going to let this go. She wishes she had her phone to show him. Then she wouldn't have to say it. "You liked a post. It was a shitty joke about me. No big deal, it won't hurt your reputation, I'm sure you can unlike it, I bet no one noticed."

She says it all very fast, as if that will make it less humiliating. A pause. Charlie has gone very still.

"I liked a post?" From his voice she can tell he knows exactly what kind of post. "And you thought it was *me*?"

Awkward. Her hesitation is too obvious. His eyes narrow.

"H-h-how could you think"—he takes a breath—"after everything, why would I do that?"

She didn't think she'd have a response to that, but the words are there, whispered, dripping from the cracks in her heart: "To hurt me."

Charlie actually flinches. "God, TJ. Why would you think that?"

"Because I hurt *you*." Especially with the spectacle during Spring Break. She put him in an awful position. "I used you."

He's quiet for a long moment.

"Yes," he says. "You did."

The confirmation hits her like a blow, but she takes it and

nods. Charlie's never been one to shy away from her rough edges. "I'm sorry—" she begins, but he cuts her off.

"I still wouldn't do something like that. Not to you, not to anybody. You have to know that." His eyes grow warm. "And whatever you did is already forgiven."

And because she knows him to be honest, she exhales in relief.

The door opens. It's the same volunteer that let them in. "We're starting." She remains in the doorway, waiting for them. Their ten minutes of extra prep time are clearly up. TJ wonders if they screwed themselves over by not using it to fix their case.

Charlie tucks his notepad into his bag. "Ready to go one last round, my *esteemed* partner?"

One last round.

After this—it's over. No more brainstorming sessions, no more antics, no more practice debates or Word Salad games, or weekend trips to tournaments with the club. No more Charlie.

He's waiting for a response, so she smiles through the bittersweet weight in her chest. "Ready if you are, my *valued* colleague."

He nods with a smile, and she gets the feeling they spent their ten minutes exactly as they should have. When he stands, so does she, and they follow the volunteer into the hallway, footsteps in unison. TJ's so busy wondering if she's matching him or he's matching her that she almost misses his last comment.

"By the way, TJ, don't believe everything you hear." Charlie adjusts his cuff links. "It was cheese, not chocolate."

TWENTY-FIVE
***

There's a steady buzz of conversation in the ballroom when they arrive. News of the delay has clearly spread fast. Maybe even the rest of the drama. There are so many layers to this debate.

TJ and Charlie head to the stage, where two cloth-covered tables sit, facing each other at a slight angle. When TJ takes her seat, she notes the judges' tables; four of them, closest to the stage. In the center is the Speaker's table. Beside it, the time-keeper's chair. Rajan is sitting in it. Really? They couldn't find anyone else for the job?

Jenna and Isaac are whispering to each other as the Speaker calls the debate to order. They don't even glance TJ and Charlie's way, they're so focused. Oh boy.

The resolution is announced to the crowd. TJ knows the Speaker script so well she can practically mouth along the words: *Welcome to the final round of the Canadian Senior Nationals Debate tournament. The resolution is: This House Believes That inner beauty is more important than outer beauty. On Side Proposition, Isaac and Jenna Turner will be arguing in favour. On Side Opposition, Charles Rosencrantz and Tejindar Powar will be arguing against. Each speaker will have seven minutes to present their case, with one minute of protected time at the beginning and end. I now call upon the first speaker for*

Side Proposition to present their opening arguments, including definitions.

Isaac rises from his seat. He stands in front of his desk and smiles at the audience before speaking. "Honourable judges, worthy opponents, esteemed guests," he begins, "we're here to debate whether inner beauty is more important than outer beauty. We on Side Proposition don't see this as much of a debate, and we don't think you will, either. To start, I invite you to ask yourselves: What aspects of yourself will remain in fifty years?" He pauses. "Think that over while I provide some definitions."

As expected, their definition of beauty is indistinct enough to encompass personality traits. TJ glances at Charlie. He shakes his head minutely. They can work with it; she nods in agreement.

When Rajan finally holds up the ONE MINUTE sign ending protected time, Isaac says, "Inner beauty, unlike outer beauty, can't lie. Think about the people you love the most. Are they always the most physically attractive? Probably not. But they're still beautiful to you, because of who they are on the inside. Now think of the people you dislike the most. They can do whatever they like to enhance their appearance, but they will never be appealing because their personalities are not. The truth is, you can hide what you look like, but you can't hide who you are."

Both TJ and Charlie stand up, chairs scraping back simultaneously. Isaac barely bats an eye. "Yes, I'll take a question."

He doesn't specify from who, but Charlie waves TJ on, so she remains standing and clears her throat.

"Honourable Speaker, inner beauty can most certainly lie. People can pretend to be someone they're not and only show their true colours later. We've all known people who talk one way and act another behind your back. Wouldn't Side Proposition agree?"

She offers a sugary smile. Isaac does not return it.

"No, we would not. It's much easier to fool someone by continually altering your appearance and lying about what you really look like. *That's* quite the lie."

Now Isaac's the one smiling. TJ keeps her face blank. She supposes if she went for a personal blow, then it was only fair that Isaac do the same. She sits down. Beside her, Charlie has a white-knuckled grip on his pen as he writes.

Isaac wraps up a few minutes later. "Side Opposition will undoubtedly try to convince you that outer beauty is what forms first impressions. But *lasting* impressions are what really matter. By the end of this debate, we are confident we will have made a lasting impression on you. And we won't do it based on our looks."

The judges smile and nod. The Speaker calls on Charlie next.

He adjusts his tie slowly before rising and strolling in front of his desk. As always, when he takes command of the stage, TJ is compelled to listen. Especially when he starts his rebuttals.

"Side Proposition's first contention was that outer beauty fades, but inner beauty only deepens over time. Their thesis question was *What aspects of yourself will remain in fifty years*? Their answer was inner qualities only. Our opponents make it sound like we'll all be corpses by the time we're fifty. We would respectfully disagree. We believe beauty is not attached to age, and to say otherwise is ignorance." Charlie flashes a smile at the audience. TJ hides a grin. Truly, a smart move to try to win over the older judges. Isaac scowls, but doesn't rise from his seat, as protected time is still going. Charlie moves on.

"Furthermore, the claim that inner beauty deepens with time only holds if you believe the passage of time automatically makes us better people. There is no correlation between those things. In fact, we would argue it's actually more difficult to remain a good person over time than it is to succumb to corruption. And while that *does* make a lasting impression, it's probably not the one Side Proposition intended."

Isaac rolls his eyes. TJ hopes the judges caught it.

"The next flaw," Charlie continues, "is the assumption that outer beauty *must* fade eventually. Allow me to remind you that Side Proposition defined outer beauty simply as how someone looks on the outside. Which means we're not only talking about the superficial here, but also things about them that might not change at all."

TJ sees where he's going, and this time she can't help but smile. He's using the vagueness of the Turners' own definitions against them.

"Think about the people you love and what about their appearance is most appealing. I bet it's not their lack of wrinkles. No, it's the sound of their laugh. The way they tap their pen against their lips when they're thinking. The way their eyes sparkle. All these things are expressions of their personality that you can only observe from the outside. And none of *that* will go away."

Finished with his rebuttal, Charlie moves on to his own contentions. TJ tenses. This first one is risky.

"Evolutionarily," he says, "it makes sense that outer beauty would be appealing. Think about what people needed back in the days when the number one priority was passing your genes down to the next generation. For example, broad shoulders in men implied strength, which can be passed down to offspring and used to protect them. Wide hips in women implied a better chance for healthy childbearing. It's all science."

Jenna stands up immediately on that one. "Is Side Opposition not aware we don't still live in our caveman days when those things mattered?"

A few titters from the audience. Charlie shrugs. "I'm just commenting on the fact that, unfortunately, these things still play a psychological role in our lives. We're not debating whether inner beauty *should* be more important than outer beauty, we're debating whether it *is*. We may have moved past our uncivilized days, but there's parts of that psyche that remain. I'm not endorsing it. In fact, I'd say it, along with most vestiges left over from our 'caveman days,' doesn't have a place in a modern society. And yet, it's still ingrained in us. That's the reality that Side Proposition is ignoring in favour of their fictional utopia where the most powerful thing is someone's personality. And therefore, it's *important*."

Jenna sits, her lips thin. Charlie's on fire.

Still, TJ can tell the audience hasn't bought what Charlie's selling. The judges haven't, either. It's simply not a very feel-good argument. If Charlie is the harsh reality, TJ will have to be the feel-good.

Charlie rounds off his arguments, and right before Rajan holds up the PROTECTED TIME card again, Isaac stands up fast, his chair screeching back. Charlie pauses in speaking for just a moment, clearly taken aback:

"Yes, I—I—I—I'll take a question."

No. TJ bites back a sigh. He already took two. And protected time was about to start. Now he's gone rigid, because he stuttered, and Isaac seems to know it.

Isaac tilts his head back, considering his former best friend for a long moment. TJ almost wonders if he had a question at all, or just wanted to poke at Charlie's confidence. "What does Side Opposition believe long-lasting marriages are based on?"

Charlie is silent for a moment longer than necessary. That's a difficult question to answer without sounding like an asshole, given his contention about the evolutionary significance of certain physical features.

"Would you like me to rephrase the question?" Isaac asks innocently.

"W-w-w—" Charlie stops and takes a deep breath.

"Does Side Opposition not agree that long-lasting marriages are based on meshing personalities, not looks?" Isaac says, his voice sharp.

TJ sits there, willing Charlie to continue. But she can tell he's blocking again.

The seconds tick by. Someone in the audience coughs.

Isaac says, "I can always rephrase again."

His voice is light and friendly for the judges. TJ knows better, though. And she wants to drop-kick him into the sun.

But maybe this was what Charlie needed, because she can practically feel the fury rolling off him. It doesn't come out in his voice, though. "If inner qualities are so important to Side Proposition, I—I—I'd suggest they learn patience."

He smiles while he says it, even through his stutter. There are a few laughs from the audience. The moment is effectively skated over. Charlie goes on.

"W-what Side Opposition would say is, while long-lasting marriages may have an element of meshing personalities, chances are that isn't what initially attracted that couple to each other. Some outer characteristic must have been com-pelling, too. We would say this is the fundamental difference between them being friends and them being a couple."

He's gained back that measured rhythm to his words again, and he goes on to wrap up his speech with his typical dramatic flair.

When he sits, she's so damn *proud* of him that she leans over and whispers, "Nailed it."

He turns to her, their shoulders brushing. "I didn't believe a word of what I said in my answer to Isaac, to be clear."

It wouldn't be the first time they argued something they didn't actually believe for the sake of a debate. In this case, though, she's not sure she understands. "What do you mean?"

"I mean you can be attracted to someone's personality before their looks."

His eyes are piercing. TJ frowns. But that's all they have time for, because the applause fades away, and Jenna is called up to speak.

"In life, in school, in your job, success depends on your own hard work. Good looks will only get you so far. We acknowledge that outer beauty often has a part to play"—she puts a hand up as if to ward off the questions that TJ and Charlie are about to stand up with—"and certainly, there are jobs where that's important. But for the large majority of things in life, you can't just be a pretty face. You have to be intelligent, and hardworking, and detail-oriented. Not just with healthy childbearing hips," she drawls, earning a few laughs from the audience. TJ crosses her arms. She should not feel this irrationally angry that Jenna's twisting their arguments. That's the whole game. But it's *Jenna*, and she's a massive hypocrite, and it's just *so* unfair that they get to argue that side.

Charlie touches her wrist, drawing her attention to his notepad, where he's scribbled some notes to use in her rebuttal. Right. She's the last person to speak in this debate. The last effort to sway the judges. Jenna's already trying to do that, now talking earnestly about how beauty and fashion trends are fickle, while a good personality will always be appealing.

Both TJ and Charlie get up to ask questions during her speech, but she answers them strongly. Then she wraps up by summarizing the Side Proposition case.

TJ's turn is announced by the Speaker.

She stands as if in a dream. Her hands are sweaty. The room seems unnaturally bright, and she swears she can hear the scuff of every boot, the clink of every spoon, every *breath* in the room. Her heart thunders.

This. This is the part she loves, right here.

She inhales.

"Honourable judges, worthy opponents, and assembled guests," she begins, "why are we so preoccupied with our favourite actors? They play different characters with different personalities. But it's what they present on the outside that draws us to them, makes us watch every movie they do, love every character. We of Side Opposition believe we should not underestimate the importance of outer beauty. To prove this, I will wrap up our case with one more contention: in our society, you have to be beautiful to get ahead."

She feels Charlie jerk in slight surprise; she's going off-script. But she had a burst of inspiration, born from his own words earlier. They don't have to be arguing *in favour of* outer beauty at all. All they have to do is prove that it's more important—for better or for worse.

And it *is* important. Damn it, this year taught her at least that.

"You can't show up in pajamas and bedhead to a job interview. Once you're hired, you still can't show up like that if you want to be promoted. Same for debate. If I came here wearing a T-shirt and jeans, no one would take me seriously. On our own honourable judges' scoresheets they're using right now, there's a score for etiquette, and that includes dress."

As she speaks, she sees Jenna and Isaac whispering to each other out of the corner of her eye. They're cooking something up. She refocuses.

"Your intelligence, kindness, and hard work don't matter if you don't look a certain way. Any person of colour applying for a job will tell you that! Far less people will even consider their internal qualities, because based on their *external* qualities, they've already decided who you are. And let's not forget trans and nonbinary folks," she adds, remembering Lulu's words, "who can actually face violence because of their gender, if people think they should look a certain way that they don't. To assume who you are on the inside will be respected from the get-go is a privilege not everyone has. Would Side Proposition not agree?" she shoots to Isaac, because he's stood up.

Isaac scoffs. "No, we would not. Besides, external qualities, and what makes them appealing, are often subjective. Whereas inner qualities like intelligence are more objective, and therefore hold more weight. Wouldn't *you* agree?"

Ah. The good ol' objectivity argument. "No. Like my partner alluded to earlier, we can't read minds, so internal qualities can *only* be measured by how they present on the outside. That can lead to plenty of misunderstandings." TJ pauses, because although she's spinning this out of thin air, it actually applies strangely well to her life. She thinks of Simran. "Say a person is having an internal feeling of guilt. How that manifests in your body language is what actually matters because that's what is going to be interpreted by other people. And they might see it as anger, for example, instead of guilt." TJ thinks of Charlie. "And another person's anxiety might come across through their appearance as incompetence to someone else. Although that's obviously not true.

"The point is, outer beauty *as defined* by Side Proposition is more important than inner beauty, because the outer beauty is what people are reacting to and judging you on, not what you're actually feeling on the inside. Now, moving back to my speech." She's spent a while on Isaac's question and has to take a second to remind herself what she was even talking about. "As I was saying, you have to be beautiful to get ahead. People who are *not* considered beautiful are placed at a disadvantage."

Jenna practically jumps up, and TJ waves her on, because she might as well get her two questions in now. "What is Side Opposition saying? Are they implying that not everyone is beautiful, in their own special way?"

Jenna's voice is all indignant, the picture of the feel-good argument trying to paint TJ as shallow. The entire room seems even more silent now, waiting for TJ's answer.

TJ could deny it. She's expected to. She could say, *Of course everyone is beautiful in their own way to someone, but . . .* and make it an empty rebuttal. It would still get her points. Or . . .

She hesitates, hovering on the precipice of saying nothing, and saying something *risky*.

Screw it.

"That's exactly what I'm saying," she says savagely. One of the judges sits back in her seat in surprise, but that's not stopping TJ now.

Amy's meaningless EVERY BODY IS BEAUTIFUL pamphlets float through her head. The unfairness of Yara being *not good enough* to be a model. How it was so—so *pick and choose*.

TJ tosses her cards behind her. "People will try to make you feel good by saying everyone is beautiful, but what they really mean is written into all those empty beauty campaigns where they only ever show people who still fit the standard or are just a tiny bit deviant from it—just enough to still be acceptable. Maybe they've got body hair, but it's only some peach fuzz and a bit of stubble under their arms. Maybe they're plus-sized, but they still have the correct chest-to-waist-to-hips ratio. Maybe they're going makeup-free, but their skin only has a few small imperfections to begin with. Then everybody pats themselves on the back because they're so inclusive, wow, everyone *is* beautiful. That wasn't so hard, was it? Let's all go home."

Rajan's staring at her, and she's fairly sure he's forgotten to put up her TWO MINUTES LEFT warning. She keeps going.

"But here's the thing. You never see the girls with tufts of armpit hair and moustaches in the ads. Or the ones with fat rolls and cellulite. Or the ones with acne and psoriasis all over their bodies. Or the ones with all three, and more. That's because society can't find a way to frame them in the beauty standards that already exist. So they don't show them at all. Because what they really mean is you can be hairy, but not *too* hairy. You can be fat, but only *this* fat. You can have flawed skin, but only by *this* much. Et cetera. And we call that revolutionary, but we're still comparing everyone to the exact same ideals, only looser."

She pauses to catch her breath. It occurs to her that she hasn't roasted the Turners in a while, so she gestures to their table. "And you know what? Not only is this resolution false, but it's also poorly worded. I mean, what *is* inner beauty even? Side Proposition defined it as 'the inner qualities of a person's character.' But why do we have to call it beauty, then? That sounds more like the definition for 'a personality.'" That earns her a few snickers. Nice. "Listen. I don't look at a muscular weight lifter and say they've got outer intelligence. I don't feel the need to say everyone in the world is funny in their own special way. Why do we do that with the word *beautiful*? I'll tell you why. It's because we've been told the only way we can feel good about ourselves is if we are somehow beautiful." Her voice catches. "We don't talk about it, but we all know deep down that being beautiful is more important than anything else in the entire world."

She's so far from the point now but she doesn't care, except Rajan has thrown up his ONE MINUTE LEFT sign. She scrambles to conclude. "In conclusion, the idea that inner beauty is more important than outer beauty is simply false. As my partner said earlier, to pretend otherwise is to live in a delusion. And to be clear," she adds, in one last bid to win over the judges, "we *wish* Side Proposition were right that inner beauty is more important. But they're not. And if we never acknowledge the truth, we'll never get there. There has to be some self-awareness first. We have to learn to see our value without it being tied to whether society would deem us attractive. You can be ugly and a lovable person at the same time, I promise. I hope that will count for more one day in the eyes of society, but it can count in yours. Being beautiful is nice, but it's not something to pin your self-worth on. And your worth is definitely *not* debatable."

She sits down just as Rajan slams his hand on the desk. "That's time."

TWENTY-SIX
***

The ballroom is breathlessly silent. The Turners, staring. TJ's sweating like she just ran a marathon. She shucks off her blazer and dares to look at Charlie. After all, near the end of that debate, she basically went on a rant. Far from irritation or even surprise, though, his expression is similar to when they first kissed: enraptured, lips parted, and his eyes nearly black.

The Speaker announces the end of the debate, and TJ looks away. It takes ages for the judges to finish their scoring, but eventually, one by one, they hand in their scoresheets to the Speaker. The Speaker takes his time reading them over.

TJ realizes she's leaning forward in her seat and forces herself to relax. It doesn't matter if they win, not really. She knows that.

But damn if the competitive streak in her isn't absolutely *killing* her with curiosity.

Finally, the Speaker leans in to his microphone. Pauses. "The judges wish to award this debate to Side Opposition. At this time, if any debaters have complaints regarding rule violations . . ."

They won.

Her mind goes blank. All eyes are on her and Charlie, looking for a reaction. Neither of them moves a muscle.

"The debaters may cross the floor," the Speaker says, and

right, that's a thing. TJ reaches for her blazer. It's chilly now, and her sleeveless blouse has left her arms with goose bumps.

Her very *hairy* arms.

She stares at them for a moment, then retracts her hand. She leaves her blazer behind and follows Charlie.

As usual, the Turners remain in their places, waiting for them to cross the floor. This time, TJ doesn't care. She grasps Jenna's hand firmly.

Jenna's eyes flicker down to TJ's arm and then up. "Congratulations," she says, voice not quite as peppy as usual. She barely shakes her hand, but TJ finds that she doesn't care.

Meanwhile, Isaac is talking to Charlie. "Great debate, Charlie. You've come a long way. I'm glad they didn't dock points for your stuttering."

Charlie gives him a bored look and walks away. TJ grins. Charlie is done giving Isaac any of his energy. She loves that for him.

TJ, however, has plenty of energy to give. She grabs Isaac's hand and pumps it up and down. "My favourite part of your speech was when you shut up," she tells him with a smile. "I think you should've gotten extra points for that."

Without waiting for a response, she turns and goes back to where Charlie's waiting. The two finals teams are directed off the stage, through opposite doors. She and Charlie calmly walk out into the hallway. As soon as they're out of sight, TJ begins jumping up and down. "Oh my god! Charlie!"

She's too hyped to care that she's in his space, hopping around like a little kid. Charlie laughs, a real endeared laugh, like she's funny; then he catches her mid-jump to hug her, lifting her clean off her feet. She flings her arms around his neck and inhales his Sunday-morning smell, hardly noticing that one of her heels is dangling off her foot.

"I've never seen you this happy to win a debate before," he says against her shoulder.

"It's not even the debate." She sighs contentedly and leans back to look at him, nose to nose. He's a reflection of her joy, for once an open book. "It's . . . what I felt, back there."

"A healthy sense of revenge?"

She snickers. "That's part of it." But it was more, too. On that stage, everything had come out, all those conflicting feelings she's had this year about her appearance. She went from wanting to believe she could still be beautiful this way, to wanting to believe her looks didn't matter at all. But they do. Of course they do. And it's strangely freeing to be able to admit that, and still do her own thing.

As Charlie gently sets her back on the floor, she says, "You were right. The fact that I deserve respect isn't a debate. I don't have to justify my existence. To anyone."

Charlie's eyebrows draw together. "I hope you didn't take that conversation to heart. I called you pathetic."

"It's okay." She half laughs. "I kind of am."

"No, you're not," he says so strongly that her laughter dies and she has to look at him seriously. "What you went through this year . . . it would've been so easy to give up. But you set out with a goal in mind, and nothing could shake you from it. That's the furthest thing from pathetic."

Her cheeks warm at his praise. But she didn't earn it; he

doesn't have the whole story. "Plenty of things shook me from it." She looks away. "You don't know how many moments of weakness I had."

Charlie puts his finger under her chin and gently turns her face back to his. There's no pity in his expression. Just steadiness. "But you're still here, aren't you?"

"Well," she says, pausing, melting. "I guess I am."

The door behind them opens. Charlie drops his hand, and they step apart. Mrs. Scott pops her head out.

"For heaven's sake, are you waiting for Christmas? The banquet's started. Everyone wants to talk to you." She pauses. "Congratulations, by the way. You did very well."

Charlie looks at TJ. "Well, we made a good team."

The past tense in that sentence whacks TJ over the head. It's really over.

Too dazed to protest, she lets Mrs. Scott usher them through the banquet hall doors.

Immediately, TJ's swarmed by people, and separated from Charlie. Yara's hopping up and down, beaming. Ameera asks, *How does it feel?* Her Ontarian opponents from a few rounds ago come by to offer congratulations. A judge from yesterday taps her on the shoulder and says he enjoyed her speech. Chandani's little brother asks her if he can go home now. There's no shortage of people who want to talk. But there's only one person she wants to talk to right now.

She looks over at Charlie. How she wishes for just one more minute alone with him, but it's clearly not to be. He's several feet away, surrounded by debaters from Whitewater who are here volunteering. He's laughing at something someone said.

TJ doesn't know the girl he's talking to. She doesn't know any of the Whitewater kids very well, really, but it occurs to her that he's certainly spent more time with his own school team than he ever has with her.

She suddenly feels embarrassed for her thoughts earlier, when she pondered kissing him. All TJ ever had with Charlie was *arguments*. And even that's over now.

As if sensing her stare, his eyes flick up and meet hers. She feels like the breath has been knocked out of her. Those amber eyes should not rattle her like this, not after all this time.

Then he's coming towards her, in the middle of the crowd.

Ameera appears at her shoulder, holding her blazer. "TJ, we can all talk later. You must be hungry."

"Just a second." TJ's focused on Charlie, who's reached her. But even he's got a distraction in the form of Nate, jabbing him in the shoulder.

"Mr. York wants to talk to you."

"Hold on." Charlie hasn't looked away from TJ. Her heart leaps. What's he about to say? Could he be—

He reaches into his pocket. "I didn't give you your pen back."

It takes her a moment. Oh. The pen they'd shared during that one debate.

She wants to laugh at herself for thinking he might say anything different. Maybe if she hadn't jerked him around so much, he would. But that's the thing. She was so concerned about how he could break her heart that she didn't realize she could break it herself.

Charlie holds the pen out. She takes it, their fingers brushing for a fraction of a second. The metal is warm from his body heat.

She never knew she could be so jealous of a pen.

Someone else calls her name from behind her, demanding her attention, so she just takes him in one last time and tries to commit him to memory. Not the way he looks, but the way he makes her feel, just by standing next to her. Safe. Anchored. Understood. Even if he doesn't realize it, he gave that to her. And she'll never settle for less.

Charlie's searching her eyes, and TJ realizes she should say something. She clutches the pen.

"Thank you," she says.

"You're welcome," he says.

And then they walk away from each other.

It takes several minutes to reach the food line. People keep stopping her to talk. Finally, she reaches the banquet table and finds herself next to Rajan.

"Nice debate." He reaches up to tug at a phantom cap, which Mrs. Scott has confiscated for the duration of the tournament, so his fingers graze his wavy black hair instead.

"Thanks, Rajan."

Of course, it's Rajan, so he can never leave well enough alone. "I really liked your point about people of colour not getting jobs and stuff. A great power move, since you were the only minority on stage and so no one could say anything about it without sounding racist." He winks.

TJ chooses not to dignify that with a response. "Couldn't they find anyone else for timekeeping?"

"The dude who was gonna do it cancelled last-minute, and I was the only one there when Mrs. Scott was panicking."

TJ rolls her eyes and puts her blazer back on. She digs her phone out of the pocket. A notification instantly catches her eye—an email from Simran.

Her heart leaps, and she clicks through to read it.

The message is short. **I just got back from camp. Thanks for the tea, definitely no sore throats around here.**

Is Simran . . . making a joke? It's hard to tell, but TJ's heart lifts. She's been anxious all week waiting for a response, but of course Simran wouldn't have emailed until she was back. And she did so on the very same night. Which *means* something. She's accepting the olive branch.

Before TJ can think of a response, Ameera nudges her. "Hey, someone's waving at you."

TJ looks up to spot Chandani and Piper entering the banquet hall. They're in hoodies, hair damp like they're freshly washed up. They're back already?

"Go," Ameera says. "I'll save your spot."

TJ thanks her and exits the food line.

Her two friends appear to be in unusually serious conversation as she draws nearer. Chandani's arms are crossed, and Piper looks solemn. But they both stop talking when they notice TJ. Piper lights up.

"TJ!"

TJ accepts her hug. "How are you here? The soccer game—"

"Was a victory, no thanks to you," Chandani finishes. "We just got back."

"We wanted to see your debate," Piper says. "We just missed it, but I heard you won." She pauses. Chandani not-so-subtly elbows her, and she takes a deep breath.

TJ looks between them, confused. Something's up. "What—"

"Jake's one of the people who liked that new post," Piper blurts. "About you, I mean. From after Spring Break."

This isn't news. "I know."

"Well, I broke up with him."

That's news. TJ stares at her, shocked. Piper looks away, anger and embarrassment clear on her face. "I wasn't even that surprised when I saw. I think I always knew he was that type of guy. But it didn't hit home until right then. I'm sorry it took me so long. And if you knew . . . I can't believe you didn't say anything!"

"I didn't want to get in between you two. I knew how much you liked him." It sounds ridiculous as soon as she's voiced it. She was really just going to let it go. As if she didn't deserve any better from her friends.

Piper sighs. "Yeah. But I don't want a boyfriend who puts down my friends. And I don't want to be someone who puts down her friends, either. Whether . . . I meant to or not. And apparently I've done it before."

TJ looks at Chandani, who suddenly looks a little misty-eyed herself. "We did a lot of talking on the way back to Kelowna."

Well, good for them, finally clearing the air.

Piper goes on, lowering her voice. "The worst thing is, I can't help it sometimes. Even though I know it's wrong, sometimes I look at you and think, *That's unnatural.* Isn't that messed up?"

"Yep," TJ says. Piper looks at the floor, at least until TJ adds, "But I get it."

A while ago, with Charlie, TJ had blamed the beauty industry for being the problem, but she's starting to realize that's only the start of it. She and Chandani and Piper and her mom and all those aunties have been made part of the problem, too. They are crucial players in their own shaming.

She can almost imagine these CEOs in their office, breaking down their business plan. Tell girls that it's actually *not* just about beauty. Tell them it's more serious than that—it's about cleanliness and health, about appearing professional, about female empowerment. To not look a certain way isn't just ugly, it's lazy and dirty and unhealthy and primitive.

The beauty industry stifled them with that message, and they stifled each other with it. It's hard to shake off. Sometimes the best they can do is recognize it and try to be better.

Chandani yawns theatrically. "This is nice and all, but now that it's over, can we finally kick Charlie's ass?"

"No." TJ sighs. This is so embarrassing now. "He got hacked. He didn't even see that post."

"What?" Chandani's eyebrows fly up. "Are you sure?"

"Yes, we talked about it—"

Chandani waves this away impatiently. "Are you back together?"

"We were never— Shut up!" TJ hisses, even though the room is too loud for anyone to have overheard. "I am *not* discussing this here."

Piper brightens. "We can talk about it tomorrow. We need to tell you about the game, too. Sunday brunch?"

They haven't had brunch in such a long time. The temptation is strong. But TJ thinks about a certain yet-to-be-composed email and shakes her head. "I have somewhere to be tomorrow."

TWENTY-SEVEN
✳✳✳

TJ switches position for the fifth time in as many minutes. She's not used to sitting cross-legged on the floor for lengthy periods of time, unlike the rest of this congregation. She's sweating and the fans on the ceiling are too high up and spinning far too lazily to help.

But not even her foot repeatedly falling asleep can detract from the experience of sitting in the grand hall, with its high ceiling and expansive space that make the music echo in the most ethereal way. It's Sunday morning, and for the first time in years, TJ is spending it at the gurdwara.

On the stage sits Simran, with a lute-like stringed instrument in her hands. She holds it with the conscious, deliberate touch of someone new to playing it. The sound is lovely and haunting, unlike anything TJ's heard, yet still familiar.

The woman beside Simran accompanies with a harmonium, and a young boy on the tabla on her other side. And when Simran opens her mouth to sing . . . TJ has to take a second to process it. Her voice is—there's no other word for it, because the perfect one comes to mind immediately—*beautiful*.

Maybe there's hope for the word after all.

Simran's eyes flutter closed as she sings, her fingers dancing lightly along the strings, head tilted, easily sitting cross-legged like she was born to be here—she's so clearly in her element,

more than TJ's ever seen anywhere else. Despite not understanding the words, TJ can't look away from her skill.

When Simran's finished, there's a hush over the crowd as the
next person moves into place to start their own performance. TJ
feels indescribably, undeservedly proud of her cousin.

She waits until the morning's proceedings are over—after
parshad has been served, and people are drifting downstairs for
langar—to tentatively approach Simran. She hesitates, because
Simran is surrounded by people, the musicians she was playing
with and members of the congregation, both young and old, and
most of all people TJ just doesn't know well. The longer she
lingers on the fringe of the crowd, the more uncomfortable she
gets. Maybe she should just go. Maybe Simran would hate TJ
intruding here for no reason . . . making everything about her
once again.

Just as she's turning to leave, her masi passes by her, doing a
double take. "TJ?" she says, quite loudly, drawing a few stares.
Then she seems to get ahold of her shock. "How are you?" she
asks in Punjabi. "Come have langar. It's so good to see you here.
Where's your mom?"

"Uh, it's just me and Dad today." And he's already disappeared downstairs.

She doesn't realize how her masi was holding her breath
until she visibly deflates. "Of course. I don't know what I was
thinking."

"She was tired from work yesterday," TJ says awkwardly. At
least, that was the reason she gave when TJ invited her.

A shrug. "Sure, sure. Come downstairs and eat."

"Actually, I was hoping to talk to Simran first."

"Well, I'm right here," a voice says from behind her. TJ turns. The crowd has cleared in the time TJ was talking to her masi, and now Simran's standing there, her hands clasped calmly in front of her. Her expression is inscrutable.

TJ's masi looks between them. "I'll see you downstairs." And then they're left alone.

TJ clears her throat. "I saw your email. Glad you liked . . . the tea."

She instantly wants to slap herself, but Simran smiles. "Oh. Yeah. Thanks for that."

A smile is good, right? Maybe TJ's been imagining Simran avoiding her at school lately. She racks her brain for anything intelligent to say as the silence stretches. "You're an incredible musician."

"Thanks." Simran doesn't sound surprised to hear the compliment. She's probably gotten it before.

"Seriously. Your voice is beautiful. You should record albums or something." TJ pulls her chunni higher over her head, cringing internally at her own words. She clears her throat. "That stringed instrument—did you learn that at the music camp?"

"The rabab? Yeah. But I'm so used to playing the harmonium. My fingers weren't ready for the pain of strings. I love the sound though, and I've heard once you build up calluses, it gets easier—" Simran pauses, perhaps seeing how wide TJ's eyes are, and shakes her head. "I heard you and Charlie won at Nationals. That's amazing. Congratulations."

"Oh. Thanks." TJ frowns; once again the conversation has

swung back to her. "I'm not here to talk about that. I'm here to say sorry to you."

Simran blinks. "What for?"

"For everything!" TJ shrugs helplessly. "Everything you said about me being self-centered was true."

But Simran's putting up a hand to stop her. "TJ. I regretted everything I said that day. I wanted to take it back, but I thought you'd be mad—"

So it's true! Simran *has* been avoiding her! "No! Why would I be mad?" Simran gives her a look, and TJ sighs. "Okay, fine, but I swear I wasn't mad this time. You were right. Our relationship has been one-sided as hell for a long time. I just didn't realize until now." She takes a deep breath. "But that's going to change now. I want to know you outside of debate, and I want to listen to you play your rabab and hear about your day and meet your friends and—and—I want to *be* your friend." Her voice catches. "I want to be the friend to you that you've always been to me."

Simran's silent.

"I get it if you don't want that," TJ adds. "I've never been the nicest to you, I always ignored you in class—"

"I do want that."

Relief sinks through TJ's body, melting her anxiety away. "You do?"

She nods. "Remember when we were little? I miss that."

Those were good times. Simple times. But then they grew up. And everything changed, except . . . "We still have debate."

Simran smiles. "Not even that anymore. But Western's debate team will be lucky to have you."

"They'd be even luckier to have you." Simran makes a face. "Oh, come on! You could go wherever you want. I don't get why you're staying here. Didn't you get accepted everywhere you applied?"

Simran shrugs. "I just did that to see if I could. I like it here. UBCO's good, too. I don't expect you to get it."

Her last statement is kind, not derisive. And she's right; TJ doesn't get it. There are a lot of things about Simran she doesn't get. But that doesn't mean she isn't willing to try. "I guess jumping right into something new isn't for everyone," she ventures, and is rewarded with a nod.

"Yeah. Starting university will be a big adjustment, and I'd rather do it from the comfort of home since I can. But at the same time," she adds, "I like that you're so ready to take risks all the time. Like going out in a two-piece suit without shaving. Or going all in if there was someone you wanted to date. You don't weigh every risk and benefit. You go with your gut."

TJ snorts. "Some people would call that impulsive."

"Or brave."

That has TJ sputtering a laugh. *Brave?* Me? Simran, I tried to go without shaving or waxing for half a year, and all the people laughing at me nearly made me lose my mind. And I was doing it to make a point, while *you* were just existing and refusing to compromise who you are."

Simran's smile fades. She takes TJ's arm and leads her to the corner of the grand hall.

TJ looks behind them, confused. "Simran, what—"

Simran shakes her head and sits TJ down against the wall,

far away from the stragglers. Then she takes a deep breath and sits next to her. "I have to tell you something. I lied to you, about whether that original meme bothered me. It did."

TJ's jaw drops. Simran hugs her knees to her chest and continues.

"Remember when I was at your house over Winter Break? While I was there, I stole one of your razors."

TJ's head is spinning. She remembers this; she remembers trying to find a razor and thinking she must've thrown it out. But Simran had taken it. "You shaved . . . ?"

Simran sighs. "Well, I locked myself in my bathroom later and watched some videos on how to do it. And then I shaved one ankle. But it felt so wrong, when I touched it. Too smooth, like plastic. And it *looked* so wrong, my hair on the floor of the tub. That's my hair. It's part of my body. And I just cut off a piece of me and left it on the floor. I was horrified, so I stopped." She pauses. "I threw out the razor. Sorry."

"Unforgivable," TJ deadpans. Simran smiles slightly, but it fades with her next words.

"I couldn't wait for it to grow back, TJ. I had this moment of weakness and my ankle showed that to the world. I felt . . . so ashamed."

Simran drops her head against her knees. TJ puts a hand on her back. Knowing the connection Simran has with her hair, she can only imagine how hard that must have been. "You shouldn't feel ashamed of what people did to you."

"I shouldn't have listened to them in the first place. But it's hard not to feel like they're right sometimes. Like maybe I'll . . .

miss out on things in life, because of how I look."

TJ's already vehemently shaking her head. "Screw those miserable people, okay? You don't have to change who you are. You can have love and happiness and—everything you want out of life."

Simran lifts her head. "Do you really believe that?"

"Yes."

"Do you really believe that," Simran asks, "for *yourself*?"

TJ pauses at the echo of their past conversation. So much has changed since then. She holds Simran's gaze. "Yes. I do."

Simran studies her for a moment before nodding slowly.

They're silent for some time after that. The hall is nearly empty now save for a few little kids running around on the other side of it; sunlight streams through the tall window behind them, warm as a blanket. TJ leans her head against Simran's shoulder. It's peaceful, at least until TJ's stomach growls. They both laugh.

"I see emotional talk makes you hungry," Simran says. "You know, I spotted some fresh pakoré downstairs this morning."

TJ sits up. "Damn it, Simran. Why didn't you say that earlier?"

TWENTY-EIGHT

***

TJ and her father arrive back home later that afternoon. As they're walking up the driveway, he pats her shoulder. "I'm glad you and Simran get along."

TJ smiles. After langar, she had given him and Simran a play-by-play of the final debate over chah. They talked in the langar hall for almost an hour. Her father, it seems, has picked up on their new dynamic. "Yeah, me too."

The front door swings open before they reach it. TJ's mom.

"How was the gurdwara?" she asks impatiently. She's dressed to go out in street clothes, her hair combed and tied back in a short ponytail.

TJ exchanges looks with her dad before replying. "It was good." Her father skirts past them both and continues on into the kitchen. "Simran played her rabab. She's a great singer, do you remember?"

"Yes, I think so," her mother murmurs. She closes the door behind TJ, eyes flicking over her face. She changes the subject abruptly. "I'm going to the salon. For eyebrow threading. Want to come?"

She asks as if hopeful, and despite everything, it stings. TJ takes a deep breath and faces her fully. "No. And you can stop asking me, okay? I'm not going to be pressured into this."

Her mother blinks. "You think I'm . . . pressuring you?"

"Well, yeah." TJ lifts her chin. "Because you are."

TJ expects her to deny it, but instead she's silent. TJ sighs and heads for the stairs. She only takes one step before her mother speaks again.

"You know, I was eighteen when I started removing my hair."

TJ stops in her tracks and turns. Well, that was unexpected. She waits, but there isn't more. "Eighteen? You waited that long?"

Her mother shrugs. "My family never let me. They didn't understand why I wanted to fit in. They thought I was letting go of our culture, and Sikhism. No one realized the pressure I was under, going to school here." She smiles grimly. "My sister especially."

"Why are you telling me this?" TJ asks slowly. Her mother's never talked about her teenage years before.

"Because I told myself I'd never shame my own daughter for wanting to remove her hair. I wanted you to feel supported when the time came, the way I wished I had. Except I think I ended up shaming you anyway." She wrings her hands together. "I didn't mean to pressure you. I just want you to be happy, but if your way to happiness is different than mine, that's okay. You should not feel ashamed."

TJ almost can't believe the things her mother is admitting—so vulnerable. Bitter. She's always seemed impenetrable to those things. Without thinking about it, TJ walks back to hug her. Her mother's stiff for a moment, but then her arms encircle her and hold on tight. Neither of them speaks, but TJ knows her mother's never going to mention her hairiness again.

Her mother clears her throat and steps away. "I should go. I'll be late for my appointment."

Right. Her eyebrows, which she regularly gets compliments on, are becoming chaotic, growing into the middle. Just like TJ, the hair always returns so strongly, despite all their efforts over the years to stomp it out. TJ almost has to marvel at a thing so resilient that no matter how many times it gets cut down, even destroyed at the very root, it eventually grows back. It refuses to have its existence erased.

Maybe she could learn a thing or two from it.

"You don't have to go," TJ says softly.

"I know." Her mother pats her arm and smiles—a real one, this time. "I'll see you later."

And she leaves, closing the door gently behind her. TJ shakes her head and ascends the stairs.

In her room, she drapes her chunni over her desk chair and sits down with the weight of all these new revelations. It makes so much sense now. Even though TJ never mentioned what she was enduring to her parents, her mother *knew*. Because she endured the exact same thing. Except she dealt with it way longer, and got judged by everyone, including her own family. Her sister.

Clearly the divide between her mom and masi runs deep. That won't change overnight, but who knows? Maybe one day it can.

As TJ leans back in the chair, something catches her eye. An old cue card, wedged between the desk and wall. She fishes it out, already knowing what she's going to find written on it. *This*

House Believes That TJ Powar can exist as a hairy girl and still be worthy of respect, beautiful or not.

She runs her fingers over the indents where her pen dug in. How furious, how devastated she had been while writing this. How desperately she wanted to be accepted.

With a flourish, TJ tosses it in the trash.

Two weeks later, TJ opens Instagram to find that Charlie's posted a story on his acceptance to Queen's University. She's not stalking him this time—they finally officially followed each other after Nationals. Ignoring the voice in her head pointing out that Queen's is only a few hours away from Western, she stops in the middle of the hallway to text him congratulations. It feels okay to text occasionally. Just like how she texts anyone else. Except with him, she has to ration herself so it doesn't seem weird.

She sighs and puts her phone away, only to find herself staring at Amy's face on one of the school TV screens. It's a photo of her receiving a certificate from the principal—OUTSTANDING CONTRIBUTION AWARD, the title of the slide reads, given for the beauty campaign. Simran is noticeably absent.

Then the slide changes to the next—an announcement of the charity soccer game in June—and TJ hears a voice behind her.

"It's awful, isn't it?" Yara walks up to TJ's side.

"What's awful?" TJ asks, although she knows.

"How she's getting the recognition for a project we all worked on."

"I don't even *want* recognition for it. Thanks to Amy, it

ended up being a complete waste of time." TJ's eyes fall to the receptacle under the TV, the one that usually holds the school paper. Extra copies of the special edition have been placed in. Amy's really milking this thing.

Just as she's staring at the receptacle, a long arm reaches in and grabs a handful. "Dude, this is heavy cardstock." Rajan waves it in Simran's face, who's beside him. "The good shit."

"Rajan," Simran says in a resigned voice, "I thought we were looking for a place to work on your math homework."

"I can do math right here! Look. Multiply résumé-building volunteerism"—he pulls out another flyer—"by unlimited access to a colour printer"—he folds the flyers neatly—"all in brackets to the power of a gigantic ego, and you get"—he slam-dunks them into the garbage bin—"Amy West."

"And where in this equation are you solving for x?" Simran asks dryly.

"X is the unknown." He tosses a few more flyers into the garbage. "The unknown of whether I'll get a smack on the wrist or a detention for this. We haven't solved that one yet."

Rajan's voice carries, and people start to stare. It's only a matter of time before a teacher comes out to investigate. Oh, what the hell. TJ joins him, grabbing a wad of flyers. She takes a vicious pleasure in watching all those perfect, filtered, fake photos fall in the garbage. "You're not so bad after all, Rajan."

He looks at her with exaggerated shock. "Dude. Are you feeling okay? You should probably go talk to the school nurse, I think you're delirious or something—"

TJ rolls her eyes. "Don't be so dramatic." Whatever grudge

she had against him is over. He was right, anyway. She *does* have a very Indian nose. It's her father's nose, and her grand-mother's for whom she was named, and she wouldn't trade it for anything. Too bad Amy had softened it in her pictures.

She crumples another pamphlet into a ball and boots it into the bin. It's deeply satisfying. Now she understands what Charlie must have felt when he blocked its distribution at Whitewater.

Yara coughs. "Um, incoming."

TJ follows her gaze. Amy is marching down the hall towards them, practically frothing at the mouth in rage. News spreads fast.

Her voice is like a whip. "What are you doing?"

Rajan fashions a paper airplane out of a flyer. "Doing a public service. There's just a lot of trash around here."

"I'm not talking to you." She wheels on TJ. "Seriously, what are you doing? You're *in* this flyer."

"Really? Can you show me where? I don't recognize any-one." TJ flips to her portrait and pretends to squint at it. Rajan laughs.

Amy puts her hands on her hips. "You're so weird, TJ. I'm talking to admin about this. Enjoy detention."

TJ shrugs. Worth it. Rajan seems to think the same, because he says, "Oh no, *detention*," and throws another wad of flyers in the garbage. Amy's lips thin into a line and she looks at Sim-ran, who's been silent this whole time. "Why aren't you saying anything?"

Her tone is reprimanding in a way TJ imagines has made

Simran stand down at many a council meeting, and it ticks her off. She opens her mouth to tell Amy to shove it. But then Simran speaks.

"Rajan, TJ, this is wrong."

TJ sighs. Rajan seems to be of the same mind. "Come on, Simran Sahiba, don't pretend you're not enjoying this—"

"These should be going into paper recycling," Simran interrupts, and reaches into the garbage to daintily pluck out Rajan and TJ's mess of flyers. She flattens them out between her hands, pauses, then rips them clean in half.

Amy's jaw drops. Simran, meanwhile, simply deposits the newly compacted flyers into the paper recycling bin. "The least we can do is give these pamphlets the chance to become something useful one day. Like . . . toilet paper." She dusts off her hands.

Rajan turns to TJ and Yara. "Was my weed laced with something, or are you seeing this, too?"

"I'm seeing it," TJ confirms with a grin.

Amy manages to rehinge her jaw. "What the hell, Simran? You were on board with this before!"

"No, I wasn't. You just didn't listen." Simran pauses, seeming to weigh her next words before saying them. "But I guess you were always more interested in hearing yourself talk."

The foyer is nearly silent. TJ wonders if Rajan was onto something and they're all experiencing a group hallucination. Because surely her cousin didn't just say that.

Amy's face has turned brilliantly red, and instead of answering, she spins on her heel and leaves. She's making a beeline for the principal's office.

"If we leave now, we can get out of lunchtime detention," Rajan says, and, well, he's the expert. So when he turns, ambling to the exit with his hands in his pockets, TJ looks at Simran and Yara.

"Come on!"

They hurry to follow him outside, into the sun. Once they're out on the blacktop, Simran stops. "I can't believe I just did that."

That makes two of them. TJ laughs. "Impulsiveness looks good on you."

"Bravery," Simran corrects, and they share an understanding smile, at least until Rajan slaps her on the back.

"Dude, that was sick. Now we can be detention buddies. I'll teach you all the ropes. Which spots in the classroom have the best Wi-Fi, which teachers will let you go early, how to make holes in the desks when you start getting bored . . ."

Simran doesn't appear to be listening. She sinks onto a picnic bench, looking slightly pale. "Detention . . . Mom is going to kill me."

TJ privately agrees, but Yara pats Simran's shoulder. "I'm glad those pamphlets are in the paper recycling where they belong. I'm embarrassed I took some of those photos."

The theme of the year for Yara, it seems. Inspiration strikes TJ. She pulls out her phone and pokes Yara. "I think we need a selfie to commemorate this. Mind doing the honours?"

Yara looks down at the phone and then at TJ. "You want . . . me to take it?"

TJ nods. "You're the photographer here, aren't you? We have to immortalize our moment of rebellion."

Rajan swings his legs off the bench. "It's just another Tuesday for me." He glances Simran's way. "Don't worry. I'll go do my homework by myself."

TJ must be living in the Upside Down. "Really?"

"If Simran auntie can do something out of character, so can I." He winks at Simran. "Well? Are you proud of me?"

TJ thinks of several sarcastic quips, but before she can say any of them, Simran answers with a gentle smile. "I was always proud of you, Rajan."

And Rajan, for perhaps the first time in his life, has nothing to say to that.

The three of them end up finding a grassy hill away from the bench for the photo, because Yara insists the lighting there is better. But she fiddles with the phone settings for several minutes after they sit down, and TJ starts to wonder if maybe there's other reasons she's delaying.

"Yara," she says finally, "just take the photo already. I don't care how bad you think it is."

Yara lowers the phone. Then: "I'm really sorry about the meme."

TJ blinks. It's Simran who responds first. "Don't apologize."

Anyone else, and TJ would question whether it was genuine, but it's Simran, and her voice is catching.

"It exposed something we all had to see, I think. And figure out." She and TJ share a smile. "I honestly wouldn't have it any other way."

Yara nods slowly, then lifts the phone again. They scoot closer to each other.

"Someone's going to make fun of this," Simran murmurs to TJ as Yara adjusts the angle. TJ shrugs.

"What's the worst they could say?"

"That we're Bigfoot's long-lost cousins?"

They all laugh. Yara snaps the photo at that moment, lowers the phone, and grins. "I think this is the one."

They all crowd around it to look at the screen. In the photo, TJ's hair is floating in her face from the breeze, Simran's squinting from the sun, and Yara's shirt is slipping over her shoulder. Their faces are turned towards each other, laughing. It's not a particularly flattering laugh they have; their noses are scrunched up, teeth bared. But it's clear that in that moment, they were too busy being happy to care what they looked like.

TJ uploads it to her Instagram and types a caption before hitting post: **That feeling when you realize there are worse things to be than ugly.**

TWENTY-NINE
***

Much to TJ's surprise, the photo becomes her most liked post within twenty-four hours. By far. Tons of people she doesn't even know leave encouragement. There are almost no trolls in the comment section, which is probably unprecedented in the history of the internet.

Charlie is one of many who like the post. Seconds after she gets that in her notifications, her phone buzzes with a new text. From Charlie himself.

Just to be clear, that was me. I changed my Instagram password.

She's alone at the time, so thankfully no one sees her grinning.

Nate likes it, too, then DMs her to say he's coming to a table tennis tournament at Northridge next week, and she should "watch her back," which she takes as an invitation to come see him. The day of the tournament, she drops in to the gym at lunchtime, hoping he'll be playing.

As luck would have it, as she walks in, Nate's engaged in a fierce match with a Northridge competitor. They're lightning fast. TJ wonders how they even keep track of the ball.

Although it's close, Nate wins the set and jogs off for a break. He tosses water back and then makes eye contact with TJ, who's found her way to the front of the stands set up for viewing. He does a double take. TJ waves.

When he comes over, she says, "Ping-pong, huh?"

He settles his arms on the railing between them. "Just say it. I'm an Asian cliché."

TJ smirks. "Did Charlie get your club that new equipment he was bribing you with?"

Nate blinks in a way that plainly says this is not common knowledge. "I've been asking for it for a year, so he damn well did. Still made me fill out an application, though. Asshole."

TJ laughs, ignoring the ache in her chest. "Yeah."

Nate takes another swig from his water bottle. In the lapse in conversation, TJ looks around the gym. There aren't many spectators—most people don't spend lunches during summer inside—but she spots Liam walking into the gym with Alexa Fisher snuggled to his hip. They're a pretty couple. But, she finds, it doesn't hurt to watch anymore.

"Who's that?" Nate asks, following her gaze. Liam retrieves a soccer ball from the storage room, and the two of them disappear out the door again.

"No one." She pauses. "My ex-boyfriend."

"Damn. That's Liam? What, you were too much of a diva for him?"

He's joking, of course, but it strikes a little too close to home. "No. I was just too hairy." The silence following those words makes her awkward. "Anyway, I—"

"I know what it feels like," Nate interrupts. "To walk into school one day and look totally different. You're the same person, but some people just can't see that."

TJ looks at him sharply, surprised he would bring up his transition last year. That was huge for him. In comparison . . . "What I did is nothing—"

He waves her down. "This isn't the Oppression Olympics, okay? Let's just agree the concept of gender is fragile as hell. People had a meltdown as soon as I put on a binder, you stopped waxing, and Charlie showed up to school with exactly one hairless leg. Isn't that sad?"

TJ grins. Charlie had never mentioned reactions to his look, but he must've been delighted to scandalize people. "Very."

He nods. "They're so disturbed they just can't help but comment on what you're doing with your own body. Or what you plan to do, someday, down the road."

There's a softer, more vulnerable edge to his voice, and she gets the sense he's been judged too many times by too many people he cares about.

"People should mind their own business," she says firmly. "You shouldn't have to stay the way you are, any more than I should have to change."

She doesn't realize how tense he's become until it clears. Grinning, he leans back, held upright only by his grasp on the railing. "Man, I think that's the most intelligent thing you've ever said."

She rolls her eyes. "Thanks. I just wish I didn't have to put myself through so much to realize it."

"It's worth it in the end. Because you figure out who your real friends are."

He looks at her and looks at her until she finally grasps his meaning.

"Wait. Are you saying . . . we're friends?"

"I would never say something that absurd," Nate says with a wink. "So, what's next? Excited to graduate in an unnecessarily long ceremony? Got your prom outfit picked out?"

"I'm not going to prom. I don't have a date, remember?" She makes a face. At the beginning of the year she thought she'd go with Liam, but—

"Wait," she says again. "How did you know Liam's name?"

Nate looks stricken for a moment but recovers quickly. "You mentioned him. And by the way, you know you can go to prom solo, right?"

But TJ won't be deterred from her line of questioning so easily. "I never mentioned Liam at any debate." She knows that for sure. Before this year, she'd put great effort into separating her debate life from her social life. "So how do you know?"

Nate makes a face but relents. "Charlie might have mentioned him."

TJ's brow furrows. She'd only said Liam's name to Charlie once. In her bungled-up explanation about why she'd kissed Charlie during Spring Break. But . . . "Why would he mention that?"

Nate's eyes dart away and then back. "It's not that deep. It's just, I sensed some tension between you two at Nationals"—TJ cringes, remembering the hike—"so I asked Charlie if it was true you two had a thing during Spring Break. He said no and that he was, um, helping you deal with an ex-boyfriend. This Liam guy."

"Oh," TJ says. "Yeah." That's a neat little explanation Charlie came up with. It's technically the truth, but implies the reason for their kiss was less that TJ was desperate and more like Liam was.

But something about it niggles at her. She frowns.

Nate notices. "You okay?"

She nods distractedly. The whistle blows, calling Nate back to his match. "Yeah. Good luck."

Nate gives her another indecipherable look before leaving. She leans against the railing, no longer paying attention to the game in front of her.

Charlie thought . . . What did he think?

She tries to put herself in his shoes. The first time she kissed Charlie, she basically told him he was a rebound. The second time, she was trying to prove something to Liam.

She racks her brain, but can't think of a single instance she ever told Charlie she was into him for *him*. But it still must've been obvious with the times she practically threw herself at him. Right?

Suddenly, her phone's in her hand and she's trying to compose a text message to him. But nothing sounds right. What is she supposed to say, anyway? Their text conversations have been nothing but occasional jokes since Nationals. It would be a little weird to out of nowhere say, *You know I like you, right?*

She puts away her phone without sending anything. Charlie might not even respond if she texted him. And even if he did, she wouldn't get to see his face.

She spends the whole drive to Charlie's house trying to talk herself out of it.

There are no vehicles in the driveway. It doesn't occur to her until she's almost at the door that this probably means no one's home. She pivots and takes a few steps away before realizing they have a garage and there could, in fact, be vehicles inside.

So she returns to the door and raises her hand to knock. But right before she can, she imagines herself asking if he knew he was never just a rebound, and him saying yes, yes he knew. And the awkward silence that would follow. TJ would rather die.

She starts back down the driveway, pulling out her phone. She needs advice. Piper! Piper knows all about heartbreak.

Piper takes several rings to answer. "What's up?"

"I'm at Charlie Rosencrantz's house and I need advice," she says without preamble. A squeal on the other end.

"Oh my god! Okay. Well, remember, foreplay is key—"

"Not what I'm talking about." TJ pinches the bridge of her nose and explains the situation.

Piper is quiet for a second. "I don't think being scared is an excuse not to ask. If you don't, you'll always wonder."

"But what if he doesn't feel that way anymore and I just look like a—"

"TJ," Piper interrupts. "Remember when Charlie told you he liked you the first time? He took the same risk, lost, and accepted it. If you can't do that, then I guess you have to make your peace with the fact that you're not as brave as him."

TJ gapes although no one can see it, her competitive side bristling. "That's *not* the same."

"Isn't it?" Piper says cheerily. "I have to go. I'm getting my nails done."

"Piper—"

Call ended. TJ is left staring furiously at her phone. Ugh. No way is she letting Charlie make her a coward as his last act in her life. She marches for the door. Let him humiliate her, then! To her face! No one can say she was scared.

She raises her hand to knock, then notices the doorbell. She giggles nervously and reaches to press it.

Pauses before she does. There's a mezuzah on the doorpost right next to it, most likely put up by his mother. What if his parents are home? She can't tell him she's into him right in front of his parents. Now, *that* would be awkward. She backs away, resolving to return later, or maybe call ahead and set a time to meet, instead of just showing up on his doorstep like a stalker—

The door swings open.

"Do you want to come in?" Charlie asks. "I'm getting tired of watching you pace around my driveway."

THIRTY
✳✳✳

TJ opens and closes her mouth several times. In the silence, he steps aside to let her in. Only his shoes are on the shoe mat. They're alone.

She notices then that he's in a collared shirt and paisley tie. "Going on a date or something?" She giggles, then shuts up. Why'd she even say that?

If Charlie notices how weird she's acting, he doesn't comment. "Going to a dinner, actually, but that's later. I just got back from school a few minutes before you showed up. Last student council meeting of the year."

This somewhat distracts her from her panic. "Yeah? How was it?"

"Very emotional. I said goodbye to the entire council and thanked them for everything. Somehow I forgot Brandon Fletcher on my list, though."

She cracks a grin. "How careless. Was he mad about it?"

"I think he was more mad when he was selected for a locker search and my old phone was found inside."

Of course. "That's an unprecedented abuse of power. How'd you manage it?"

"It had nothing to do with me. Apparently there was a complaint about the smell of a certain illicit substance emanating from his locker." He blinks innocently. Right. "Are you planning to explain why you're here?"

She gulps. Straight to the point. To buy herself time, she kicks off her shoes. "Um . . ."

She trails off pathetically. Charlie takes this in stride. "Want something to drink?" He moves through the living room towards the kitchen, almost businesslike, like he's hosting her.

That's what gets her moving. No. She doesn't want that—for him to treat her like everyone else.

She catches him by the arm in the middle of the living room. The words fly from her mouth without a filter. "Charlie, I wanted to kiss you."

She says it to his back. He goes very still. Recklessly, she plunges on. If his reaction hurts, if it's humiliating, well, maybe that finally makes them even. "I wanted to kiss you every single time. At Provincials, and on deck, and below deck. It was never just about getting back at Liam or getting over him. It was about *you*."

He still doesn't move. Doesn't say anything. She steps closer. "Do you still feel the same way?"

He wrenches his arm out of her grasp. "I don't know. Why don't you just tell me how I feel? That seems to be your favourite pastime." His voice is cutting, harsh.

"What's that supposed to mean?" Narrowing her eyes, she moves around him to see his expression.

But he backs away from her swiftly, putting a couch between them. "Don't come any closer. I—I—I—I can't think," he snaps when she moves to follow, and she stops, confused and hurt. "You know exactly what I meant. We've been through these motions more than once. I tell you I like you and you tell me I couldn't possibly feel that way. We kiss and then you tell me to go take a hike. And now here you are again. *Make up your mind.*"

"Charlie, I—" She gapes. "I'm sorry. Back then, I couldn't understand why you would like me when I look the way I do. And I know—I *know*—I am so much more than the way I look," she adds when he opens his mouth. "I know I'm brave, and decent at debating, and that I have a killer penalty kick. I know those things matter more. But in the dating game, it feels like nothing matters if you're not pretty, too."

He's quiet for a moment. "Did I ever give you that impression?"

"No!" Her vision blurs with tears. "But I've been burned before, and I couldn't be sure. But now I think I can be. I trust you."

It's the biggest leap of faith, to not question his feelings, to let him in. But it feels like the right one, after everything.

Charlie still doesn't move. There's something in his expression—he's not completely convinced. She takes a deep breath. "Remember that theory you had about me? You never did tell me what it was."

He doesn't speak.

Maybe he doesn't remember. "It was that night after—"

"I know what night." His voice is low. "I think it went back to being a hypothesis, after everything."

"No." She holds his gaze. "I promise you, it's still a theory."

Her words are followed by a long pause. Then:

"Enough of all the technical definitions." He sets his jaw. "Let's just call it a debate resolution. 'This House Believes That TJ Powar likes Charlie Rosencrantz.'"

He says it strongly, just like any Side Proposition speaker would. But there's an undercurrent to it, something vulnerable she sees in his expression.

She smiles to encourage him, and presses one knee into the couch cushion, drawing closer. He doesn't move away this time. "As Side Proposition, you need to provide some definitions."

His eyes are nearly black. "We define the terms as follows. 'TJ Powar' is the girl in question, who seems to think my attraction to her is inversely proportional to the amount of hair on her body."

Her smile becomes a scowl. "You little—"

"We define 'likes' as . . . *like* like."

"Very elementary school of you."

"Always best to keep definitions simple. We define 'Charlie Rosencrantz' as . . .'"

"My *esteemed* opponent. My *valued* colleague," TJ puts in, drawing her other leg up onto the cushion and bracing her hands on the backrest, facing him fully from where he stands behind the couch. "My partner."

A warmth enters his eyes. He touches her cheek, knuckles brushing over her skin and then falling away. "Yes," he says. "That."

TJ hooks her fingers under the knot of his tie and tilts her head up, bringing their faces close together. "Well, don't just stand there. List your contentions."

Charlie leans closer. TJ's eyes flutter shut, waiting for the touch of his lips. Then he puts a finger on her chin and pushes her away. She blinks, affronted.

"If I kiss you," he says, "will you freak out after?"

"No." She's breathless.

"And will you run off without talking to me?"

"What? No!"

"Will you go tell your ex-boyfriend we hooked up to make him jealous?"

"No! And I was never trying to!" She's getting annoyed now. "What is this, cross-examination?"

"If it is, you're not doing a very good job. All these one-word answers. So easy for me to spin."

"I'm not *trying* to do a good job! I'm not on Side Opposition! Charlie, I *like you*—"

And then he kisses her, hands sliding over her neck to slant her head towards his, swallowing up whatever else she was going to say. Her stomach does an odd swoop. Then some part of her wakes up and remembers what to do. She pulls at his tie and kisses him back. He still smells like Sunday mornings. He still feels like a safe place. He touches her like she's precious to him, rough edges and all. And when she runs her hand down his chest and he holds her tighter, she thinks maybe she makes him feel that way too.

He breaks the kiss this time. TJ keeps her eyes closed for a second before opening them. His face is inches away. His cheek-bones are tipped red—*she made him blush!*—but he's studying her like she's a science experiment. She giggles breathlessly, because she knows what he's looking for—a sign of a freak-out, that she's going to run away. To dispel that notion, she flings her arms around him and rises up on her knees to properly hug him.

Charlie exhales and wraps his arms around her. His body is warm and sturdy and so very comforting. They stand like that for a moment until he turns his face into her neck. His lips move to her pulse, and she doesn't think about the hair on her face, just his nose brushing against her jaw and the long, slow suck to her neck that makes her arch into him. "There's my first contention," he murmurs.

She shoves him away with a scoff. He lets go surprisingly easy. So easy that she loses balance and falls back onto the couch, nearly sliding off onto the floor, but she catches herself just in time.

He's laughing at her. TJ finds she doesn't mind. She's splayed all over the couch in a ridiculous fashion. His eyes find hers, and then flicker down.

She realizes then that her shirt has bunched up around her stomach, exposing it and the happy trail. She reaches automatically to pull the hem back down.

His voice stops her. "Don't."

She freezes. Her breath stalls as he comes around the side of the couch and crawls onto the cushion with her, hovering over her. Then, carefully, deliberately, he leans in and plants a soft kiss to her navel.

She shivers.

He notices. "Contention two." He slides back up to look at her, grazes his fingers over the raised hairs on her arm. "By the way, the dinner I'm going to tonight is the event for—I mean, *against* polio."

TJ finds her voice. "I'm glad you switched sides."

"Well, you're very convincing." Charlie pauses. "Do you—you—you want to go with me?"

"Of course I do. Because I *like you*, in case you forgot."

And she kisses him right on his stuttering mouth.

"Well, then," he says when they part. "Side Proposition rests their case."

EPILOGUE
***

June is sweltering hot. It makes everyone at Northridge restless, no one more than the grade-twelve class. There's a sense of finality in the air to everything they do leading up to the end of the year. The final assignments, final field trips, final week of school. And of course, for TJ, the final soccer game.

Well, technically it's a charity game, but TJ didn't go to the real last game, so this will have to do. Besides, it's against Whitewater, so it's still deadly serious, as Coach makes very clear in their pre-game huddle.

"It's our *final* chance to stick it to Whitewater," he says at the end of his five-minute hype-up speech. "Particularly for those of you graduating this year." He clears his throat, surveying the twelfth graders. "I'm proud of you girls."

Everyone exchanges shocked looks.

"Now, don't make me regret saying that!" he barks, making them jump, and yep, *that* sounds more like him.

They do their cheer, and half the team jogs onto the field. TJ turns to the bench, but Coach stops her.

"TJ! Weren't you listening earlier? You're on."

TJ definitely hadn't been paying attention, but—wait. She stops in her tracks. "I'm . . . starting?" She'd assumed that, as usual, she wouldn't play until later in the game.

Coach appears to be repressing a smile under his moustache. "Kiddo," he says. "Get on the field before I change my mind."

TJ grins and obeys.

On the field, she plants her cleats in the grass and inhales deeply. Her teammates are all already in position. Chandani's stretching her hamstrings. Farther down the midfield line, Piper sticks her tongue out. TJ returns the gesture, then focuses on her opponents. Even though it's a charity game, the Whitewater forwards look like serious business. Just like any contest between their schools would be. TJ's heart kicks into gear, that familiar adrenaline coursing through her.

The ref blows the whistle, and she takes off.

"You're rusty," Chandani says after the game.

TJ flips Chandani the bird because she's too winded to talk. She collapses in the grass, shucks off her shin guards, and rolls down her socks. Sighs in relief. Chandani sits beside her and does the same.

Piper approaches, and they make room for her between them. "I'm glad we scored. This would've been embarrassing otherwise."

TJ had passed to Chandani, whose foot had been waiting at just the right place to nudge it into the goal. It had tied them with Whitewater at the last moment. TJ pokes Piper. "We couldn't have done it without you."

Piper scoffs. "I didn't even touch the ball."

"But you faked out that one defense player. I never would've gotten the pass to Chandani otherwise."

"Yeah." Chandani kicks Piper's foot. "Don't think you're not important."

That's as emotional as Chandani's going to get and TJ thinks Piper realizes it, because she smiles and nods.

"I wish you guys were coming to UVic with me." She picks at the grass, sounding wistful. "We could've played together there, too. But instead . . ."

She trails off. A heavy silence falls. Piper's going to Victoria for a business major, Chandani's staying in Kelowna where she got picked up by UBCO (major undecided), and TJ will be all the way in Ontario doing political science. Everything will be different. Exciting and scary all at once—TJ doesn't think it's ever going to stop feeling that way.

While she's staring aimlessly ahead, a pair of jean-clad legs steps into her vision. She looks up.

"Simran?"

Simran smiles. She's got a cashbox tucked under her arm and is wearing a fundraiser T-shirt. The charity game had been a collaboration with student council. And more importantly, it was Simran's project. "Thanks for keeping the game tight. The tension really boosted concession sales."

TJ grins. "Our pleasure."

Simran's eyes shift away from TJ, to Chandani and Piper. She nods at them.

Piper waves. "Hi."

TJ cringes inwardly; she introduced them to each other a few weeks ago, but the awkwardness is still deadly.

Chandani looks Simran up and down. TJ only has time to pray she's not about to make some kind of callous comment before she speaks. "Your hair is gorgeous. What's your routine?"

Simran blinks. "Um, just coconut oil."

"Genetics. Got it." Chandani eyes her. "Want to come for ice cream with us? We're headed to the waterfront."

TJ could cry. Chandani, making an *effort*?

Simran shakes her head. "I've got money to count." She hefts her cashbox for emphasis. "Say hi to Charlie for me, though."

Chandani whips her head around to TJ. "*Charlie's* coming?"

Piper starts choking on her water. TJ thumps her back and sends Simran an evil look, because she's clearly enjoying this reaction too much. "He's picking us up. Why is this so surprising? You kept begging to meet him."

Piper finally recovers. "Yeah, but we didn't think you'd *agree*."

"We thought you were keeping him as your little secret summer fling," Chandani adds, wiggling her eyebrows. TJ rolls her eyes.

"It's not like that." Okay, maybe a little bit. But she's just trying to make their short time together count.

They bid goodbye to Simran and head off the field with their bags. Chandani sighs as they near the pickup zone. "I'm so single. Maybe *I* should ditch my razors and get me a hot debate nerd, too."

TJ snorts. "You wouldn't last five minutes without your perfect eyebrows."

Chandani jabs her in the ribs harder than necessary. "So what now? You proved your point, didn't you? To yourself? Are you going to start waxing again?"

TJ shrugs. She's gotten used to hair brushing against her fingers when she touches her skin. She sort of understands what Simran was going on about—it makes her skin feel alive.

Then again, if she chooses to head back to Lulu's parlour, it'll have to be different this time. It's just another fun thing she can do for herself if she chooses, like getting a new pair of shoes, or a lipstick that speaks to her. But the nice thing is, whether she does it or not, no one who's important to her will care.

A familiar grey SUV is in the pickup zone when they arrive, the driver's-side window rolled down. As they approach, Charlie pokes his head out and slides off his sunglasses. His eyes find TJ's.

It's ridiculous how her heart jumps, seeing as she just hung out with him yesterday.

"Good game," he says, and she blinks.

"You were watching?" She'd only asked him to pick her up afterwards. She hadn't thought he'd come to the match.

"I wanted to see my jock girlfriend play at least once. Is that a crime?"

It shouldn't please her this much to hear him call her his girlfriend, but it does. "Well? Was it everything you hoped?"

"No, it was better."

His eyes have darkened. Interesting. She sort of wants to explore this further, but then she realizes Chandani and Piper are snickering behind her.

"TJ," Chandani drawls, "aren't you going to introduce us?"

TJ envisions strangling them both but pastes a fake smile on her face instead. "Charlie, this is my friend Piper, and that freak over there is Chandani."

Charlie, unfazed as usual, extends his hand through the window to them both to shake. It's so formal she has to restrain a laugh. What a nerd.

He gives Chandani a second look. "I actually think we've met before."

Chandani blinks. Even TJ's surprised. He goes on.

"You were timekeeper for a debate once, weren't you? I remember because you let me go overtime." He flashes her a charming grin. "Thanks for that, by the way."

"Who *wouldn't* let you go overtime?" Chandani purrs, a hand on her hip.

Kill Bill sirens go off in TJ's head. She steps on Chandani's foot. "Get in the back seat *now* or we aren't taking you anywhere."

Chandani mutters an insult under her breath. But she and Piper move, throwing their soccer bags into the back. TJ, however, leans into Charlie's window. She's sweaty and dirty and smells like grass, but judging by his expression, it's working for him. "I didn't see you on the sidelines."

"I stayed in the car. I didn't want to distract you."

She scoffs. "I would've liked to see you there. You wouldn't have distracted me."

"Are you sure? You distract me. All the time." He looks at her mouth. "Your lip gloss is distracting me."

She's surprised she hasn't sweated it off by now. "I bet it would look even more distracting on you," she says, and kisses him.

When she leans back, his lips are smudged cherry red. He

looks in his rearview mirror with interest. "You're right. It does."

She laughs. "I'll give you one for Christmas."

As soon as the words leave her mouth, she wants to take them back. Why'd she say that? They're not going to be together by December. She's already resigned herself to, as Chandani said, a summer fling. Just for fun.

But Charlie doesn't miss a beat. "Make it Hanukkah and it's a deal."

She can tell, from his meaningful gaze, that he understood what she meant. "Really?" she breathes as her friends clatter noisily into the back seats. He nods. "Are you sure? I'm going to Western. You're going to Queen's."

"Like we've never gone to different schools before." His lips quirk up. "Besides, it's not like there's no opportunity to meet. They do plenty of debate tournaments in Ontario."

That's true. With so many universities in the province, there are tons of intervarsity competitions. Her heart lifts with hope. "It's British Parliamentary Style in university. Heckling's allowed. Ready to get owned every time you face Western?"

She can just imagine what it would be like. Being on the opposite side of the floor once again. The battles they'll pick with each other. The competitiveness that will rise when they face off during questioning. Same old, same old.

Except new, and better.

His eyes sparkle. "But there's two teams per side. Maybe we'll end up on the same side of the floor."

"And if not," she says with a grin, "there's always World's."

ACKNOWLEDGMENTS
✳

Honourable judges, worthy opponents, and assembled readers: the resolution before us today is *Be It Resolved That it takes a village to publish a book.* As Side Affirmative, I can confirm getting my debut novel into your hands took the efforts of many, many people. They are the reason why this resolution must stand.

Kelsey Murphy, my wonderful editor at Viking, took this story on, put me at ease with her warmth, and helped me shape it into the best book it could be. Some of my favourite details are ones we added together. Several other editors were also involved in various roles: Cheryl Eissing, Gaby Corzo, Ginny Dominguez, Gerard Mancini, Marinda Valenti, Krista Ahlberg, and Sola Akinlana. And our sensitivity reader Shenwei Chang's insight and thoughtful critiques greatly helped in my attempts to make this story more nuanced and inclusive.

I may have written the book, but other people made it an eye-catching package for potential readers to pick up. I have Lucia Baez to thank for the adorable interior design. The amazing cover is courtesy of designer Kristie Radwilowicz and artist Fatima Baig, who made my hairy girl impossible to ignore. TJ Powar would approve!

Many other folks have touched this book in some way or another from the publisher's side: Vanessa DeJesús, Samantha Devotta, Shanta Newlin, and Elyse Marshall; Christina Colangelo, Emily Romero, Kara Brammer, Felicity Vallence, Shannon Spann, and James Akinaka; Carmela Iaria, Trevor Ingerson, Venessa Carson, Rachel Wease, Danielle Presley, and Summer Ogata; Felicia Frazier, Deborah Polansky, Todd Jones, Jennifer Ridgeway, Drew Fulton, Joe English, Cletus Durkin, and Trevor Bundy; Robyn Bender and Pete Facente; Vicki Olsen; and, from the pub office, Jen Loja, Jocelyn Schmidt, Jill Santopolo, Ken

Wright, and Tamar Brazis. As well, fellow authors Adiba Jaigirdar, Emily Wibberley, and Austin Siegemund-Broka were kind enough to give this book wonderful early blurbs.

My hardworking literary agent, Jennifer Azantian, championed this book (and shout-out to Ben Baxter for his behind-the-scenes work, too!). When I first shared this story with her, Jen's enthusiasm made me cry happy tears. And once it sold, she guided me through many parts of the traditional publishing process that were new to me, fielding my questions with great patience and compassion. She cares so much and it shows.

Several years ago, Meredith Ireland took me on as her mentee, helped me revise my first manuscript and has supported me constantly on my journey since. She was the first person in the industry to see potential in me and give me a chance. It meant the world to me then and still does now. And Beth Phelan founded the Twitter pitch event #DVPit that connected me with my agent. What an amazing opportunity she created for me, and for many others.

The very first people I shared this book with are good friends of mine, and each made their mark: Rachel Merritt read the whole thing before anyone else and took the time to write me an honest-to-god edit letter. I can always count on her to give in-depth feedback and be completely straight with me. She has also reliably been there when I needed someone to bounce ideas off of quickly, which I am eternally grateful for. Meha Razdan read the revision right before I sent it to my agent—the way she devoured it and instantly adored the characters is something I don't take for granted. She has been overwhelmingly generous with her love and support over the years, and it makes me want to be better, too, to deserve it. And of course, Mariel Jorgensen. She helped me find the heart of this book while I was still on the first draft. Her influence is weaved into the pages—I can always trust her instinct, and there's no better validation of my story choices than hers. I can't imagine getting here without her.

Then there's the online fandom communities I've been a part of (they know who they are!): I don't know where I'd be if they hadn't hyped me up and encouraged me to keep writing. Their kindness to me, a complete stranger on the internet, gave me the courage to try. Never underestimate your ability to change a life.

My parents have supported me in multiple ways, allowing me the peace of mind to do full-time school while simultaneously pursuing a writing career. As a kid, my mom was the one who made sure I became a reader, and also made sure I pulled my nose out of the books once in a while to experience life. Learning that sense of balance was vital in the years I worked on this story. My dad was the very first fan of my writing. I'll never forget his encouragement when I first started out (and to this day). He's also given me some solid advice which has been invaluable in navigating the business side of being an author.

Lastly, my brother Gurbind. He's the one who inspired me to reach for my dreams in the first place, when we were little. Publishing is full of ups and downs, and every step of the way, he's been my nonjudgmental confidant, my greatest supporter, the person I can share anything with. No one listens like he does.

Of course, there are many more people who've contributed to my debut journey than I have mentioned. Some will never know they were part of it. Some even I will never know. But that's the nature of paths like this; there are always more people behind you than you think, and people before you who paved the way and made it easier. It's not a journey anyone truly takes alone. Which is, of course, why this resolution cannot fall. Thank you for your time, esteemed reader. I now stand for cross-examination.